ALSO BY A.K. CAGGIANO

VILLAINS & VIRTUES
Throne in the Dark
Summoned to the Wilds
Eclipse of the Crown
A V&V Tale: Celeste's Story: Bound to Fall
A V&V Tale: Xander's Story: Bound and Tide

Summoned to the Wilds

VILLAINS & VIRTUES BOOK 2

A.K. CAGGIANO

sourcebooks casablanca

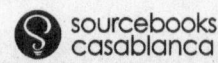

Copyright © 2022, 2026 by A.K. Caggiano
Cover and internal design © 2026 by Sourcebooks
Cover art © Jyotirmayee Patra
Internal design by Tara Jaggers/Sourcebooks
Internal Illustrations © Charlie Bowater
Map Illustration © Emily Sudar
Chapter opener image © Anastasiia Zvonary/Getty Images

Sourcebooks and the colophon are registered trademarks of Sourcebooks.

All rights reserved. No part of this book may be reproduced in any form or by any electronic or mechanical means including information storage and retrieval systems—except in the case of brief quotations embodied in critical articles or reviews—without permission in writing from its publisher, Sourcebooks.

No part of this book may be used or reproduced in any manner for the purpose of training artificial intelligence technologies or systems.

The characters and events portrayed in this book are fictitious or are used fictitiously. Any similarity to real persons, living or dead, is purely coincidental and not intended by the author.

All brand names and product names used in this book are trademarks, registered trademarks, or trade names of their respective holders. Sourcebooks is not associated with any product or vendor in this book.

Published by Sourcebooks Casablanca, an imprint of Sourcebooks
1935 Brookdale RD, Naperville, IL 60563-2773
(630) 961-3900
sourcebooks.com

Originally self-published in 2022 by A.K. Caggiano.

Cataloging-in-Publication Data is on file with the Library of Congress.

The authorized representative in the EEA is Dorling Kindersley
Verlag GmbH. Arnulfstr. 124, 80636 Munich, Germany

Manufactured in the UK by Clays and distributed
by Dorling Kindersley Limited, London
001-357791-Mar/26
10 9 8 7 6 5 4 3 2 1

Dear Reader,
If you're going to throw me, please
aim for something soft.
    —The Book

AUTHOR'S NOTE

This book contains sensitive content, including but not limited to sexual assault.

Please see a complete list of sensitive content at akcaggiano.com.

CONTENTS

CHAPTER 1—*Humble Altruism and What It Entails* 1
CHAPTER 2—*A Dissertation on Unfinished Thoughts* 21
CHAPTER 3—*Measuring the Might of Reeds* 30
CHAPTER 4—*Ironic Trust Reprise* 40
CHAPTER 5—*Misogyny and the Misguidedness of Imps* 55
CHAPTER 6—*Bad Company and Worse Discourse* 64
CHAPTER 7—*The Creation of a Thousand Forests Can Be in One Acorn, but That Acorn Can Still Fall on One's Head* 81
CHAPTER 8—*More Like Duren-Drag* 91
CHAPTER 9—*The Advantage of Being Literal* 112
CHAPTER 10—*Multiple Critical Failures in a Row* 128
CHAPTER 11—*The Practicality of Establishing Base Understanding* 140
CHAPTER 12—*Innkeepers and Imbeciles* 153
CHAPTER 13—*In Defense of Acting Foolishly* 168
CHAPTER 14—*A Thinly Veiled Analogy* 186
CHAPTER 15—*Talis-Whatsits and Doohickeys* 202

CHAPTER 16—*In Which Expectations Are Hopefully Met*	220
CHAPTER 17—*Denial Isn't Just a Spell in the Lux Codex*	241
CHAPTER 18—*Attachment Issues, A Case Study*	252
CHAPTER 19—*On Finding and Being Found*	268
CHAPTER 20—*No, Well, Maybe, Probably, Yes, Definitely*	282
CHAPTER 21—*Defining What Constitutes a Chore*	296
CHAPTER 22—*The Immutable Wisdom of Trees*	313
CHAPTER 23—*Well-Placed Exposition*	332
CHAPTER 24—*Tracking and Trespassing*	342
CHAPTER 25—*A Court of Ice and Irrationality*	358
CHAPTER 26—*The Care and Curing of Blood Mages*	371
CHAPTER 27—*The Incessant Desire for a Passage Back*	383
CHAPTER 28—*Broken Vows and Fixed Numbers*	406
CHAPTER 29—*The Very Sinews of Villainy*	424
CHAPTER 30—*The Various Shapes and Sizes of Heroism*	435
CHAPTER 31—*When One Considers the Alternative*	451
CHAPTER 32—*A Eulogy for Alleged Chivalry*	456
CHAPTER 33—*The Spoils of Servitude*	468
CHAPTER 34—*A Second Lesson in Futility*	474
CHAPTER 35—*The Illusion of Safety*	485
CHAPTER 36—*Despicable Callousness*	498
CHAPTER 37—*Summoned to Yvlcon*	510
BONUS CHAPTER—*Alone in the Wilds*	517
ACKNOWLEDGMENTS	529
ABOUT THE AUTHOR	531

CHAPTER 1

AMMA

Humble Altruism and What It Entails

THE MOST SUPERLATIVELY GOOD being to have blessed the realm of Eiren was Evangeline Temperance Virtulios, more colloquially known as Eva the Congenial. While other good beings were spoken of in Eiren's history—the descendants of dominions, conquering kings, priests to any of the one hundred and seventeen gods of goodness and light—there was no argument that Eva held the highest-ranking place for three reasons: One, it was well established by the Holy Order of Osurehm that her deeds had been monumental, selfless, and, most importantly, in the interest of serving the gods; two, there was a song about her altruism and consequently the death she suffered for never wavering from her morals, which was quite popular amongst schoolchildren and those seemed to really stick; and three, she had in fact been dead for almost one thousand years so couldn't ruin her own ranking by slipping up and saying something untoward on a bad day.

The legacy of Eva the Congenial was often taught to children in theology as a way to both define good behavior and instill great guilt at considering taking part in that which was bad, so it was perhaps not strange that Ammalie Avington, daughter of the Baron of Faebarrow, thought of the holy figure as she walked toward a dark tower in the middle of the Accursed Wastes beside not one but *two* blood mages. Amma had just faked her abduction, and it wasn't even the first time she'd done that, but the most recent performance did have an awful lot more death and destruction, and that made wonderful fodder for the guilt that roiled in her belly. Eva the Congenial would have never trusted one blood mage, let alone a second rival demon spawn, so Amma couldn't help but measure herself against the well-known deeds of the realm's most virtuous woman and recognize that she was coming up significantly short.

But considering Amma's upbringing, all those shameful thoughts were perfectly normal and expected. What was perhaps strange and unexpected, however, was the next thought that popped into Amma's head about the legendary, infallible figure, which was really more of a dawning realization that should have perhaps hit her a few years earlier and not at the ripe old age of twenty-five: Eva the Congenial was a complete and utter fabrication.

Because if she actually had existed in the exact way the religious scholars said, the stories about her life would have been significantly more fraught with doubt. In her tales, Eva was routinely faced with a moral quandary and consistently chose the path of goodness and light as if she were a hound and virtue smelled of treed raccoon. While knowing exactly what to do and always having the perfect path to follow didn't make for particularly good stories in the *interesting* sense—and likely contributed to Amma's boredom with theology—Eva's conflict-free decisions did make for good stories in the *moral* sense. But they were only stories, Amma realized, as having an easy answer every time just wasn't realistic.

Not that there was a parable in which Eva had been faced with the decision to hitch her cart to a blood mage who intended to slaughter the king, free his demon father from prison, and call up infernal vengeance on the entire realm, but if there were, Amma was sure Eva wouldn't have chosen to help the man who had just unleashed an undead army on her hometown. Then again, if Eva had seen how that blood mage looked when doing it—and *for her* nonetheless—she might have actually surrendered all her virtue on the spot.

Amma surely would have if they hadn't been interrupted.

Damien Maleficus Bloodthorne's muscled but exhausted form strode along at Amma's side, violet eyes set forward and unblinking, black hair mussed and falling in his face, hard, clean-shaven jaw clenched and unreadable. He had smartly used a stone imbued with a translocation spell to take them away from her home in Faebarrow. The stone provided the quickest escape, certainly, and if any enterprising Holy Knights or priests tried to suss out the magic left in the stone's wake, it would all match the lie he had told, that he was a different blood mage who was stealing Amma away.

Slightly less smart was the fact that they were now actually standing in the Accursed Wastes, the place Xander Sephiran Shadowhart, Damien's archrival, made his home. But Xander had been delighted to see the two of them, especially since they had successfully stolen and were carrying the Lux Codex—another bad deed to heap onto Amma's growing moral predicament—and a truce was struck between the half-demon blood mages.

Xander's tower was all obsidian and sharp, and looking at it made Amma feel like a blade was pressing against her skin, just on the verge of slicing through it—not cut exactly, but just nicked enough to be painful in only the most annoying ways. The tower stood stark and tall amidst a flat field of red and gray, dried claylike soil with rocky outcroppings scattered on the horizon. The clouds overhead were heavy, but the air was dry, and a violent wind swept them over the dual moons and many stars.

But despite the troop of imps at their back and Xander leading them inside, Damien didn't appear worried. There had been a flash of fervor at Xander's offer of working together, and then a pall of apathy settled over him. In the pallidness of his skin and dark circles beneath his eyes, he was wearing the exhaustion from what he'd done in Faebarrow keep: releasing the Army of the Undead and clashing with Cedric. The

Brineberth marquis and his occupying force had surely been staved off by the skeletal soldier, perhaps even wiped out so that Faebarrow would be in the hands of its own people again. It had been an incredible expenditure of power.

But that...that wasn't why Damien did it. Not really. He had of course told the army what it *would* do—drive out Brineberth troops and protect Faebarrow—but he had also explicitly said, "fuck the barony," and told Amma she was going with him when it was all over because it wasn't safe for her to stay there. Amma had been willing, there was no questioning what her heart and body wanted, but what Damien truly wanted with her—that was still curious.

Except she did know one thing now for certain, revealed by Xander: Damien intended to release a demon in Eirengaard to destroy the realm.

Up the main stone steps that circled the exterior of Xander's tower, they were finally brought inside, out of the whipping winds and dry air, and into a grand and imposing receiving hall. The blood mage's shadow creatures remained shut outside, but Damien's violet eyes darted around as if looking for more, though the rest of him remained stoic. Only Kaz crept along behind them, a lone imp in the tower. Xander's too-light and cheery steps guided them into a smaller chamber just off the main hall, a receiving parlor of sorts, where a cozy fire was already lit along a curved wall.

With a small flourish, Xander pulled a chair away from a table in the room's corner, motioning to it as he stood over the back. "Kitten, please, have a seat."

Amma hesitated, glancing at Damien. When he nodded, she went to it and sat, because despite now knowing his treacherous plans, even tangentially, she still trusted him. Xander, though, she trusted much less, and when he stepped around the chair and gave her a look up and down, she shivered, squeezing the Lux Codex tighter against her chest.

"I'm very flattered the two of you have dolled yourselves up so much to come see little old me."

Amma took a hand, dried blood smeared across it, to the fluffy skirt of her dress, the hem of the light blue tulle dusted heavily with red soil. It felt bizarre that only hours earlier, she was sitting uncomfortably as her hair was done, her face painted, and her body cinched into the gown. She'd been sweating, yelling, and even forced out a few tears during their charade as she pretended to be Damien's unwilling abductee from her own home, so she knew her face and hair must look a wreck now, eyes red-rimmed and blonde strands falling free from the curls piled atop her head.

Damien, similarly, was "dolled up" in a dress uniform common to Faebarrow. The military-style jacket fell open at Damien's collar, exposing his chest where he had cut into his own skin to cast blood magic. It was a look Amma was familiar with, but she'd never been so attracted to it as she was now. His hair had been pushed back at one time, but it had predictably fallen in his face—a face that was growing more severe by the minute, jaw interminably clenched in Xander's presence. Even the long scar running from his forehead to cheek looked angry.

He had been so similarly angry when he fought Cedric, but there had been a moment out on the balcony, before all the madness, when his face was softer. When he said all that mattered was that she knew he was doing all this for her. And then there were other moments when he addressed the assembled, when he played the part of a villain *so well*, when he said he would destroy everything and take her with him, when his face was wild and wicked. Amma couldn't decide which was the real Damien. Maybe none, maybe all.

Xander took one of the two seats before the fireplace, folded his hands in his lap, and slung a leg up over the other. He sat back too comfortably, an amiable smile across his lips. In stark contrast to the other blood mage, Xander's white hair was pulled into a knot at the back of his head, his sharp features were clean, and his dark eyes were filled with elation. The fire flickered across his tanned skin, warm and full of life, and he gestured for Damien to take the seat across from him.

Damien remained unmoving for a moment, staring at Xander and then the empty chair. His throat bobbed with a swallow, a bead of sweat dripping down to his collar, and he finally sat, hands on his knees to bolster himself. It was then Amma realized he was injured, but he never let it show on his face, pushing the pain away to sit up fully.

At her feet, Kaz scurried up in his true imp form. He'd curled his ruddy tail about himself, fiddling with its pointed end in his claws, little leathery wings pulled in. When he sidled up to the leg of her chair, she could feel heat off his body, and his eyes were wide, never blinking. Kaz was almost always nervous, but never had he taken solace in being close to Amma, and that only heightened her unease.

Damien sat back, tipping his head down, narrowing his eyes, and glaring at Xander as if he had been insulted. In return, Xander's placid smile curled up on one side, and his fingers steepled, knuckles cracking as he pushed his hands together. Damien cocked a brow at him, frowning deeper and huffing out a hearty sigh. Xander tipped his head to the side, the foot propped on his knee bouncing lightly.

Between them, the fire crackled. Their forms grew more shadowed, more sinister with each passing moment as they continued to do nothing but stare at one another as if in some unspoken contest. Firelight fell into their deeply hollowed cheeks, reflecting in their eyes as if the very pits of the infernal plane burned there. Neither spoke, simply trading half smirks, wicked glares, and increasingly aggressive poses in the stiff-backed, too-elaborate, probably uncomfortable chairs. What in the Abyss were they doing?

"I can't take it anymore!" Amma squeaked, and both men jerked toward her, thrown from their ridiculous game. "Someone say something!"

Damien snorted, a flicker of amusement on his face. "I've blackened your name," he said, delivering the news with a satisfied lilt. "The Army of the Undead has been unleashed under what has been declared as your order. The forces of Brineberth March of the realm of Eiren have been, by now, decimated. I expect the crown will consider it treason and put a call out for your head."

Xander stared back, unmoving, hands folded again, and then his lips twitched until he broke down into full-bellied laughter. "I would expect nothing less from you, Bloodthorne. Basest beasts, the Undead Army? No one's used that thing in centuries! Skeletons are sort of passé though, don't you think? They're not my style anyway, but they sure do make a point, I suppose."

Amma leaned forward, jaw hanging open. Xander was *laughing* at the fact Damien had blamed the treasonous act on him.

"It served its purpose," said Damien, finally settling back and pressing the tips of his long fingers together.

"But I imagine that scroll would have been a bit more useful in Eirengaard to liberate dear old daddy, no?"

Damien's cool confidence waned, eyes flicking to Amma at the mention of his father, the demon he intended to free. He swallowed.

"So you must have something *much* better up your sleeve to get him out, and as I said, I want in." Xander's dark eyes were wide, set on Damien expectantly, his smile tight-lipped. He knew he had him—and Damien knew too.

He shifted in the tall-backed chair, bringing a hand up to his chin and rubbing it, looking into the fire. "You'd like your mother out too, I wager."

"Always sharp as a horn, you were," said Xander. "I've been considering it ever since I figured out what you were doing. Imagine this." He sat up, holding his hands out in front of him, fingers spread. "We head into the capital together, side by side—no one will see that coming. I'm thinking maybe we bring a few wyverns. I know a guy offering a good deal—oh, don't look like that. They're impressive, okay?"

Damien was apparently not doing a very good job of hiding the unease on his face at the mention of winged serpents.

"Maybe we'll even get a dragon if we can convince one, and I know what you're thinking, but *not* an infernal one—I'm actually interested in turning one of those divine things. Of course, all my shadow imps will come along, and you can bring your little draekin army or whatever it is you keep up there in the mountains, and we march right up to that dominion spawn, cut off his head, and then we'll break out my mother with whatever it is you've got planned, and I guess your father too, and *then* they can duke it out to decide who gets to reign supreme over the realm from the throne in Eirengaard. Whoever wins—Mother, of course—will be pleased with both of us either way since we did it together, and I'm fairly sure they'd let the loser's son live. At worst, you'd be a trophy, but at best, you'd be a ward—you remember, like the good old days in Aszath Koth?"

Damien cocked a brow at Xander, eyes shifting back from the fire when he was finished speaking. Amma's mouth went dry at that look.

Xander waited a moment longer, then dropped his hands into his lap, pouting. "Well, I thought it was a marvelous idea. You, kitten, you think it's a good idea, don't you?"

With his dark eyes on her, willing her to agree, Amma

just pressed back into the chair on the room's far side. "You both have a parent trapped in Eirengaard?"

Xander nodded. "His Majesty Archie, that king you serve in the realm, is a prolific if not picky demon hunter. My mother, Birzuma the Blasphemed, Ninth Lord of the Accursed Wastes and Nefarious Harbinger of the Chthonic Tower, is one of the most, if not *the* preeminent prisoner."

Of course, Amma had just heard Damien rattle off the same thing to the assembled in Faebarrow, though she had sort of thought he was making it all up.

Xander turned back to Damien and smirked. "The better ninth lord of anything."

"Please." Damien's eyes rolled with an untensing of his shoulders. "How difficult is it to lord over the Accursed Wastes? There's nothing here. The Infernal Darkness is significantly more complex and evolved. It's not even on this plane."

"Oh yes, it's so difficult to be an Abyssal Tyrant, I guess." Xander crossed his arms, sticking out his tongue. "We're all blood mages, Damien. I don't know why *you* get to have the Sanguine Throne."

"It's not mine, just like this tower isn't yours, and you know it." Damien sat forward slightly.

"Isn't it?" Xander also sat forward but quicker, his smile sharper as he nearly sprang from his chair. "Isn't it yours to defend in Zag's stead? Just as this place is mine?" He slipped a hand into the neckline of his top and revealed a thin vial of blood.

"Moronic," said Damien, eyeing the vial. His lip curled, disgusted, and he leaned farther forward. "You can defend nothing if someone gets their hands on that blood of yours that you've preserved. All because you're not willing to endure a little pain."

"Who said I don't like pain?" Xander perched just on the edge of his chair. "And if this is so simple to take away, then why don't you come over here and show me how easy I am?"

Damien took a deep breath, veins in his neck bulging, violet eyes on Xander like they could burn him alive, and then, all at once, he threw himself back into his chair with a huff. "We can argue for millennia about who's the better blood mage, but the truth is both of our parents are trapped in that bastard's vault, fallen to a divine mage who calls himself a king, and we can't prove a damn thing."

Xander remained on the edge of his seat a moment longer, holding his breath, but finally relaxed back as well. "And killing you now won't prove anything either—you're so weak after that ruckus you caused, it would hardly be fair. I will admit I'm impressed you got my translocation portal to work so cleanly though. You didn't even fall down the steps or anything. *And* you brought the human and the imp with you. Quite the expenditure of arcana, I imagine." Xander stretched, arms behind his head, casually glancing in Amma's direction. "So much so that I wonder if you've got much left in you to protect anything at all."

Amma's knee began to bounce nervously, bloodied fingers curling around the edges of the Lux Codex.

Damien sat forward again, quickly this time, face pinched as he tried to hide the pain he'd just caused himself. "When I agreed to your terms, it was for all of us. We have a bargain, but only for as long as you keep your hands to yourself. We're obviously not leaving tonight to storm the capital, so first: our asylum."

"Aw, sleepy?" Xander pouted, but he stood, stretching before the fireplace. "I suppose I am as well. Come on then, why don't we retire—"

"To our own rooms," Damien cut him off, standing as well.

"Still no fun, as always. You'll want clothes too, yes? And what else? A warm bath? *Food?* Darkness, so needy." Smirking, he looked him up and down. "I know just what to put you in at least."

"Nothing you own will fit me," scoffed Damien: he was wider-shouldered. "Not in size or style."

"Oh no, not my clothes. I just had someone recently who's almost your identical build. Amazing in bed, if his fashion sense is a little…meh." He started to walk off, crooking a finger at Amma. "Someone your size too. If only I'd gotten them both together, now that would have been a good time, though it does seem the opportunity has presented itself again, hasn't it?"

Xander wandered back into the main hall, calling out orders with a cheery lilt to make his guests comfortable, addressing unseen servants. Amma eased herself over to Damien, who was rubbing a temple and focusing very hard on putting one foot in front of the other now that he was no longer under Xander's eye.

Amma gently touched his arm, and he stiffened. "Everything will be fine," he assured her without her asking and continued on as if there were no problem at all, and she followed.

The tower had a set of stairs built into its center that wound upward in a spiral, each level set along a rounded balcony. As they traveled through the eerily quiet place, shadows moved at the corners of Amma's vision. They took shape to look like a human or creature and floated ahead, anticipating Xander's needs. Sleeping chambers were near the top, up even more of those steps. No wonder Xander was so thin; he was constantly climbing these things.

When they came to a single door, Xander paused briefly. "You'll both find what you need inside. And if you need anything else"—he pointed upward—"you know where to find me." He continued upstairs, his light footsteps disappearing overhead, and they were left in silence.

Damien and Amma glanced at one another and then at the single door, but when Damien swung it open, there was a small parlor inside with two bedchambers off it. Amma wasn't sure if it was relief or disappointment she was feeling, but when Damien shut the rest of the tower out and the hollow silence of the stairwell was replaced by the more cloying silence of the closed chamber, she was overcome by intense trepidation.

She went to step forward, but Damien threw out a hand.

"Wait." There was a pulse of arcana, one that he didn't spill blood for but that she could feel. It crackled out into the room like tendrils sweeping over everything, and then there was a yelp from each of the bedchambers.

"Unless you'd like to be banished, get out now," Damien called into the space, and slips of shadow scurried through the doorways, keeping to the edges of the walls. Kaz flew upward to wrench the door open by its handle, and a darkness tripped over itself to escape. Kaz shoved the door closed again with a shiver.

"Even you don't like those things?" Amma asked the imp, rubbing away the chill from her arms through the thin fabric of her ruined dress.

Kaz shook his head, looking at the door. "They're a whole different kind of imp. Sneaky and weird." He clacked his claws together, placed himself low to the ground, and started scurrying off through the space. "I'll check for anything else, Master."

When he was gone, Amma looked over Damien standing limply beside her, gazing off into the fire burning blue in the parlor as if in a daze. "You look exhausted."

He blinked over at her. "I'm fine."

He wasn't.

"Well," she said softly, "thank you for…everything."

"For stealing you?"

Her heartbeat sped up at the thought of truly being abducted, but that hadn't been what happened, even if she was in a strange and frightening place. "For besmirching your name. Well, Xander's name, I guess, but so many people saw your face, someone will put it together that you were lying eventually, and now you can never—" She cut herself off before going on, knowing what she wanted to say was…silly. Why would he ever want to go back to Faebarrow? "Well, you've just made things complicated for yourself."

"It was nothing, really," he said ruefully, taking a few slow steps deeper into the small parlor, giving it a look over. "I might not have actually been attacking your home or taking you against your will, but I *am* evil after all."

Amma's stomach clenched as she stared at the back of him, hands clasped, tall and looming as he blocked the fireplace, body like a shadow in the low lighting of the room. She wanted to scream at him to stop saying that, especially after what he had done for her, but then Xander had given away the secret Damien had been keeping, the plans he had made, the prophecy he was set to fulfill, and Amma had to remember she was a hitch in those plans—a hitch that needed to be resolved.

"I think I should go to bed," said Amma, weary, and she started toward one of the rooms.

"Wait." Damien's voice cut into her, making her stop. "The Lux Codex. Sleep with it."

Amma turned to him fully, gripping the book to her chest.

"Don't just keep it nearby but in the bed, against you. It will be the best deterrent."

What exactly did he mean to deter? "You think Xander will come into our rooms?"

"I don't know what he'll do, but other than me, that book is the best protection in this place. It will keep anything infernal from touching you, including blood mages."

Amma glanced down at the Lux Codex, trying to hide the warmth on her face and her preference for his body over some hard-edged book in her bed. She swallowed. "All right. I will."

Kaz was just skittering out of the bedchamber as Amma went into it. He gave her a frustrated look but confirmed there was nothing else inside. When she closed the door after him, she looked around as if she could identify the kinds of things Kaz might suss out—as if she could even do anything about potential dangers—and then gave up.

Only the red, arcane glow of a pile of rough-cut rocks on a table at the foot of the bed lit the space, but it was an opulent room even in the dark and exactly Xander's style. There was crimson and gold woven into everything: tapestries on the floor, the bedding, the wall hangings. She caught her reflection in a massive mirror with a gilded edge in the corner of the room and pushed off the door to go to it. She could see the room behind her, and even though she was wearing a pale-blue dress, she didn't necessarily look out of place. She was just as done up, just as opulent as everything around her, she just *also* looked like she'd been dragged through the Abyss.

She was careful to put the Lux Codex right beside her as she finally reached around her back and wrestled with the cords to shuck off the poofy gown. It fell to her feet like a thick fog, but her body immediately felt better, the itch of the fabric gone, the weight of the layers gone, all of it *gone*, just like—she winced suddenly at the realization—just like her: She was gone. She had left...no, she had *abandoned* Faebarrow. Again.

Amma tripped, staggering out of the pile of fabric on the floor, catching herself on the edge of the bed before sinking to the ground. She sat there in her thin chemise—her dagger strapped to her thigh where she'd secured it before the banquet—suddenly cold in the empty room. This was what she wanted, she knew; she'd asked for it even.

Amma had spent a lifetime doing everything right only to have things go so wrong, and even as she had tried to fix things, they only got worse. Running away had been her only option before, so she did, on a desperate quest for magic to protect her home. But even if she had gotten the Scroll of the Army of the Undead back to Faebarrow on her own, how would she have read it without knowing Chthonic? How would she have commanded a skeletal army? She would have gotten everyone killed, including herself. Or there was the much worse alternative, she realized: surviving the ordeal and being stuck with Cedric. She would have never been able to do anything for Faebarrow or herself without Damien.

But what about this decision? Accepting Damien's offer to use the scroll on her behalf and then spiriting her away from whatever gruesome aftermath they left behind? And now she was sitting in the Chthonic Tower in a place called the Accursed Wastes with not one but *two* blood mages, not to mention all the imps.

Her eyes snapped back up to the small table where the Lux Codex was, and she scrambled on hands and knees to it. But when she reached for the book, the sight of the dried blood on her hands—Damien's blood—made her freeze. He'd hurt himself for her, but he'd done that for himself too, hadn't he? He certainly looked like he was enjoying the mayhem he'd called down on Faebarrow, the chaos, the death.

Amma shook her head and grabbed the Lux Codex, crushing it to her chest as she squeezed herself into a ball on the floor. What was she thinking? Moments before, she had been pining over Damien, been wrapped up in his arms, almost kissed him, and now?

She had seen how his eyes flashed with eagerness at Xander's offer. She had heard him say he was evil more times than she could count, and now she knew exactly what he was destined to do. It wasn't enough that he had made himself the villain in her home, the place she had sworn to protect and love; he was planning on razing the entire realm to the ground.

Amma squeezed the book even tighter between her knees and her chest, wrapping her arms around her legs as her vision blurred with tears. Damien had told her, and she had refused to listen. It was easy to ignore the bloodcraft and his ominous if vague words when the plan wasn't laid out before her, but his father wasn't just an idea now, harmlessly living in some unreachable plane. He was a demon, the vilest being in existence save for the dark gods, and King Archibald had trapped him in a vault beneath Eirengaard to protect the realm for what had to have been a good reason—every crusade the king's holy men went on was to drive evil from the land. Damien's goal, the prophecy given by the Denonfy Oracle, was to release him.

And he had to kill her to do it.

CHAPTER 2

DAMIEN

A Dissertation on Unfinished Thoughts

DAMIEN MALEFICUS BLOODTHORNE TORE off the once-pristine dress coat now stained with his blood, throwing it to the ground as he paced through the bedchamber after booting out Kaz. He whipped about when he got to the room's far end, and then his vision blurred. Hand to his head, he staggered into the wall.

"All right, enough," he said to himself, stumbling to the bed and falling face-first onto it with a groan.

She knew. Damn it, now she knew all his plans to release his father and destroy the realm that was her home, and he had seen it in her eyes—Amma was terrified.

"Fuck you, Shadowhart," he growled into the incredibly soft linens, and he was sure he imagined it, but there was a faint *Fuck you too, Bloodthorne*, that echoed somewhere in the back of his mind.

With eyes closed, he saw Amma's face again—no, Lady Ammalie Avington, daughter to the Baron of Faebarrow—the fear in it at knowing Damien's intentions, the shiver of realization at what she had gotten herself into, and he rolled himself onto his back. There was a mural painted above him—massive, across the whole ceiling—of Xander depicted as a god surrounded by maniacally laughing shadow imps, fire, and destruction. Xander wasn't just a prick, but he was a prick with terrible taste.

Damien ran his hand down his face. He had expended so much arcana he was surprised he hadn't already fallen deeply asleep, but he supposed his burning hatred for the blood mage could spur him on to do anything.

And there was also the *excitement* at what he had just done. Xander might think skeletons were mundane, but he hadn't seen their glinting-white bones climb from the ground, he hadn't watched them cut down the living with graceful ease, and he hadn't felt the immense power of wielding an unbreakable, compelled army with words alone. And he hadn't seen the look of adoration on Amma's face when he had done it.

He had been too long keeping a low profile, holding in every intense, dark desire he had—including those for Amma herself—playing at whoever he needed to be to slink from place to place on his quest to Eirengaard. But he hadn't made it. He'd not even gotten close. And truthfully, had he even been trying?

If Xander was good for anything, it was reminding Damien of who he was: a creature filled with that seething hatred, that powerful anger that reminded him of his demonic blood, that desire to slice that stupid, smarmy grin right off Xander's stupid, smarmy face. And now Xander had trapped Damien there—and Damien hated to be trapped—but more, he had revealed things to Amma so ungracefully and then dared make a pass at her.

The light in the room wavered then, and Damien sat up with a start. His head spun, a shadow swirling about, but it didn't feel sinister or oppressive. This felt…cathartic. It was not Xander's magic or some imp infiltrating the room but his infernal arcana, the noxscura, seeping out again without permission.

"Dark gods," he mumbled, falling back flat again and willing the darkness to disperse. "I've got to get a handle on that."

He supposed there was really no reason not to trust Xander in the moment. Well, of course, there were infinite reasons, chief among them that he was a total twat, but at the crux of things was Xander's discovery of Damien's plan—or semblance of a plan—and how Xander intended to use it as an in to get his own mother out of Archibald's vault. If Xander intended to use him, and that was certainly the case, he wouldn't do anything to jeopardize his life, and if he was smart enough, not Amma's either.

Of course, the translocation stone was charmed with an additional seeing spell—*of course* it was. That was Xander's way: sneaky, spying, deceptive. But he didn't know of Bloodthorne's Talisman of Enthrallment, and he didn't know enough about Amma to risk doing something stupid to her—not tonight anyway. Not only did she have the Lux Codex, but she was the only one who could touch it. Without her, they'd end up as dead as Malcolm, the ancient blood mage who had tried and failed to do the very same thing.

But now Damien had to grapple with getting Birzuma out as well as Zagadoth, something he'd been actively putting off since it would take Amma's death to do it. And being here with Xander wasn't helping get the talisman out of her, was it? But where both he and the alchemist Anomalous had failed, the Lux Codex stood as a possible solution, which had been the whole point in fetching it in the first place. And even if the book held nothing, he still had other options, one being an answer to his raven he had yet to act upon.

But his father still waited…

Damien pulled himself up to sit, blinking. There was food on a tray beside the bed. He didn't bother to check that it wasn't drugged or enchanted, simply grabbed the indiscernible meat and took a messy, starved bite. In a moment, it was gone, washed down with wine that was too sweet and boozier than he expected. The goblet refilled itself arcanely—of course Xander wanted to get him drunk, especially so late at night—but Damien pushed it away. With a deep breath, he dug into his pocket for the sliver of occlusion crystal and held it up.

He had just enough magic to call on the arcana in the

crystal to finish the work of summoning his father. He sliced a finger on the crystal's sharpest edge, smearing blood over it, and whispered in Chthonic. Zagadoth the Tempestuous's eye blinked into life from between Damien's weak fingertips.

"Kiddo!" the demon lord's voice boomed, and Damien winced at the sound, skull ringing. "Oh, sorry there, champ. I'm just jazzed to see ya. It's been a while. Thought you forgot about me!" He laughed in a wary sort of way.

"No, never, Father," Damien half lied, rubbing a temple. "It's just been a long day."

"You're looking a little haggard. Where are you?" Zagadoth's slice of a pupil darted to the edges of the crystal.

"Uh, well…" Damien took a look around, only half believing it. "I'm actually in the Chthonic Tower."

"The Chthonic Tower? What in the deepest Abyss happened? Who took you? What souls must I crush to retrieve you from—"

"Dad." Damien shook his head, dropping his chin down, but he half—no, *quarter* grinned. His father often threatened things he couldn't do from inside the crystal, but it was comforting nonetheless. "I actually came here. It was my doing."

"Isn't Birzuma's boy there? Oh, unless you've killed him?" There was an excited jolt to Zagadoth's voice.

"Not exactly." Damien lay back again, holding the crystal up over his head, grip weak. He ran his other hand through his hair and tugged at it. "I've sort of come here due to a… complication. I may have accidentally pissed off an entire barony, unleashed the Army of the Undead, and may have besmirched my name in the realm a few moons too early. It might throw things off course."

"You what now?" Zagadoth chuckled. "I can't really blame you for having a little fun on the way. But this wasn't actual fun, was it?"

"No, it *was* fun," Damien admitted, the side of his face twitching. Scarcely able to believe it had only been hours ago and not moons, he remembered the blood that had gushed from Cedric's arm, the hundreds of undead soldiers piling in, and the flush to Amma's cheeks when he had stolen her away. Now *that*—that had been exceptional. How her body had felt against his, how she had so breathlessly answered him with an eagerness to be taken. And then, when the chaos was behind them, how she had run her fingers up the back of his neck, how she had told him what he'd done with his blood magic and infernal arcana was wonderful, and the way her blue eyes had sparkled at him in the dark, hungry and full of admiration.

"What's wrong, son? Did that little Shadowhart prick drug you?"

Damien tugged the corners of his mouth down, eyes flicking to the plate of food and back. "No, Dad, I'm not that stupid."

"Huh, well, I've never seen you look so cheery, so I thought—"

"Never mind. I just needed to explain that I'm off schedule."

Zagadoth's eye blinked, waiting. "And?"

How his father was so perceptive from another plane of existence was beyond even Damien's arcane abilities. "*And*...I think I might need some advice."

Zagadoth chuckled, a warm, homey sound that reminded Damien of being very small and safe and made a different kind of ache rise in his chest.

He pushed whatever that feeling was right off the closest theoretical ledge. "I'm considering something. Something that might be idiotic." He rolled his shoulders against the bed, arm throbbing from holding up the crystal shard. "We spoke before about calling in assistance from allies, but have you ever worked with someone you shouldn't have? Formed an alliance with an enemy?"

Zagadoth was quiet for a long moment. After telling him he was in the Chthonic Tower, there was no hiding that Damien was speaking about Xander, the son of Birzuma, who Zagadoth famously loathed and in turn who Damien did as well. The hatred was as inheritable as his blood. Zagadoth's brow narrowed, pupil going sharper, and Damien tightened his grip on the crystal, swallowing. Then the demon lord said carefully, voice taut, "Yes, I did. Once."

Damien's stomach clenched, unable to parse out what was coming next. He tried to inject casualness into his voice, but it only cracked on the words. "And how...uh, how did that go?"

Zagadoth's piercing gaze softened, and he sighed. "Best thing that ever happened to me."

Smacked right in the face, Damien cried out and jolted upward, heart racing. Then he swore and grabbed the occlusion crystal shard from where it had bounced across the bed. His weakened grip had dropped the bloody thing right onto his nose. Rubbing the sore spot, he held the crystal up again and squinted at Zagadoth's eye. "Sorry, Dad, I—"

There was a mumbled, fuzzy sound, and the eye blinked in and out.

"Father?"

"...juice...stronger..."

Damien shook the crystal, but he could feel the magic draining out of it. "Shit, this damn thing's almost out of arcana." He listened a moment but could only hear Zagadoth faintly, though whatever he said sounded jovial enough. "Sorry, Dad." He swiped a hand over the crystal, and the eye was gone.

Damien fell back again. It was inevitable that the crystal would lose most of its ability to connect back with the rest of it in Eirengaard once the shard was taken out of the Infernal Mountains. It also didn't help that Damien was currently so weak.

"Enough," he said again to himself, shoving the shard back into its protective satchel and stripping off the rest of his bloodstained and uncomfortable clothing before climbing into the bed. He lay there, staring at the ridiculous ceiling mural, arms crossed over his chest, suddenly angry, but with what? Xander? His father? His own dwindling power?

He rolled to his side, the bedchamber's door in his view as his lids drooped. He imagined slipping out into the parlor, knocking softly on Amma's door, being invited inside, attempting to explain. There were imagined tones of Amma's voice in his mind, soothing and sweet, because surely she would understand. She would accept things as they were no matter how terrible because she was soft and compassionate and forgiving and…and she deserved so much more than whatever the fuck he had dragged her into.

CHAPTER 3

DAMIEN

Measuring the Might of Reeds

THE MORNING CAME DULL and heavy, the curtained window in Damien's bedchamber of the Chthonic Tower letting in no light. When he pulled it back, there was little to see but a ruddy landscape and a gloomy sky threatening rain. Just how he should have liked it. There was a *plunk* against the window as the first drop fell. Even better. But Damien's insides were twisted into knots, and he would bet it had little to nothing to do with the food Xander had provided the night before.

There was a trunk full of clothing at the foot of the bed, all black, thank the basest beasts, and not ill-fitting but not entirely his style either. The tunic didn't button or tie all the way up, and the pants were tight and hip-hugging, but none of it should have been a surprise when Xander was choosing what they'd wear. Damien bathed quickly and dressed, then dragged himself out into the parlor where Kaz had been huddled under a blanket before the arcane fire in the hearth. The imp immediately jumped to attention.

"Master! The shadow imps have been in." He was hissing and nervous, claws clacking. "They left food. I haven't touched it for fear of poison, but I would be willing to take the risk for you, and there is a message from that *nasty*—"

Damien lifted his hand, hushing the imp as the door to Amma's chamber cracked open. She stepped out into the room carefully, head bent and eyes flicking away as soon as they landed on his face. Much sleeker than the ball gown she'd worn the night before, the deep-sapphire dress wrapped around Amma's body and looped over her neck, arms and shoulders bare. The skirt fell to the floor in a clinging, silken wave, and when she took a step, her bare leg peeked out a slit running up from the floor to just shy of her hip. She had her silver dagger strapped to that thigh. *Smart girl*, he thought, then realized she must have armed herself before going to her parents' banquet if she had it now. His chest hitched. *Bloody brilliant*.

Amma tugged the skirt back over her leg, head still bent, gnawing on her lip. She'd pulled her slightly damp hair into a thick braid over her shoulder, her face clean and pink.

"Good morning," she said, voice breathy as she shifted the Lux Codex to cradle against her body.

Fuck me, thought Damien, mouth going dry as he

wondered if there was a spell to change himself into a book, just for a moment. And there was yet another complication for the day. "The note," he said, pulling his eyes away from her.

Kaz scurried over and pressed a piece of parchment into his hand. It was written in an overzealous, loopy script, almost impossible to read for its flourishes, but Damien could ascertain from Xander's too-formal message that their presence was requested in "the study." Damien crushed the paper in his fist and sighed, looking back up at Amma. "We've been summoned."

Together, they exited the parlor. A shadow imp was waiting for them, and they followed it silently as it dodged and skittered around the balcony to the stairs, its amorphous body flitting from shady alcove to gloomy corner. Down one winding flight on the next balcony, there was a set of double doors that the wispy creature phased through. The doors opened themselves with a smattering of broken smoke and shadows onto a large chamber.

There was a crash of thunder, and a bolt of lightning lit up the space through the massive windows at the room's far end. The chamber was grossly extravagant, multiple tapestries overlapping one another on the stone floors, the walls lined with glass cases and overly designed, hand-carved shelving, pedestals holding vases, busts, crystals, floating miniatures of entire cities, and in the center stood Xander, that stupid, smarmy grin plastered on his infuriatingly pleased face.

Hands clasped behind his back, the blood mage sighed at the sight of them. "I could barely sleep last night, just waiting for this moment."

"How long have you been standing there?" Damien snorted, eyeing the room's single shelf of books.

Xander's head cocked. "Not so long that I felt I needed to come get you."

Damien strode to the shelf, reading the spines with a quick glance. Nothing of great interest, though some of the books appeared ancient while others looked pristine and unread.

"Kitten, how lovely it is to see you especially. Come here, have a seat."

Damien snapped around to see Xander pulling a chair out from a table near the windows. This time, Amma did not look to him for approval or help. She only squeezed the Lux Codex tight to her chest and crossed the long room in a scurry, head still down. Damien abandoned the shelf and stood at her other side, meeting Xander's gaze as he pushed the chair in under her. The Lux Codex made Damien's insides crawl as she set it on the table before her. As Xander's dark eyes widened and he peered down at the book, it was clear he could feel its divine arcana too.

"Delightful," he whispered and then fell into the chair at the table's head. "Now, first, the plan." Xander dragged a hand against the wood grain, and from beneath, a spark of light scurried its way to the table's center. A vivid image took shape to hover just over the wooden top, tiny buildings springing up in miniature, and in the center a grand castle: Eirengaard. "So how do you intend to do it?"

Damien watched the image of the city subtly spin before them, the divine arcana off the luxerna-infused threads woven into the Lux Codex's spine oppressive on his skin. He remembered the city, but the vision in his mind was odd, a nostalgic sort of prickling at the back of his head and something like fear pressing in on his spine.

He looked down at Amma just beside him. Now that—*that* was fear shining in her doe-like eyes, her hands clasped tightly in her lap, goose bumps on her bare shoulders.

"You said it yourself." Damien stepped away from her to the third chair set at the table's other end, across its length from Xander. "Storm the gates, cut down the king, and take the vault. Simple."

"No, no, no!" Xander threw back his head to stare at the ceiling with a childish huff. Xander had two years on Damien, yet he always acted so much younger. That at least gave Damien the tiniest bit of leverage. "That's not it. That can't be it. You're so much *smarter* than that."

Damien remained stoic as he sat, resting his elbows on the table, folding his hands together, and placing his chin on them. He looked over to Amma, who was still watching him, the fear in her eyes lessening as they narrowed. "Am I?"

"Of course!" Xander sat forward violently, grabbing the table and making Amma jolt back into her chair. "Now, tell me *exactly* how you're going to do it—it's part of our bargain."

Damien only stared back at him, barely putting effort into shrugging. "I already did."

"I can call off the truce *any* time," threatened Xander.

Damien knew that, but he also knew he wouldn't. He sat back, cracking his neck to cover another glance at Amma. It was perhaps obvious the woman had something to do with Damien's machinations, but Xander could never guess what. He'd only donned one piece of armor that morning, his bracer with the dagger he used for bloodletting, and he turned his arm so its hilt caught the light. "Go ahead. Your accommodations were quite restorative."

Xander stared back at him over the shape of the city they intended to infiltrate as it slowly spun. Another flash of lightning lit up the side of his face, highlighting the deep curve to his brow and the anger there. Thunder rumbled again, farther off, but the plunking of rain against the window intensified. "Fine," he finally said, blinking away to look out at the growing storm. "But you'll tell me eventually. And in the meantime, we have plenty of work to do with this." He gestured to the book.

Amma was visibly relieved at that, hands loosening from around one another. Her eyes flicked to Damien, and there was even a hint of a smile on her lips.

Damien returned it, just as small, then cleared his throat. "Well, none of us have looked at it yet, so, Amma, if you would, please?"

She sat forward and laid her hands on the cover before carefully opening to the first page. Her eyes followed the script there, thin brows knitting, head tipping slightly to the side in thought. Her fingers skimmed the edge of the page, thumb rubbing over the corner as she prepared to flip to the next one. Deep in thought with the soft glow of the candles on her, she was even more beautiful than usual. Damien leaned on the table, gazing at her, tension wrung out of his muscles. He could have sat there all day, the rain pattering against the window, just watching her read.

Xander huffed out an impatient breath. "By the basest beasts, kitten, tell us!"

Amma jumped. "Right! Um—"

"She has a name," Damien spat, hating the slimy diminutive, especially on Xander's tongue.

"Yet she answers." Xander grinned back at him.

"The thing is," said Amma before Damien could tell Xander to properly fuck off, "it's all written in Ouranic." That was the language of the gods in Empyrea, the equivalent of Chthonic to the dark gods in the Abyss.

Xander laughed ruefully. "How the fuck did Mal read it?"

"He didn't—he died." Damien knew a number of languages himself, but Ouranic was a challenge that most infernal creatures couldn't overcome: It was cursed or blessed—depending on one's persuasion—to tell the reader's intent, and if Ouranic disapproved, the symbols could get up and move around.

Amma made a small, nervous sound in the back of her throat. Overall, there were very few pages in the Lux Codex, and Amma flipped through several of them before hesitantly looking up. "I know Ouranic. Sort of. Or at least I had lessons in it..."

Damien couldn't help but grin. "Boring lessons?"

"*So* boring," she said, huffing and rolling her eyes.

Glad to have chased off a little of her anxiety, he leaned

toward her. "I seem to remember that priest-in-training, Perry, saying something about how rubbish you were at paying attention in theology?"

She let out a wary laugh. "I may have sneaked off a time or two. I definitely missed the classes where we learned what a lot of these words mean."

Damien sighed. "Hmm, very naughty."

"Oh yes, she's *absolutely* nefarious," Xander scoffed, disgusted by probably a few things at that moment. "Next thing you know, they'll be inducting her into the Grand Order of Dread. Look, kitten, are you saying you can't read it and you'll need to make your usefulness up some other way?"

Amma shook her head. "No, I can! It's just going to take some time, translating and puzzle solving. Every word has multiple meanings because of all the anagrams from Key. Maybe if I had some help?" She turned to look behind her and focused on the singular shelf of books. "May I?"

Xander waved her on. Damien watched as Amma walked away from them, captivated by the exposed skin of her back, the dress tied at her neck and open down to her waist, then he quickly pulled his gaze away.

The blood mage across the table smirked knowingly, mimicked gripping himself with a fist, and pumped his hand at the table's edge. Damien growled, pointed to himself, dragged his finger across his throat, and jabbed it at Xander. Licking his lips, Xander only grinned wider and nodded, more intensely working the hand gesture.

When Amma turned, they both straightened and froze,

but she was focused on a thick, old tome in her hands, so big she had to carry it like a tray. She placed it carefully on the table, but it was heavy, and when she opened it to its middle with a rougher *thunk*, dust erupted from the long-unopened pages. Damien and Xander both backed away, and Amma waved off the dust with quick apologies.

"I did pay a little attention in some classes, and I know these Empyrean songs by heart—well, mostly—so I can use these to fill in the translation gaps."

Xander looked pleased enough at that, sitting back and squinting at her. "I find it interesting you were well-off enough not just to be taught but to blow off lessons in your gods' language."

Amma avoided his gaze, shrugging as she flipped another page.

"You're not just some little peasant girl looking for a leg up in the world who moronically tied your cart to a blood mage," Xander observed correctly, "so why *are* you hanging around Bloodthorne?"

Amma squirmed, looking up to Damien, eyes glassy in the candlelight. He wasn't going to tell Xander the truth—that she really had no choice but to hang around—not at that moment certainly, but as he opened his mouth to yet again tell Xander to fuck off, she took a deep breath and turned to Xander herself. "I'm helping him."

The blood mage stared back as if trying to will out more, but she only grinned in a self-satisfied way that made Damien want to hand over the world to her.

"Now"—she cleared her throat and sat straighter, focusing on the books—"I'm going to need some parchment and reeds and a little better candlelight if I'm going to get through any of this."

CHAPTER 4

AMMA

Ironic Trust Reprise

THE WORK WAS LONG and tedious, but that was the crux of translation. Amma's hand cramped midway through the day, and Damien took over, writing as she dictated. He often had to cross things out and rewrite when she discovered she'd made an error or changed her mind about the order of letters, flipping between the Lux Codex and the old tome of Empyrean songs. But he only grumbled once, and playfully, about how she should have been punished for paying such poor attention in class, giving her a look as if to say he'd be happy to do it himself. There was a flash of heat all over her body at that, and she was grateful for the sleeveless dress even though the redness showed more prominently on her skin.

Picking out what to wear that morning had perhaps been her least difficult decision—all the dresses in the wardrobe were nearly identical. Much more difficult was convincing herself to walk out the door and face Damien. Her night had been wrought with indecision and fear, startling her awake from shadow-filled nightmares. But then she had seen him that morning, and the concern swallowed itself up, packed away for a later time. His face did that to her somehow, scar and all.

Damien had moved his chair closer to Amma in the study, though he still kept his distance as he copied down in Key the things she said. His handwriting was lovely and careful, and she'd found herself staring at it as he wrote, the scratch of the reed filling up the chamber as rain pattered softly on the massive windows. How could someone with such a nice script want to ruin an entire city? A whole realm? It seemed quite preposterous, and when she caught herself glancing up at him as he waited for her to go on, the gentle bend of his smile only convinced her further that things just weren't as they seemed.

Xander was significantly less helpful, though also less threatening, as the day wore on. He wandered about the chamber, poking at his own artifacts, picking them up and admiring them as if they were brand-new, and then he would pull down a random book to thumb through it and replace it on the shelf without having read a page. And of course, there was the sighing, like they were putting him out by not instantly doing whatever he expected with the Lux Codex.

"This word doesn't have a translation," Amma said as she

came across one she didn't recognize at all. "But there's mention of it in both books, and it's the same in Key and Ouranic, but the letters are funny."

"Luxerna," said Damien. The letters didn't read that to Amma, but there was a symbol amongst them she'd never seen before that she assumed changed the word's pronunciation.

"Ah, finally!" Xander shot across the chamber to lean over their shoulders, and Damien scowled at him when he got between the two. Too excited, Xander backed up just as quickly—it seemed neither of them could get too close to the book without physical harm.

Amma had heard the word *luxerna* before. Damien had mentioned the codex being dipped in it, and something familiar tickled at the back of her mind, like it had a place in a childhood fairy tale. She blinked, thinking of the Everdark and the stories from the fae's plane, then shivered. Fae were purported to be dangerous, though not as dangerous as blood mages, and Amma was sharing a tower with two of *them* safely. So far.

Marching around to the far side of the table and leaning over it to look at both of them, Xander snorted. "Well, go on. Does it say where we can find it?"

Amma skimmed the page, flipped through the other tome, and frowned. "No, it's just listed as an ingredient in a spell that I haven't quite…wait." Her eyes widened as her breath caught. "Flip these letters and—*spirit resurrection!* Oh, that makes so much more sense than what I puzzled out."

Damien chuckled, crossing through the note he'd originally taken. "*Sinister erotic purr.*"

"Well, we know where her mind's at," Xander grumbled. "So there's a spell in there for resurrection? And all those divine mages are always going on about how evil necromancy is."

"Just like the elf said." Damien cocked his head as he read over the translation he'd been taking down. "This isn't necromancy though. This is supposedly true resurrection without degradation of the body, enthrallment, or loss of the soul. It just returns the spirit and completely heals the vessel. Theoretically."

Xander made a thoughtful noise, the first true one that day. "Do you think…do you think you could substitute noxscura in that spell for the luxerna?"

"Noxscura?" Amma sat up. She was almost certain she'd heard Damien use that word before, but she knew neither of the ingredients the two spoke of.

Damien only shook his head. "You can figure that out on your own time."

Xander clicked his tongue. "Fine, that's not what I wanted the book for anyway. Maybe you two can skip ahead to the good parts? This is already taking forever."

"How can I skip ahead if I don't know where the good parts are?" Amma flipped a page to see more dizzying Ouranic filling up the parchment.

"Indeed," said Damien dryly. "You can't have expected this to go quickly, though it would go a fair bit quicker if we had additional help."

"Oh, fine," Xander huffed, falling into his chair in a heap and pulling fresh sheets of parchment from the stack. "We need to translate all this to Chthonic anyway. I'll start in on that."

"Oh no." Damien cut through the air with his hand. "I've seen your Chthonic. It's abysmal."

"Of course it's Abyssal," Xander snapped. "That's where it comes from."

"*Abysmal*," Damien stressed. "Terrible, illegible, bad. I'll do the Chthonic translations, and you take a turn at dictation."

The three of them worked into the evening, shadow imps bringing them a meal that they picked at while they dove deeper into the Lux Codex, discovering healing spells and blessings, the translation and anagram solutions coming easier to Amma as she went.

When she read over a specific song in the old Ouranic book, she began laughing, and the two blood mages urged her to tell them what was so funny. Amma had to admit that she and Laurel had made up their own words to that particular song about a farmer who had too much interest in his herd of goats. That made both men laugh, and whether it was at the idea of a prayer song about goat-fucking or if it was directly at her embarrassment at having to sing a few lines, she didn't really care; she was just glad to ease the room's tension a bit.

The storm had mostly cleared itself out when night fell. Xander announced he had reached his limit taking direction from Amma and told Damien it was time for the two of them to go elsewhere in the tower for some friendly sparring.

"No." Damien stood, gathering up the parchment he'd written Chthonic translations on.

"Come on, it'll be fun! Just like when we were kids."

Damien glared at him, violet eyes boring a hole into his head. "Of course you think that used to be fun." He rolled up the parchment and pointed at Xander with the scroll. "And I'm not stupid enough to spar with you in your lair, surrounded by your minions."

"I'll play fair."

"That would be a first." He turned and headed for the door, gesturing for Amma to follow.

She gave Xander a quick, apologetic look, but the blood mage scowled back at her. So much for any camaraderie she might have thought they'd fostered. Hugging the Lux Codex to her chest, she followed Damien back up the stairs and to their shared parlor, leaving Xander behind to pout alone.

"He wants to speak with you," said Amma when they were behind closed doors, "and he doesn't want me around for it."

"No, he wants to see how many times he can stab me before the wounds stop healing." Damien stretched his arms above his head and yawned. "At least that was his idea of fun when he was about seven years old."

She watched him stretch, eyes lingering on the sliver of stomach he unwittingly revealed with his pants slung so low on his hips. It was nice to see him out of armor and even nicer when he was relaxed. "He can't do that," she said quickly, snapping herself out of the stare. "He still needs information from you."

Damien hesitated. "Maybe."

It was true, of course, and she wanted to ask if he intended to hand that information over, if he would tell Xander that she had the talisman inside her that they needed to do…the thing she did not want to think about.

"You've known Xander for that long?" she asked carefully, wondering if she could discern whether all their sniping at one another was truly hatred or something else.

"Unfortunately." Damien cleared his throat. "Amma, I've been thinking: You must be concerned with what's going on in Faebarrow, yes?"

Amma's heart shot up into her throat—that was a good way to get her to change the subject. "Yes," she said desperately, moving to stand right before him. He took a large step back, away from the aura of the codex. She dumped the book onto a sofa and closed the distance between them again. "Do you know? Is there a way to tell?"

"There is, but it won't be quick. We're in the Accursed Wastes, and west of here are the Wilds and then Eiren's eastern border. We're about as far from your home in the west of the realm as possible. But we can send a message to someone there and hope for a response. Would you like to do that?" His violet eyes were searching her face, hesitant.

Amma nodded vigorously. "Very much so."

"All right, good. I considered a message to your personal guard, Tia, but she has likely had enough of ravens berating her. Your friend, the half-elven woman Laurel, she was not at the banquet when things occurred, but would she be privy enough to other goings-on to offer a useful response?"

"Oh my gods, yes, Laurel is the biggest gossip. Also, she loves animals, so if you send her a raven, she'll be thrilled."

"Well, it's an arcane manifestation of a raven, but Corben is real enough." Damien gestured for her to follow to a door at the back of the room that led to a tiny balcony outside. A cool wetness swept in, the smell of rain and clay thick in the damp air. "I think the message would be received best and most likely to be responded to if it came in your voice as opposed to mine."

"My voice? How?"

"Magic."

Of course that was how.

Damien unsheathed his dagger slowly, surveying it like he wasn't intimately familiar with the blade. "I haven't done this with anyone else before."

A chill crawled up Amma's exposed back, and she felt the urge to step closer to Damien on the already cramped balcony, despite the fact that he was brandishing a weapon. "You shared magic with me that time at the Faebarrow gates," she said, touching her lip where he had smeared his blood and then changed her face so she could hide from the guards. He had gotten so close then that she had thought he would kiss her. Maybe he would do the same again.

"Well, it won't be exactly like that," he said, pushing up a sleeve to expose his forearm. "This isn't entirely infernal."

Amma wasn't sure what that meant. She knew mages typically learned a single kind of arcana, whatever the gods blessed them with, and could sometimes pick up other spells with intense study, but Damien was a blood mage, and as he'd told her, his magic ran through his very veins.

He was tapping the tip of his dagger to his forearm, thinking. "I summon the raven with my blood and communicate with it through touch. When Corben reaches his target, my arcana slips into their mind to deliver the message and extract a response if the target wishes. If you allow me, I may be able to turn you into a conduit to manifest the message. The magic would go...well, it will go *through* you, I think, and it *is* infernal, but also something else. Would you...allow that?"

Amma nodded without a moment longer of consideration. *Of course*, she thought. *Anything.*

Damien cut into his forearm, fist clenched, and a drop of blood slid down to splash onto the already wet railing of the balcony. He watched the Accursed Wastes, the darkness, the ruddy landscape, all shadows, and Amma watched him. He was offering her a way to communicate with her friend, something much safer than a letter that could be intercepted. When Amma had refused to comply with Cedric, he had threatened to have Laurel killed, to do away with everyone she cared about, until she gave in to him. If Damien were truly evil, if he were anything like that, he surely wouldn't allow her to speak to her friend, let alone propose the idea.

A raven alighted on the railing and pecked at the droplet of blood before its sharp, black eyes fell on Damien. The bird twitched only once and then held still.

"All right, let's experiment." Damien brought his hands to either side of Amma's face, thumbs sliding against her cheekbones, fingers grazing over her temples, her ears, her jaw. She held very still, not even breathing, and then she felt it, a strange prodding that climbed over her skull, down the back of her neck, and across her shoulders.

Like a thick mist caressing her, the feeling lightened over her limbs and simultaneously squeezed her around the middle until it found purchase at the base of her sternum, and then it—whatever *it* was—was inside her, moving up through her chest until it rested thickly in her throat.

"Place your hand on Corben."

Amma looked down at the still bird and gently touched his head, much fluffier than she expected, and then ran her fingers down to nestle in the feathers of his back. The raven clicked his beak and gurgled out a contented purr, flicking his head up to look at her.

"What would you like to say to Laurel?"

Amma's mind went blank. "Shit."

"Well, I wasn't expecting that." Damien let out a deep chuckle.

"No, I just..." Amma inhaled sharply, the arcana coating the inside of her throat. When she took another breath, the magic shifted in tandem, eerie but also comforting, like it was learning how she moved to become an inseparable part of her.

She lifted her eyes to Damien's, and his focus on her was intent. She could see how hard he was working to make this possible for her, and she focused intently back.

"Laurel," she said, wringing the tension out of her voice, "it's me. Please let me know the state of the barony, if there are any Brineberth soldiers left, if Cedric is gone, if there is still any threat. Are you all right? Is Perry? And Tia and Mother and Father? And are the undead soldiers and Tia... getting along?"

Damien grinned at that.

A little more comfortable, Amma went on. "Did the liathau sapling survive? If so, please let one of the gardeners know to take special care of it, maybe even hide it away. And speaking of hiding, I hope you put those poisons somewhere no one can find them. Ask Perry to help if you need a good spot, and please try to convince him to go to the exams in Eirengaard—he's going to use all this as an excuse to stay home, but if it's safe by the time they come around, he absolutely has to go. Oh! Also, there are these two horses—well, they're not really horses even though they look like horses, but their gas is exceptional—at a place called the Too Deep Inn. If you can, bring them home and take care of them. Bring along something sweet to convince them to go with you, they like sugar best and—"

Damien's face twisted a bit, signs of an internal struggle crawling across it, and Amma sucked in a breath.

"And please be safe, Laurel." She nodded at him.

Damien stared at her for another moment, and she waited, unsure what he wanted. He cleared his throat and murmured, "And tell her how *you* are so she knows I've not done anything too nefarious to you."

"Oh! And I'm fine," she squeaked out. The magic pulsed over and through her, a gentle caress against her skin and

insides, and Damien's fingers, still on her head, felt especially nice then. "Actually, I'm more than fine."

Damien hummed. "And, Lady Laurel, one more request if you are able. There was paperwork on the desk in the rooms Marquis Caldor was using—a lot of it. I know you are a sneaky thing like your friend here. Gather as much of it as possible, read it, report back, and keep the pages hidden away."

Amma squinted back at Damien.

"Is there anything else?"

She swallowed, the words thick in her mouth with guilt. "I'm sorry that I did this. Again."

Damien stared at her a moment longer, his arcana caressing her throat, warm yet odd. She wanted instead to be wrapped in the tendrils of his magic, her whole body heating up at the thought. Her skin beneath his actual touch prickled, craving more.

Then it all dissolved, the arcana pulled out of her too quickly and Damien's touch gone. She was alarmed at how urgently she longed for it to return, the places left behind hollow, and she took a deep breath to try and fill them again. It wasn't enough.

The raven moved under her fingers. He swiveled his head from one of them to the other, and there was a flash of something white against his chest, a single feather hidden within the black. The raven turned himself on the railing, clicked his beak, and shot off with a flap of iridescent wings to disappear into the night.

Alone then, the two stood on the tiny balcony, the damp chill of the wind brushing over their skin, buffeting the warmth of the fire from inside the tower. Amma's heartbeat was pounding, and she felt like she'd been running for miles. "I've never experienced anything like that before," she said breathlessly. "That wasn't infernal?"

"Ah, no, not entirely," he said, tipping his head. "I picked up the spell when I received a message once, something I believe was accidental, but the origin of the spell I've twisted to use on Corben is actually divine, believe it or not."

She absolutely believed it.

They were inches apart, and Amma's body screamed at her to do...*something*. Anything. *Just make him yours*, she silently urged herself, the selfishness of those words not lost on her but meaning them all the same. *If he's yours, he won't want to hurt anything anymore.*

Damien turned from her then and pushed back into the parlor. Gods, was she really so stupid? She had almost the exact same thought once before about a man, and it had been the worst endeavor of her life.

There was a low rumble of thunder out over the Wastes, and Amma shivered, going inside herself and closing the doors on the cold.

"The raven will return to us if Laurel sends a message back, though it will be days, weeks maybe—we're very far from your home."

"Thank you, Damien." Amma rubbed warmth back into her arms, feeling lonely even in the room with him.

Damien gave her a weak nod and collected the parchment full of Chthonic translations he had taken from the study. "Remember to take the book with you to bed," he said, not looking at her as he went for his chamber.

Amma grabbed the Lux Codex from where she had abandoned it on the couch. Hugging it to her chest, she felt like it was her only friend now, and the stupid thing couldn't even talk. "What *is* the plan?" she asked sharply. "The one for Eirengaard and your father?"

Damien paused in his stride away from her, staring at the ground. "The talisman," he said, voice flat. "You are aware how it can control the actions of another. It was meant for Archibald. Only your king has the power to unbind my father from the crystal he's trapped within. I would use it to command him to release Zagadoth the Tempestuous, and then my father will extract his revenge on Archibald and the realm of Eiren."

Amma stared at the back of him for a long moment, saying nothing. What was there to say? Damien had just told her plainly, with no attempt to make it more palatable to hear.

"And now Birzuma the Blasphemed as well," he added, voice taut. "Another demon, another devastation."

Amma was gripping the Lux Codex so tightly her fingers ached. "And you want to do this?" she asked, voice small.

Damien's head snapped up, but he didn't look at her. "I must." And then he swept through to his chamber and shut the door.

CHAPTER 5

AMMA

Misogyny and the Misguidedness of Imps

S TORMS CONTINUED EACH DAY, heavy and dark, a persistent cloud hanging over the tower, but the rain was a soothing backdrop by which to study and transcribe, and the three fell into a routine of reading and discovering what the Lux Codex held. A week passed with no sign of a return raven, but Damien told Amma not to worry—it was a very long way across the entirety of the realm, and Corben was only so big.

That was about all he said to her, though, outside the study. While the three of them were together working, he was friendly enough, though not quite as friendly as that first day. That friendliness even extended to Xander occasionally, if still punctuated with sniping and passive-aggressive comments.

But when they were alone, Damien was reserved and contemplative, unlike how he had been even when they first met. Then he had been cranky and bordering on cruel, but at least he talked to her. Now with each day, he grew more reclusive as he sank further into himself.

One evening, Damien had shut himself up in his room but came storming out, a wicked snarl on his face, muttering, "Damn you, Soren!"

Amma had been sitting in the parlor, hoping he would join her, but not like this. "What's wrong? Who's Soren?"

"Soren bloody Darkmore!" He stalked to the fireplace and threw something into the flames.

"Soren Bloody Darkmore? That's got to be another blood mage," she said, twisting to look into the fire.

"No, it's just Soren Darkmore," he grumbled, turning to stomp back to his chamber. "A blood mage wouldn't bind up all his fucking research into a journal just to tear the concluding pages out." With that, he went back into his room and slammed the door.

Amma sighed. "Actually, that sounds exactly like what a blood mage would do." She grabbed the fireplace poker and fished out the book he'd thrown in, finding that it was that exceedingly boring one he'd gotten from that alchemist's tower in the swamp. The flames had quickly eaten up the dry parchment, and only a few lines of the slanted writing were still legible. "Oh, Maribel," she said to herself, recalling the earth mage's name from Damien's reading on their travels through Eiren, what felt like ages ago. "I hope it was worth it."

Kaz had taken to following Amma everywhere while Damien insisted on being alone. The imp's hatred of Amma even seemed to wane ever so slightly in the presence of the shadow imps, which he much more openly detested. Amma had come to recognize some of them, though not by their forms, which remained inconsistent, but by their affect. Far from a monolith, the shadow imps each had a particular way of doing things. They all served Xander, and most did as Damien requested as well, but some were aggressive and sharp while others were placid and apathetic, and a few even hid in corners with docility.

After a week of this, Amma had worked up the courage to talk to one of the meeker shadow imps and requested a dress that didn't leave her quite so exposed. "And," she added when the imp vigorously nodded the dark, hazy blob that was its head at her request, "if it's maybe rose-colored or lavender or something, I won't complain."

The imp obliged her instantly, bringing her a dusty-pink-colored dress that, while still formfitting, didn't risk one of her breasts slipping out if she moved too quickly. But it only bolstered the annoyance she had been harboring at both blood mages—this dress had been available all along.

She privately enjoyed the soft, slinky fabric of the clothes she had to pick from in the tower, and even the low necklines and cutouts were growing on her, but not when she had no choice and especially not when Xander had picked them out. He was a brat, a conman, and lazy to boot. She didn't like the way he looked at her, and she especially didn't like the way he looked at Damien, like he would kiss him while he drove a knife into his heart.

Before the helpful imp could leave her that evening, Amma asked it to stay. Hesitantly, it curled in on itself into a little shadowy blob and bounced closer to where she sat on the end of her bed.

"Thank you for this," she said, gesturing with the dress. "I was just wondering, have you served Xander for a long time?"

"Yes." Its voice was breathy, something like a mouth opening in the hazy shadows of its head. "I've been with the Blasphemed bloodline for centuries."

"That's Xander's mother, Birzuma?" When the imp nodded again, Amma swallowed. "So you must have been around when Xander and Damien were young. How well did they know each other?"

"There was a time when they both lived in that city of beasts, north of the realm."

"Aszath Koth?" Amma's grip on the dress tightened. "Birzuma and Xander lived there too?"

"After Master Shadowhart was spawned, yes. They remained when the Tempestuous family abandoned the city and Master Bloodthorne."

"You mean Birzuma took care of Damien after his parents left?"

The imp shrugged the parts of it that could have been called shoulders and nodded.

"Lies," Kaz hissed from the room's corner, and Amma and the imp jumped. She had forgotten he was there, but with

Damien often kicking him out of his chamber, Kaz seemed to prefer being with Amma to being alone in the parlor.

The shadow imp curled in on itself a little more. "The dark lordess commanded the city in Zagadoth's stead," it said in a shaky voice, "and Master Bloodthorne was her ward."

Kaz grunted. "Until the dark lord saw what became of Aszath Koth and his son and then had her chased away. *Again*." He turned to Amma. "Master Bloodthorne didn't need her anyway."

"Master Bloodthorne was very young and unruly, and—"

Kaz growled openly at the shadow imp, whose hazy form shrank.

Amma sat straighter, eyes narrowed. "Wait, I thought the draekin took care of him? And what *actually* happened to Damien's parents anyway?"

"Your king happened," Kaz spat at her. "The dark lord was forced to march on Eirengaard to retrieve his spawn, but he could not return, and Aszath Koth and Master Bloodthorne were left unprotected through treachery and the betrayal of humans like *you*."

Amma blinked back at him, unsure what to say. "To retrieve his spawn? You mean Damien?"

"The humans took the young blood mages," said the shadow imp, voice still quavering.

"Enough! She is a human woman, no different from the others. The more she knows, the more she can use against demonkind." Kaz stomped forward, and the shadow imp shot across the room, its hazy body dissolving through the door.

Left alone with Kaz, Amma sighed. "Kaz, I don't want to hurt anybody, especially not Damien. I just want to understand."

"That is what they all say," Kaz grumbled and then added, "trollop," for good measure before stalking out into the parlor.

Amma fell back onto the bed with a hefty sigh. Wonderful, now even the imps wouldn't talk to her.

The next morning, the seventh day of their incessant studying, Xander finally jumped up at one of Amma's dictated translations.

"This!" he shouted, poking a finger down at the book and making contact. Twice as quickly, he pulled his hand back, shaking off the fire that lit itself on his fingertip. "Oh, you bastard of a book," he swore, finger in his mouth.

Damien glanced up, little concern on his face. He had been scrawling furiously, so hard and fast his handwriting had lost its neatness. The midday sun was just barely peeking through the clouds, lighting his face on the side through the massive windows. Though his skin was pallid, it was still nice to see warmth reflected on him. "What?" he asked with a heavy sigh.

"This is what I was hoping for," said Xander, gesturing much more carefully to the page Amma had been translating aloud. "A corruption spell."

"It's a blessing," Amma said carefully, biting her lip. "Almost an exorcism, actually."

"Sure, but *reverse* it." Xander was grinning like a cat. He grabbed a new piece of parchment and began to scribble, drawing out a diagram of sorts, then he stood suddenly to gather something from the other side of the room.

While he was gone, Damien stepped around to look at what he'd done, visibly impressed with the diagram. When Xander returned, he was frantic with more energy than he'd had in days, slipping back into the chair under where Damien still stood. He dropped a small handful of smooth rocks on the table and finished scrawling on the parchment. Then, with a flick of his hand, he called up shadows from the table, the rocks moving with them, and his marks lifted off the parchment. Damien leaned forward over his shoulder, watching, mesmerized.

"The original of this spell is meant to cleanse, but theoretically it can be used to take the most innocent, purest object and absolutely debase it."

As he explained, Damien's violet eyes flicked all over the smoke diagram that Xander had conjured, leaning even closer over the other blood mage's shoulder, transfixed. "You're speaking of reversing the spells."

"Reversing all of them, yes, but *this* is the one to try out, to see if any of this work can actually be done at all. We're doing this one. Together." Xander's gaze slid over to Amma across the table. "And all we need is a target."

Her throat clenched around the protest she wanted to spit out. She'd been convincing herself this work had been theoretical. She never intended to take part in making any of it a reality. Even Damien's plan to take the crown and destroy the capital—she'd pretended like it was just some dream or joke or far-off thing that would never really involve her. And now Xander was looking at her like he would be casting his new corruption spell on her very soul.

"You think this is what Malcolm was doing?" Damien asked, his voice filled with wonder as he gazed back down over Xander's shoulder at the parchment. It was the closest the two had been to one another since they'd arrived.

"I have a feeling, yes." Xander sat back in his chair, tipping his head up. "I only need an evening of preparation, and then we can leave."

Damien squinted down at him, curious and intrigued.

"To steal our vessel—the thing we'll corrupt. I have the perfect target in mind, something I've wanted for a while to add to my collection, but I'll need your help in getting it."

Amma relaxed at hearing the target wasn't her, but she wasn't thrilled at how Xander turned slightly in his chair, bringing his face even closer to Damien's.

He lowered his voice, his grin turning down. "It's only a few days' journey from here. Seizing it will be effortless if we work in tandem, and then we bring it home and perform the spell. Together. How's that sound?"

Damien stared back at him, swallowed, and then pulled back, standing straight. "I don't like it."

Xander's face shifted into a deep frown, but only for a moment. Then he crossed his arms and leaned back fully. "Well, that doesn't really matter, does it? Because you're in my home, and it would be quite rude, not to mention much too risky, to say no to me now."

Damien paced to the far end of the table and flipped through his own paperwork. "I suppose this is the least destructive way we can test the practicality of reversing—"

"Fabulous!" Xander shot up from his seat, cutting him off and pleased again. "We'll leave at first light."

CHAPTER 6

DAMIEN

Bad Company and Worse Discourse

DAMIEN HAD TURNED DOWN every offer of Xander's to speak privately thus far, but the blood mage was persistent, and things had changed. They would be leaving soon, and Damien knew he had to take a chance. He lingered in the study's doorway, watching Amma as she took to the stairs. She wore another of those long, sleek dresses that hugged her and highlighted every careful step she took, but this one suited her even better. Its dusty pink color reminded him of the brief time he'd spent in her home in Faebarrow and the oddly comforting feeling he'd had there despite knowing he did not belong.

The past week had been painful, watching her move through the tower as his desire for her grew with every long look and traded word. But Damien kept himself away, encouraging her to carry that damn book around everywhere as a fail-safe. He wished bloody Corben would come bloody back with some bloody good news every time he caught her looking melancholy. He wanted to bolster her spirits but also wanted a reason to go against his self-imposed exile from her presence and touch her under the excuse of arcana once again.

Not that his touch could be anything but chaste, not while the talisman was still inside her.

Damien's ability to translate from Key to Chthonic was lightning fast, so he had plenty of time to take his own notes while Amma dictated to Xander and Xander complained or fucked off somewhere else in the study. He was glad for Xander's distraction, calling for his help only a few times, but the blood mage had given it to him freely. Now, Damien had a scroll full of notes, bits from other spells found in the Lux Codex, translated and partially reversed, and he was very close to coming up with something that could get the talisman out of Amma. But the pieces didn't quite fit together yet.

Xander was a little shit, but even shit was useful in expelling problems. How he had twisted the blessing Amma had translated that afternoon into a thing of vile beauty—it was brilliant, though Damien would never say. With enough time and the right pieces from the codex, Damien could craft something similar, a bastardized spell meant to rend rather than mend, but to cast it on Amma? Not when the risk of his own failure would be hurting or, gods forbid, killing her. And so if he was going to get the talisman safely out of her, he may actually need Xander's help.

There was only the small problem that he still hadn't told Xander that Bloodthorne's Talisman of Enthrallment existed at all.

Xander came to stand beside Damien in the doorway of the study as Amma climbed the steps. She cast a glance back at the two of them before entirely disappearing, curiosity in her eyes, the Lux Codex tight in her grasp.

"I know you don't trust me, but I promise this will be fun."

Damien squinted back at him. Did he trust Xander? He'd been sleeping under his roof for a full week, and not once did he experience anything untoward. Xander had, so far, kept his word. While he'd been annoying and avaricious, he hadn't tried to stab Damien in his sleep, with a dagger or anything else, and save for daily propositioning often followed by dirty looks behind her back, he hadn't touched Amma either.

"We need to talk."

Xander's eyes widened. "Do we?" He pushed past him and began down the spiraling staircase.

Damien sighed, following. "We have known one another for a long time. In fact, I'm fairly certain you are in some of my earliest memories. You were being a little bastard, but you're there nonetheless."

"Is this the part where you recap our long-standing rivalry as if I am unaware?" Xander took the stairs quickly, his hand skimming the railing, the other flitting above his head. "Because if you do that, I'll know you're asking me for something that you think I don't want to give you." Then he whirled around at the next landing, stopping Damien short. "And there are very few things in that category."

"That doesn't sound like you."

"Doesn't it? Death's at the top of the list."

"That's more like it."

Xander turned again and continued downward. "Go on then—tell me about *us*."

Well, not when he said it like that. Damien groaned, calling up Amma's words in his mind. "It's just occurred to me over the last week that we may be...friends."

Xander stopped short at the foot of the stairs. Even the back of him looked uncomfortable. Xander, who would gladly bed anything on two legs and describe the act in full detail to a stranger, cringed at the thought of actual companionship. In some ways, Damien understood that, and for that reason alone, he knew they almost definitely *were* friends.

Taking in a long breath, Xander glanced back over his shoulder. "You owe me a sparring session."

Damien ground his jaw. "Fine."

Xander's dark eyes twinkled, his grip on the railing tightening for a moment so that the metal beneath his hand looked to bend with the tiniest of escaping shadows. "Excellent."

He led Damien to a room he'd not yet been in, a wide, empty space with stone floors and walls. It wasn't made to be elegant and pretty like so much of the rest of the Chthonic Tower. This space, with its dim lighting and old bloodstains, was meant for one thing.

Xander was already taking off the long dress coat he'd been wearing that day, the linen tunic beneath undone at the neck and falling open so that the vial of blood he always wore danced against his chest when he moved. He threw his arms out, and the white coat was flung across the room and into the waiting arms of a shadow imp who disappeared with it. Xander backed into the space, eyes on Damien. "Let's see, let's see…we need some rules…"

"Oh, you haven't already thought this through?" Damien rolled his shoulders and pushed the sleeves of his tunic up. Neither had on armor, which was a little more dangerous but at least balanced.

"Only every night," mumbled Xander with a chuckle. "We ought to keep faces off-limits, and no conjuring—the shadow imps aren't fond of other infernals, and it's bad enough your dinky little fire imp's here. Oh, and do you still use those squishy, bindy tentacles?"

Damien undid the button at the top of the tunic to expose his chest. The more skin he had available, the better. "Sometimes."

"That's what I was hoping for. Don't hold those back." Xander grabbed the vial about his neck, popped off the cork, and held it up in salute. "And if you really insist on talking, you have to earn it."

A cast of red smoke immediately filled the room before Xander had even spilled any of his own blood from the vial. Damien's dagger slid into his hand like an extension of himself, flipping around his fingers as he got low to the ground and crossed the room, eyes on where Xander had been. He called up arcana to reach out and feel for Xander's presence, but in his own home, Xander's stink was already on everything, and then there was no point, as Xander was cutting through the smoke with a blade brandished, swinging it down right at Damien's head from above. So much for avoiding faces.

Damien dodged him, slashing, but at himself instead of Xander. His blood spurted out down along his arm, and with it, his own faithful blades. They sailed toward his opponent, the smoke cleared in their wake—a nice theatric but short-lived and ultimately a waste.

Xander dodged two of them, but the third caught his elbow. He hissed from the pain, his own blood spilling, then he grinned. "Faster than I remember. So"—he flicked his wrist, and the arcane sword he was holding lost its rigidity, the blade falling in a loose coil on the floor—"it's time you tell me how you're going to free our parents."

Damien clicked his tongue at the new weapon. "Very subtle."

"If you're using ranged attacks, so am I." Xander cracked the whip made up of arcana and then struck out with it.

Instinctively, Damien shielded himself, and the arcane cord wrapped around his forearm but at least avoided his face. "Enthrallment," he said, addressing Xander's request for a plan while reaching over and grabbing the corporeal magic, giving it a tug, and pulling Xander off-balance toward him.

Xander tripped, tall but light, and then grunted as his weapon pulsed, the whip wrapped around Damien's arm sizzling. "Enthrallment?" Xander ducked as Damien swiped at him with his dagger, then popped back up. "Like Tilly and my other infernal girls?"

"On Archibald? Please, I need the enthrallment to last longer than a succubus's charm. Stay still." Damien struck out again, but his aim was thrown when the burning of the arcana wrapped around his other arm intensified.

Xander snickered, wrenching backward and taking Damien along with him. "So no ubi infernals. Then what? You think you're going to convert Eiren's king away from that ridiculous god Osurehm? His domain includes honor, last I checked. You expect to get Archie to drink some newfangled infernal wine in devotion to whom exactly?"

The pain in Damien's arm was too much, and he stabbed the dagger through the weapon hard enough to pierce it down to his own skin. He felt his blood seep out beneath it, and with it, black tendrils crawled out over Xander's magic to choke it back. "The succubi's captivation is short-lived and based on desire, and sects like the Brotherhood rely on their followers' desperation and willingness to drink that arcane sludge," he said, grinning as Xander jumped back, losing his weapon completely as it was gobbled up by Damien's arcana. "I crafted a talisman that bends the victim to my will. If the target simply touches it, their body absorbs it wholly, and they can be ordered to do anything I wish, interminably."

Xander scoffed. "No, you didn't."

Blood still dripped from his forearm amidst coiling burn marks, but Damien whispered Chthonic instead and commanded shadows from the edges of the room to sneak up behind Xander and jab him in the back. "Yes, I did."

Xander straightened, frowning, and grabbed the vial around his neck to tip blood onto the ground. "Say you did manage to do that. What good is it?" He pulled his boot through the small pool, and from it, a black haze emerged and flew at Damien.

Freezing and all-encompassing, the shadows Xander conjured were too fast to dodge. Their squeeze was tight around Damien's body, and he inhaled sharply at the shock of cold, the air forced from his lungs. The sound about him was all gone, and the light too, but that was just fine—in the silent darkness, he could easily focus on the arcana Xander had sent to consume him, and with his dagger in hand, he sliced down through the shadows, bursting out.

With a deep breath, Damien blinked into the light. "The king absorbs the talisman, and I order him to free Zagadoth. The deed is done."

Xander stood on the shadow's other side, arms lax, head tipped. "Just like that?"

Damien shrugged.

"Won't his lackeys notice something's wrong? And couldn't he call on someone to stop him?" Xander seemed to forget they were sparring, face screwed up.

"He won't even know the talisman is within him, nor remember the orders given."

"You're saying this thing you supposedly made can't be overridden by the target's will?"

"I know quite a willful creature that doesn't fight back," Damien mumbled, using the blood from his weeping arm before it healed to cast another volley of arcane blades.

He caught Xander again on his shoulder, the other man hissing out in pain. "You know, of all people, Archibald has years of blessings being heaped upon him, *and* he's a descendant of one of those ridiculous dominions. His will is like iron."

"That's the beauty of the talisman—it's crafted around *my* will. It allows me to place *my* blood inside the target, so it doesn't matter what the target wants, it simply makes them an extension of me."

Xander was frowning in that very specific way he had always done when he was jealous. It was a look he'd mastered when they were quite young. "Well, if it's so good, then why in the Abyss aren't you already in Eirengaard and figuring out how to get it into the dominion spawn's hands?"

Damien gestured to the room. "Because I'm here."

Xander squeezed his bleeding shoulder, and Damien prepared to dodge a ranged attack. "Show it to me."

"No."

"But I wanna see how it works!" There was a yank at the back of Damien's tunic, and he was wrenched downward by unseen hands, slamming into the ground.

"Fuck." He coughed as shadows sprinted away from him. "You said no imps."

Xander pounced before he could stand, getting right in his face. "Show it to me!" And then, just for fun, he slapped him across the face.

Rubbing his cheek, Damien grunted. Why Xander couldn't just break his rib or stab his thigh, he'd never understand. "I can't."

Jumping to his feet, Xander held the vial of his blood over Damien's face. "How am I supposed to believe these claims if you can't show me this supposed talisman?"

Damien curled his lip at the drop threatening to land on him and spat, "Because it's inside Amma."

Xander froze, blood hesitating at the mouth of the vial, and then he recorked it. "You put an enthrallment talisman inside our sweet little kitten? Nice."

"No, it's not nice at all." *And she's not ours, she's mine.* Damien swept his leg along the ground, taking Xander's feet out from under him. The blood mage landed with a hard *thunk* on the stones. "And I didn't *put* it there. It just sort of happened." Damien pushed himself up as Xander lay on his back, taking a sharp breath, the wind knocked out of him. "Regardless, it is inside her. Whatever I tell her to do, she'll do, whether she wants to or not, even if she's not capable."

"Basest beasts, Bloodthorne, you're right. It's not just nice—it's fucking wonderful." Xander coughed breathlessly as he attempted to laugh.

"Well, the complaints aren't wonderful. I made the mistake of telling her about it, and she's obviously unhappy to be my experimental vessel."

Xander blinked, breath finally caught. "If you think it's so *not* wonderful, then why haven't you taken it out?"

Damien groaned quietly.

Xander's eyes pinged all the way open. From his spot still on the ground beneath him, he put on the most shit-eating grin Damien had ever seen. "Oh, you didn't...but you did?" He laughed and then ran a finger across his throat. "You've gotta kill her to get it back, don't you? Of course! If I made the thing, that's exactly what I'd do too!"

Damien drew his dagger just below his collarbone and released another barrage of blood blades straight downward. Xander's eyes lit with shock for only a moment before his form completely vanished from beneath him. "Shit."

There was a crack against Damien's back, and he jerked forward, pain searing up his spine from what had impaled him. Dark gods, that was bad, paralyzing even. Of course, Xander was obsessed with translocation, even the most minor instances of it, and he'd been saving that to get him at the perfect time.

Damien couldn't move; something like a blade was wedged at the base of his spine as Chthonic was whispered behind him, and then Xander's arm came around his chest, pulling him back and up against him. "Just like this," said Xander into his ear, and he pushed Damien's arm up to his own throat, still gripping his dagger. "You can use this little knife you adore so much and slice right across her pretty neck. Would be fitting, poetic even."

Damien should have known how much Xander would revel in the idea of killing her. The feeling came back into his body all at once, Xander's arcane blade dissolving—he never could keep it up for very long—and he threw Xander off him.

"Too complicated," he growled, spinning and striking out with his dagger, catching Xander right across the chest and severing half the cord his blood vial was suspended on.

Xander gasped, snatching the vial before it fell to the floor. "Minotaurshit. You just don't want to tell me because your complications are all mushy and stupid, even though you know as well as I that you can't *really* feel those things."

Damien covered his hesitating response with another dagger slash, but it was messy and wild and all too easy to dodge. Xander would certainly consider any sentiment toward Amma a detriment—Damien even recognized that it was—but there might be another appeal for her life that would work. "She's more important than you think. She comes from a noble house that's become entangled with a much more powerful magic. Something the elves call the One True Darkness."

Xander stared at him a moment, the two men breathing heavily, and then he threw the vial to the floor, where it shattered, blood pooling as frigid, shadowy blackness rose around them both. "Tell me about this One True Darkness."

As if they'd been transported to another plane, the cramped space suddenly felt cavernous, and only the flecks of noxscura floating in Xander's eyes shone back. Damien swallowed, unsure if the connection he only marginally thought was there mattered. "Have you heard the name E'nloc before?"

"E'nloc?" Xander coughed out a single laugh in the dark. "Actually, yes. Whispers of that name came out of Briymari's Tunnel in the Kvesari Wood a moon or so ago."

Damien hadn't paid much attention to the northeast corner of the realm, but that was what the elves had said too. "And?"

"He's a demon, sort of. My mother spoke of him once, said never to trifle with him." Xander blinked, dousing the only light in the darkness for just a moment. "He was wiped out with the Expulsion, and Birzuma would normally hate that sort of thing, lament it, ya know? But she actually seemed more relieved when she told me that particular fairy tale about him. He, uh, is meant to consume the world if I remember correctly. Tried once, in fact, but considering we're all still here, he apparently failed."

Damien sheathed his dagger in the darkness. "So there's an evil out there that's too evil? Even for Birzuma? For you?"

"Oh, those bedtime stories are all half untrue and half lies to keep little blood mages in line. *If you don't finish all your dark rituals, a Holy Knight will banish you too!* You know it's all nonsense." Xander swiped a hand through the air, and the darkness around them dispersed. "Or maybe you don't—I wouldn't know how draekin keep their hatchlings in line."

Damien took a step back, but in the room's clarity, it seemed the sparring was over. Birzuma hadn't been imprisoned until Xander was nearly an adult, so he'd had more time with her in person than Damien did with his own parents, though there was no shard of Birzuma's occlusion crystal to converse with her now. "So even if there's talk and evidence of him in the realm, you'd be fine with him existing and *consuming* the world?"

Xander snapped, and a shadow imp flitted from the edge of the room, bringing his coat. "Oh, sure, why not?" He dressed carefully, wincing with pain from the last blow. His cuts, however, were already mending.

Damien looked at his arms and the places he'd sliced, mostly closed now, even the arcane burn going silver as it dissipated. With his eyes averted, he tried to sound as casual as possible. "You wouldn't be worried about the...*implications* of letting something like that wreak havoc on the realm?"

When there was no response, Damien looked up. Xander was simply staring back, utterly bewildered. "I don't understand the question."

Damien rolled his eyes with a hefty sigh. "You know what I mean. We've all got our self-imposed limits of villainy—it's part of the Grand Order's damn charter, and you're not supposed to criticize the height of someone else's bar."

Xander groaned. "Are we really about to have a discussion about *morality*?"

"Don't act like you're below it. You've chosen not to make an attempt on my life this last week. Even now, you and I both held back."

"Right. Because you're worth something to me alive."

"That's it? There isn't some...fondness?"

"Depends on how you define fondness." Xander scrunched up his nose with a smarmy grin, then blew out a breath and sauntered past him to the door. "But no, I suppose your romantic interests lie elsewhere, with that little bird, just like that raven you adore so much that's not actually infernal." He glanced back at him with an eyebrow cocked. "That's right, I know about that smidgen of divine magic you picked up. But our kitten's more like a sparrow, isn't she? So tiny, so delicate, so like prey. The exact kind of creature a raven would pick apart with its talons and devour."

A twinge rolled in Damien's guts. "I am talking about us, Xander. We're the same. Birzuma and Zagadoth hate one another, but we are here, working together, and you can't lie to me: I know you prefer my company to an empty tower. And you enjoy Amma's company too."

"I do *not*," he said in a huff, swinging around with Abyssal fire flickering in his eyes.

Damien bit his lip, hating what he was about to say, but if it could help protect Amma, he would admit it. "I have this memory of you, Xander. One from when we were very small."

"Beating your ass?" The blood mage's grin went wide.

Damien wanted to roll his eyes; he wanted to say that two years was an awful lot of difference to a five-year-old, but instead he just swallowed. "No, not that. Before all that. You and I were alone, and we were far from home, and we were both…scared."

Xander's grin faltered, recognition in his eyes, but his face twitched in a way that seemed to say he was disgusted at the very thought.

"Sometimes it feels like it was just a dream or a nightmare, but other times it feels like a memory. I don't know where I was, but it was far from home in Aszath Koth, and you were with me. You told me everything was going to be okay, and I believed you."

Xander's throat bobbed. "Does that sound like me?"

"Not really."

When the blood mage gave him a shrug as if that answered things, Damien groaned. Perhaps that had been a waste.

"Regardless, the two of us, we've got a shared existence. You know that we're human just as much as we are demon, and don't you ever question that? What it means?" He scoffed. "Don't you ever wonder who your father is?"

"Do I *wonder* who my *father* is?" Xander's face changed then, every bit of amusement he'd had at Damien's questions gone. "The human part of me isn't something to mull over and romanticize. It's a necessary good. The demons, our *true* creators, they're immensely powerful, more so than you or I will ever be, but because of what they are, they're flawed. They're only on this plane because some other being summoned them, but they can be banished against their will or worse, chained and subjugated. I know you've gotten a taste of that yourself, fucking with a nox-touched, but imagine it being permanent." Xander had moved closer, poking him in the chest, lips curled down with vicious disgust. "It might take you moons, years even, to break free of the noxscura if your will is too weak, but you *can*. Demons though? The price they pay for their power is relying on someone else to break them out. That's the only reason they deigned to lie with humans to bear us—to free them from the idiotic situations they've gotten themselves into."

Damien had never heard Xander refer to his mother in such a way, and he was sure he never would again. He didn't even bother to knock Xander's hand away.

"So yes, I suppose I've briefly considered why I am what I am, half human, and what that means, and it's this: Humanity is a necessity solely to be free from enslavement. Otherwise, we're just demons, Damien, and we're meant for evil, nothing else."

Damien just stared back at him. It wasn't a conversation—it was never going to be. It was simply Xander's truth. "It must be nice to have it all figured out."

"Until you understand that, we won't really be the same," said Xander, sighing wistfully, more gently placing his hand on Damien's chest and giving him a pat. "That's why you always end up losing."

A blast of cold arcana caught Damien in the chest and knocked him to the ground. Pain seared up his back, and he lay there, coughing, the sound of Xander's laughter echoing out into the hall as he walked away.

CHAPTER 7

AMMA

The Creation of a Thousand Forests Can Be in One Acorn, but That Acorn Can Still Fall on One's Head

When the door to the parlor opened, Amma jumped to her feet. She'd been sitting on the edge of the couch, worrying the binding of the Lux Codex with sweaty fingers, and Kaz had been pacing at her feet silently, doing his best to ignore her even as he consistently checked that she was still there.

Damien stood in the doorway, taken aback as if he hadn't expected her to be waiting. His hair was mussed, and there was blood spattered on his chest, his hands, and his cheek.

"What happened?" she breathed, held to the spot.

He took stock of himself, then closed the door behind him, shrugging. "Xander and I got into a bit of a scrap."

Amma abandoned the Lux Codex on the sofa and went to him. "Let me take a look at that."

"No." Damien caught her hand before it could reach him, holding it tightly. She would have pulled back if she hadn't missed his touch so much. "I'll heal as I always do. This is nothing."

"But—"

"You should be resting." He released her as if he'd been burned and eased out from between her and the door to head for his chamber. "We're leaving early tomorrow."

Amma glanced back at Kaz, who gave her a smirk and followed after Damien, only to have the chamber door shut in his face. Amma waited there, hoping he might come back, but there was only wind buffeting the tower windows and the popping of the blue fire to fill up the silence left behind. Frustrated, she grabbed the Lux Codex and went to her own room, the knot in her stomach tightening so that she wondered if it would ever come undone.

But when she woke the next morning, she was determined and requested clothing appropriate for travel from one of the nicer shadow imps. Dressed in a comfortable tunic with a particularly flattering leather vest that laced up the front and a pair of tight, knee-length breeches that allowed her to strap her silver dagger over instead of against her skin as she'd been doing, she felt a boost in her confidence. She'd also acquired a new belt with a set of pockets. There wasn't storage large enough on it for the Lux Codex, so she left it in the parlor with the shroud beside it, but she did still have the raven feather Damien had given her in Elderpass, to be used in case the two were separated, and the shard of pottery from the upturned cart in Faebarrow, a reminder of her home, however fraught it was—those she had squirreled away inside her dress the night of the banquet.

They set out on foot over the Accursed Wastes, hoods up since it was drizzling again. Amma offered Kaz a ride on her shoulder to hide from the rain, but he only sneered at her and trudged along behind them, dripping and grumbling instead. Damien and Xander marched on either side of her, and without the Lux Codex, both could get close, though the strangeness of the Wastes kept Amma from minding the proximity. They were accompanied the entire way by shadow imps that flitted about at their sides, barely seen, but their presence ever ominous.

Half a day's walk through the cloudy Wastes brought them to a gate that stood in the middle of nothing. The storm had abated, but the land about it was still cracked and dry, and it went on in every direction—forever, it seemed—broken by small copses of trees or rock outcroppings and not much else. The gate was tall and made of twisted metal, thin bars wrapping around one another, but it was connected to no fence. It stood closed, but one could simply walk around it.

Xander went up to the center where the doors came together, half a circular pattern on each side meeting in the middle, and put a hand at the convergence. There was a burst of arcane energy that rattled through the metal bars, crackling over it and down into the ground. The doors swung open, away from them, and a dark image formed on the other side, illuminated just at its edges from the Wastes' low lights to reveal rocky walls. Xander walked through without a word, only a satisfied glance back.

Damien clicked his tongue. "Yes, yes, I'm sure your mother is very proud of *her* work."

Xander scoffed, flicking off his hood as he stalked into the dark.

"He didn't make that. This translocation is more advanced than what he can do," Damien told Amma. "Plus, this portal's older than him by at least five centuries."

She smiled warily but said nothing—Damien speaking to her was welcome, even if it was to belittle Xander, and she didn't want to ruin it. The two followed, Kaz and a small group of shadow imps trailing after.

On the gate's other side, the air was cooler, the dampness different. A gentle glow of light silhouetted Xander's form ahead of them. He was removing his wet cloak as he walked, and they did the same, reaching the end of the rocky tunnel to step out into a dense wood.

Amma glanced back at the opening they'd come through, an eerie cave built into a rocky outcropping in the wood. It gave her a chill just to look at it, something telling her to stay away even though she'd just walked through. That was likely by design. But there was gentle birdsong in the trees and wind in the leaves, and it seemed at least some of her unease was left on the other side of the tunnel.

Xander took a deep breath of the forest, squinting into

the sunlight that streamed through the branches, then made an exaggerated retching sound. "About two days in that direction and we'll be in Durendreg. It's a shithole, but we won't be spending any real time there."

Amma didn't recognize the name, and that likely meant it was outside Eiren's borders. The Accursed Wastes certainly were, and even though they'd gone through a portal that translocated them, there were still a lot of places that weren't protected by the crown.

"Are you intending on ever telling us what we're going after?" Damien ran a hand through his hair, damp despite the hood, and brushed it out of his face. The look he was giving Xander wasn't friendly, but seeing him under the dim sunlight and not glowering and depressed made Amma's heart hitch. She remembered him on the road not so long ago and hoped their new surroundings might inspire him to return to who he had been before Xander's tower.

"There's a temple, tucked away in Durendreg, and every fifty or so years, they devote a new sacred vessel to their goddess," said Xander, as if they should have known. He eyed Amma a moment, then went on. "The newest one was just created, and I want it, so that's what we're fetching. I'm sure Yannveceny won't mind."

"Yannveceny?" Damien looked to her with the expectation that she would know the goddess.

Amma winced. Yannveceny wasn't Abyss-cast, but the goddess still wasn't well-loved in Eiren, at least not for direct worship. She only knew the name because of a particularly nasty parable told to warn against taking retribution that had stuck with Amma over the years and how Yannveceny could help with retaliation—for a price. "She's the goddess of vengeance," Amma said, heart speeding up.

"You've got one of those?" Damien cocked his head.

"And doesn't she sound lovely?" Xander was folding his cloak. "But she's not terribly popular it seems, so her followers all converge in one boring little town in the middle of this awful jungle. Only benefit is they condense their power to place a radiant essence inside their vessel-type thing, where it's housed for half a century and then just sits around being worshipped. Useless, they do nothing with it, but the last one was too difficult to get, too evolved. Plus, I didn't know what to do with it exactly. But now, thanks to the two of you, we've got a splendid corruption spell to turn it."

"And then?" Damien asked.

"Who knows!" Xander threw up his arms, continuing ahead through the trees. "We could fail, I suppose, and accidentally destroy it, but that's part of the experiment. If we succeed, then we have a weapon. Maybe we use it in Eirengaard, or I'll just keep it safely tucked away in the tower. The shadow imps can care for it until it's more useful."

"What's that supposed to mean?"

"Oh, it's just quite fragile, and weak too at first." Xander was smiling. "That's why now is such a good time to take it."

"I don't feel good about stealing something," said Amma carefully, even as Damien shot her an unbelieving glance.

"Of course you don't," mocked Xander as he led them

through the wood. "But if it helps, the thing's already been stolen once."

While she tried to puzzle out what that meant, Damien grunted. "And how are we supposed to get this thing these zealots care so deeply about? Walk into town and start blowing the place up?"

Amma's eyes widened, flicking from Damien to Xander. At her side, Kaz's tail flicked madly with excitement.

"Ah, you know me so well!" Xander chuckled. "That's what I'll be doing, yes, and all their attention should be on me since I told them I'm coming."

"You what?"

"I leaked my whereabouts, used the shadow imps to run along ahead under an illusion to spread whispers that the terrifying blood mage Xander Sephiran Shadowhart was making a trek to Durendreg, intending to burn it to the ground. I sort of declared an anticrusade against Yannveceny, I guess. Hope I don't get smited. Or is it smote? Smitten?"

Damien had caught up to him, hands out in bewilderment. "Why?"

"They'll be focused on me, and the two of you can sneak around back to their temple and snatch the vessel."

"You don't think they'll have increased security at their temple too?"

"Probably, but I assume you can handle whatever's there. Can't you?"

"Of course I can. That's not the point."

The two of them continued to bicker as they walked

along, and Amma let herself fall a few paces behind. She took a deep breath of the woods and stretched her arms above her head. The Accursed Wastes had been heavy on her, and for all the tower's comfort and luxuries, she had missed the freshness and wilds of the outdoors. There were massive sable oaks here and ashes with wide trunks, like they had in the northeasternmost duchy of Eiren, but a species or two she hadn't seen before too, further suggesting they were outside the realm proper. When a small something fell out of a tree and bonked her on the head, she grunted, but that too she supposed she had missed.

She picked up the acorn that had attacked her. Holding it between two fingers, she rubbed its exterior, the smoothness of the shell and the rough dappling over its top, and then there was a third feeling, something that pulsed into her fingertips. Amma came to a stop, lifting up the acorn as a slight vibration worked its way down her hand. That was…that was new.

She blinked, eyes refocusing ahead instead of on the seed, and Damien was looking back over his shoulder at her, head cocked, watching. She grinned and tossed the acorn over her shoulder, continuing on.

The day fell into night earlier in the forest than it would in the open plains, and they made camp around a small fire. Xander and Damien continued to argue about the plan to sneak into the temple, but Amma was too distracted to properly listen. Instead, she lay on her back on her cloak, now dry, and blinked up at the tree branches overhead. They swayed lightly in the breeze, dark against the deep blue of the evening sky. She had the urge to wave back at them, but that was incredibly silly, she knew, and she kept her hands firmly folded on her stomach until the sounds of the forest lulled her into sleep. Her dreams that night were vivid, filled with colors and moving trees and breathlessness.

Amma woke suddenly, blinking into the dark. The fire had gone out, and she held still, listening. There had been a noise, something, that had woken her, and her heartbeat was pounding hard in her chest. But there was nothing but the gentle night sounds of the forest: crickets, wind, and an owl calling far off in the trees, too low to be alarming.

Amma dared to sit up in the dark. She could make out the forms of Damien and Xander sleeping opposite one another. Kaz was gone, likely prowling the perimeter as he had when they'd slept on the road before, and if the shadow imps were about, they had the perfect spots to hide in. The weariness was all out of Amma though, and she leaned back on her hands to gaze up at the starry sky between the branches.

Under her palm, there was a hard knot, and she pawed at the bump in the dark, gathering it up and bringing it to her face. Between her adjusting vision and the feeling of it, she could tell it was another acorn. Well, not another, the same acorn as what had fallen on her before—that was what her mind told her at least, even though it was impossible.

No, of course it was a different one; it was only that all acorns looked pretty much the same.

"You want to stay with me?" she asked it in a whisper, chuckling to herself but needing the absurdity of the idea after the solemnity of the last week.

Yes, please, a voice whispered back, and Amma nearly chucked the seed as hard as she could into the dark, but she continued to hold on and just stare.

"O...okay," she said, and into her pouch it went, alongside the feather and the piece of pottery.

Wide-eyed, Amma lay back down, folding her hands over her stomach and staring at the tree branches again. This time, when they bent, she did indeed wave back. Then she quickly rolled over and squeezed her eyes shut.

CHAPTER 8

DAMIEN

More Like Duren-Drag

DURENDREG WAS, AS XANDER described, small and, from the looks of it, quite backward. It reminded Damien of the boggy town outside Tarfail Quag where Amma had accused him of having resting villain face. He moved his lips around, feeling for a frown, but the tight line he'd pulled them into was just his deep-peering face, the villainousness more difficult to access lately, if not the grumpiness.

Xander was kneeling beside him in a cramped space between two huts, but he was grinning, and wickedly at that. They had quietly waded into town from the thick wood at the outskirts and remained unseen despite the brightness of the early afternoon. Xander had finally revealed why he'd chosen the date and time that Damien had been railing against for the last two days: Durendreg had engaged in some sort of festival the night before for their goddess so that they would be hungover and weary that day, and indeed, there were very few people about.

There wasn't much to the homes that dotted the village, but the buildings fanned out from its center in concentric circles, allowing for good cover in the daylight. A wide, winding dirt road cut through the town, leading to the temple at its very middle, the most elaborate building, standing on a small plateau. It was clear what they valued here, with symbols of their goddess Yannveceny nailed up on doors and painted on walls.

At Damien's other side crouched Amma, back against the building, a small frown creasing her face. He wanted to suggest she wait at the edge of the wood, but knowing he would be heading into a temple gave him pause at sending her away. It would be safer for her if she didn't engage, but holy buildings were sometimes…*difficult* to maneuver, likely why Xander had decided he would stay outside while Damien languished within. Damien would possibly need an anchor to do this, something to tether him to reality if the divinity in the temple was too much, and Amma, who would be completely unaffected and, well, just being *her*, would serve that purpose. At least they would both be free of Xander for a bit.

"Speed is of the essence for you two. I'll stretch it out as best I can, but this place won't take long to terrorize." Xander squinted around the corner from where they stood and then eyed the two of them. "I expect you'll be in the wood waiting for me by the time I'm done. But don't show up without the *ancast erfind*." Xander was carrying another translocation spell with him that they would use to go directly back to the tower instead of the multiday trip it would take on foot to find the forest's portal in the cave back to the Accursed Wastes.

"Was that Ouranic?" Amma asked with a sharpness to her voice that Damien didn't expect. "I don't recognize the meaning of those words."

"The vessel of Yannveceny's holy light, yes. That's just the relic's Empyrean name." Xander stuck his tongue out. He then gave Damien a wink. "See you on the other side, *friend*." The word held none of the camaraderie it should have.

Hood up to cover his white hair, Xander stalked away from them, headed back to the farthest edge of Durendreg where he would begin raising the Abyss and drawing as much attention as possible. Shadow imps flitted along behind him, and Xander was already uncorking his blood vial to summon more as he disappeared. Kaz was sitting at Damien's feet but had taken on the form of a ruddy-colored squirrel with a jutting underbite just in case they were seen. His puffy tail flicked and then relaxed when Xander was finally gone.

Left alone to wait, Damien grumbled, hating being given an order, but was surprised to see a similar frustration on Amma's face. He wanted to give her words of reassurance but had none. "It's not so strange," he said with half a shrug. "Just like the last time we went thieving together."

She sucked in a breath. "I'm going to need an even stiffer drink after—" Her eyes narrowed as if she had just remembered something, then she shook her head. "Why wouldn't Xander tell us this relic had a name until now?"

Damien groaned. "For drama's sake, I expect."

"He wouldn't give us any details, he just said it was a relic, like that was supposed to mean something, but now, all of a sudden, it has a name?" She glowered at the ground, fingers tapping quickly against her knee like she was counting. He had seen her do something similar when she worked on the translations out of the Lux Codex.

"What do you expect? He's a di—"

There was a scream off in the distance, and they both straightened. Xander's terror had begun.

Damien only looked at Amma for a moment more, her angry pondering replaced with a frightened glint in her eyes. "Come on," he said, standing and heading for the shadows of the next building, but she didn't move. She could only stare out above the roofs at the smoke rising from some unknown place at the town's outskirts. Damien gritted his teeth. "Sanguinisui, follow me."

Amma jolted as if being dragged, a visible lurch to her step and shock on her face. It had been quite some time since he'd used that Chthonic word, and it tasted bitter on his tongue, but he couldn't dwell on the discomfort he was causing her. Damien darted to the next building, and she did the same, Kaz skittering along at their feet.

And then they were running, the chaos enough of a distraction for the two to make it down another road toward the temple, blending in with villagers who had come out of their homes bleary-eyed and frightened. Amma was moving in a way that looked like her own accord now, keeping up and watching him, mouth pulled into a tight frown.

They came to an alley with a stack of barrels and crates to crouch behind. There was a sour, rotting smell and small piles of abandoned clay cups and bits of clothing, as if a wildly good time had been had the night before. Despite the stench, the stupor most of the civilians would be in would indeed be helpful, but he'd never tell Xander that.

Damien could survey the temple from their spot hidden in the shadows. It was a tall building with columns running along its front and sides and a currently open entry for villagers to come and go as they pleased for prayer. But at the doors stood five larger men, clad in armor and with semiformidable weapons strapped to their sides. They were slightly disheveled though, and one even looked to be somehow sleeping as he leaned against the wall with his eyes closed. Xander's warning had likely put them there, another obstacle for Damien and Amma, even if the obstacle was hungover.

"I'd rather not cause a scene," said Damien. Though it would be easy, the idea of striking them all down irked him. "We need time inside since we don't know exactly where this relic is, and if we kill them, it might just bring more."

"Oh no, please," whispered Amma, her hand finding his forearm and squeezing, "can we not kill them?"

Damien swallowed, glancing down at her hand, then back up. How she could still do that, still touch him so gently as if he hadn't been cold to her since stealing her away from the home he had rained destruction upon, he didn't know.

The victims in question fidgeted at the far-off sounds in their city, though they weren't roused completely. Xander and whatever he was doing were still unseen from where they stood, and they were so bleary-eyed, they might not have really seen anything even if he were close.

Then there was a shriek, and from the opposite end of the street, a young girl came running, a shadow imp on her heels. Xander adored having minions; his were grossly devoted, so it was no surprise they'd been ordered to slink off into town and cause additional chaos. The shadow imp tore claws through the air, barely missing the girl, and she tripped, stumbling forward and landing in the dirt. Damien glanced back at the temple. The guards had to be able to hear her, but they weren't moving to do anything.

Another shriek, and he knew the imp had struck her. "Bloody stupid incorporeal beast," Damien growled and called up arcana with more Chthonic words, no blood to spill just yet, and reached out toward the infernal creature. He could speak to most infernal things, even those loyal to Xander, if need be, and he sent it a message to halt.

Its head like blob popped up, spindly, black arms extended over the defenseless villager, ready to really do damage. Damien cast with instructions to find Xander and to stay by his side, and the imp dispersed. The girl scrambled up to her feet, clutching a bloodied arm, and fled inside the closest hovel.

"You helped her." Amma's voice was just behind him as she leaned in close.

"Her cries were distracting." He sniffed and pointed to the guards. "Now, what to do with them?"

Amma crept around him to the edge of the barrels they hid behind. "I know what we can do."

When she stood, Damien reached out, grabbing her wrist. "What are you doing?"

"Getting rid of them," she said. "Trust me, you gave me an idea."

He hesitated, then released her. They hadn't spoken of the arcana she'd demonstrated back in the Grand Athenaeum, their escape from the library and all that came after a good distraction, but perhaps she was finally ready to reveal whatever magical secret she'd been keeping all this time.

Amma cleared her throat, took a massive breath, and then bolted at top speed right toward the guards.

"The fuck?" Damien groaned, using the last bit of his patience to stay still. "She's *not* going to attack them," he reassured himself, though he was coming to realize he didn't have much confidence in ever really knowing exactly what Amma would do.

At his side, Kaz chirped. "Maybe she'll get herself killed!"

Damien blindly swatted and connected with something furry but kept his sights on Amma as she ran right up to the men and skidded to a stop, breathless. "Dead!" she screamed. "They're all *dead*!"

The guards questioned her all at once, bumbling their words, hands hovering over hilts and squeezing halberds.

Amma didn't give a straight answer, her voice frantic as she continued to shriek, "You have to go now! They're being attacked! Please, do something!"

Damien nearly jumped at the urgency himself, uneasy at hearing Amma distressed at all.

Three of them took off in the direction she pointed, leaving her there with the other two. Brilliant. Two, Damien could handle without anyone else seeing, but then one of them grabbed her, proclaimed something about taking her to safety, and all three sprinted inside the temple. Massive doors slammed shut behind them.

"Shit." Damien dropped his head forward and thunked it against the barrels. In the wake of Amma's screams, the city fell into an eerie quiet.

With the villagers dispersed, darting inside at the chaos, and no more guards standing watch, Damien lifted his head again and stood slowly. Alone, he simply wandered up to the front of the temple, cautious but pointlessly so—there wasn't even anyone about to stop him. He squinted up into the sunlight, then at the doors. There were distant screams again, men fighting off imps and, presumably, Xander himself, muffled from the far side of town. With a sigh, Damien gave the door a gentle tug, but it was sealed shut. He gave it a heftier jerk, but still it remained closed.

Growling, Damien began to circle the stone structure, Kaz scampering unhelpfully beside him. There would be another way in, hopefully still unlocked. Sprinting from one column's shadow to another just in case there were prying eyes, he took in the large, stained glass windows, breakable, though that wouldn't be terribly stealthy—the attention needed to stay on Xander.

In the shadow of a column near the corner, he placed a hand on the stone of the building, arcana gathering in his palm and seeping outward as he cast a simple spell to locate Amma inside. The whole temple pulsed back, and he was thrown against the column. He would have been on his ass had the stone pillar not been there. Groaning at a twinge in his back, he steadied himself. It was no wonder Xander had no intention of going inside. Goddess of vengeance or not, the divine energy in the place was intense, suggesting priests and protective spells on the building.

But luck did smile on him in the form of another door. When the handle didn't budge, Damien's frustration took over. Amma was inside, and he'd been apart from her for too long. Taking a step back, he pulled out his dagger and sliced into his palm. Taking down the door would require a stronger spell, and it would be loud and messy, but it was the only way to take him to Amma.

And then the door opened.

Damien closed his fingers around the arcana, which was about to burst from his hand. "Amma," he hissed, staring at her diminutive form standing in the open doorway.

"Hey!" Her smile was bright, as if she had not just almost been blown to bits with infernal magic. "Come in, quick—I told those guys I had to pee, but I've just been wandering around looking for a door, and they're going to wonder where I went."

Damien fully snuffed out the spell and stepped toward the door, but Kaz yelped and backed away. "Wait around back," instructed Damien, and the imp scurried off, fluffy tail disappearing around another corner. "It's too holy for all his infernal blood."

She watched him step inside, a small pout to her lips. "But you're in here." She closed them in and dropped the lock bar back into place with a *thunk*.

"Well, I'm not a—" Damien clicked his tongue. He'd almost said he wasn't an infernal creature but chuckled instead. "I'm not as susceptible as he is." He had his humanity to thank for being able to stand on the hallowed ground inside and not immediately catch on fire in any case, but how he would hold up remained to be seen.

They stood in a small hallway that ended in another hallway that crossed it. The building wasn't particularly large from the outside, but it was housing at least two guards and gods knew how many holy people. He didn't need to put out any feelers to know the place was thrumming with divine arcana, and he pressed a hand against his own chest, his heart thumping a little harder.

Amma began down the hall, pointing. "There's a big worship chamber that way. A priest and priestess were praying up at an altar."

"Of course they were." That was perhaps some of what Damien was feeling. "Using my arcana in here may alert them to our presence."

"The guards are in there too, but the room was pretty bare otherwise. I didn't see any relic that could be the *ancast erfind*. Would have been nice if Xander had told us exactly what it looks like."

You'll know it when you see it, he had so unhelpfully told them.

"What's that way?" Damien nodded toward the other end of the cross hall, the small move making him slightly dizzy.

"Let's find out," she said, creeping down to the end.

Damien followed, disappointed that how he felt was distracting him from fully appreciating her willingness to misbehave. The room they entered appeared to be completely dark; only a faint glow around the windows that lined it near the ceiling was evident, but Amma was apparently seeing things better, gesturing for him to follow when he stopped on the threshold. There was an oppressive pressure on his temple and his vision was blurry, but he could tell the next chamber spanned what seemed to be the width of the entire building, with a ceiling that was twice as high as where they'd been.

He swallowed, breaths coming too shallow for comfort as they hugged the darkened wall of the space. The floor was scattered with tables and many benches. Moving shadows and glints of strange light filtered through the colored glass of the windows above, though it was difficult to tell what might have only been in his head.

A hand took his, and Amma tugged him a step closer to her. "Are you all right?"

He nodded instinctively, though it wasn't true.

She squeezed his hand and then let go. He would have asked her not to if he thought opening his mouth wouldn't lead to vomiting. "I bet what we're after is hidden up there," Amma whispered, pointing to the far end of the room.

A statue on the back wall was set into a deep alcove, with stairs running along an arch on either side of a massive set of wooden doors. The statue was presumably of Yannveceny, a thin-limbed goddess draped in robes and holding out a pendulum. A blade attached to it on a chain swung in perpetual motion.

"Is that what you lot do?" Damien asked, strained. "Put your important religious things up high?"

"Or underground," she said. "Wherever is least convenient for thieves."

Damien felt the presence before seeing or even hearing it—a holy person of some deep persuasion was headed their way. He grabbed Amma and pulled her into an alcove, sliding the two of them into a shadow just behind the bent arm of another statue. He felt the breath go out of her, shocked at the sudden movement, but she made no other noise, just pressed her back up against him.

There were footsteps that found their way to the largest statue of the goddess. Damien knew he shouldn't use the arcana to hide them like he had in the Grand Athenaeum, especially not when the priest's sibilant whispers began to fill the chamber with prayer. They were not loud, but they swelled in his head, stabbing at his mind, and there was a constant pulse, the cadence of that pendulum, growing with every swing.

Then there was another feeling that pressed on him, but from the inside, pushing out. Noxscura. The urge to release the magic, to strike out and kill the man, to level the whole temple, flooded his being. With the hand not wrapped around Amma's middle, he reached up and rubbed an ear, trying to block the prayers out, but they only became louder, and that rhythm intensified, knocking at his brain like it could crack his skull right open and release the deepest evil within him.

Amma shifted around to face him, pressing close to remain in the darkened space. She slipped a hand upward and placed it on the side of his face, rubbing her thumb across his cheek. He could see her lips moving, saying something, but couldn't hear over the muffled prayers echoing in his head.

Save for the spell to send Corben off to Faebarrow, Damien hadn't truly touched Amma since he had taken her away from her home, both at her request and his insistence. Not since he had held her close and looked into eyes intoxicated with what he had done for her, high on the chaos of releasing the Army of the Undead, of terrorizing a royal house, of spilling the bastard marquis's blood, and even higher on the way she had clung to him and pulled him close. He had a brief if mad thought back then that the rest of the world might actually give the two up. They could escape from whatever vows they'd made to anyone else and only be beholden to one another.

That, of course, was impossible.

But now he had her again after days and nights of holding himself back, of convincing her to keep that damn book close to ward him off. But the Lux Codex wasn't an oppressive force between the two anymore, and he could finally feel the soft touch of her fingers on his face. No one had ever been so gentle with him, and he wished he could just trap the two of them there so he never had to give up that touch.

Fuck, what was this bloody temple doing to him?

But the noises had all stopped, and the pain too. All he could feel were those soft fingers on his skin, and he was reaching up, wrapping a hand around her wrist, being just as gentle, not to pull her hand away but to lean farther into it.

With newfound clarity, the sounds inside the temple came back, but the priest's prayers had stopped. Damien's eyes snapped to a figure trekking across the room. That overwhelming feeling removed itself fully, and Damien squeezed Amma's hand as he carefully removed it from his face. The robed priest left the way the two of them had come without noticing either one in their shadowed alcove. So much for divine arcana.

"Let's go," he said, and the two hustled to the stairs beside the statue and upward to the large set of doors.

After opening the door with a low creak, they eased their way through the smallest crack possible and slipped inside the room. This space was not meant for worshippers, the shelving on the walls holding bound tomes and parchment rolled up messily but no apparent effigies or religious artifacts to make

Damien feel especially awful—only a desk and chair in the room's center. It was strange to keep an office above an altar, but then it wasn't really an office, he supposed, when he saw what was sitting on the desk: a finely woven basket holding a satiny turquoise blanket, and nestled inside that, the still form of an infant, fast asleep.

Damien's eyes darted around the rest of the room—empty. Even without casting, he would know if others were hiding inside, especially priests, but to find a child so small all alone was strange. At least he was fairly certain it was strange, but Damien would be quick to admit he knew nothing about child-rearing. Then again, there was a mad blood mage afoot, attempting to break into this very temple, so why anyone thought to leave their spawn here at all was a mystery.

"Oh no." Amma crossed the room on silent feet to lean slightly down and look at the infant. "Oh. No, no, no…"

Damien glanced back out the cracked door, but no one was in the chamber below. "What's wrong?"

"The *ancast erfind*." Amma began to gnaw on a nail. "This is it."

Damien wasn't typically so slow on the uptake, and he could blame the oppressive aura of the temple, the recent brush with Amma, or his annoyance at being there under Xander's direction for his cloudy mind, but the truth was much more likely that what Amma was saying was just rather preposterous. "Well, I'm sure we can move the child without waking it to grab the relic."

"Damien, the baby *is* the relic."

No cloudiness of mind could misconstrue that and yet...
"I don't understand."

"The Ouranic *ancast erfind*, it translates to *sacred infant*."

Damien ran a hand down his face as he stepped toward the desk and stopped abruptly when the floorboard beneath his boot creaked.

"Damien," Amma hissed as the human relic stirred with a whining noise.

"I didn't mean to."

The baby's whining began to escalate.

"I said, I didn't mean to," he hissed directly to it as if that might convince it to stop.

The baby began to squall properly.

"Amma, do something."

She held her hands out. "Like what?"

"Why are you asking me? Shouldn't you know?"

Amma's hands fell back to her sides, and all the anxiety went out of her voice. "Why would I know, Damien?"

He glanced back to the chamber through the door's crack, still empty, but for how long with the spawn's cries rising? "Because you're, you know, *kind* and...and nurturing? Also, you happen to have breasts."

Amma glared at him and poked herself in the chest. "These aren't *working*. They're just for show!"

"I just, I mean—" Damien rubbed his forehead, the child's cries, the temple's aura, and his own stupid words making him as inarticulate as he'd ever been. "They're warm and nice to be pressed against. That's what spawn are fond of, no?"

Amma's indignation didn't recede until she glanced about the still-empty room. Beyond the cries of the child, there were no doors opening elsewhere, no footsteps headed their way, no worried voices calling out. "It doesn't really seem like this baby is used to being cuddled against anything," she said, looking back down at it.

Amma reached into the basket, awkward at first, face pinched, and then she lifted the baby out and held it to her chest, slipping a hand underneath, the other cradling its head. She whispered to it, something Damien couldn't hear over its cries, but then, as the infant quieted, he could make out her voice, softly lilting a few honeyed words of appeasement and reassurance. The child's eyes, deep brown and large, roved up to her and studied her face with a strange and sweet wonder.

That was what Damien had meant—it was that Amma was a soothing presence. The breasts were just a nice perk.

With the room quiet save for Amma's low hum, the pressing pain on Damien's head lifted again. Strange, he thought, so close now to the *ancast erfind*, but even as he took steps toward where Amma stood gently rocking the infant, the cloudiness and pain didn't intensify. Yet he could feel the child had been blessed, not so he couldn't touch it, but it was *prepared* somehow, and his stomach turned over. It had to be like Amma herself and the talisman, housing something arcane within it but blocking the aura with its very body.

"Damien?" Amma's voice broke just on his name as she stared down at the baby. She cleared her throat and opened her mouth again but wasn't capable of getting out what she wanted to say.

"I know." He sighed heavily. "Xander knew what this was—he had to—but chose to keep the details from us. A holy relic is one thing, but this is a person." Damien poked at the baby's hand, and it grabbed at his finger. "Barely a person, but one nonetheless."

Shadows were moving in the chamber below, and a voice commented on the door being open.

Amma hugged the infant closer. "Do you think they won't be mad if we just tell them we only meant to steal their holy relic, but since it's a baby, we don't want it anymore?"

Damien grunted. "Doubtful."

There was a shout from below and the ringing of unsheathed metal. Damien pulled out his dagger, ready to defend them.

"We shouldn't hurt these people. It's going to look real bad," Amma said.

"I don't think we have a choice. They'll be here in a moment." Boots scuffed up the stone steps outside.

Amma shuffled backward, knocking into the wooden desk and grabbing its edge with a hand to stay steady, the other firmly wrapped around the child. "We just need a little more time," she said in a whisper, and then the doors to the room slammed shut with a resounding *thud*.

Damien had been prepared for them to burst open, and the shadows that were headed up the stairs certainly suggested that was about to happen, but instead the light was blotted out, and there were only surprised but muffled cries from the other side.

"I didn't do that," said Damien, hand and dagger still raised but no blood spilt. There was a latching sound, and when the handle jiggled, the door remained tightly shut.

"Well, neither did I."

Damien narrowed his eyes at her. "You've done that before."

"Not *that*—not to a door I didn't touch. And that's not even liathau anyway."

Up against Amma's shoulder, the child was beginning to fuss again.

"It may not be, but"—Damien gestured to her other hand gripping the wooden desk, gaze traveling down its leg to the wooden floors and along them to the wooden door, a good conduit for whatever kind of arcana she was capable of—"I do believe that bit of magic was all you."

Amma held her breath, taking a shaking hand up to the baby's back to pat it as she stared at the door. It bulged slightly as shouting came from the other side, and then she shook her head. "It won't hold forever. We need to find a way out of here. Take this." In one swift and too-nimble move, she passed the infant off to Damien, and he had no choice but to be saddled with it.

The baby stared back at Damien, something both expectant and suspicious in its eyes. He held it at arm's length, little feet dangling from the bottom of a simple gown. "What am I supposed to do with it?"

Its whining began to evolve from annoying to aggressive.

Amma hurried along the room, running her hands over the shelves and pulling things off in a mad search. "It might be cold?"

Damien awkwardly brought the spawn to his shoulder, one hand enough to hold it there. The baby's tiny hands clumsily pulled at a strap of his armor, and it let out a happy sound as it bit down on the leather. *Disgusting.* But that was better than crying, he supposed. Its ridiculously small feet were still bare, so he grabbed the turquoise blanket from the basket and bundled it up around the spawn as best he could one-handed.

With it no longer on the verge of wailing, he went to the opposite side of the room, and the set of shelves there was filled with religious tomes and a few ledgers. He touched the wall above them, calling out arcana and pressing it into the structure. If there were another way out of the room, his infernal magic would want to escape through it, and perhaps they too could use it to flee the temple.

"Look at this," said Amma, crossing the room to him with a set of scrolls, interrupting his work. "Didn't Xander say the *ancast erfind* was already stolen? I think this is what he meant."

Damien traded the infant for the scrolls in one deft move before she could protest. Unfurling the parchment, he read a list of names. Beside each one was a small family tree drawn across the page and additional dotted lines running from one person to another as if pairing them off. Further along the page, the names were written in sets, most crossed out, and finally, there was a pair circled and a date written below that only nine moons past. He looked up at the infant in Amma's hands. If he had to guess, it was likely nine moons old.

Though the banging on the door grew louder, Damien's thoughts were suddenly filled with the shard of occlusion crystal in his pocket and, curiously, the last memory of his mother before she disappeared. He shook his head at the terrible timing. "Bloody Abyss, these are its parents, aren't they?"

Amma nodded, and behind her, the door began to splinter.

CHAPTER 9

DAMIEN

The Advantage of Being Literal

D AMIEN'S INFERNAL ARCANA FLOWED back into the chamber walls, hateful and angry. It jerked along, searching for escape, and then began to flood toward a corner of the office. Places like this always had second exits, and behind a hutch was a panel that could be lifted off the wall, a winding set of stairs within. He ushered Amma and the baby through, then followed, pulling the hutch back in place as best he could but not bothering to be exact. Those banging on the door would know where they'd gone; the two of them simply needed to get out. And he very much wanted to be out.

The temple was making him want to vomit, and his noxscura wanted to burst out too, but much more destructively.

For a moment, he had let the magic play of its own accord, and it had felt quite good, but when he cut it off, it dangerously prodded at him to be free once again. That wasn't how any arcana was meant to work—it was supposed to be his tool, not use him in return.

They met a wall at the foot of the tight staircase, but a lever sticking out was simple enough to pull. With a grinding sound, a passage opened up into a bedchamber, likely where the head priest slept, as it was adorned a bit more fancifully than any priest would profess to live.

But it was empty, and after shuffling through it and into a back hall, they found an exit to a courtyard full of thick hedges that kept them hidden until they were free of the temple's shadow.

A red squirrel jumped down in front of them, then recoiled. "How long were you in there?" the squirrel hissed in Kaz's gurgly voice, eyes on the baby in Amma's arms.

Damien clicked his tongue, the fog in his mind clearing. "Too long. Where's Xander?"

"The shadow imps have set fire to the southeastern corner of the village, but many of them were banished. Xander is parading what's left through the streets just west of here." There was a crash from the far side of the temple and a scream.

"He's still alive, eh?" Not terribly surprised, Damien frowned at the row of residences before them, darkened with no movement through the windows.

Kaz chuckled nervously. "He seems to be having a very good time."

"To the meeting place," said Damien, heading off into the alley behind the houses, away from the city center and toward the woody outskirts.

"But, Damien." Amma remained still, holding the baby against her.

"I understand your trepidation, but we may not have a choice," he said hesitantly. When she still didn't move, he sighed. "Please, Amma, we should go now." When he headed off, he could hear her behind him, and he was thankful he didn't have to use the Chthonic word again.

Traversing the forest was as simple as weaving their way back to where Xander proposed they meet, trading words in hushed but sharp voices about the *ancast erfind* and what to do with it until they reached a dubious agreement.

They waited, Damien pacing slightly, Amma sitting on a fallen log, the bundle in her hands held tight to her chest. Her knee was bouncing despite the fact that he'd told her to calm down multiple times, which, of course, only made things worse.

"Ah, you've succeeded despite my doubts!" Xander's voice boomed into the forest, jovial and high as he pushed his way between two ferns.

Amma inhaled sharply, jumping to her feet and glaring at the blood mage.

"Not happy with me, kitten?" Xander's smile turned down into a playful pout.

"This is unconscionable," said Amma, and though her voice was shaky, she held firm to the spot. Well, she was certainly jumping right into it, wasn't she?

"Spare me," spat Xander.

"You knew," she said, a fire in her eyes he hadn't seen before, "and you still want to experiment on him?"

Xander shrugged. "Yes?"

"On a *baby*?" She was absolutely aghast.

"Really, kitten, it's as if you didn't just spend the last week with the two of us." He held out his hands, grabbing for the wrapped-up spawn. "Come on now, hand it over. No use getting attached."

Amma shook her head, holding the bundle tighter to her chest. There was a muffled child's cry, and Amma gasped at the sound.

"Enough of this," Damien grumbled, turning away from her. "I'm sick of this wretched village, Xander. Open the portal so we can get out of here."

Xander scoffed, then reached into a pocket with one hand, revealing the translocation stone. As he held it up, the other remained out, waiting for the child.

"Amma, hand over the relic."

She swallowed hard. "But it's not a relic."

Xander rolled his eyes. "Is your pet being purposefully dense, or did she hit her head in that temple?"

"Amma." Damien injected threat into his tone in place of words he didn't really want to say.

"No, I changed my mind." She stepped back, knocking into the fallen log, voice shaking like a thin branch in a storm. "We can't do this. Damien, tell him we can't do this."

He couldn't look at her, the sway of her presence almost

overwhelming as it was. "We don't have time for this—they'll be out looking for that thing. Xander, open the bloody portal."

"I adore it when you're so domineering." Xander dropped the stone, and the ground split where it fell just before him, the smell of brimstone filling the air as the ruddy darkness of the Accursed Wastes opened beneath their feet.

"But, Damien, please." Amma's pathetic voice cracked, and Damien practically felt it splintering into his own chest.

"Sanguinisui, hand what you've got over to Xander now."

Amma's body snapped to attention. Compelled, she marched toward Xander, hands no longer possessive around the squirming bundle as she held it out.

The blood mage's dark eyes lit up as he hopped over the portal. "So that's how your talisman works? Dark gods, that is nice!"

Amma deposited the swaddled thing into Xander's eager hands. Dazed, she wavered when the order was carried out, and Damien took her by the elbow, jerking her back so she wouldn't do anything stupid in her post-enthralled state.

Xander was much less gentle with the spawn, predictably, pulling at the turquoise blanket to reveal its face, but Damien wouldn't give him the chance to express the shock he was about to have. Without heeding the bundle or consequences, Damien kicked Xander squarely in the stomach.

The idiot had already positioned himself perfectly before the raised earth at the edge of the portal, and it barely took any effort to send him back where he belonged. He swung his arms, shocked with not one but two surprises right after one another, and fell backward.

The blanket unfurled as Xander tried fruitlessly to stay aloft, and Kaz was only caught in it a moment, wings flapping to be free and fly up and away from Xander's snatching hands as he fell. But it was no use—it had happened too quickly, and Xander hadn't even thought to use arcana to keep himself upright. The portal swallowed him, just as it was meant to do, and in a shock of white hair and a tumult of curses, Xander was gone, nothing left but the vague smell of burnt cinnamon and the echo of a betrayed voice.

Amma took off in the same instant for a copse of thick foliage. "Oh, I'm so sorry!" she cried, lifting the actual infant from where he had been stashed. Ruddy-faced and beginning to bawl again, she held him close. "I know, I know, we didn't mean to leave you for so long, but it's all right now."

As she bounced the baby gently, she looked at Damien. She had been convincing, red still rimming her eyes from forcing out tears, but she smiled at him. He returned the grin momentarily, then snatched up the swaddle from where it fell. Half of it had been burnt away, trapped in the portal as it closed up. "Well, that's one problem solved. Now for the second."

They meandered through the forest toward the town more slowly. Xander would appear back at his tower in the Accursed Wastes, and he didn't have a direct way to return to Durendreg, so they'd bought themselves days. Slower was also preferable, as the village itself was still likely in the midst of chaos, though Damien expected the shadow imps were all banished with Xander's expulsion. Kaz was even trudging along beside them with a newfound lightness.

"You just *kicked* him," Amma was saying to Damien, but her voice was syrupy sweet as she poked at the baby in his arms, somehow his turn to carry once again. The child had taken to waving clumsily, and every time Amma waved back, it let out a high-pitched squeal of delight. Annoying, yes, but perhaps Amma was not completely incorrect when she called it *adorable* as well. "You didn't use magic or anything, just your boot. And then he was gone, just like that! Bye-bye, Xander!" She waved again, and the baby waved back.

"I couldn't call up arcana without him realizing something was amiss. You were quite convincing as well." Damien readjusted the infant. "I don't think I can ever trust your tears again."

"It wasn't all an act. I was a little afraid you might change your mind," Amma said, chuckling as the baby bit down on the strap of Damien's armor.

"You were?" He slowed, turning to her. Pretending to argue about handing the spawn over, then tricking Xander with a swaddled Kaz and sending him through his own portal had been a joint plan and a good one; no reason to second-guess.

The amusement at the spawn crawled away from Amma's face. "Um, well, things in the tower were…tense, and you didn't really want to send Xander away, did you?"

Damien's brow pinched. Injuring Xander was actually

great fun—he would have done that regardless—though he *had* hoped the blood mage could be reasoned with instead. Despite how ambitious that goal was and how their sparring session proved it might have been impossible, Damien was willing to prolong being in Xander's presence in exchange for his help in perfecting a spell to remove the talisman from her. As it stood, all Damien's translations and notes from the Lux Codex still needed quite a lot of work, and unlike Xander, Damien was unwilling to test out hastily crafted magic on living beings—least of all on Amma.

Amma, who walked beside him, smiling for the first time in too long. Amma, with her golden hair and her blue eyes and her gentle voice and a touch that had thwarted all the horribleness in the temple. That—that hadn't been magic, though he'd seen her do a bit of that as well. That had been something else.

Something he had no business thinking about.

"I'm glad he's gone," Damien told her, starting off into the forest again. There were other options to free her, and Damien still had associates eager to help, ones that were not even very far off.

Kaz, more comfortable in his imp form, grunted out an agreeable noise from behind.

"But you miss him," Amma ventured carefully. "You look sort of sad, and I know he's your friend."

"Xander?" Damien scoffed, maneuvering over a log with the infant in hand. "Amma, we have only known one another, what, a moon? I would hope then that you of all people would understand length of acquaintanceship does not equate to depth of friendship."

Amma gasped, falling still. "Damien, are you saying *I'm* your friend?"

He groaned but did not stop alongside her. Being Amma's friend was preferable, he supposed, to being her adversary, but it didn't feel quite right. At least it wasn't exactly what he wanted. Not that what he wanted mattered. "I did kick someone I've known since birth into a hole through existence and space at your behest, so you may define that however you see fit."

She quickly caught up and gave him one of those smiles that made him bite the inside of his cheek to keep from returning. Then swiftly shifting her features, she groaned. "I was going to say friends don't usually kill friends to get talismans out of them, but seeing as you and Xander are always talking about killing one another, your version of friendship might be very different from mine."

Damien chose to ignore the mention of the talisman. "It's not exactly that simple. Xander and I are at odds because it's in our blood. We were raised together for a short time, but that only instilled a deep, mutual hatred. This is how villainy and dark lordship work after all. One needs rivalries and nemeses and grudges."

"That seems sort of silly."

"Does it?" He pulled the spawn away from his shoulder to assess it, as it had made a little fussing noise. When it grinned at him, he smirked back, lifting his voice to mimic the one

Amma used when speaking to the infant. "Almost as silly as ridiculously fluffy ball gowns and pretending to be kidnapped so you can go outside for once in your life and being betrothed to a self-absorbed bastard that you don't particularly like very much, eh?"

Amma's voice fell low. "There is a certain unkindness to our duties in life, isn't there?"

The spawn's face squished up, reddening. He looked as if he was about to scream, but then broke into a squeal and a smile. And then he suddenly smelled absolutely foul. "Indeed, quite unkind," said Damien, handing him off to Amma.

She took him, then gasped. "Oh, no way, Damien. This happened on your turn!"

"But you're already holding him," he said as if that was it, continuing through the forest. Kaz gurgled out a laugh at their feet.

Amma planted herself before him, pulling her shoulders back and standing up to her full height, which was not at all formidable. But how she glowered up at him from under a pinched brow still made him stop abruptly. "Damien, I am the daughter of a *baron*. I don't *do* this."

He appraised her: how she jutted out her chest, how her eyes had darkened, how she stood there so defiantly. He would have liked to run that defiance right off her features by tying up her hands behind her back and whispering halfhearted threats against the shell of her ear, though not because her brazenness vexed him—just the opposite.

Instead, he only smirked. "I imagine it was painful being unable to wield your noble birth against me our entire trip down from the infernal mountains."

"Oh, you have no idea." She chuckled, pressing the baby into his chest, and he had no choice but to take it.

He dropped his voice to its lowest, most villainous pitch. "Well, I am a dark lord, Lady Ammalie. The son of Zagadoth the Tempestuous, Ninth Lord of the—"

"Your dad's stuck in a crystal," she said, waving at him and wandering off. "Save it for next time."

He would have argued if he didn't realize her flippant tone could have very easily been instead a rebuke for the not-so-small secret prophecy he'd been keeping from her, so Damien resigned himself to his fate. He considered having Kaz deal with the mess instead, but only for a moment, knowing the imp could never be gentle enough. It was lost on him that he would have thought the same about himself not so long ago. But learning a sort of base tenderness didn't come with inherent child-care techniques, so Damien assumed a quick dunk in a nearby river took care of things well enough, and he rejoined Amma, finding her staring up at a tree.

Her head was tipped back, the light breaking through the branches shimmering on her, lost in whatever thoughts ran through her mind. She reached a slow hand out to touch the tree's trunk, but just before connecting, she pulled back. As if she felt his eyes on her, she turned then and smiled like she hadn't been up to something.

He considered prodding her about the temple and the arcana she'd performed but instead just held out the slightly-damp-if-mostly-clean spawn. "The forest thins ahead, and Durendreg is just on the other side."

Amma had kept the scroll with the names of the presumed parents, and she was careful in walking them through the town, asking quietly after who they thought should have the child. The village was still coming down from the chaos of only an hour or so before, but that seemed to be a boon; no one wondered why two strangers with a baby were looking to find the parents who had lost their child to the very temple that had been raided. However, Damien assumed the priests wouldn't put the word out immediately that their sacred relic was missing—the panic of shadow imps and a blood mage was great enough.

When they found the home the parents were said to be in, Damien insisted on waiting outside. Amma was gone just a short time, and when she came out, she was wiping at her face. She sniffled only once, then put on a bright smile. "Okay, let's go!"

It was a dash then for the border of town, the more space between them and the place they'd brought a certain ruin to, the better. Avoiding the direction Xander had taken them through the woods, they chose instead the southern path out of the village on a well-traveled road.

Amma was quiet as they went, lips drawn down since they'd gotten rid of the smelly, loud thing. Damien waited until they put enough distance between themselves and the village that turning back would be a problem. "Please don't tell me that you miss the spawn."

She snorted and shook her head. "Oh no, nothing like that. We have Kaz anyway." She reached down to pat the imp, and he recoiled and hissed, taking a swipe that he was very lucky missed. "See? Almost as good."

"But you are still melancholy. You feel bad about the fires and things, don't you?"

Amma's eyes widened at the road ahead like she had just remembered. "That was a little our fault, huh? Well, I guess so, yeah."

"It's not Xander you miss, surely?"

"Ew, no." She stuck out her tongue.

Damien nodded to himself, covering just about every possibility except the fear that had been niggling at him since they'd decided to return the child. He peered back, the town too far off now to see, then to the small hill ahead and a thicket running down each side of the road. "The spawn," he said carefully, scratching at his neck, "when you returned it, its mother *did* want it back, didn't she?"

Amma made a small, shocked sound, and then laughter bubbled up out of her. "What? Yes, of course! Why wouldn't she?"

"Well, you can't really be sure about these things. Maybe it smells funny now." Damien shrugged, searching the ground for good reasons. "Not everyone desires to have children, and even if that one was wanted, she could think, after being away from it, that it's broken."

"Broken?" Amma laughed louder then. "Damien, why on all the planes of existence would you think..." The words trailed off, her amusement following, her eyes finding him and looking much too deeply. "Why would you think that?"

The space between them was sliced through, and they recoiled from one another.

"Halt!"

With a *thwack*, an arrow pierced the ground just before them, narrowly missing Kaz, who pulled his tail in and squalled. Damien scanned the road. At the head of the hill stood a tall and menacing figure. Wide shoulders plated in armor glinted in the sun. It couldn't be Xander, not so soon and not with that build, but magic crackled in the air with a familiar, stifling spell, hot even before it was cast.

"Fire." Damien swept his hand across them, Chthonic on his tongue as he called up a wall of shadows, pulling Amma close.

Heat and flame burst on the other side of his infernal barrier, and Amma shrieked into his chest. That would have been quite damaging without a shield, and he was as incensed as he was confused: The attacker didn't appear to be coming from the direction of Durendreg.

When the shadows cleared, the figure once at the end of the hill's top was barreling toward them, weapon brandished overhead. The longsword caught the light of the day, the full plate armor of the warrior clanging as he charged, a gleaming beacon of metal and rage and—to attack a blood mage—foolishness.

Damien shifted Amma behind him, pulled out his dagger, and sliced into his palm. He called up his own arcane sword, crimson and dripping with his blood, ready to meet the man. But the assailant was still running.

He'd started his onslaught too soon, it seemed, and Damien waited, shoulders drooping a bit as he glanced around with his weapon. Two other figures had crested the hill, a woman in light-blue vestments leading a small contingency of horses, hands clutching a pendant around her neck, and a thin, robed man holding an open book.

Something about the scene felt vaguely familiar, and he eyed the man with the book, knowing the spell had come from him. Still with a moment to spare before he was attacked, Damien flicked a hand and woke a shadow being cast from a nearby tree to flip the tome from his hands.

The sword wielder finally reached him and brought his weapon down against Damien with a mighty force. Against the taller and broader attacker, Damien wavered slightly under the brunt, metal ringing against his arcane blade, but he didn't use the magic itching inside his weapon just yet. The man's face was close enough now, tanned and covered in dark stubble, with eyes that were all too serious. "Do I know you?" Damien asked, releasing the pulse of arcana and sending the man staggering backward.

The sword wielder regained his footing, difficult in the heavy armor, and held his blade aloft again. "Vile villain," he called and once more charged at Damien. "This day, evil will not escape from our righteous hands!"

Damien once again caught the blade with his own, keeping him there and ducking under where they crossed to take in the man's face a second time. "Oh, it's *you* lot." He risked releasing his blade with one hand, losing the leverage and allowing the man to fall forward with his own momentum right onto Damien's already sliced palm. Infernal arcana hammered out of him and into the attacker so forcefully the man was lifted off the ground, sailing backward thirty paces and then skidding at least twenty more when he landed, sword clattering away from him in the dirt. Damien sucked in a sharp breath between gritted teeth, forgetting how powerful some of his spells were against even above-average humans.

Amma grabbed his arm, and he allowed the blood blade to melt away.

"What's going on?" she asked.

"Hold on, there's meant to be one more." Damien peered into the bushes along the edge of the road behind them, catching the shadow there. "Aha." With the flick of his wrist and the cast of a bind, black tendrils wrapped around his target, and a crossbow clattered out into the road.

CHAPTER 10

AMMA

Multiple Critical Failures in a Row

"Do you know these people?" Amma looked from the small figure wrapped in tendrils—she knew what that was like—to the huge man still unmoving in the ditch his body had made from Damien's spell.

"Uh, well?" Damien scratched his head. "Yes, though it has been many moons since we've…collaborated."

A woman still stood at the hill's crest, clutching her necklace and shaking before a few horses, the thin man who had been at her side now cursing and searching through the weeds for where his book had been thrown.

"You've worked together?" she asked.

"No, no, more apart." He had his nose scrunched up in contemplation. "It's difficult to explain, but I believe that *they* believe that I am their..." His hand wound through the air, searching for the word.

"Nemesis!" cried a voice, and the man in the robe stumbled up to his feet, book finally in hand. His long pointed ears gave away his elven heritage with a fall of silvery hair and limbs that could be snapped if they were looked at the wrong way. He flipped through a few pages, swore again, and flipped backward until his finger jabbed the presumably correct spot. "You shall not triumph this day, not in the presence of the Righteous Sentries!" A light began to form between his spindly fingers and the page.

"The Righteous Sentries, that's it!" Damien snapped his fingers and sent another shadow to knock away the book once again, spell doused.

"Oh, come on, man." Shoulders slumping, the robed elf traipsed off the edge of the road, diving into the weeds.

"You're their nemesis?" Amma gave Damien a long look. He stood there to his full height, shoulders back, swathed in dark fabric and armor. With black hair falling messily around his temples, deeply violet eyes, that long scar across his face from forehead to cheek, and the last vestiges of shadows smoking off his hand, she supposed he looked at least a bit like a villain. But it wasn't the first thing she saw when she looked at him. It wasn't even the second or third, to be perfectly honest.

The blood mage shrugged. "I needed something once, so I went and got it, and some feelings were hurt."

"You stole the Azure Hide of Ruvyn!" called the elf from the tall grasses.

Damien rolled his eyes. "That was years ago, and the thing's basically just a rug. You'd think they would be over it by now."

Amma craned her neck to see that the woman in vestments had run over to the fallen knight to lay a hand on his chest. There was a dull radiance under her palm, and the armored man finally began to twitch and groan. "Well, maybe you could just give the hide thing back?"

Damien frowned. "But it's the only color in my bedchamber, and it really ties the whole room together."

"Damien," she hissed, "you *stole* it."

"Oh, fine, but it's all the way in Aszath Koth, so there's nothing to be done right now, and even if there were, we've sort of been running into one another since, and things have…escalated." Damien focused on picking an invisible piece of dirt from his chest.

With two members of their group nearly incapacitated—one still wrapped in tendrils thrashing on the ground and another half-conscious—Amma could imagine what that escalation entailed.

"This is no accident," murmured the knight as he pulled himself up from the crater his body had made, reaching out blindly for his sword and not finding it. "We came hunting a notorious criminal and happened upon our greatest rival. It is fate we end the abominable Damien Maleficus Bloodthorne this day."

The woman who had healed him scurried to get his

longsword. The thing was nearly as big as she was, and she dragged the blade through the dirt to him.

"Thanks, Pippa," he said, taking the weapon as if it weighed nothing and brandishing it in one hand. "Xander Shadowhart will have to wait until our nemesis has been destroyed."

"Hold on, hold on—you're going after *Xander* now?" Damien had been grinning when he'd heard the word *abominable*, but that grin fell sharply off.

The knight charged again. Amma didn't know much about sword fighting, but she didn't think it was meant to be so…big. She went to step back, but Damien grabbed her and pulled both of them out of the way, the weapon striking where Damien had been standing with enough force to have cleaved him in two, but it left the knight all out of breath.

The blood mage strode back over and tapped the exhausted knight on his shoulder this time, sending him across the road in the opposite direction. Dirt sprayed up in his wake. "Bloody moron." Damien grunted, going back to Amma and latching on to her arm. "That big one's the worst."

Pippa gasped and scurried after, giving the two of them a wide berth as she ran to the once again fallen knight.

"Wait!" The elf bounded once more out of the weeds. This time, no magic crackled between the pages of his book, so Damien did indeed wait. "That woman. It's her." He pulled out a tattered piece of parchment that had been tucked into his tome, and Amma nearly choked at seeing her own visage—one of the posters that had been tacked up all over Faebarrow—dangling from the stranger's hand.

"Oh, by Osurehm, not this again," she murmured and rubbed her face.

"You!" The elf gestured wildly with the parchment. "You've stolen the Baroness Avington from Brineberth!"

Damien tipped his head, squinting. "Well, maybe, but she's not technically a baroness yet, and she's not from Brineberth at all. Amma, would you consider yourself stolen?"

Amma wasn't entirely sure what the correct response was. *Was* she stolen? And did it even matter? Damien appeared unconcerned about being blamed, which was quite different from back in Faebarrow when he had discovered her truth and how he'd unknowingly been roped into the lie she'd told. She simply shrugged.

"We have been charged with the reclamation of the abducted bride of the Marquis Caldor from one Xander Shadowhart. We followed the whispers spread through the realm that the most nefarious blood mage who had taken her would be attacking Durendreg."

"Well, I don't know about *most* nefarious," Damien grumbled, a hand on his hip, the other still protectively on Amma's arm.

"How unexpected yet fortuitous we would find her with *you* instead, Bloodthorne." The elf gestured with a flourish, and a flame crackled in his palm once more.

"Kaz, do you mind?"

The imp squealed with delight and charged toward the

elf. The spell was redirected at Kaz as he bolted, wings and legs working in a blurry tandem, and he was struck dead on. Amma shrieked, sure that he would be burnt to a crisp, but Kaz only sailed through the flames with a graceful, leathery flap, all claws and talons as he knocked the elf to the ground with a gurgling battle cry.

"The book, Kaz, just get the book," Damien called, and the imp sprang off the elf's chest and grabbed the tome. He scampered to the edge of the road, holding it up in his long arms in triumph. "Fire mages," Damien scoffed, releasing Amma and striding over to the still-entangled form on the ground behind them. "You'd think they'd learn that fire imps are incombustible."

"They're here for me," she said, heart speeding up even as she blinked out at the others scattered along the road in various states of near ruin. "They think Xander took me because that's who you told them you were, and Xander put word out that he was going to be in Durendreg, so they found us."

Kaz had taken to running in a circle with the book, the elf chasing after.

"Seems like it." Damien was altogether too nonchalant, not with so little space between her and actual abductors, no matter how benevolent they thought they were being. He picked up the crossbow from where the fourth member of the Righteous Sentries had dropped it. "Amma, would you like this?"

"Release the woman, and we will...uh," the knight said before she could respond, sitting up again and bobbing dizzily.

The priestess was crouched at his side, biting a nail. "And we will let you go…unscathed-like."

Damien didn't even glance at him. "I think you should have it." He brought the weapon to Amma. "It's a good weight, compact, and look—extra arrows."

Amma hesitated, but when he pressed it into her hands, the wood thrummed under her fingers, and the realization that it could defend her on her own terms bloomed pleasantly in her mind. Even if she couldn't load and fire it, it was hefty enough to knock someone out if she swung it right. Amma gestured to the tangled-up woman. "Won't she need it?"

"She'll make do."

"Demon spawn," spoke a new, wavering voice. Pippa, the priestess, had her hands on the blade of the knight's sword as it turned a shimmering light blue. "Prepare to be banished back to the infernal Abyss."

Damien sighed. "I thought we'd established that doesn't really work on me." He had his dagger out and casually sliced into his palm. "Amma, you may want to take a few steps back." When he drew his hand through the air, the crimson sword made of blood took shape yet again.

The knight barreled toward him, this time with sweat on his brow, covered in the dust of the road, and absolutely Abyss-bent on destruction, if incapable of running in a straight line. Damien had to maneuver himself into the man's way to meet him with his own blade overhead but was pushed down and back with the force of the weapons clashing. Amma staggered back, hugging the crossbow to her chest.

Damien groaned under the weight, back bending, then shadows seeped out from behind him and threw the man off. "That divinity does sort of sting." He shook out one of his hands, smoke coalescing there like when he had discovered which tome was the Lux Codex in the Grand Athenaeum. He was really scowling now.

"You've stooped to an all-time low, Bloodthorne," scolded the knight, wrenching his longsword overhead and wavering under the weight, slurring slightly. "Kidnapping an innocent, young girl for your dark machin…machin…dark plans."

"All right, to be quite clear, I've not done anything *that* depraved with her. Furthermore, Amma is an adult woman who's admitted herself she's not *that* innocent, and—" He dodged another swing and deflected the blade, a spark of arcana cutting between the weapons.

"And I don't *want* to go back," shouted Amma, voice echoing down the road.

The knight froze mid-swing, sword hovering in the air over Damien's head. The elf halted in his circular chase of Kaz. Even the bound-up woman on the ground stopped thrashing.

"You don't?" As he wavered, the knight's shoulders relaxed, blinking at her like a drunkard. Damien took one long step to the side, out of the weapon's range.

"No! None of you must be from Faebarrow, which is where I belong anyway, not Brineberth, or else you'd know," she spat, a warm rage bubbling up inside her. "Cedric, the marquis who sent you, is awful. He's a liar and a monster, and he's the villain you should be after, not Damien." Amma snorted, squeezing the crossbow so tightly she thought it might splinter in her grasp. She should have probably expected this—a baron's daughter could only fake her own kidnapping so many times before an entire adventuring party was sent out after her—but Cedric's audacity incensed her nonetheless.

The Righteous Sentries traded glances from their spots scattered all over the road. The elf made a confused sort of noise, the knight returned it, and the entangled woman groaned against her binds.

"She's bewitched," the priestess, Pippa, finally squeaked out. "She...she doesn't know what she's saying. Demons, they can enthrall, and they can possess, and I bet Bloodthorne's doing that to her."

"Oh, bloody Abyss," Damien mumbled.

The elf pointed down the road to Pippa. "Yeah, and there's that thing that happened in Dyoktev, you remember, with the centaurs? Where the hostages overempathized with their captors and didn't realize they were in danger anymore?"

"Dyoktev disorder, yes!" Pippa shook her head. "She's definitely got that too."

The knight roared, pulling his sword down through the air and leaving a trail of bright arcana in its wake.

"All right, enough of this." Damien finally struck out and attacked, slicing up under the knight and cutting into the plate on his chest, leaving a smoking, violet slice that sent the man reeling backward, knocking into the priestess as they both tumbled into the bushes. "Come on, we're leaving."

Amma followed Damien down the road, away from the

bound-up woman and passing where both the priestess and the knight groaned in the thicket. "Why aren't they listening to me?"

"Because they're idiots." Damien reached the elf, who, without his book, took a huge step back but clapped his hands together, hastily trying to whisper out a spell. "More fire?" Damien asked, plucking the book away from Kaz as he scurried up. "For what? So you can again attempt to mangle the lady you're failing to rescue?"

The elf's mouth fell open, eyes darting to Amma as she kept pace with Damien. "F-foul creature," he stuttered even as he backed up. "This won't stand."

"Pick your favorite." Damien gestured to the contingent of horses as he flipped through the elf's book. Amma slipped the crossbow over a shoulder, choosing a sleek but short mare with a ruddy coat and black mane.

"You will rue the day—"

"That we met? Believe me, I already do." Damien ripped out a page.

The elf shrieked as if his skin had been sundered from his body. "My book!"

"Have it back." Damien tossed it in the dirt before climbing astride a pale stallion dappled with gray, and Kaz flapped his wings to land on its rump. "You really ought to learn those spells by heart." With a sizzle of arcana through the air, he propelled the entire lot of horses—the riderless two running in opposite directions—and he and Amma took off, leaving the Righteous Sentries scattered and dazed in the dirt.

The horses galloped, and whatever loyalty they might have had to the others was gone. Amma squeezed the reins as they sped down the road, away from her would-be abductors, away from Durendreg, and away from the portal that would take them back to the Accursed Wastes. The open road came at them fast, meandering ahead between hills and through lands unknown to Amma outside the realm of Eiren. Beside her, Damien was leaning low over his stallion, lips turning up into a very satisfied smirk.

Villain, they'd called him, and yes, perhaps with that glint in his eye at stealing from them, making fools of them, leaving them mountless, she could see how they might think such a thing. But he could have done much worse. *Should have*, she thought, when they were so clearly intending to kill him. But he hadn't. He had instead saved her—twice now—from Cedric. And anyway, how could someone so utterly handsome be evil?

Amma laughed. It bubbled out of her bright and high and happy as the wind blew back her hair and stung her eyes.

"What's so funny?" he called over the sounds of galloping hooves and rushing wind.

"You made fools of them," she called back, "but you didn't kill them."

"They're too pathetic to be worth it." He snorted. "But I would have if they'd actually gotten their hands on you." Damien's gaze narrowed on the road ahead as if he could see the Righteous Sentries doing just that, bloodshed glinting in his eyes.

She bit her lip, a fluttering in her stomach, but kept her voice raised so he could hear. "Oh, would you?"

He looked at her from the corner of his eye, fighting off a smile. "You are *my* captive after all. No one's touching you but me."

CHAPTER 11

AMMA

The Practicality of Establishing Base Understanding

DAMIEN'S THREAT LINGERED IN Amma's mind like a cat looking for attention but not wanting to let on what it was doing. It lounged in every corner, making her wonder if it just wanted to be fed or if it was genuinely looking for human affection, but it was impossible to really puzzle out when on horseback.

They rode for the rest of the day over rolling terrain that meandered in and out of thickly treed fields. Durendreg had been outside the realm, but the flora was most similar to the northeast of Eiren, and when she shared that information, coupled with the sun's orientation, Damien affirmed he knew relatively where they were.

It was a place with no name, but Amma knew it as the

Wilds. The realm of Eiren reached to the sea on its westerly side, but the border on its eastern edge ended at a thick forest that ran from the frozen marshes in the north to the archipelagos of the south; the land beyond that—*this* land—was unprotected by the crown. The Accursed Wastes were even farther east, Damien explained, though the terrain made it abundantly clear they were far off from the flat plains Xander called home.

Here, the trees were thick, and even in the chill of autumn, the vegetation was lush and verdant. She didn't know the names of every species they passed, and as the acorn bounced along in Amma's hip pouch, she wondered if it might grow into a kind of oak she had never seen. There were, in fact, many trees she'd never seen before, and maybe that meant wild liathau could be growing outside Faebarrow despite what she'd been told all her life. It was too much to hope, though, that she could replenish the barren orchards of Faebarrow, and she shook that thought away.

Sundown came sooner than when they were on the road before—fall had come all at once while they were locked away in Xander's tower. Kaz lit a fire behind a copse to protect from the chilly breeze, and Amma was reminded of that night, the one she'd used to get close to Damien that had ended so horribly. She sat across the fire from him as he looked through loose pages this time, face twisted up into deep contemplation, and she weighed the merits of seduction against searching for the truth.

"Damien?" she asked, voice feeling heavy, though it was quiet.

He blinked up at her, firelight warming his features, no annoyed pinch to his brow, and not even a frown creasing his face.

She swallowed. "What, um…what are you going to do with me?"

His mouth opened, eyes flicking over to Kaz, who had curled into a ball with his tail tucked in around him, not yet asleep. The imp's black, bulbous eyes glared back, and Damien fidgeted for a moment, scratched at his neck, and then huffed. "I'm taking you somewhere to get that talisman out of you."

Amma pressed a hand to her chest as her body went cold. The strap of the crossbow cut into her palm, and her hand tightened around it. "You're going to take me somewhere to kill me?"

"What? No. Why would—oh." He cleared his throat, sitting straighter. "I did threaten you with that quite a lot, didn't I?"

She nodded, but her grip loosened.

"Amma, you are…" Damien stared deeply into the fire as his words trailed off before he really said much at all. She leaned forward, waiting, but then his head snapped back up to her. "Well, you're not some common street thief, are you? I don't need the headache of a royal's blood on my hands, so I've decided to find a cleaner method to retrieve Bloodthorne's Talisman of Enthrallment from inside you. One that leaves you breathing and, you know, talking and smiling and doing all those other annoyingly thoughtful things you tend to do."

Kaz groaned, but Amma grinned.

"It's going to be arduous though, so I hope you're prepared

to suffer along with me until we can resolve this." He rolled up the parchment he'd been looking over. "I reached out with Corben to some associates of mine a bit ago, and they've agreed to assist. As your god of luck would have it, they happen to be located just south of here. They have skills that are very similar yet drastically different from my own. I actually think you'll like them quite a bit."

Amma's interest was piqued at the mention of both Damien's messaging spell and these associates. She pulled the crossbow off her back and set it beside her. "You sent a raven to them from Xander's tower? If it came back that fast, does that mean I'll hear from Laurel soon?"

"Oh, no, no, I didn't do this recently. They returned my message back in—" Damien caught himself, brow narrowing. "Well, who can remember exactly when?"

It had been back in chapter twenty-nine of book one, but neither were privy to those specifics.

She sat back, a little disappointed but knowing that if he asked for help with the talisman before the tower, then he'd made a decision about the worth of her life before knowing she was nobility. She wanted badly to point this out but settled instead on eyeing him and clarifying, "So you're really *not* going to kill me?"

He met her gaze. "Provided you refrain from irritating me."

Amma snickered. "I'll do my best."

"I'm sure you will."

Their gentle laughter fell away into the quiet din of chirping insects struggling to outlast the changing season. Amma picked at her cloak, which she sat atop. "You know, it's sort of funny that those Righteous Sentries said I was enthralled by you and that's why I didn't want to go back with them."

Damien grunted. "If you consider what that makes me out to be, it's not really *that* funny."

"Well, it would make you evil, and isn't that your whole thing?"

"I have standards, Amma," he insisted. "I'm a much more civilized villain than that."

"But I am enthralled. Technically."

"Technically," he repeated.

The fire popped between them.

He looked up at her finally. "I am confident the Army of the Undead chased out the Brineberth occupiers from your home, but I know you want to set things right there, and I know I am keeping you from where you belong, but as soon as the talisman is out of you, you can truly go home. You'll be able to see your family, Laurel, Tia, and that nervous acolyte too. I will take you back there." Damien pressed a hand to his chest. "It may not mean much coming from me, but I swear it."

Amma's heart hitched, unable to look away from the sincerity he was desperately trying to show her. Faebarrow—home—was so far off, and as much as she loved it and did want to set things right, she wasn't sure she actually wanted to go back, as horrible as it felt to admit.

Fleeing down the road on horseback had been exhilarating, her heart racing in her chest, her mind sparking with endless wild thoughts, and when she looked at Damien, even under the calm of the night sky and the firelight, those feelings rushed into her with a vengeance. They pulled at her, an amalgam of danger and refuge, of trepidation and peace, and a fondness that she was frankly embarrassed to feel so deeply for someone who had professed to loathe her not so long ago and even now someone who had only promised to not kill her, as if that was some impossibly high bar.

Damien was right: With Cedric expelled from Faebarrow, her home was where she belonged. It was the place her parents were, her friends were, what was left of the trees... But home didn't have him. And it couldn't possibly after what he'd done there, both because his presence would be unwelcome and because, well, why would he *want* to be there? Because of her? Had she really not learned she couldn't convince him—couldn't *change* him or anyone, for that matter—when he was on such an Abyss-bent path?

Amma managed a weak smile. "Thank you, Damien," she said, wanting very much to mean it but only feeling ungrateful and foolish. She pulled her cloak out from under her and wrapped it around her shoulders.

"If you find yourself cold tonight," said Damien as he focused intently on a patch of the ground that couldn't have been nearly as interesting as he made it seem, "you can, um... you should let me know."

Amma's pulse quickened, but she shook the thoughts that were flooding her mind away. "Okay, I will."

She curled into herself and closed her eyes, listening to him bed down on the fire's other side. An owl called out into the night, and though she knew exactly what it was, she contemplated using the sound as an excuse to get closer to him.

I don't think I can ever trust your tears again, he had said, and that probably extended to fear too.

"Amma?"

Her eyes popped back open. "Yes?"

"The thing I said, about killing you if I find you too irritating?" Damien cleared his throat. "That was a...a joke."

She clicked her tongue. "I know. That's why I laughed."

"I just would like to confirm that you completely understand." There was patience levied in his voice along with a strain as he struggled for the words. "Feel free to be, you know, as irritating as you like without fear of imminent death."

Kaz retched from the shadows.

Amma giggled lightly. "Yes, Damien, I do understand. Thank you," she said, and this time she meant it.

A few days headed southward brought them to craggier lands. They did not come upon another village, instead taking less-traveled roads and seeing very few others. When they slept, they remained on opposite sides of the fire, a thing Amma reminded herself was for the best, even with Damien friendly-ish once again. So he had promised not to kill her and to eventually bring her home—even if it was true, then what? She would be left without him, and he would be headed to Eirengaard to...well, she did not want to think about *that*.

Once the talisman was removed, that would be the end of things. She would return home to what was hopefully a still-intact barony. When the raven came back from Laurel, she would know what was waiting for her, and whatever it might be, she couldn't very well rely on Damien to assist again, no matter how that thought wormed its way into her brain. He would be gone, a stranger and a villain to boot. That she'd gotten so used to being at his side in only one moon's time was a matter she could mourn later.

But meeting Damien's associates would come first. She would like them, he had said, which was a thing she couldn't imagine but was open to hoping for.

Rocky formations rose up alongside the road they followed. White stones stood at jagged angles, growing taller as they went and blotting out the plains and forests that stretched to the eastern horizon. At first there had only been a few, but they had grown larger and larger yet remained distinct from mountains, steep and straight, no trees or shrubbery upon them save for a deeply green moss at their bases, anchoring them to the ground as they towered tens and then hundreds of feet into the sky.

Eventually, they came to a lake nestled at the foot of the stone cliffside, and Damien dismounted. The pool was deeply maroon under the cloudy autumn sky and generous in size. With such access to water and the natural defense of the stones to one side, Amma would have expected at least a small village to have sprung up on its shores, but there wasn't another soul or even a structure about, only a cave on the lake's far end. Amma had been expecting a tower like Anomalous's or Xander's, but when she saw the opening into the colossal stones, she knew that was where they were headed.

"Stay," Damien was saying to his horse, hands out and face twisted up as if it was a struggle to command in such a soft voice. The pale stallion only looked at him lazily and then went to drink from the lake. "They're not as bright or commandable as the knoggelvi. I'm afraid they likely won't be here when we come back, as this may take a few days."

Amma slipped down from her ginger-coated mare and spied a bushel of clover that she quickly tore from the ground and offered to the creature she'd taken to calling Winnie. "That's a good girl," she said as the horse snuffled at her hand and ate. "You were so sweet to take us this whole way, even though we're not your actual people. We'll be back, so if you two can find it in your big horsey hearts to stick around, we sure would appreciate it." She took the horse's muzzle in her hands and planted a kiss on its velvety end.

When she looked over at Damien, he was staring at her dumbly, and there may have even been a bit of color to his cheeks, but he turned away too quickly for her to tell. "They don't speak Key, Amma," he murmured, then headed toward the ledge of rock that ran along the back half of the lake's shore.

Amma giggled and followed after. "So what is this place?"

"They're only known as the karsts. Most do not venture here for fear of the rumors alone." Damien ran a hand along one of the smooth stones that rose up hundreds of feet. Scaling it would be impossible.

Kaz was careful as he crept along, holding his tail up to avoid the water, though it was unnecessary. He actually led the way with some vigor she wasn't expecting.

"Seems like this might be a pretty serious detour," she said, leaning out around Damien's back to spy the imp. "Kaz, you're okay with this?"

As they worked their way around the lake to the jagged opening in the rock wall, Kaz sneered back at her but said nothing. There, on the shore at the mouth, sat three small canoes, the lake continuing on to spill into the darkness of the cave.

Damien planted one boot into a boat, the other firmly on the shore. "Kaz has never minded the karsts. There are supposedly other imps here, but they stay hidden away." He extended a hand to Amma as he held the canoe still.

She hesitated then, unsure why. He'd touched her dozens of times, but mostly to pull her out of danger. "He didn't like Xander's imps." When she slipped her hand into his, she tried not to grip too tightly. It felt right to only use him as temporary leverage, like if she held on, she wouldn't be able to let go.

"These are fire imps, not shadow," said Damien as she stepped into the boat with his help. "And not that one can really decipher, but I'm fairly certain most of them are of the female persuasion."

Kaz pounced off the shore for the far end of the canoe, landing hard enough to rock it and knock Amma off-balance. She lost her footing and tumbled into Damien's chest. He clung to her hand, his other arm around her waist, and the two stood there up against each other as the boat swayed.

Wind swept over the lake and through the mouth of the cave, urging Amma to nuzzle against him. Her hand was already gripping his side and could so easily be tangled up in his tunic if she just slipped it to his neck. Damien wasn't moving, even when the canoe fell still.

Kaz snickered, and Amma relented, carefully slipping out of his grip to take a seat. The blood mage sat at the other end, lips pulled into a thin line, hands flexing as if he didn't know what to do with them.

There was no oar, but the boat began to float, pushing itself off the shore.

"It knows the way," said Damien, and they both glanced across the lake to the horses, indifferent to their riders' pending disappearance.

Amma was sitting so that she could see where they were headed, into the mouth of the tunnel, with jagged rocks that hung overhead like so many fangs. The light was slowly doused as they passed under the toothy curtain. The echo of running water and a steady drip from deeper within was magnified by the rounded rock walls.

But as they came around a gentle curve in the river, there was color. Specks of teal light dotted the cave's ceiling like stars in a night sky. As they went deeper, the lights multiplied until the entire ceiling was clustered with a soft cerulean glow that was reflected in the lapping water, casting the whole cave in an ever-moving sparkle.

"It's beautiful," Amma said, the words pulled out of her with a heavy and wondrous breath.

"Is it?" Damien's voice was far away, its bass lost in the cave's echo. "I never quite noticed."

"How could you not?"

"Well, they're not what you think." He raised a hand slowly above his head, and from the darkness, something alighted on his fingertips. He extended the hand toward Amma. She had to lean in to properly see, bringing her nose about an inch away, and even that almost wasn't enough. There, stretched out over his palm, were eight spindly legs attached to a pinprick of a body hovering just in the center.

She inhaled sharply but didn't move even as the spider took a careful step toward her. "Oh," she said in a tiny voice, holding her breath so she wouldn't blow the fragile thing away.

"Their threads are very thin, but if you know what to look for, you'll see them," Damien said, as if he hadn't just stated that there were thousands of spiders dangling above their heads.

When she glanced up again, she could just make out how their silky strands were also illuminated in that soft glow. "Those lights are their webs?"

Damien turned his hand over as the spider moved with a delicate grace onto its back. Amma watched its needlelike legs bending to feel for stability before taking each careful step. He nodded. "They catch things that mistake the light for a way out."

She leaned back carefully, the knowledge that the luminescent webs harbored husks of dead things not really changing how she saw them. "It's still beautiful."

Damien hummed a thoughtful noise to himself, and the boat took another turn to reveal a wall of rock where the river split off past it in two directions. The boat bumped gently into a narrow shore, and there, amidst the naturally amorphous and jagged stone, was a distinct carving in the shape of a door.

Kaz propelled himself from the boat, Amma following, and Damien reached up to a low-hanging stalactite where the spider disembarked from his hand. When he stepped up to the image of the door and knocked, it made almost no sound—it was only a carving after all, and it wouldn't open, surely.

But then it did.

CHAPTER 12

AMMA

Innkeepers and Imbeciles

THE ROUGH SOUND OF stone dragging against stone, like a tomb being opened, filled the cave. The door that had only been a carving moments before slid out and away from the solid wall of rock, and in the shadowed entry stood the most beautiful woman Amma had ever seen.

Skin as dark as midnight was pulled taut over a tapered jaw and angular temples, and lips full and deeply maroon curled into a smile. "Lord Bloodthorne," she said, voice as smooth as the silken webs that hung from the cave's ceiling, "we've been expecting you."

She stepped back from the door, disappearing into the shadows like a figment, and Amma was unsure if she'd imagined her or not. But Damien stepped through the doorway, and she followed, afraid she might be shut out and left alone there on the shore with the ghost of an entrance carved into the rock wall.

A stone floor polished so intensely that Amma's reflection stared back from below ran down a wide but dimly lit passage, walls left craggy and natural, climbing up and away to tunnel overhead in stark contrast. Along the rough walls, a curious liquid that held its own illumination seeped from above and ran through the crevices. The moving light danced over the reflective surface of the floor to pool in narrow troughs on either side of the hallway. Amma could not make out its end, though something was there, black and swaying.

Ice pressed into Amma's shoulders, and she jerked beneath the touch. A deep, throaty chuckle answered her jolt as one hand slid to the back of her neck, even colder on her bare skin, the sharpness of a nail playing along its length. The woman from the entry was behind her, leaning her face down just beside Amma's and taking a deep breath, and then those freezing fingers wrapped under her chin. The woman's touch was gentle if frigid and would have been easy to pull out of. However, Amma had been struck still by both the starkness of the woman's beauty and the growing fear that pulling away might be considered rude, despite the intimacy of the touch definitely not being something Amma considered appropriate.

The woman's skin was so smooth that the glowing water reflected off her pointed cheekbones in a blinding glint as she circled Amma, appraising her. Eyes the color of gold—an exact match for that strange ooze she'd seen in the alchemist's tower—held her gaze. "So small," she said, her other hand coming around to meet the first so she could tip Amma's face up to her own, "but so warm."

"Yes, yes, she's like a hearth." Damien's voice cut through the long stare Amma had been giving the woman, and that frigid touch was suddenly removed, though the iciness lingered on her skin. The sounds of the hall intensified then, like the world was waking up around her, and Amma could hear the soft shuffling of fabric, the tinkling of the water, and even the unseen breeze as it whistled over the rocks.

Damien had taken the woman by her wrists to remove her, but a shiver still crawled up Amma's back, as though she would be left permanently cold. She clenched her hands into fists at her sides to keep from embracing herself and rubbing warmth back into her freezing limbs, another thing she thought might be a tad bit rude.

"Jealous?" The woman's attention was now on Damien, and free of her touch and mesmerizing eyes, Amma could see things a bit clearer.

She didn't like what she was seeing.

The woman swept her long fall of auburn hair over a shoulder, sidling right up to Damien and taking another deep inhale, ample chest heaving up against him. "I didn't forget about you. How could I?"

Maybe rudeness was relative.

Amma frowned, looking to Kaz for some kind of loyalty, but the imp was paying no attention, just tapping a taloned foot and craning his neck to the hallway's end, spindly arms crossed.

Damien hesitated under the woman's touch but didn't step back. "I do appreciate your quick reply to my raven and your willingness to help me with my"—his eyes flicked to Amma—"problem."

His words fell like a stone into the pit of her stomach, a hollow splash coating her insides with irritation. So she was a *problem* then? Fantastic.

"I would love nothing more." She looked down a long nose at Amma, a piteous knit to her brows.

Amma felt about as small as Kaz.

"Come," the woman said, turning from them sharply and leading them to the curtains at the hall's end.

Feeling Damien's eyes on her, Amma couldn't return his gaze, already embarrassed enough. Discourtesy be damned, she wrapped her arms around her middle and hurried along, needing to jog to keep pace with the long strides of both Damien and the stunning woman who was just as tall.

The curtain pulled itself away as they approached and revealed a massive chamber that had Amma coming to a full stop at its entrance, arms falling limply at her sides. More of that luminescent liquid crawled in thin rivulets down the walls, but candelabras dotted the space to give it a warmer glow. An exquisite amalgam of every style of furnishings was set in matching groups atop extravagant rugs and animal hides: couches, chaises, and high-backed armchairs, each with fine detail along their ornate legs or backs. The smooth, reflective stone spread out on the floors, an inverted echo of the chamber, mirrored back like a perfectly still lake. And then there was the slightest movement, and Amma realized the space was filled with people too.

Their bodies melted over the furniture and one another as if they had grown right out of the cave itself. Draped in rich, dark fabrics, jewel-toned or velvety black, many were poised with books and languishing on sofas while others sipped wine, but no one spoke. In fact, the room was nearly silent if not for the gentle popping of candles and a stringed instrument that echoed throughout the space, its origin unseen. But there was a flicker of golden lights as eyes moved to settle on the entry, and Amma's blood went cold under their metallic gazes.

Their hostess stared out over the dozens of still bodies, then tipped her head upward almost imperceptibly. Two women who had been seated together at the back of the room stood in unison as if being lifted. Their eyebrows twitched and lips curled in silent speech, and then the two finally approached, eyes set on Amma.

"This is Ivory," said their hostess, running her knuckles down the cheek of a shorter woman with ghostly white skin and black hair in massive curls, "and Asphodel." She touched the other one under her chin, a remarkably slender woman with silver hair pulled into a slick bun to reveal the pointed ears of a half elf. Amma could not decide which of the two earned the title of second-most beautiful woman she had ever seen.

Asphodel's sharp eyes flicked to Damien and then to Ivory, who moved quickly to return the look, and then the two began to snicker.

Gods, how on all the planes of existence did Damien think Amma would *like* these people?

Their hostess then turned for them, and they both fell silent.

"Apologies, Rapture," the two said in unison.

"Well, do try to remember. Our visitor will think you very rude if you only communicate telepathically." Rapture winked at Amma, or at least she thought that was what the woman intended, but her heavy lashes moved as if coated in honey. "Now, Lord Bloodthorne and I have some terms to discuss, not to mention a bit of catching up to do. Please keep our sweet guest company in the meantime, and be sure to look after her."

"We will." Asphodel's voice was as eager as it was sultry. Beside her, Ivory reached out and took Amma's hand in another frozen grasp.

"Lovely." Rapture hooked her arm into Damien's and began to guide him away. He shot a glance at Amma, but Ivory was tugging her in a different direction, and Asphodel crowded into her other side. As they parted, Kaz's crotchety form skittered off to disappear into the shadows. Amma had never been so loath to see him go.

The women moved quickly, though it seemed they put no effort in. "What are you called?" asked Ivory in a breathy, high voice.

Mouth gone dry, Amma lost every bit of confidence she'd ever had, whispering her name into the quiet of the huge room.

"Oh no, I don't think so." Asphodel drummed long nails on her lips in thought.

The room's other occupants twisted to watch them go, moving like they were swimming in syrup. Almost every one of them was female. "Er, yes, I—well, my name's actually Ammalie, I guess."

Ivory gasped playfully. "Now, that's perfect." She rested her head on Amma's shoulder. "Such a pretty name. Just like you—so pretty."

Amma's stomach flipped over. She wasn't uncomfortable with her own looks, but she was a realist—these women were inhumanly stunning, and especially after days on the road, Amma wasn't exactly looking like she was ready for one of her parents' banquets. "You think I'm pretty?" she scoffed with a bit more bite than she meant, but surely they were just being sarcastic.

"Of course," said Asphodel with all the conviction in the realm. "Just deliciously beautiful."

It was strange how believable that was—particularly the *delicious* part.

Still with arms linked on either side of her, the women walked Amma out of the massive living space and into another long hall. This one had archways built along its sides in the natural stone. "Rapture says you'll be with us for a few days. Maybe longer," said Asphodel, brows shooting upward in anticipation. Well, that was a conversation Amma certainly had not heard. "We'll show you around so you feel at home."

"Don't wander off though," said Ivory quickly with a giggle. "You'll get lost on your own. Forever."

Despite their frigid skin, Amma held on to the two a little tighter.

"Do you like books, Ammalie?" Ivory pulled her ever so gently, and all three of them crossed the hall to stand in an archway that led into a room brightened by twice as many candles. The walls were still made up of rock, but here shelves had been carved directly into the stone, running up into the darkness of the ceiling and filled with hundreds of leather spines.

"Whoa," Amma breathed. There were two women inside the room, one of them sitting up, the other lying with her head in the first's lap. Both were reading but turned with that slow purposefulness of all the others to look directly at Amma. One of them inclined her head to sniff the air.

"I think she does," said Asphodel, voice right beside her face. She chuckled darkly when Amma jerked at the frost that tickled her ear. "But she's also covered in weapons."

Amma supposed she was covered, as they said, with a dagger strapped to her thigh and a crossbow slung over her back, but they didn't know she had very little idea how to use either one for protection beyond swinging them very hard—a fact she wouldn't divulge.

Regardless, she was towed again to a different arch that led into a vast space, the walls inside adorned with weapons. Two women in tight breeches crossed needlelike swords, the sound sharp in the otherwise silent room. Their gazes were intent on one another, but that concentration was turned on Amma the moment they took up space in the entry. A third woman, this one in a long gown, was lying on a bench at the back, watching, and there was a man, perhaps the first Amma had seen in the cave, lounging beside her.

Amma's eyes darted around at the weapons, gleaming under the firelight that burned in a hearth at one end of the long room, though it gave off no warmth. Amma's mouth dropped open, and her heartbeat sped up at all that shining metal and potential danger.

"If you think *this* is exciting, have we got something to show you," said Ivory, and she tugged just a bit more intensely, pulling them away and back to the center of the hall. They passed a few other arches, and Amma noted each was filled with some sort of amusement: musical instruments in one, easels in another, even a massive loom and spinning wheel in a third filled with fabric and thread.

As they continued on, Amma found her voice. "How did you get all this here?"

"It's brought to us," said Asphodel.

"On that river? In those little boats?"

"It's not easy, I imagine."

"This way." Ivory gave her another gentle if insistent redirection.

The archway she brought them to opened up into a smaller space, a table in its center and five women gathered around it, leaning in.

"I should stab him in the heart, shouldn't I?" one of them asked the others, and Amma's chest tightened.

"Should you?" asked another. "With your dagger? In front of this entire crowd of people?"

"Well, it's a mercy killing, isn't it?" The original faltered as her eyes searched the other faces at the table and gestured to a ginger woman. "He's lost his arm, and Marisha just turned him down."

The one called Marisha's eyes widened. "That doesn't mean he wants to die. Wait, does it?" She turned sharply to the woman beside her, lips curling into a wicked smile. "Did I break his heart that badly?"

Amma's brows knit, utterly confused. There was no armless man in the room, and in fact, there was no dagger either, and the five of them hardly constituted a crowd.

The woman central to the others took a deep breath and lifted her hand, a set of dice bouncing across the table. "He does look exceedingly sad, but not fatally so. He is still bleeding out though."

The table erupted into shouting, the women shuffling through small stacks of parchment and throwing dice at one another.

"What's happening?" Amma asked quietly, surprised by the sudden shift in demeanor from the languidness she'd become used to.

"It's a game," said Ivory. "We sort of tell one another a story and take on the roles in that story. The goal is to see who can survive the longest while doing the most good deeds—you know, the kinds that usually get you killed. It's called Innkeepers and Imbeciles, and it's great practice for reacclimating to the world."

Amma watched as the argument at the table escalated.

"I want to heal him," one woman shouted.

"Well, so do I," cried a second.

"The healing power of *true love* isn't a thing, Laura," mocked a third. "Unless, wait—is it?"

More yelling erupted from four of them, arguing whether there was any kind of arcane power behind love, romantic or otherwise.

Ivory giggled. "Shall we join them?"

There was a scuffle then as the central woman stood suddenly, brandishing an actual dagger that she plunged into the center of the table. "Who makes the rules?"

The others fell silent until the one called Marisha finally sighed. "You do, Ash." The others begrudgingly agreed.

Amma's heart was beating very hard at the sudden show of violence, and she leaned back from the room's entry.

Asphodel clicked her tongue. "She's too frightened."

Ivory pouted, reaching into her cleavage and pulling a vial of something out, then tucking it back away just as quickly when Asphodel glared at her. Instead, Amma was led away, and all the archways were left behind as they reached the hall's end. It stopped in a room as large as the main sitting space, only this one was filled with plants.

Without sunlight, they were nothing like Amma imagined plants to be—instead sprouting ghostly white petals and silky, black leaves—but the underground garden pulled the breath and the nerves all out of her. Amma slipped out of the grasp of the two, feet taking her forward as she marveled at the sprawling tendrils, the climbing vines, the twisted trunks of spindly trees that grew right out of the rocky ground.

"We've found a winner." Ivory caught up to her, and Asphodel was at her other side, again with one silent move. The air was heavy and humid, but the mist was cool, and even the long, placid stares of others strolling by didn't upset Amma from her joyous meander through the pathways between the plants.

She didn't recognize a single thing, and both Asphodel and Ivory admitted to knowing very little about horticulture but were happy enough to indulge her. When Amma ran a finger over the slick surface of a flat leaf covered in naturally occurring holes, there was a quiet voice in the back of her mind that said a word that sounded quite a bit like *Dead*. Though nothing there looked dried out and expired, she suddenly thought about the undead kalsephrus trees outside the Ebon Sanctum Mallor back in Aszath Koth, which kept growing thanks to arcana, and she tucked the thought away for later.

How much time had gone by, Amma didn't know, but eventually her stomach panged loud enough for the women to hear. Ivory gasped in her overly dramatic way, apologized profusely for not feeding her, and Amma was whisked off yet again, this time down a much narrower hallway to a room significantly smaller than any of the others. There, the ceiling was a normal height, and there was only one long table and a set of benches at which the three sat, a not terribly impressive dining hall considering how immaculate the rest of the place was.

Asphodel whistled long and low into the air, and a woman appeared at a small door at the back of the room. "A meal," she said, and the woman disappeared again. Staring at her with kind smiles, neither spoke, but their eyes did flick to one another momentarily.

The woman they'd ordered the meal from returned. She was comparatively plain, a servant by the looks of her clothing, clean but nowhere near as ornate or fine as the others, and there were circles under her eyes and an exhausted pallor to her face. She set a plate in front of Amma, a portion of red meat, a bed of dark, leafy greens, and a deeply brown, nutty-smelling grain.

Ivory urged Amma to eat, leaning forward and folding her hands under her chin. Amma hesitated, but it seemed there was no expectation that the other two would dine with her. She cut into the meat, red juices flowing out, and popped a piece into her mouth. "Holy Osurehm," she said, mouth full, then slapped a hand over her face. "Sorry," she squeaked out from behind her fingers.

Asphodel shook her head, still grinning. "No apologies necessary. We insist on the highest quality, and it's nice to hear about it every once in a while."

"Drinks," Ivory ordered, and the servant fetched full wineglasses for the two of them. She waited a step back from the table in case anything else was requested, features tranquil if detached.

Amma was so invested in her food that it took her a moment to notice she'd been given a light-colored ale rather than the red wine the others had, but perhaps it simply paired better this way. "Aren't you two going to eat?"

Asphodel took a sip. "I'm not terribly hungry, though you do make it look appealing."

Amma slowed in chewing her next bite, careful to swallow fully, and then apologized for what she assumed was how barbarous she looked when eating, explaining meekly that days on the road could do that.

"Oh no, did we do it again?" Asphodel shook her head, her smile fading slightly. "Sometimes we're not sure how to sound sincere, but we do mean it when we say we're so happy to have you here."

The concern in her voice felt genuine enough even as her golden eyes sparkled eerily. It was unfair, perhaps, for Amma to have judged them so early on. They were quite likable, but their intense beauty had simply blinded Amma, not least with jealousy.

"You're right—we're not being very accommodating." Ivory had just finished off her wine. "You know what? I think I will join you." She gestured to the servant, and the tired woman came to stand just beside her.

It happened so fast, Amma didn't even stop chewing until there was a spray of blood across what was left on her plate. Ivory had the servant bent at the waist, her teeth were sunk into the woman's neck, and she took a long, slurpy drink from her throat. The hand clutching the servant had changed, fingers transformed into claws with bony, thickened knuckles, and blue veins pulsed up her arm.

When she wrenched the servant's form back to stand upright, blood ran down the woman's neck to pool at her collar, and the same slick crimson stained Ivory's chin.

Amma had seen a lot of blood in her life; she was a woman after all, and it was especially unavoidable when following a blood mage all over Eiren—but it wasn't really the blood that made Amma's vision tunnel so much as the grin Ivory was sporting afterward, canines elongated and dripping.

I suppose you've never seen a vampire, so those must not exist either, echoed Damien's voice in the back of her mind, and then the room went dark.

CHAPTER 13

DAMIEN

In Defense of Acting Foolishly

DAMIEN HAD NEVER BEEN quite so aware of Rapture's friendliness. When he was near the karsts, he frequently bartered his company with the woman when he needed something in trade. Misgivings only weaseled their way in about how he had struck a deal afterward, but those were easy to brush off—it was just how things were done in their circles.

Sometimes, Rapture only requested blood or assistance with a mundane task, such as someone captured or killed that required daylight to be endured, the usual, but companionship was never offered without a caveat. Rapture was an ally who could always be counted on, and during Damien's *indenturement* to another, she never pushed for anything he wasn't willing to give, but she also never…what was it?

Well, she never really cared about him, did she?

Of course, Rapture had clung to his side as she walked him along the den's halls to a private chamber where they could have their *discussion*. She chose to sit them both on the smallest of seats, running fingers up his arm to his neck and behind his ear, all things he normally liked, but she always did that when he first arrived, and it wouldn't last.

Rapture's private room had been refurnished. The style was changed from the deep reds it had been last time and the unfortunate white she'd gone with for a short-lived and messy time before that. She'd chosen green presently, rich and vibrant like the heart of a humid forest, and had added golden accents that reminded Damien of Amma and her penchant for trees. Amma would like the room, especially the vase of pink lilies beside the door. Except—Damien glanced down at how Rapture was lightly rubbing her shin against his own—maybe Amma actually wouldn't like what was in the room at all.

Rapture had just finished saying something about a disturbance in the Innomina Wildwood to the south when Damien focused back on his host's face—her captivatingly beautiful face. "The assistance I need from you…it is no small ask."

The woman turned her head slightly, her expectant smile sliding off her face, and she pulled her feet up on the short sofa they shared to fold beneath her. Now she was really looking, yellow eyes scrutinizing him in that way he hated. "Tell me what you want," she said, voice losing all its throatiness.

"Lycoris."

Rapture did not move for a full minute, features refusing even to twitch, but then immortality could do that to a person, making them forget time had meaning.

"I hope you're not attempting to speak to me telepathically because it's not working if so."

Rapture blinked heavily lidded eyes, pushing herself up off the couch. Warmth returned to the space she left as she flitted to the far side of the chamber and poured herself a drink. The tinkling of the crystal carafe filled the room as thick red liquid filled a matching goblet. She replaced the carafe upon a metal holder suspended over the flame of a stubby candle and turned back to him, resting her hips against the table. "You want me to wake Lycoris ahead of schedule?"

"It's only a few decades."

"Sixty-six years is more than a few decades." She took a drink, steam from the viscous liquid inside rising from her cold fingertips against the goblet. "I can't imagine what could be so imperative. Or what you would be willing to barter."

Damien stood, finding it impossible to sit there under her eye any longer. He was glad Kaz had fucked off somewhere else in the den and wasn't around to grouse at him. "A favor. From Zagadoth."

"Zagadoth is in no position to be granting favors," she said with a bite but grinned. She had to know what was coming—he had shared with her his plans once, years ago.

"Not yet."

Rapture suddenly appeared in front of him, though he hadn't seen her move. The blood in her goblet sloshed as she stood still before him, nails tinkling against the crystal. Its contents smelled of human, predictably, but this time the stench made Damien anxious instead of amused. They really preferred the stuff fresh, and he had just abandoned a human in their midst that he knew had to taste exceedingly sweet. But their agreement would be honored—it had to be—and like Damien himself, Rapture and her kind had standards.

"Not…yet?" Rapture's tongue darted over her lips, considering the deal.

"I'm closer than ever to freeing him, but there are complications. Lycoris may be able to rectify those."

"Your ambiguity is riveting," she said, the throatiness returning to her voice as she lifted the goblet between them and took another drink, crimson staining her pointed teeth as she smiled. "I almost want to grant you this just for the Abyss of it."

"Almost?"

Never one to actually pace, Rapture went back to her makeshift bar and set down her glass, leaning back against the table, hips cocked to one side. Her dress hugged her rounded curves, the fabric so thin and taut there was little left to the imagination, though with his memories, he didn't have to imagine. "Something this audacious isn't up to me alone. You'll need the other elders to agree your father's favor is worth it, but my sway with them is heavy. Convince me."

Damien clasped his hands behind his back, taking a step as he thought. "The power a demon lord holds is immeasurable. A favor from him—"

"No, no," she said, humor in her voice as she crooked a finger at him. "*Convince* me."

A few more steps brought him up to her, the familiar distance of nothing between them. She pushed off the table and settled her arms on his shoulders, hands in his hair so that her nails slid over his scalp. He steeled himself for the pain of her fangs and waited.

Rapture's kiss tasted of blood, the heat of it mingling with the frigidity of her lips. It was rough, as always, inviting in all the ways Damien usually gave in to, but he immediately pulled out of it.

"No?" she asked, brows knitted with curiosity as she studied his face, fingers still scratching at him like they wanted to dig right into his mind. Her kind could glean flashes of one's desires from physical contact, and Rapture was especially good at getting to the truth, but his violent reaction likely made further prodding unnecessary. "You're not involved with that awful Delacroix woman again, are you?"

"Darkness, no." He wiped at his mouth, a smear of blood on the back of his hand and something like regret in his gut. "But I would still rather persuade you with the alternative."

Rapture pouted a thick, dark lip, then curved it up into a grin, canines glinting in the candlelight.

When Damien's eyes opened onto the darkened room later, he had no sense of how much time had passed. He lay on

Rapture's bed, still fully clothed but drained in a different way. He'd let her feed off him in the past, little nips here and there when they'd come to some agreement, and then, when he was really desperate, deeper drinks. Those had been low points, disgustingly vulnerable both before and even worse after, but she and her kin had always proved trustworthy enough, not attacking him when he was weak. Their laws didn't exactly protect blood mages, but it would be stupid to kill him off, he reckoned; once he was gone, the well would be dry.

A new corked bottle of deep crimson was sitting beside Rapture's carafe on the bar, and she was lounging alone on her sofa again, as disinterested as always after she was done with him.

Damien rubbed his neck and sat up. The marks there had already healed, but the pain remained. When administered with no other distractions, her bite left quite the sting.

Rapture's eyes were even more vibrant than before, flicking up to him quickly, impatience floating in them. "Finally feeling better?"

"Good enough." His head only spun a moment, and he yawned.

"I'll convene with the elders over your request tonight, and I'm sure they will want to hear from you tomorrow. You're welcome to stay in the den, of course." She licked her lips. "And if you've changed your mind, you can stay right there and wait for me to return."

He snorted, even that making him woozy. "I think you've depleted my ability to be much more use tonight."

Chuckling, she led him to the door. "I had a room prepared while you were napping, just in case. It's beside the one they put your human in."

"Amma." He hadn't considered recuperation time along with negotiations. "How long was I out?"

"Oh, *hours*," she said a bit too gleefully. "But not to worry. Just a small warning: She did have a teeny, tiny accident."

His eyes went wide as he followed Rapture into the hall. He had to grab the doorway to remain steady. "Where is she?"

"Calm down, Lord Bloodthorne. You don't want to swoon out here now, do you?" She chuckled again. "There wasn't even much blood, I'm told. And we were sure to clean up every drop."

Damien pushed off the wall, dagger sliding down into his palm. "When did your laws change?"

Rapture brought a claw up to his face, its sharp point pressing against his cheek, not in reassurance but in warning. "They haven't. You can see for yourself. Second hall that way, third door on the right."

"If anyone has touched her—" Threats left unsaid were often more daunting than those well-defined. Damien swept away from Rapture and followed her directions without another word because his worn mind simply could not come up with one. Sheathing his dagger, he staggered bleary-eyed the way she'd said and slammed the door open. "Amma?"

"Damien!" The pile of blankets on the bed exploded, and a small figure jumped out of them. From behind the sheer curtains hanging around the four-poster bed, arms moved about like those of a feral animal, searching for a break in the drapery. She was frantic, but she was alive.

"Thank the dark gods," he muttered, falling against the door as it shut behind him, head spinning.

"By Osurehm," she said, finally finding where the curtains met and ripping them apart from one another. Her hair was mussed, and her tunic was askew, falling away from a shoulder. She was trying to climb off the bed but getting tangled in the many blankets she'd apparently been hiding beneath. "Did you know that—ah!" She finally managed to free herself, but it was as much a surprise to her as it was to him, and she toppled right off the edge of the bed to the floor.

Damien straightened, too dizzy to have caught her. She had none of the exhaustion or pain of someone who had been bitten but all the coordination of a victim nearly drained.

Amma growled, flipping onto her back to kick the last blanket off, then tipped her head to eye him upside down. "Did you know that these women are *vampires*?"

Damien blinked. "Uh...yes? Did you think I did *not* know this?"

"I don't know!" She scrambled up onto her knees. "Because you brought me, a human, here. You know vampires eat humans, right?"

He squinted out into the room she'd been put in, well furnished with a fire lit for warmth that the rest of the den was missing. A comforting sort of drowsiness crawled over him, even with her excitable exaggeration in the middle of all of it. "Well, these ones have a certain code, and really, they only drink blood. There's no ingestion of flesh."

"What's the difference?" she squeaked, finally back on her feet.

"You get to live afterward, usually. And it can be quite pleasurable if you're in the right mood." His vision evened out as he looked her over. She'd taken off her boots, that tight vest from around her middle, and abandoned her weapons too, so he assumed she couldn't be that rattled by the whole thing, but she was breathing rather hard, and then he remembered Rapture's warning. "They told me you were injured. What happened?"

"Injured? No, I, um"—Amma took a big breath, her frenzy reining itself in—"well, I did sort of pass out when I saw Ivory munch on somebody, and I scraped my elbow a little."

Damien rested his head against the door again. "So I don't have to kill anyone for biting you?"

She looked about the room like the answer might be in there with them, then shrugged. "I guess not."

He nodded to himself. "Of course not—they would be fools to do so when you're…"

Mine. The word echoed into his mind. She wasn't meant to be, and he'd only just promised to return her to Faebarrow, but the desire to keep her still ate at him, the word so eager to be free from his throat that it burned.

Amma was still standing by the edge of the bed, face changed from the overwhelmed look she'd been giving him while she delivered the not-so-new news of their hosts' origin. Now she was anticipating what he was about to say, but he'd cut himself off to save both of them from it. She ran a hand through her hair, eyes lingering on him, still wide with something like fear.

"I suppose I should have warned you that we were entering a vampire den, but I thought—well, it doesn't matter what I thought."

Amma said nothing, but he could see an unease in her face that he wanted to chase away.

"Would you like me to find Kaz and have him sleep in your room?"

She squished up her features but quickly wiped the grimace off. The imp wasn't even there, yet she was still trying not to offend the horrible little beast. Darkness, why did she have to be so thoughtful? "He doesn't really like me very much," she said, quite reasonably. "And I think he's busy with the lady imps. I haven't seen him at all since we got here, and I've seen...a lot."

Damien huffed, a little jealous of Kaz, though glad for his absence if it left the room to just the two of them. Then again, Rapture had said he had his own chamber next door. "Well, that only leaves me, but certainly you don't want to sleep together. That is, uh, have me in your bed." Basest beasts, why did he have to go and say it like that? He could have had Rapture with so little as a look, but here, now, with Amma, he was tripping over words and feeling like an absolute idiot. "Beside you," he clarified, perhaps unhelpfully.

Amma took a very slow breath as her shoulders rose, working up to something that turned out to be only a small noise that was neither confirmation nor declination—a wonderful time for her to be so brilliantly clear.

Damien tapped his fingers on the door, testing that it was closed completely, then slid his hand to the latch. The sound of it locking cut into the air. He pushed off the door, taking careful, measured steps to where she stood, giving her time to tell him to stop, to back up, to show him in any way that she wanted him to leave. Amma only tipped her head up when he was finally standing right before her, small frame trapped between him and the edge of the bed.

She'd say *something*. She had to.

He leaned closer, watching her features soften in the low light of the room. The chill of the den was chased away, her body giving off the heat he'd been seeking earlier. He may have been nearly drained, but he wasn't so spent that he couldn't lift her up and dump her backward into the nest of blankets she'd hoarded, climb atop her, and make good on the torture he'd promised when she had been drunk.

But while he held himself back, the noxscura made its own decision. Despite being so close to exhaustion, the dark arcana slipped out, wrapping invisible tendrils around Amma and touching her in his stead. His magic felt her blood as it pumped mercilessly in her veins, heartbeat wild though she held herself very still.

Damien's hand found its way behind her to the bed, and she still didn't move, didn't speak, but her pulse was frantic.

His fingers closed into a fist around a linen, holding tight as he willed the noxscura to leave her, and then all at once stepped back, bringing one of the blankets with him.

"Sleep." He gestured with his chin as he turned away. There was a chaise before the fireplace just off the foot of the bed. "This will do," he said and sat.

"You're just—" She cleared the husk from her throat. "You're just going to sleep there?"

He shrugged, pulling off his boots.

"But you can't. You'll be so uncomfortable, and it's stupid for me to be afraid, like you said."

"I did not say it was stupid," he insisted, removing his chest leathers and relieved to have the weight off him. "And this is a fair bit more comfortable than the forest floor."

Amma worried her hands on the edge of her loosened tunic, fallen further askew down her arm and exposing more of the soft curve of her shoulder and the thin strap of her chemise beneath. She wouldn't sleep in those clothes, and he wasn't sure if he should be thankful or morose he hadn't suggested once more they share the bed.

But he reminded himself sharply as he unstrapped his belt, Amma was still the vessel for a talisman that allowed him to override her will completely with a single word. Even asking her outright wouldn't have been sufficient. Damien paused his modest undressing. "Unless you want me to leave, then I will go."

She bit her lip, eyes averted, but shook her head forcibly.

"All right then. I have reading to do anyway." He pulled from his satchel the parchment he'd kept from Xander's, the notes he had taken on the Lux Codex translations, and the ripped-out page from the fire mage's book, and lay back, feet up.

From the corner of his eye, he saw Amma hesitate, then climb onto the four-poster. The bed was high and large, surrounded by sheer curtains. Her silhouette against the drapes stole his attention no matter how hard he tried to focus on his notes. His writing was a blur, but every movement as she undressed was sharp, cutting into his peripheral, reminding him of when he'd been alone with her in that tiny tavern room in Faebarrow and she'd stripped down to almost nothing.

Apparently, Damien wasn't quite drained of as much blood as he'd thought. He readjusted as he rolled to his side to turn his back on her shadow. He squinted at the pages, firelight behind them, making the script even more difficult to read. The sounds of Amma moving about quieted, and his eyelids felt heavy, thoughts about how to reverse his own arcana inside her mingling with fantasies of just being inside her at all.

"Damien?" Amma's voice jolted into him, though it was just a whisper. "Are you awake?"

He was, but he hesitated. If she'd changed her mind about where she'd like him to sleep, he couldn't sprint into the bed as, well…as *eager* as this, but then she could just as easily be about to tell him to leave. He rolled onto his back again and blinked up into the glow of the fire reflecting on the rocky ceiling. Hopefully, whatever she would say would douse his wanton thoughts. "Yes, Amma, I am still awake."

"Did you say that, um...when a vampire bites you, it feels *good*?"

Bloody Abyss, she really needed to listen to him a little less. "I'm fairly certain I did not."

"Yes, you did," she insisted a bit louder, though her tone was gentle. "You said it can be, what was it? Pleasurable?"

He squeezed the bridge of his nose. "Look, don't get any ideas."

"I was only wondering—"

"Well, don't." Damien picked up the pages again, needing the distraction of laborious translations from the way he was imagining her mouth would form the word *pleasurable*.

She huffed from across the room, the sound of one of her fists falling into the blankets. "Look, I just want to know if that Rapture woman bit you."

He clicked his tongue but was intrigued by her tone. "Yes, that *vampire* did indeed bite me."

"She did?" The alarm in her voice made it waver. "And you *let* her?"

"Well, no one's going to bite me against my will, Amma," he droned, then thought that may not have been the response she was looking for.

She scoffed, and he didn't have to see her to know she was crossing her arms and pouting. No, that had definitely not been the correct response.

"You are...upset?" he mused quietly.

"No!" Her quickness was wholly unconvincing. "I just, you know...I don't think it's a good idea. Not for a *blood* mage."

"Oh, you've become an expert in sanguine arcana now, have you?" Damien chuckled.

"Well, isn't that where your magic comes from? Won't it be dangerous for you if they have your blood?"

"Ah, I see." Damien laid the parchment on his chest and sighed—her query was much less interesting than he'd originally thought, but he should have gathered as much; Amma did seem ever-concerned about his well-being. And that was...well, it was meant to be nice when someone cared about you, wasn't it? "Once my blood is spilt, it loses nearly all its magical properties. It must be preserved with a spell, like what Xander the great buffoon does with that vial about his neck, to be dangerous in another's hands...or mouth. Regardless, I did it as part of a trade. My blood for their help."

"Help with the talisman?"

"Yes."

"Oh."

That seemed to satisfy her, and Damien picked up his pages again. He'd hoped to coax the essence of what she was getting at out of her but was strangely disappointed she was only worried about the potential risk of his actions.

Amma remained silent as Damien read, long enough that he thought she had fallen asleep, but silence rarely lasted in her presence, and her quiet voice cut into the air once more. "But did you also *enjoy* it when she bit you?"

Damien grinned into the dark. Now that would be difficult to explain, even to a woman who had gone to mush in his hands when he'd tied her up. "I don't see how *that* matters."

"I just want to know," she said with exasperation she hadn't really earned.

"And *I* just want to know why *you* are so concerned?"

That garnered no quip back, the popping of the fireplace the only thing filling up the room's palpable silence.

"Ah, so Lady Ammalie is absolutely full of questions, but she is not so keen to offer any answers."

She clicked her tongue. "Fine, don't tell me. If we're going to be here for a few days, I'll just ask Asphodel or Ivory to show me how *pleasurable* being bitten can be."

He growled at the thought, suddenly incensed. "Being bitten is incredibly painful, Amma, and it can easily lead to your death—you know, the thing we are trying to avoid by being here? It's only if you engage in other intimate activities when being bitten that—"

Amma gasped, and her small shadow bolted up behind the sheer curtain. "*That's* what you were doing with Rapture?"

And there, that was the crux of all her circular inquiries; he *knew* it. Damien let her question hang in the air, then sighed. "Your concern is endearing but irrelevant. My virtue was ruined long ago."

She was still sitting up, and he could feel her eyes boring into him, the room's temperature dropping even though the fire still crackled at his side. All the fun was swept from his teasing as a strange, guilty sensation dug its way into him, odd especially since he had actually refused Rapture's advances.

"To be clear, Rapture and I did not participate in anything except a *very* painful bloodletting." He winced, the sting traveling from his neck to his gut where it settled, prodding at him to be totally honest. "Though she did...press her mouth against mine."

"She did?"

"For a very brief moment," he said quickly. "I should have been expecting it, but she acted without invitation."

"Oh." She was quiet, and he feared what question, or worse, what anger might come next, but then she totally surprised him. "Are vampires susceptible to silver like werewolves?"

Damien actually laughed. "Why would you ask a thing like *that*, Amma? Surely you don't intend to stake one of them."

Grumbling, she fidgeted on the bed, the linens shuffling. "Well, did she stop when you told her to?"

"Yes, of course she did." He snorted, grinning wider. "Do you intend to defend my honor, Lady Avington?"

Amma's shadow fell still, and then she shifted to lie back down, her form disappearing from the drapes. "Well, someone should if need be."

He expected her to begin laughing, to signify how ridiculous her own suggestion was, but she didn't, and as unnecessary—and frankly unhelpful—as it would be if she attacked any of the vampires, something in Damien's chest cracked at the thought of Amma courageously defending him. It was just a narrow fissure, but when he let his mind truly consider what she meant, it grew deeper than the Abyss.

"That won't be necessary," he said, throat hoarse. "Nothing further occurred. She only collected my blood and agreed to convince the elder council to strike a deal with me."

He listened to Amma shift under the blankets. "Thank you," she finally said.

"No, thank you, Amma," he replied, likely too quiet for her to hear, but—and of this he was curiously relieved—it felt quite *good* to say.

CHAPTER 14

AMMA

A Thinly Veiled Analogy

AMMA WOKE IN THE soft, downy comfort of a bed, covered in many blankets to keep out the cold and feeling curiously blissful considering the shock of the day before. She'd been left with eerie strangers, seen a woman's neck split open by fangs, and fainted. But then Damien had finally returned, and he'd stayed with her.

She sat up, slow and deliberate, the linens and furs falling away so that her bare shoulders were caressed by the frigid air of the vampire den below the karsts. Without windows or the sun, time was difficult to keep track of, but the candle left on the bedside table was down to a stub to suggest the night had passed. Amma slipped forward onto her knees and crawled silently to the foot of the bed, where she pushed the sheer curtain away.

Sprawled out on the chaise before the dying fire, Damien had an arm hanging off to trail the ground and a small stack of parchment on his chest. His head hung to the side, hair falling in his face, lips slightly parted, out cold. She'd seen him asleep before, but never quite so relaxed.

Brow unpinched and mouth not pulled into a frown, he was so much more handsome, if that were even possible, and for a moment, her chest actually ached. What was she thinking? Damien Maleficus Bloodthorne was the son of a demon, a demon who was imprisoned by the king of her realm, and she was ordered to marry another man for the supposed good of her barony and people. But, gods, did she want *this* man instead.

She'd been fighting it, telling herself she was mad to think it could ever work, but the night before, when she had thought, even for an instant, that he had made love to someone else, a burning anger propelled her upward. Then, as soon as it rushed into her, it rushed back out, leaving her cold and empty and bathed in grief. As if her heart had shattered, tears welled up at the thought that he had chosen to be with someone else, and she had lost him.

And that *was* madness, she knew it, madness beyond the very simple and obvious reason she shouldn't have had any of those feelings at all: She had no claim on him. Damien didn't belong to her—and the way he acted suggested he didn't want to belong to anybody—but it wasn't just jealousy clawing away at the wall of good sense she'd been building up since learning of his destiny to destroy Eiren. It was how completely foreign the heartbreak that had followed felt.

Even when Amma had to tell her former suitor Thomas they couldn't be together, she hadn't experienced something so all-encompassing, and she'd barely ever touched Damien in comparison. And, gods, did she want to do more than just touch him, especially when he growled about how she belonged to him and loomed over her with a protective presence that somehow made her feel safe from everything else in every plane of existence.

Amma fell forward from her position on all fours, burying her head in the blankets and letting out a long, muffled groan. He was everything she should have run away from: domineering, brutal, and, chiefly, evil, but—

"Amma?"

She sat up with speed, back straight, as if she'd been doing something she shouldn't have—which was accurate if pining after him counted.

Damien was blinking awake, wiping at his mouth with the back of his hand. "How'd you sleep?" he asked in a drowsy, tender voice with none of the sharpness it normally carried.

Her heart fluttered. "G-good."

Damien stretched, arching his back and groaning, still half asleep as the blanket he'd used fell to the floor. She watched with wide eyes, his muscled form writhing there in front of what was left of the fire, tunic undone to the middle of his chest, sleeves pushed up over muscled forearms, the tops of his hips and the hard lines running down his abdomen exposed when he stretched back completely.

Amma swallowed hard—to speak of ruining someone's

virtue, the sight of his navel could have done that to her all on its own. She regretted interminably not inviting him right into bed the night before.

When he pushed up onto an elbow and blinked those violet eyes fully open to set them on her, the chill that worked its way across her back wasn't from the room's temperature. "So is it safe to assume you did not go on a murderous rampage, staking the whole den last night?"

"No, of course not." She pouted, embarrassed, then sat straighter. "Did you?"

A lazy grin crawled up the side of Damien's face, gaze drifting down her body as he leaned against his elbow. "Did I..." She watched his throat bob, chest rising with a deep breath, and then his eyes quickly shot back to her face. "Hmm—what?"

Amma glanced down at herself, chest barely covered in just her thin chemise, the dying firelight not quite shadowy enough. She fell back onto the bed and pulled a fur over herself. "Nothing, never mind!"

From her hiding place, she listened to him shuffle around. "It appears to be morning," he said after a few moments.

Amma popped her head out and pushed the draperies away.

Damien had his things over his shoulder, parchment in hand, boots on, still looking disheveled and sleepy. "I've got to meet with the elders today, so..."

"I'll be okay," she assured him, and with another glance at her and then the room, he left.

Amma groaned again, covering her face with the blankets and collapsing. Right—another day surrounded by gorgeous, capable, and, most importantly, *powerful* women. With that clarity, she realized she should be thankful for her nerves the previous night; they had saved her from the mortification of his rejection.

When she had composed herself, bathed, and dressed, Amma spent another day with Asphodel and Ivory. Now that she knew just what surrounded her, Amma found it difficult to relax, but not for lack of the vampires trying. They spent more time in the garden, and then she was taken on a tour of their denmates' artwork, which consisted of plenty of nudes, of course, but landscapes too, notably all nighttime depictions, and some fantastical scenes she was sure couldn't be real. When they again brought Amma to eat, Ivory assured her she wouldn't give her reason to pass out once again.

"She is still very uncomfortable," said Asphodel with a slight frown as if she knew plainly this was a fact.

Ivory stuck two fingers down into her cleavage and pulled out a vial again, holding it up. "This would help!"

Asphodel sighed but was less annoyed than the last time her companion had fished out a tincture from between her breasts. "Perhaps, but I think Rapture would rather we assuage her fears naturally."

Amma hesitated with her next bite of buttery shellfish, eyes flicking toward the man who had served them. She was keener today, noticing the servants tucked into shadowy corners, appearing immediately when a vampire called for them.

They all had deep circles under their eyes and dead expressions and were quite thin, following commands like how Amma imagined she probably did when Damien would use that Chthonic word on her. They actually were enthralled, it was explained, a mixture of blood loss and vampiric arcana making it temporarily possible, but not quite like Amma's predicament.

An icy hand wrapped around Amma's wrist, though it didn't hold her there. Asphodel's fingers only pressed in gently as she spoke. "You feel a sort of...empathy for them?" It was like she was unsure how to explain it.

Amma cleared her throat, setting down her utensils and gently tugging her hands away. "There's not a lot of difference between me and those servants," she whispered. "We're all just human."

Ivory laughed at that, loud and sharp as she tucked the vial back into his hiding place. She flicked a hand and sent the man back into the kitchen, leaving the three alone in the small dining space. "We took that man from a prison in Eirengaard," she explained when he was gone, her laughter falling away. "He was there because he raped the daughter of someone important, but who knows how many others?"

"And the woman from yesterday?" Asphodel tipped her head, smiling. "She beat her child to death. It was meant only to be a punishment, but it went, as she said, *too far*."

Amma sat back from the food, stomach turning.

"Now they're here in servitude and our fodder." Ivory shrugged. "It's not forever—they wither away after a while—but there's no shortage of warm, deserving bodies out there to replace them."

"I'm sure you're delicious, and the temptation isn't lost on us, but you don't meet our requirements for food." Asphodel pursed her lips. "Some of us asked to be cursed in this way. Many also did not. We do what we must to survive, but to join our den, an oath must be taken to abide by our laws and minimize needless suffering."

"And it's *very fun* to seek out the wicked and exact revenge," Ivory said, fangs glistening. "Especially when you get to tell them what's going to happen and that there's not a thing they can do about it."

That was not at all what Amma had expected, but Damien mentioned they had standards he approved of. After their run-in with the werewolves in the swamp, she had assumed that vampires were much the same, ferally feeding off whoever they wanted. She wondered if there were clans of werewolves who hid themselves away and fought their cursed instincts too. "So you're enacting justice against evildoers?"

The two nodded.

"But Damien…he says he's evil."

"Well, he's a blood mage. He manipulates the very thing we need to survive, so it's a little more complex than that," Ivory told her, "but can you think of anything that would get him in trouble with us?"

Asphodel's golden eyes flicked about. "If there is, he's probably made up for it with all the tasks Rapture sends him on. Oh, once he brought a whole cartload of slavers to us. Do you remember that?"

Ivory squealed. "My belly was distended for a week afterward!"

Amma's queasiness was overridden by laughter at how Ivory slapped her stomach.

"You could join us, you know," said Asphodel, folding her hands before her.

"Yes!" Ivory leaned forward, grinning wickedly. "Then, if you really feel he deserves it, you could exact your own revenge against the blood mage. You would probably lose, but it might be fun to try!"

Amma's eyes flicked to the kitchen door where the servant had been dismissed. "I don't think he's as bad as…" Then her mind clouded with a rush of thoughts. She really didn't know, did she? Whatever Damien had gotten up to before her, it was all shrouded in mystery. He simply *told her* he was evil, but did he mean because of his actions or because of the circumstances of his birth? She'd thought vampires were evil right up until a moment ago, and now…well, now she didn't know what to think.

"The offer stands," said Asphodel.

"I'll think about it."

Amma discovered then that she really did like the vampires. She was introduced to Henri, a slim man with eyes as golden as the rest of them, who looked over the crossbow, made some slight modifications, and taught Amma how to use it. He told her she proved adequate, however, "all one ever needs to be is threatening."

When Damien showed up in the training chamber at day's end, Amma insisted he watch. Henri was just behind her, helping to steady her arms as she aimed at the grass-filled figure at the chamber's end. This time, he didn't correct her but simply hovered there, and Amma pulled the trigger. The arrow zipped through the air and planted itself just at the edge of the target. She squeaked out a sound of excitement and turned fully to Damien, arms out, wiggling the crossbow in one hand. "Look, I'm threatening now!"

"I see," said Damien, pleased until his vision narrowed on Henri, who took a long step away from Amma. She thought to correct him, that no one had even so much as sniffed her neck, but when he strode up to her with another appraising look, her insides went a little too melty to form words.

But then Rapture was just behind him, and Amma soured, biting her cheek to keep the look off her face and her finger off the crossbow's trigger.

"Congratulations, Ammalie, the council has agreed to assist. It is not for just any human that we would wake the dame of our kind early." She ran a hand through Damien's hair, and he remained stoic beneath the caress. "Nor just anyone who could convince a blood mage to appeal on their behalf."

Amma didn't know of what exactly the vampire spoke, but she knew it had to be good. Damien explained, as they left the others to retire for the evening, that after a day of preparation, there would be a ceremony to wake someone called Lycoris, which was, as he said in that ominous way of his, *a considerable occurrence.*

"How will this person help us?" Amma asked when they reached her chamber door.

"That is not...entirely clear," said Damien in a way that made her both believe him and not, but then he changed the subject abruptly. "Your day—was it acceptable?"

Amma nodded, then eagerly told him of the artwork and the gardens.

"Then you feel safe here, yes?" His eyes flicked to the chamber door.

She nodded again, grinning at how silly she had perhaps been to think otherwise.

"Right. Good. Then I'll just..." He took a step backward, awkwardly rubbing his neck and reaching out blindly for the next door along the way. "I'll leave you to it."

"Oh, uh?" *Shit.* Amma looked about, but the hall was quiet; there was nothing even remotely frightening about the polished stone floors or the pretty glowing water in the walls, and he'd found the other door, opening it and watching her hesitantly. "Yes, of course! I'm fine. I don't need anyone to... to sleep with me. I, um...I've got this now!" She pulled at the strap over her shoulder, yanking the crossbow forward and grabbing for it. There was a click and a snap, and an arrow shot off right into the floor.

She jumped away from where it landed, and the arrow rolled to a stop a few feet away. Damien had gone very still, watching her with wide eyes.

Amma grumbled a minced oath and retrieved the arrow. "Right. Henri did say to never leave it loaded. Forgot." She pushed her way into her chamber with half a wave at Damien before shutting herself inside where she could properly curl into a ball and try to stop existing until she felt slightly less like a complete fool.

The following day, while the vampires prepared things, Damien and Amma worked on her aim in the morning, and he blessedly did not mention the mishap the night before, but he was vigilant when she had the crossbow in hand, frequently correcting her stance. That was more than fine with Amma, preferring how he gently pressed fingers into her back to make her straighten or ran his hands under her arms to raise them up, and she found herself purposefully getting the stance wrong so he would touch her all over again. Perhaps it wasn't subtle, but Damien never complained that she couldn't comprehend the simplicity of standing correctly, nor did he point out how she was curiously capable when he stepped away to observe her from afar.

They then spent the afternoon in one of the many studies where Damien was engrossed in his notes and a few books he'd picked out from the shelves. Left to wander the room without him paying attention, Amma found things the Grand Athenaeum would have hidden away for their debauchery. She curled up in a chair with the most promising one—a story that really had no plot but did an extraordinary job of immersing her into the lasciviousness of a relationship neither character had any business being in.

When the candles had burned down, it was time, though for what, Amma was still slightly foggy. Taken deeper into the caverns than they'd yet been, Amma walked in shuffling silence alongside Damien, flanked by many vampires. The procession was hooded, long shadows of thin forms moving all around them, and at the back, a row of servants carrying crates. Their slow march made Amma feel as though she were suspended in water, the ground gently sloping as the ceiling rose up into a forever darkness above them. The glowing water was in shorter supply, the troughs at the edge of the walkway narrow, and they traveled by following the lanterns carried at the front of their procession.

Amma's breath swirled before her with every exhale into the frigid air, her nose and fingertips going numb. The wind in the height of the cavern whistled, mimicking whispers that tickled at the back of her mind. There was magic the deeper they went, a sort of latent arcana that seeped up from the black pit they stalked into, and it buzzed around in the cold, reaching out like it had its own hands, assessing the forms as they drew nearer to its source.

The procession stopped, and Amma crossed her arms, rubbing her fingers but failing to work warmth back into them. Then a flame sparked to life and chased around a chamber, jumping from newly illuminated golden brazier to brazier.

Firelight danced over the craggy walls and floor; the cavern was ancient and plain save for the braziers fixed to the walls, and though the space was mostly empty, it was filled with something that pulsed in the massive crystal jutting out of the cave's center. With a smoky, rose-colored hue, the ice-like crystal stood at a slight angle, disrupting the earthen floor beneath, a bed of smaller, jagged crystals breaking through and crawling away like rocky tendrils.

When the lanterns were carried up to it, the shadow hidden inside was revealed. Vaguely human but taller than those who illuminated it, the shadow remained unmoving as the lanterns were placed at the crystal's base. The five who had led the procession, elder vampires though there was nothing about them that made them appear any older than the rest, approached the crystal, Rapture amongst them.

Silence filtered through the chamber as the five turned to address the rest of the assembled, allowing the arcana to grow louder. It was buzzing in Amma's mind like the faint sound of voices somewhere far off, Rapture's voice specifically, and then another she did not recognize but was so deep and booming that Amma could only attribute it to one of the elders who was male.

She turned to look at Damien, and he returned her gaze, eyebrow cocking as if to tell her he heard it too. The vampires communicated telepathically, so she could only assume that was what it was and continued to try to listen. Though none of the words were clear, there were many voices then, coming together to respond in a sort of chant that seemed to finish whatever they had started.

The elders moved in unison, lifting an arm each, fists clenched, pressing it into their chests with a reverent bow. It was a solemn move, and Amma kept her own hands clasped, watching through the steam of her breath. And then the elders lifted their wrists to their mouths, and crimson poured down their arms, seeping from the wounds they made with their fangs.

Amma would have wavered had she not been so used to blood, but as it stood, she simply watched each elder take a turn approaching the crystal where a basin was carved into its center. Scarlet spattered onto the pink stone, drop by drop, their wounds healing when each was finished.

When the elders completed the bloodletting, they stepped back, and the other vampires went then, one at a time—a careful walk to the massive crystal, a bite, a drip, and a retreat to rejoin the mass. Amma watched in fascination as each one completed the ritual so fluidly, with no hesitation to wound themselves, to sacrifice something so hard-won and rare. Then a thought occurred to her.

Voice as low as possible, she leaned very close to Damien. "Are we supposed to…contribute?"

He brought his lips to her ear. "Only vampiric blood will wake Lycoris, though I do intend to make a ceremonial offer for us as a show of good faith."

"For both of us?" she asked, watching Asphodel approach the crystal and complete the ritual.

"Yes." His voice was barely a whisper in the quiet of the chamber. "You are welcome to as well if you desire, but it is not necessary or expected."

Asphodel rejoined the rest, but her golden eyes flicked

right to Amma, finding her amid the crowd. She flashed her a covert grin with bloodstained fangs.

Amma leaned into Damien again. "I want to."

He pressed his hand to her lower back and urged her forward. Amma and Damien took their turn, slipping smoothly between the others to the crystalline structure. Closer, with the light glittering off its many clefts, the outline within was clearer, human. But it wasn't entirely human, Amma knew.

Beside her, Damien pulled out his dagger. Like she had seen him do many times, he pierced his flesh with the blade, cupping the blood in his palm and unfurling fingers over the quartz basin, now filled with the offerings of many vampires. Dripping down to mingle with the rest, his blood was a shade darker as it swirled atop the others. He turned to Amma, extending his hand, the wound already closing.

Her heart was racing, blood rushing in her ears. She wouldn't heal like the others, and she reckoned it was going to hurt her quite a bit more too, but it was the least she could do—endure a little pain for the aid they were all coming together to give her—so she placed her hand in his.

Damien studied her palm, the dagger hovering over it. She was reminded of the frantic moment she'd absorbed the talisman, the mad rush he had been in to try and cut it out, how he had pressed the same blade to her skin then, and how he had ultimately hesitated.

This time, he didn't grip down and force her hand open but very carefully slid upward to take only her forefinger in his own. He gently squeezed its tip, though in the frigid depths, she barely felt it. Damien pressed the dagger's point to her mounded flesh, eyes intent, throat bobbing as he swallowed. When he didn't advance and break her skin, as if he was afraid, she took a deep breath and instead pressed upward, piercing herself on the blade.

Brilliant red blossomed on her fingertip when he removed the dagger. He continued to squeeze, teasing the blood to the surface, and then guided her hand to the crystal basin. A single droplet fell to disappear in with the others, no different in the sea of red inside.

There, it was done, and Amma's skin prickled as if alive with a magic all its own. Full of a nervous vigor, her heart pounded to be free from her chest, urging her to flee—she had just spilled her very human blood in an inescapable cavern filled with vampires after all—but the silent solemnity of the chamber kept her from bolting, and Damien hadn't yet released her. He whispered a sibilant phrase she recognized as Chthonic, more of those words that would have made her cold if she weren't already freezing, and guided her hand up to his mouth.

She watched him, her apprehension vanishing as he pressed the tip of her finger to his tongue. Arcana wrapped around her, gliding into her wound and rushing along her veins. This time the magic was warm, *so* warm, filling her whole being with the heat she'd been craving since entering the karsts, and she felt the slight wound mend itself.

There was nothing to be afraid of, she realized, not here and not anywhere. Not when they were together.

CHAPTER 15

AMMA

Talis-Whatsits and Doohickeys

THE CAVERN IN THE heart of the karsts filled with a growing hum as the vampires completed the ritual. The basin of blood set into the rose quartz crystal had been filled, the liquid inside falling still after the last drop had been contributed. And then there was a resounding crack as the darkness in the bowl began to drain away.

Damien's warmth at Amma's side grounded her in the frigid space, and she shuffled closer to him as the cavern began to shake. The blood drained from the basin and filtered through the pink crystal, seeping along its crevices as if running it through with veins, brilliantly red and full of life. Amma watched her own blood along with the rest feeding whatever might emerge, and she waited with mounting eagerness.

The crimson rivulets pulsed and sank in, and the cavern's hum fell silent. No one moved, the vampires as still as statues, waiting. And then there was another sound, hollower, lighter. Rapture's head tilted, and another vampire lifted their chin in response. The sound repeated, twice this time, and it was much clearer that it was a knock.

"Hey, ladies," a muffled voice called from the crystal, "a little help?"

The elders rushed forward. There was a flurry of less-than-graceful movements as they grasped at the quartz, hands sliding off its slick surface until they finally wedged claws into what was a front lid and hefted the thing to swing open. A foggy cloud of steam escaped, and spindly fingers rose out of the hollow to grip the crystal's edges. Knobby and sinewy at first, the corpse-like appearance of the hands shifted as they grasped tighter, filling in to form long, slender fingers with pointed nails.

A face, sculpted so that every edge was sharp, emerged from the mist with eyes like a cat's, sleek and brilliantly golden, lips deeply red and thick, and hair as black as night. She took a husky breath, chest heaving, and then she spoke. "I know I say this every time, but *somebody's* gotta oil these hinges at least once a decade!" The woman who could only be Lycoris snorted then, sucking in a breath and bleating out a high nasal laugh so loud that it disturbed a flock of bats from the highest spot of the cavern. "Oh. My. Blood!" she squealed. "Look at all of you, still so young and fresh! Come 'ere, it's been too long!"

Throwing her arms out, she stepped from the crystalline casket, waiting to be embraced, and it was only then that Amma realized just how truly big the woman was. With at least an inch on even Damien, her sleek, black hair was piled up high on her head, so she seemed like she towered above everyone. She had wide shoulders and generous hips but a tiny waist and was draped in a black fabric that moved like satin—skintight with a neckline that plunged all the way to her navel. Whatever arcana kept her generous breasts from popping out was impressive, as they seemed to have a life all their own, bouncing as she wrapped arms around each vampire in turn, pulling them in to deliver wet kisses on cheeks and greeting everyone by name.

Lycoris was older than anyone would say—a definitive number wasn't allowed to be spoken—so her accent was impossible to place, lost to time. She kept the corners of her lips tight and her tongue high, so she spoke almost exclusively through her nose, adding sounds where they were unneeded and taking them away from where they were, and her pitch flew up and down like a bird battering up against a rainstorm. Unlike the other vampires, she actually spoke, and her movements were big and loud, eyes rarely blinking, excitement palpable.

"Oh, what do we have here?" she said, pulling Amma to her fluidly. "You didn't come for dinner, did you?" Amma's heart stopped beating as if in protection as Lycoris took a huge sniff of her neck, and then her eyes lit up in a different way as she tapped a sharp nail on Amma's nose. "Oh, no, I already got a little taste of you, didn't I?"

Amma was released, and she stumbled back against Damien, holding very still and hoping that if she didn't move, the woman might not bother with her again.

"Hmm, but I *am* starving—I could eat a whole priesthood!" She shrieked out another peal of that intense laughter, and then the grin fell off her face. "Seriously, though, what's a dame gotta do to get a snack around here?"

From the crowd, the body of one of the servants was thrust forward, a brawny-looking man too dazed to react as Lycoris dropped her claws onto his shoulders. "Oh, you'll do just fine, honey."

He was dead in seconds, and Lycoris was drenched from her chin to her navel, though her dress remained unstained. She tapped gently at the corners of her mouth, doing nothing to the mess she'd made on her skin. "Well, what are we waiting for?"

The assembled vampires broke into motion, and the crates that had been dragged down the tunnel were thrown open. Stringed instruments and bottles of thick drink were pulled from them and passed around, and music was struck up. The vampires seemed renewed with liveliness, speaking aloud, laughing, and dancing, and a few of the servants were pulled into the darker corners of the cavern for reasons Amma did not want to think about.

Ivory brought Lycoris a full, wide-mouthed goblet and backed away quickly to stand just behind Amma. "Looks like you get to live. Congratulations," she whispered before flitting off with a snicker.

Amma didn't realize the alternative was possible, but before she could think long on it, Lycoris eyed Damien.

"You," she said, pointing a dangerously long nail at him and twirling it about as she thought. "You're not one of mine either. You're that taste of noxscura I got, aren't ya?"

Rapture appeared at her side, and the two made eyes at one another. There was an anxiousness to Rapture's posture, straighter than before, as she communicated silently with the woman.

"No! Really? Zag's boy? He *can't* be!" All arms and breasts and nasally shrieking, Lycoris handed off her drink and slapped either side of Damien's face, pulling him right to her by the cheeks. "But you're *so* big! By all the night beasties, last I saw, you were just this teeny, tiny, little blob of a thing, and now you're almost as beautiful as your mother!"

Damien held his breath and stared back as if he didn't know what to do, and then he swallowed that uncertainty down. "Dame Lycoris, it is an honor to be in your presence."

"Aw, shucks, honey, it ain't that big a deal." She pinched him, bringing color to his pallid skin, and glanced about. "I gotta say, though, I did not expect to *ever* see you again—I shoulda out-slept your whole life. Somebody wanna tell me what's going on?"

The five vampires who had initiated the ritual surrounded her, Damien backing away as she listened to their telepathic thoughts. Shining eyes darted from one to another. Amma could hear it again, the whispers, like their voices were echoing off the walls even though they were completely trapped in their own minds. Not a word could be understood, but there were feelings, some sharp, others dulcet, until finally it seemed things had been explained.

Lycoris's golden irises swirled about like they were filled with liquid metal. She walked up and dropped a clawed hand on Amma's shoulder, the other thrown upward, breasts bouncing. "Everybody out!"

The grip on her told Amma she was not meant to follow the vampires in their mad dash from the cavern, but, gods, did she wish she could. Lycoris wasn't supposed to be awake yet, and she knew how angry her own mother could get if roused too early, but Constance Avington didn't have fangs nearly as sharp.

The others had abandoned their instruments and drinks to flood out of the rounded chamber and back into the tunnel. Amma watched them go, Ivory and Asphodel amongst the rushing crowd. She would have even accepted Rapture sticking around, but she was helping to usher the last of them out.

"And you too," said Lycoris, a long nail pointed at Damien.

He looked very much like he wanted to protest, but the fact that it would be pointless was as thick as the arcana in the air. Amma nodded at him to urge him on, not wanting to further upset the woman who had talons resting on her shoulder. Ivory had said she was allowed to live, and Amma had to believe that would remain the case.

Damien finally went, and Lycoris flicked a hand at the cavern's opening. A thick wall of black smoke rose up to cut off the rest of them from the room, Damien's form blotted out just on its other side.

The hollowness of the cavern rang in her head, and even next to Lycoris, Amma felt alone. An echoing wind bounced around somewhere high above them, the pop and flicker of flames in the braziers too loud, but then Lycoris filled up the silence with a sigh as she wandered over to her quartz tomb turned throne and sat on the ledge that jutted out of it.

"Come here, honey. I *do* bite, but I'm full now." She laughed in that piercing way again. "Let me take a look at the reason my beauty sleep's been interrupted."

That had to be a joke, of course; Lycoris had skin as smooth as marble, complete with blue veins that ran like delicate, meandering rivers about her temples, over her jaws, down her neck, and across her chest, each as beautiful as the rest of her.

Even sitting, she was imposing, and Amma did her best not to stare at the breasts right in her face, cleavage still blood-stained, but Lycoris's face was equally challenging, her light eyes both frightening and alluring, and her fangs glinting as they hung over the edge of a dark lip.

Clicking her tongue, she reached out cold palms to cup Amma's face. "Oh, don't you just feel so warm, so alive, so—" She cut herself off, face pinching in thought as her voice lowered. "Well, that's strange: It was *you* with the old arcana. Mmm, yes, I like that very much."

"You can feel the talisman?" Amma asked, trying to keep her teeth from chattering.

"Oh, yeah, that's in there too, but this is something else. It's the kinda magic you humans used to have, what the witches dabble in out in the Innomina Wildwood, making the trees bow and the earth rumble, all that. Show it to me, would ya?" Lycoris leaned back, releasing her face, and gestured for her to go on.

Like it was what she was meant to do, though she didn't know how she knew, Amma slipped her hand into her hip pouch and pulled out the acorn. It stared back as if mocking her, no difference between its smooth seed and coarse cap against her numb fingers. Had it really been the same one that bonked her on the head that first day in the forest, somehow following her? And had she really heard it speak?

"Well, we don't get a lotta living things down here, but that's not what I meant exactly," said Lycoris, grin playful. "*Show* me the magic."

"I don't know how." Amma shrugged a shoulder. "I'm not blessed by the gods, it doesn't run in my family, and I've never been taught."

Lycoris shook her head and stuck out her tongue. "Yeah, and nobody ever lived like *this*"—she gestured to herself—"before I did either. There's a different way to get there, honey. Find it."

If it were only so simple, thought Amma, grimacing at the acorn. Damien had been hinting at this too, that there was something inside her she was refusing to access—he didn't understand either that she *couldn't*. Just like doing what she pleased as a baron's daughter, just like being stuck in Faebarrow forever, just like choosing who she would marry, just like... But then, she had escaped Cedric, she had left

Faebarrow, and, for a little while at least, she was doing, *sort of*, as she pleased.

Hey, you can hear me, can't you? she asked silently, eyes narrowing on the seed.

There was a rustling of leaves in her mind, like the memory of the sound, but it was clear.

If ever it were important, I think I need to be kinda impressive here, seeing as we're in front of the plane's first vampire, so do you think you could…or, um, we *could do something?*

Heat bloomed against Amma's fingertips, and even numb, she felt it. The acorn split, and from the crack in its shell, she saw the briefest flash of a golden glow. It was like Lycoris's eyes, the metallic glint, but also like the box of yellow goo Kaz had spilled in Anomalous's tower too, and strangely like those flickers of silver she had seen when Kaz crawled out of the infernal plane and when Damien had opened the fissures over the ballroom in her home's keep.

But then the light was gone, and in its place, translucent white tendrils poured out of the seed, growing and expanding as they crawled all over her hand, her wrist, her arm. The acorn's top shattered, and a stem blossomed out of it, skinny at first and then growing thicker. Amma's gasp caught in her throat, the seedling coming into existence in an instant, hot and wet as it covered her hand, the weight of it suddenly just *there*, its roots pulsing with life, and at its very top, a group of three maple leaves unfurling.

"Now, that's more like it!" Lycoris clapped.

"Uh, what do I do with it?" Amma asked, voice quavering,

heart beating hard. The roots were still squirming up against her skin, and the edges of the leaves curled up and down as if it took a breath. It was impossible, of course, so Amma's mind refused to fully embrace the feat she'd accomplished.

With a chuckle, Lycoris patted the armrest-like protrusion of her crystal.

Amma spilled the seedling forward, and it crawled off, wrapping its roots around the crystal and falling still. In the same moment, her knees went weak, and her vision tunneled.

"Oh no, you don't," said Lycoris, grabbing her by the arm and giving her face a slap, not terribly hard but enough to shock her into forgetting she was about to pass out.

She rubbed the burn in her cheek, but there was magic there too, jolting between the skin of Amma's face and her hand. Her body was suddenly sluggish and her mind cloudy, but she remained awake.

"You need to go see the witches in the Innomina Wildwood—they'll teach you how to not exhaust yourself every time you want to make a flower bloom. It'll come in handy, I'm sure. That's not why you're here though, is it?" The smile Lycoris gave her then wasn't full of hunger or excitement but a gentle kindness, the kind a mother might give her child. "You're here for my help with that little doohickey that's latched itself onto your heart."

Amma's bleary eyes took in the seedling once more, but it remained still, and she nodded, head heavy.

"They tell me it's sorta like our magic, makes you do things you don't really want to, but it doesn't affect your mind, unlike vampiric enthrallment. Oh, how nice it would be if our thralls weren't so damn vacant. I mean, all I want is a little fear when they're about to get their throat split open. Is that so much to ask?" She wrinkled her nose, one of her hands brushing through Amma's hair, fingers caressing her scalp. "But your thoughts are all your own, aren't they? I don't feel even a tinge of arcana wiggling around in there. Problem's the talis-whatsit wasn't ever meant to be inside you, and you're sorta stuck with Zag's boy because of it, huh?"

Stuck? Amma bit her lip, then tried to nod again, the movement difficult. She'd thought she was stuck once, but she had never felt as free as she'd been in the last few days. And with what she had just done with that acorn... Her eyes found the sapling again and marveled at it.

"So you believe in at least one of them gods, don't ya?"

Amma's mouth went dry, blinking back to her, and her voice came out hoarse. "Uh, well, I guess? All of them, actually."

"Aww, that's cute." Lycoris sat back and held out a hand, taking up one of Amma's and squeezing it. "All right, honey, you're gonna swear on whichever one's your favorite that, when I ask you my next question, you'll tell me the honest-to-all-the-gods-but-especially-your-favorite-one truth. Okay?"

Sestoth immediately came to Amma's mind. She was her favorite, of course, as the goddess of trees who had gifted Faebarrow with the liathau during the Expulsion, and seeing as she also oversaw the domain of oaths, it felt doubly appropriate.

"Ready?" Lycoris's fangs pressed into her bottom lip.

"I swear on Sestoth's Roots, I'll tell you the truth."

"Oh my blood, now *that* is adorable." Lycoris snickered, thumb rubbing the back of Amma's hand, making her that much sleepier, though the arcana fought it. "All right then. There is a way for me to remove the talisman and leave you not just alive but better than you are now. The question is this: Do you actually *want* me to take the talisman out of you?"

Amma's mind went blank. Of course she did…not. Didn't she? *Yes!* The answer strained at her throat, but it wasn't coming out, as if Damien had used that Chthonic word on her and ordered her silent. She struggled against the arcana that wasn't there, mind reeling. Who would even ask something like that? Did she *want* it out? Of course, it was obvious, they'd come all this way, risked so much, woken an ancient vampire, and now…now…now Amma couldn't even answer a simple question!

Pain pricked behind her eyes, her breath hitched, and in a swirling mist, her voice finally fell out of her mouth. "Yes."

"Liar!" Lycoris hissed and then exploded into more of her rapturous laughter, throwing her head back. "Oh, your god's gonna be so upset with you when you meet 'em!"

The woman's voice jolted through Amma, chasing away the drowsy feeling and replacing it with panic. "No, I'm not lying: It has to come out, it just *has* to. Damien needs it, and if you can do it, you should. I can't hold on to it just because I—" There was a lump in her throat, the selfish words, the ones that admitted she might actually want to keep it because that meant keeping Damien too, catching.

Lycoris recovered from her laughter, one hand on the bloodied skin of her chest. "No, don't worry. The gods don't pay all that much attention. And I'm a little bit of a liar too. See, I can get that thingy outta you, and, hon, would I *ever* love to have you for my own, but you'd need to, ya know, *want* to be like us."

"You could make me like you?" Amma asked, swallowing back the lump. To be like Lycoris and the rest of them meant many things: It meant being undead, it meant giving up her humanity, it meant feeding off the living to survive, but it also meant becoming something more. "You could make me powerful?"

Lycoris made an excitable sound in the back of her throat and lifted her wrist to her mouth like the vampires had done to wake her. She bit down absently, then drew her fingers into a fist, willing out a drop of blood that she sprinkled over the roots of the sapling Amma had just brought to life.

Amma's chest clenched. *Death.* She saw it happening all at once, the roots shriveling, the leaves curling inward, and she thought of Faebarrow's liathau orchard hacked to stumps, the greenhouse barren, but then the tiny tree twitched. The roots filled themselves out again, shifting to a blue-gray coloring, and the leaves spread themselves back out, this time with lacy, delicate holes throughout and covered in a sheen of black.

"Hope you don't mind," said Lycoris, "but it never woulda survived down here without the sun anyway. Now, though, it's got another chance."

If Amma were like these women, if she were powerful, she could do so much more. She could ensure Faebarrow remained in good hands, she could protect herself from anyone who wanted to touch her against her will, and no one could stop her from leaving when she was done. It might not even matter if she had the talisman; she could go wherever she wanted, do whatever she wanted, be with whoever—

"But immortality and power come with a price," Lycoris warned. "You gotta die, that's how the talisman would come out, and dying is no small thing. Everybody remembers it differently, and there's risk too. Sometimes the negotiations with those god folk just don't work out, but I can get almost anybody back, better than before, but also a little worse at first. It usually takes a couple of decades to get a handle on being a vampire, overcoming bloodlust, reining in the rage, getting control of the claws." She held up a finger that contorted into a blackened talon and back terrifyingly quickly.

"So my family and everyone I know...I would have to leave them?"

"They'd go on living and aging, yeah, but I suppose, once you're sane enough and figure out how to travel only in the darkness, you could see 'em again! Vampirism is a little more of a problem if there are people you love out in the world, I guess." She shrugged. "But listen, don't stress. I get that favor from Zagadoth whether the talisman comes out or not, so it ain't no blood outta my veins if it stays inside you, but changing you against your will is not my idea of a good time, and I can feel every little bit of your soul holding on to that thingamajig like it's the only thing keeping you alive."

Amma didn't intend to tell her that keeping the talisman inside her meant Zagadoth remained locked away. "What about Damien?"

"Oh, I don't really care what he wants. Don't get me wrong, I can glean a *lot* from a person by their blood, and he seems like a *very* sweet boy, not to mention his father and I go way back, but if you are gonna be mine, I put what you want first, got it?"

It wasn't frightening then to look back into Lycoris's spectral eyes. There was something like empathy there, or at least a recognition of whatever was going on inside Amma, and it swirled around in the molten gold like moving stars. Lycoris may have been the eldest vampire, which may have come with inherent evil, but putting not just Amma's needs but her *wants* first? The idea was so foreign, she had to force it from her mind, leaving just enough room for another, much worse thought: Damien brought her here, and he had to know this was the solution. Had he intended to leave her?

"But I'm not—"

"But you *would* be mine, honey, and since I can basically read your mind, I'm not gonna make you say it." With a wink, Lycoris was flicking her hand, and the shadows at the mouth of the cavern dispersed. Dozens of waiting bodies flooded back in, retrieving their glasses and striking up their instruments again, but Damien remained at the opening, looking especially pale.

Lycoris stood from behind her, taking her goblet and bumping Amma with her hips, knocking her off-balance and back into her senses fully. "I'll let you break the news to the demon spawn however you'd like." Her frigid form was gone, leaving Amma to stand before the throne that had been a casket and was now a planter for a new, undead tree.

Damien finally crossed the cavern. Amma had her hands clasped into fists, and she quickly opened her palms to show they held nothing. He released a breath, chest crumpling in. She couldn't tell if it was disappointment or relief.

"I'm sorry," she said. "The talisman, it's not—"

"You're the same, yes?" Damien swept a hand over her shoulder, pushing her hair away from her skin.

"Yes, I think," she squeaked as he brought his face close to inspect the other side of her neck.

His fingers roved over her throat, tipping her head back. He was so close that his breath warmed her skin as he explored every inch of her from ear to collar.

She stood still under his long inspection, the gazes of more than a few lingering on them. "Uh, Damien," she whispered, "I think you're offending the vampires."

He righted himself, and they stood in awkward silence for a few moments, him not pressing her to tell him more and her not offering it. It didn't feel particularly good to not blurt out the entirety of the truth—that she turned down the ability to help him, that she was choosing to keep the talisman inside her after he had promised not to kill her and to bring her home. She struggled with the right words, another apology playing on her tongue, but how to word it?

"I'm sorry," he said suddenly, biting his lip and looking

down at the ground. If her own confusion and fear at what to say hadn't rendered her mute, what she was seeing and hearing—Damien, fidgeting and apologizing just like how she always did—absolutely would have. "Do you want to go? We can leave right now if you want. I just need to quickly do one thing, and then—"

"Damien, it's okay." She touched his arm lightly, then pulled back. "I mean, I think it's nighttime outside the caves anyway, but everything's fine. We can stay until morning."

"You're sure?" He hesitated. "You won't continue to consider their offer any longer if we stay, correct?"

She tipped her head. "I...no?"

"Because there are other ways," he said quickly. "Magic and spells and arcana..."

"Aren't those all the same?"

He nodded, screwing up his face. "I do need to speak to Lycoris, and we can spend the night here if you are still amenable, but if you give the word, we will leave, all right?"

"Yeah, all right," she said carefully.

Damien nodded once, succinct, though there felt like so much more left to say, and he refused to look right at her, but he did point over her shoulder. "Is that...did you do that?"

Amma whipped her head back to see the undead tree attached to the quartz.

"That? Oh no, no, no..." Amma stretched her arms out, trying to block his view as she forced out a yawn. "If we're leaving soon, we should really sleep, huh?"

He moved her elbow out of the way. "Amma, there aren't

any plants like that down this deep, and you know I did see this, treeless, just a moment ago."

"Hmm? Oh, you mean, did I do *the tree*?" She grabbed his arm and pulled him away from the sapling in question. "I guess that was me. I thought you meant making it all black and pretty. That was Lycoris. Neat, huh? She did it with her blood. Anyway, I'm exhausted."

Damien frowned, then slipped his arm from her grasp. "Wait here a moment, and then I'll walk you back to your chamber."

Amma watched Damien cross the cavern to speak with Rapture. The vampire responded with a sultry grin, though she seemed incapable of smiling any other way.

A freezing touch brushed against Amma's arm, and Ivory appeared beside her. "You're nervous again," she said, wiggling fingers into her cleavage and flashing her the tip of the vial she kept there.

Amma looked about for Asphodel, but she must have been off in the shadows, nowhere to be seen. "What is that?"

"A boost of confidence." Ivory pulled it out fully, and when it caught the brazier's light, a shimmer of blue glinted from within.

Amma's eyes flicked to Damien and Rapture, and then she stuck her hand out, receiving the freezing vial and stuffing it down her own cleavage where the shock of cold made her breath catch.

"Use it wisely," said Ivory, tugging on Amma's earlobe before flitting off into the crowd.

CHAPTER 16

AMMA

In Which Expectations Are Hopefully Met

THERE WERE A NUMBER of things Amma could not have known as she sat on the edge of her bed in the vampires' den. She had never wittingly used arcana until Lycoris demanded it. With that expenditure, she should have been rendered completely unconscious, but the vampire dame slapped her with magic, a mixture of her centuries-old enthrallment and something so ancient there wasn't a name for it. Amma recognized a spell had been used on her but not that it was still in effect.

Amma also couldn't have known exactly what was in the vial Ivory gave her, though she wasn't so ignorant that she believed *a boost of confidence* to be completely accurate. As the god of irony, Nisicroniy, would have it, the potion truly *was* meant to boost one's confidence, but it was so highly concentrated that it should have been considered a poison. Ivory, of course, didn't see it this way—so it was perhaps appropriate Nisicroniy lorded over sincerity as well. Coupled with Lycoris's magic still floundering inside Amma, the result of ingesting the little tincture threatened to be more than even Ivory would have intended.

And then there was the book Amma had read much earlier in the day, the one that had been salacious in all the best ways. Though it was not arcane in nature, not in the traditional sense anyway, the effects of the words she consumed while peeking up at Damien could never have been negligible; words were meant to make women dangerous—that was, in fact, one of the best things they did.

However, Amma was certain she *did know* one thing as she sat, twirling the potion nervously between her fingers: She wanted Damien for herself.

The vial was easy to uncork, easy to throw back, and the tiny bit of liquid slid down her throat so quickly, it was like she hadn't swallowed anything at all. Amma blinked, sitting straighter. Then she stood, slipping the empty vial into a pocket and pacing the room. Was she supposed to feel differently? Perhaps she wasn't supposed to actually drink it. Ivory hadn't said, and Asphodel had been rather cautious about her having it at all. What if she was supposed to—no.

Amma grinned, falling still.

No, she hadn't made a mistake.

She couldn't *possibly* make a mistake.

Amma trotted to the huge wardrobe that stood in the corner of the room, flinging the doors open, a rush of elation flooding her veins. Quickly stripping as her eyes trailed the clothing hanging inside, she grabbed the first black thing she could find—*favorite color, check*—and pulled it on over her head.

She shivered like she was still naked; the fabric didn't cover much—a single strap around the back of her neck, arms completely exposed. She couldn't find a mirror, so she simply looked down. With a deep plunge between her breasts, the silken material clung to her body, little left to the imagination. She swiveled her hips and stepped forward, the light material flowing around her and a generous slit on either side of the skirt to reveal each leg as she walked. "Perfect," she said to herself, sweeping across the room to the door, grabbing a fur from the bed as she went.

Outside Damien's chamber, she took only a moment to compose herself in the empty hall. Though she was unsure how long she'd pondered things before taking the vial's contents, she knew he would still be inside. Readjusting the fur wrapped around her so that it fell askew off one of her shoulders, Amma knocked. "Damien, can I come in?"

"Amma?" his voice called back, alarmed. "What's wrong?"

She pressed a hand against the wooden door, and there was a click at the latch, the tiniest bit of arcana sparking at her fingertips, and she entered.

Damien was just standing from the bed, parchment in his hands and a candle lit on the nightstand, the room otherwise dark and cold. "Thought I locked that." He stood shirtless and bootless, his pants still belted but low on his hips.

Amma took a long look at him, grinned, and dropped the fur, not remembering the point of it in the first place.

Sitting back on the bed as if he'd lost his footing, Damien coughed. "I thought you were tired."

She shook her head, crossing the room to stand right before him. Damien's eyes caught the single candle's light, flicking down her body quickly, nervously, mouth slack. She slipped the stack of parchment from his grasp, more easily than she'd expected, and dropped it to the floor. "No more research," she said, the skin of his bare shoulders warm under her frigid fingers as she grabbed him. She slid a knee over his thigh through the dress's slit and onto the bed, then before he could react, she shoved him onto his back, climbing up to straddle him.

"Amma, are you sure—"

"No more talking either," she said and crushed her mouth to his like she had wanted to do for so long.

Damien's lips were soft, his breath warm, and after a moment of utter stillness, his mouth moved against her own to match her vigor as his hands came around her waist and gripped her tightly.

Gods, it was like being filled with light and fire and wings unfurling, finally indulging in what Amma had been imagining since she had laid eyes on the blood mage. She was initially frightened of the tall man who stalked the shadows in Aszath Koth, but when she'd gotten closer and really seen him, there was no denying how handsome she'd found his dark, messy hair, his light, knowing eyes, and that fucking smirk. And then, closer still with every quiet, shared moment between the two, every long look, every touch, her hunger only intensified, threatening to devour all her good senses and willpower until now when his mouth was on hers, his breath mingling with her own, his tongue slipping over her lips.

Of course, the little vial certainly helped, shrinking the enormity of Damien's plan to bring ruin to the realm and the role she was playing in all of it. But really, demons, dominions, evil, goodness, even the gods—none of it mattered. What did matter was how hard Damien's chest was under her hands and how eager Amma was to feel how hard the rest of him would be as she trailed her mouth down his neck to the soft hollow of his throat.

He mumbled her name, gruff and broken as he inhaled, his touch falling to her thigh and squeezing the soft flesh there. "What are you doing?" he husked, his voice vibrating against her lips.

But he knew very well—there was no need for an explanation.

She ran her hands down his sides to press against his firm abdomen and lowered herself onto his lap. "Whatever I want." When she bit his shoulder, he sucked in a sharp, pained breath, but his hips answered in exactly the way she expected, the hardness of his length thrusting against her warm like kindling.

Moaning, she devoured his mouth before he could ask any more questions. He kissed her back eagerly, hand slipping through the slit of the silky dress and around to palm her ass and crush the two of them together, fingers digging in so roughly she knew they would leave marks. But the two were not so tightly pressed that Amma couldn't wiggle a hand between them and under his belt.

It was Damien's turn to moan, but he broke apart their kiss with a jolt. "Amma, wait, stop."

She had only just grazed him but pulled away. "What's wrong?"

"This," he said, breathing out raggedly. "You."

"Nothing's wrong with me." She trailed fingers down from his navel to the edge of his belt, making him squirm in a delightful way right up against her. If only she could get rid of the layers in between. "You gave up your blood to help me, and I didn't even get you the talisman. You have to let me give you something in return."

Damien grabbed her wrist, holding her wandering hand still. "You don't have to barter anything for my help," he said sharply. "Especially not this."

"But you want it too." She wriggled against the bulge between them, heat building as if they'd soon start a fire. "This part of you does anyway."

He groaned, hold weakening. "What in all the planes has gotten into you?"

"I'd like it to be you," she purred, leaning in to kiss his ear lightly and whispering, "Make love to me, Damien." She watched him swallow, gritting his teeth, hips falling still. He was stiffening in exactly the wrong way, which wasn't at all how this was supposed to go. "Mmm, that's not what Rapture called you. It was Lord Bloodthorne, wasn't it?" Amma dropped her voice low against his ear again. "Fuck me, Lord Bloodthorne."

"Holy gods, Ammalie," he swore, releasing her arm and taking her roughly by the hips, but instead of thrusting himself against her, he lifted her up, putting hateful space between the two. "What does it matter what Rapture calls me?"

"Because that's what you like." She nipped at his jaw. "I just want to please you, and if what you want is someone like her—"

"I don't want someone like her, I want—wait." Damien sat up swiftly, shocking Amma as she was taken along with him. The arm around her waist tightened, holding her there in his lap, the other hand taking her chin to pull her face close. "Are you drunk again?" He sniffed her breath.

She shook her head, barely able to move in his grip on her jaw.

His brow pinched with confusion. "You don't smell like ale at all. Did someone do something to you?"

She shook her head again, but it was clear he didn't believe her, eyes darkening.

"Tell me the truth, Amma. Now."

Her heart hitched, the threat in his voice that should have sparked fear only deepening her desire. "Or what?"

"You will not like it."

Somehow, she doubted that very much. Amma squirmed herself forward, closing the gap in their laps, and her core pulsed with pleasure.

Damien growled, though his length persisted. Chthonic spilled out from between his lips in a mad rush, a sibilant spell wrapping around Amma and climbing up her spine. As the magic writhed its way inside her, Amma put up no resistance, welcoming it in. His fingers still dug into her jaw, and flooded with Damien's arcana, she melted into the tight embrace both inside and out.

She'd been so certain of what she wanted moments ago, and that desire hadn't left, but it shifted as she watched his face, the confusion at her actions, the mistrust. She longed to crush that doubt, to obliterate it with her touch. It didn't matter how she'd gotten here, just that she was here, and she was finally able to show him what she wanted—*him*—and wasn't that enough?

Amma lifted a hand to Damien's temple and swept back the fall of his black hair. She let her fingers trail down to the space between his brows that he nearly always held so narrow and angry, and she lightly touched the place where his scar began. The spell was still swirling inside her, tickling behind her navel, beneath her shoulder blades, under her breasts, and she tenderly ran her fingers along the silvery, raised skin over his nose and across his cheek.

"Why don't you believe me?" she asked, feeling a frown crease her lips.

"Because someone's poisoned you," he said, his grip on

her going tighter though he released her chin. "I can feel it wreaking havoc in your body."

"No, you're wrong," she said, shaking her head vigorously, and then she snickered. "Come on, Damien. Show me if you have a tail or not."

Damien clicked his tongue, frustration mounting.

She grabbed his free hand then and used her nimble fingers to slip it into the scooped neckline of her dress and cup it around her breast. "I want you," she breathed, shifting his other hand from her waist to bury it somewhere even warmer. "Let me show you."

His eyes fluttered closed, fingers sliding over her, then froze. "Sanguinisui, tell me what's happened to you."

Amma's body went lax, mind clouding, words falling out. "I saw you talking to Rapture. I didn't want you to sleep with her. I wanted you to choose me instead. Ivory gave me a vial filled with something she said would make me less afraid, and here I am."

"And here you are." He sighed, pulling his fingers away from her most sensitive spots and making her draw a sharp breath.

The spell flooded out of her, an ache balling itself up in her stomach. "I thought you weren't going to do that to me anymore."

Damien groaned, this time with discomfort. "Apologies, but I didn't expect you to poison yourself and lie to me."

"I'm not—" Amma swallowed, mouth dry. "I'm not *lying*. I do want you."

He tipped his head, appraising her, then lifted a hand. The tips of his fingers were slick in the candlelight, and he grinned. "Well, I suppose so. But you're still intoxicated."

"It was a good idea," she insisted, pouting, but couldn't look right at him.

"No, it was not." The smirk fell off his face. "You ingested a potion from a stranger so that you could come in here and do something you wouldn't have done otherwise. I would say that's actually very, very bad."

"That's not true." She pawed at his bare shoulders, exasperated, but as the last of the talisman's magic left her, she was suddenly flooded again with the confidence to turn things around. She lifted her eyes back to his and grinned. "But don't you like it when I do bad things?"

Jaw tight, Damien swallowed, mumbling between gritted teeth, "I swear to all the gods, you will be the death of me if you keep pushing me like this."

She took him by the back of the neck and jerked his face just to hers. "Oh no, are you angry with me?"

"Getting there." He strained to keep space between them, but his hips shifted again, hands falling to her thighs, fingers digging into her skin.

"So punish me."

Damien fell still beneath her, and his face changed, the irritation wiped off it, traded in an instant for what she could only call villainy. A chuckle crawled up out of his throat, and his laughter was so dark, her vision dimmed. "What an absolutely wicked idea." His hands came around hers, and in one swift move, they were caught behind her back. "I think I will punish you, Amma."

She arched her back to press her breasts against him. "Uh-oh," she lilted in a breathy voice, but only grinned deeper.

"Oh no, no, no," he said, trapping her wrists in just one of his hands, pinning them to her low back. A finger came under her chin as his eyes narrowed. "You are *not* going to enjoy this."

Damien stood, and Amma slid backward, surprised her body hadn't completely melted and she could still plant her feet on the ground. Hands still bound behind her in his tight grip, he spun her around and gave her a slight shove.

She only stumbled a little, kept steady in his grasp. "Why are we going away from the bed?"

"No questions," he growled and walked her to the door and right out into the hallway. It was colder there but thankfully still empty, and then he shoved her into her chamber instead. When the door clicked shut, Damien released her wrists and swept past to the bed where a candle was still lit. He blew it out, dousing what little concentrated light was in the room, the fireplace only smoldering and casting a dim, orange glow. "Take that dress off."

Amma stood stupefied for a moment, then did exactly as she was told, slipping out of the thin fabric and letting it pool around her feet. Somehow, she was still cold even as a flash of heat took her at being completely naked in the same room as Damien, but he was focused on picking something up off the floor, back to her. "Now what, Lord Bloodthorne?"

"Put this on," he said, holding out his arm.

Amma crossed the room, cold air making her already shallow breaths harder to take at all. With every step toward him, her heart pounded in her throat, body alert to even the slightest shift in the chamber, air especially cool on the places that had been made so warm by way of friction.

When she finally reached him, he didn't turn to look at her, but in his hand, he held out her own chemise. So he wanted her as she normally was? Fine, he could have her any way he liked. She tugged the chemise on, smoothing it over her stomach, its edges grazing the tops of her thighs. "Done," she said, pleased with herself.

His voice was low, back still to her. "On the bed."

Amma brushed up against him as she slipped herself between where he stood and the bed. She sat on the mattress's edge where the curtains were already drawn and slid backward, locking eyes with him. His features were hard to read in the shadows, but he seemed to be holding himself very still, so she lifted her knees up and slowly began to drop them away from one another.

Damien grabbed her, and she gasped, the heat of his hands burning against the chill of her shins, and then they slid up, grasping her knees and holding her in place so she couldn't reveal herself. Amma whined in the back of her throat, and he chuckled again in that dark, heavy way of his that she wished he would do right up against her skin. "Patience," he said, staring down at her, lips parted, eyes trailing over her body.

Amma settled back, gazing up at him, waiting. After a painfully long moment, he finally climbed up onto the bed, tentatively releasing her knees and coming to kneel beside her. Unable to stand it any longer, Amma reached out, but her wrists were snared once more, and she was pushed into the downy blankets.

"What did I say?"

Amma bit down on her lip, a grumble rising up in her throat.

But Damien overcame her irritation with his own, clicking his tongue and dragging her upward, making her squeal with surprise as she was drawn over the bed. Before she realized, her arms were stretched above her head, and he'd swung a leg over her middle, trapping her beneath him.

Amma's eyes widened at the length hovering so near her face. Damien took his free hand to his belt, and she practically salivated at the thought of what was coming next. Breasts and core aching, she knew she was whining pitifully but didn't care. He paused for only a moment to look down on her like a feral animal about to devour his prey, then grunted as he pulled the belt free.

Damien's hands weren't as quick or nimble as Amma's, but they knew what they were doing. He expertly wound the belt around her wrists, pulling it tight as he lashed the excess somewhere over her head. The leather cut into her skin, rough but not unpleasant. In fact, Amma was surprised at just how not unpleasant the bindings were. He gave her wrists a tug to be sure they were secure, and she tried to squirm, to get some relief in the warmest, achiest parts of her, but found it impossible, completely helpless underneath him.

Now there truly was no escape, and it should have terrified her, but nothing like terror came. Her quickening heartbeat and buzzing thoughts only made her body more responsive and her anticipation deeper. Damien's control of her was complete, arcana irrelevant, and perhaps it was mad that she had allowed this, that she trusted anyone this much, and that the someone who held her captive was a blood mage who had promised to punish her, but Amma had never felt more secure.

Damien was the darkest shadow in the dimly lit room as he dipped his head beside hers, lips caressing the shell of her ear. "I'm pained by what you're forcing me to do to you, my sweet Ammalie, but I do appreciate how easy you make yourself to deceive when you're aroused."

"Deceive?" Her contented grin faltered.

"I know, it's not very nice, deception," he said, hand cupping the side of her face and thumb running over her bottom lip, "but you should remember what I told you when we first met: I'm not very nice."

"Now you're the one lying." She breathed against the pads of his fingers as they trailed back over her lips.

His violet eyes flicked up from her mouth to meet her gaze, and the villainous bite softened right out of them. Damien pressed his mouth to hers, so gently that she forgot she had her wrists bound, barely clothed, and trapped beneath him.

His kiss was not like the starved, needy ones she'd been giving him or the forceful, voracious ones he used to answer her back; it was restrained and sweet and made her stomach flutter with a whole host of butterflies. Like he was doing it for the first time, unsure and curious, his lips lightly skimmed hers and then came together with a soft press before pulling back.

Damien's throat bobbed as he sat back with another long look at her, and then he swung off her, climbed off the bed entirely, and headed for the door.

"Wait!" she squeaked. "Are you leaving? Don't go, Damien, not after *that*."

He cleared his throat, and his voice rumbled through the room. "You think your misbehavior earlier tonight has earned you something else?"

Stranded on her back, Amma had to press her shoulders back and crane her neck to see that he wasn't leaving but instead was gathering up the black dress she'd shucked off. "Well, I…I just didn't know what else to do."

"You didn't have to *do* anything," he mumbled, crossing the chamber again to the open wardrobe and hanging the dress back up. Gods, he looked so good—wasn't striding around half naked in the dying firelight enough torture?

Confidence waning, Amma whined, "Do you…do you want me to beg?"

He paused as he shut the wardrobe, smirking as he gazed back over at her. "If you'd like to," he said, chuckling again as he came nearer to the bed only to pick up her normal clothes and rummage through them.

"Please, Lord Bloodthorne?" Amma made a valiant effort to put on a sultry voice, but it cracked as she struggled for the words. "I promise, um...I'll be good for you?" Her heartbeat was quickening in a less-than-enticing way, panic setting in that this had all gone very, very wrong.

"Ah, there it is." Damien held up the tiny vial between two fingers. He inspected it closely, clicking his tongue against his teeth. "Got this from that Ivory woman, you said? No wonder it's made you this way. She's built up a tolerance for hundreds of years. It was only a small dose though—should be wearing off right about now. Bloody Abyss, you are going to be quite embarrassed by all this, not to mention exhausted."

Amma swallowed, glancing down at herself so scantily clad. Embarrassed? No, she wouldn't; she refused. But she *was* going to be inconsolable that her attempt to seduce him had failed. Heart sinking, she watched him wander across the room again and pluck something off one of the shelves in a dark corner. "Will you at least stoke the fire before you leave me here all alone?"

"Leave you? Why would I do a thing like that?" Damien returned, a book in hand, and actually climbed up beside her on the bed. With a flick of his hand, the candle on the side table lit itself again, and he sat back as if he was not reclining next to a nearly nude woman, tied up, helpless, and begging him to do whatever he wanted with her. He opened the book, and the jerk actually began to read.

"Well, I just rubbed myself all over you." She groaned, face flushing in a way that definitely wasn't embarrassment but could be interpreted as such by incorrect blood mages. "And you clearly don't want to be with me."

Damien was quiet, and she chanced a glance up at him, difficult from her tethered spot, but the candlelight made his features much more readable. The corner of his mouth twitched. "Oh, why the fuck not? You won't be allowed to remember this anyway," he mumbled with a snort and placed the book down to turn to her. "Amma, the only thing that is clear is that I prefer your company, even when you are infuriating, to an entire cave full of vampires. I'd like nothing more than to be with you, but not when you've had to coerce yourself into it by way of magic. I do want you, but not like *this*."

His face had gone very soft, and in it, Amma saw all the sweetness she'd always known was there, which should have been endearing, but unfortunately, learning that Damien indeed wanted her was a natural boost of confidence, which made the waning potion inside her flare up in one last death rattle.

She thrashed against the bindings around her wrists in a useless effort to escape them and cried out, "Gods, Damien, for goodness' sake, that's so stupid and noble! *Please* just take advantage of me!"

"Basest beasts, Amma, no!" He leaned down, bringing his face to hers as it twisted with frustration. "And it's your own bloody fault. I'm a villain. I shouldn't care about potions or talismans or *feelings*, but your presence in, what, *a moon*? In *just* a moon, your painfully sweet voice has challenged all my darkest thoughts, your wildly inaccurate yet optimistic outlook has clouded my sight, and your incessant kindness to me—to someone who deserves not a drop of your patience and affection and good will—has undone twenty-seven years of training to be evil. For darkness's sake, woman, you've made me *good*, and believe when I say that it feels like falling interminably through the Abyss every moment I am not burying my cock in you, but I could not bear it if you woke tomorrow and thought I had hurt you."

Amma's eyes went wide, breath refusing to come. And then a giggle broke out of her without permission.

Damien's features turned to utter distress. "I am trying to be quite sincere, Amma, so why, on all the planes and beyond, are you laughing?"

She gasped. "Oh no, Damien, it's just because you said *cock* and not, you know, something more you, like pulsing manhood or rigid pleasure spear or—"

"All right, all right, don't remind me." He grunted and readjusted himself before dropping back against the bed, arms crossed, scowling out at the room.

Amma bit her lip. "Oh, Damien, I—"

He grunted loudly, scowling harder.

She clicked her tongue but shifted her knee to rub it up against his leg. "Don't be grumpy—I wasn't laughing at you. I would never laugh at those things, and you already know I think that you're very, *very* sweet deep down."

"I am *not*," he barked, waving his hand into the air. "I would just gladly be swallowed by endless darkness upon endless darkness if it meant not hurting you because I have never cared so deeply for another being. I cannot explain or understand how you have broken me in this way, but you have made me feel...*things* that are maddening."

Though his words had been said with a bite and he was glowering into the darkness like his nemesis stood there, Amma's whole chest heaved with the admittance. "What kinds of things?"

He whipped back to her and stuck a finger in her face. "Ah, no, this is *not* a discussion, and I will not be answering any further questions."

She snapped her mouth shut but smiled up at him, tight-lipped.

Damien grimaced, and in the low candlelight, she could see how red he had gone. He cleared his throat and sat back again, reopening the book. "Also," he said with a hitch, "engaging in such intimate activities would be unwise when the horses likely will not be waiting for us when we emerge from the karsts."

Amma's body sank into the blankets, exhaustion sweeping over her. "What's that got to do with anything?"

"If I do to you what you want me to do, you're not going to be able to walk for at least a week, and I'm not carrying you through the Wilds."

"Is that supposed to be discouraging?" she cried, squeezing her thighs together, all the relief she could get with her hands tied. "I can't believe it—you really are evil."

"I know," he droned. "I do keep saying."

Amma couldn't help but grin up at the ceiling. She was

frustrated and increasingly exhausted, but there was a giddiness in her, poking around under her skin. *My sweet Ammalie*, he'd called her. She had broken him, made him feel, and he cared. Deeply. "Damien? I need to tell you—"

"No." Damien held the book up to his face, blocking her from eyeing him. "We can converse all you'd like tomorrow, but only if you don't say another word now and go to bloody sleep."

Amma blew out a long and sorrowful breath, but that didn't count as talking, she was sure, even as the so-called poison finally wore off. *Tomorrow*, she said only in her mind and closed her eyes.

Amma could not know that once she fell into a deep, arcanely spent sleep, Damien would carefully untie her wrists, position her more comfortably with chaste hands, and pull warm blankets over her before whispering into her ear, "Sanguinisui, forget this night." Damien would then pause, shrug, and add, "Sanguinisui, actually *do* remember this night but only as a dream."

She could also not know that he would do a final sweep of the room, removing any hint of what had happened, including pocketing the empty vial, and then go back to his own chamber, lock the door, and take advantage of himself. Twice.

Tomorrow would come, and with it, there would be embarrassment, but only suffered in her own mind at the obscene and vivid fantasies she'd had while asleep. It had been a very nice dream, but then it was only a dream, one in which Damien had made a promise that he wasn't beholden to keep, so she was unable to discuss with him the things he'd admitted to her as, disheartingly, Amma didn't believe any of his words had actually been spoken at all.

CHAPTER 17

DAMIEN

Denial Isn't Just a Spell in the Lux Codex

DAMIEN WOKE, BODY AND mind already spent, sweaty, and, well, *sticky*. The desire to fall back into a dream-filled sleep where he hadn't been such a noble idiot tugged at him, but time was short. Amma would not rise early, not after *that* display last night, the one he couldn't even needle her about as he'd arcanely ordered her to believe it was a dream, but at least he had chiseled the way she looked lying there beneath him on the inside of his skull to keep permanently.

Amma had kissed him. *Kissed* him. Damien had experienced plenty of tongues down his throat, but when Amma had pressed her mouth to his, it felt like he had never had someone else's lips on his own before. Though she'd been fervent and tipsy on arcana, it had still been *her*. And as much as he insisted she was too intoxicated to follow through with what she was asking—begging—for, it was undeniable some earnest part of her was climbing onto his lap to whisper delectably indecent things in his ear because she had also been so *fucking* sweet. When she'd taken his face in her hands, touched his scar like she adored it, and told him, even when she should have been terrified, that he was kind, that was truly *her*. She had been so bloody convincing and ardent that he had felt almost…good.

No, not almost. That wasn't what he said. He told her outright. He was good, and she had made him that way.

But she had asked him to make *love* to her, and he wasn't even sure he *could* do that.

Thank the basest beasts he could act as though none of it had actually happened.

Damien bathed in a rush and dressed quickly, hurrying out to the den's massive receiving parlor. With Amma still asleep, this would be his only opportunity to speak with Lycoris alone before they left the karsts. The vampire dame was commenting loudly about the decor, pointing out what she approved of and even more boisterously what she wanted replaced, but she sent away the others when Damien approached.

"Headed to the Innomina Wildwood?" she asked as if it were expected, voice echoing into the large chamber as she picked up a copper mug, steam wisping off its top.

"Perhaps." Damien hesitated, looking about for others,

hands clasped behind his back, but they were alone. "I do have an additional request to make before we leave."

"Really pushing it, eh?" She took a sip and snickered. "Lemme guess, you worship that god of luck, what's his name? Ryck?"

"Definitely not." He exhaled, going to stand before her. The god of luck resided in Empyrea and wouldn't have listened to Damien, regardless of whether he thought the gods listened at all. Plus, he was fairly certain he was called Turlecki—the name Ryck wasn't nearly ridiculous enough. "This is only a request for information if you'd be willing to give it. About an…ally of Zagadoth's."

"Oh, gossip? Honey, I always have time for that!" She flapped her free hand, taking a seat on the closest sofa and urging him to sit beside her. "So what do you wanna know?"

"Well, it's, uh…you said that I…" He looked her over, how she sat eagerly with her legs crossed, leaning in, eyes wide. He wished he were as eager to ask what he wanted to know, but the sun was rising beyond the caves, and he just had to say it. "Am I correct in assuming you knew my mother?"

"Oh my blood, yeah!" Her mouth opened wider, fangs glinting red in the candlelight. "Real nice lady, just the sweetest thing, you have the exact same eyes and all those beautiful, black locks—just to *die* for." She reached out and fluffed his hair. He didn't pull away, as there was no one around to be embarrassed by, and really, it wasn't terrible, the way Lycoris doted on everyone. But then she froze, face changing. "Wait, wait, I'm remembering something…"

Damien tried to hold his features still, not letting whatever oddness was roiling in his gut show on his face. "That she left?"

Lycoris pulled her hands back and sucked in a breath through her teeth. "Oh, honey, yeah, that's it. Sometimes the very last bits come back slowly when I wake up, and I did have to go back into hibernation right after your pops was locked away. Immortality ain't what it used to be. That musta been tough too, your dad stuck in that big rock, huh?"

Damien squinted—had no one told her Zagadoth was still trapped in Archibald's crystal? Perhaps now wasn't the best time she find out, with a favor promised to her by him. "It wasn't ideal."

"Ya know, that whole thing was real strange." Lycoris shook her head, all her hair moving along with it. "I was at their wedding, and your ma and pops were happier than a salamander in a volcano. And then you came along, and they were over both the moons!"

There was a flutter in Damien's chest, a spark that had no business being as bright as it was, but it persisted even as his mind told him what Lycoris was saying made absolutely no sense. "Did you say 'wedding'?"

"Uh-huh. Tiny thing, only the worst of the worst were invited, but it was so sweet."

"You're telling me they were *married*? So they...they *enjoyed* one another's company?"

"Yeah, it was almost a little unbelievable. A human and a demon getting along like that?" She snorted, her laughter joyous despite being so raucous. "Usually creatures like you are the result of an arrangement—or *worse*—but with them, it all seemed so real."

"But it...it *was* just a deal," said Damien, absolutely bewildered. His father didn't allow there to be any discussion of his mother. They had struck a bargain to bring Damien into existence, and she had promised to care for him but hadn't followed through. Zagadoth had a talk with him about it once when he was much younger, only to say that there was nothing to actually say: She was human, she was supposed to stay, she didn't. Simple.

"Friendliest deal I've ever seen." Her tone was flippant as she blew a breath out between her lips, then she cocked her head in thought. "But I suppose there was something fishy about it all since she fled Aszath Koth and stole you away to Eirengaard. Took that other one too, the one with the white hair. You know, Zane...Darklung?"

"Xander?"

"That's the one! He was always such a little shit."

A memory flashed in Damien's mind of him being too small to wriggle away from a woman who had grabbed him but desperately wanting to. And then a young Xander sitting beside him in the dark, uncharacteristically soothing an even younger Damien, telling him things would be okay in the end. It was...it was all real? "You're saying my mother *abducted* me away from my father and took me to the capital of Eiren?"

"Well, yeah. I might not remember everything in perfect detail, but I answered Zagadoth's call to march on the capital to get you back, that's for damn sure. The big fool just wouldn't wait for all of us to arrive, and he went in on his own, and it was over before it even began. They did manage to get you back though, with the help of that other demon, the little shit's mother."

"Birzuma," he said, eyes falling to the ground. He'd been her ward for a few years while she oversaw Aszath Koth until the Brotherhood rescued a chunk of Zagadoth's crystalline prison and reinstated him on the throne. To say Zagadoth had been unhappy with her when he "returned" was an understatement, not least of all for how bruised Damien was, and there had been bad blood since, her hand in Damien's rescue never spoken of. But then, Damien's kidnapping hadn't been mentioned either.

"Anyway, hon, what did you want to know?"

Damien's mind was scrambled. What did he want to know? He hadn't even known to ask the things to get him the information he suddenly had; his questions were only of his human half, of what it meant and what he still had yet to understand. "I think I was going to ask if you knew where my mother might be."

"Oh, revenge, right," she said in a whisper that was still loud enough to fill up the whole parlor. "I understand. So a couple hundred years ago, there used to be this teeny, tiny little village south of the capital where the humans worshiped this goddess. Can't remember her name, she lorded over birds, of all things, but they believed she healed the sick too, and maybe she could, I dunno, but it was the priestesses doing all the healing, if you ask me. Crazy good warriors too, I tell ya. When I'd go in to collect my confused little vampires who didn't know what they were and just thought they'd caught some nasty disease, it was *work*. Anyway, that place was called Orrinshire, but it's sort of been absorbed by the capital since. That's where your ma was from, so if you're looking for her, you might want to start there."

Damien sat back. Thoughts of his mother had plagued him since he'd left Aszath Koth. He'd always known she was human, but that felt heavier lately, as if it meant more than weakness and vulnerability. It likely had something to do with the human he traveled with, who, admittedly, was often weak and vulnerable herself but also much more than just those things. If he were as much his mother as he was his father, then perhaps he shared more of those qualities that he admired in Amma—the exact ones that had made him so perplexed the night before. Meeting his mother could assist in making sense of it all.

Or it could absolutely shatter any hope he had of being different from what he'd been taught he was.

He touched the pouch on his hip where he kept the shard of Zagadoth's crystal. Asking his father felt completely out of the question. A twist of anger at not being told the truth dug into his gut. When it had just been a broken deal, things made a little more sense, but to know his parents may have, what, *cared* for one another in a way that it was insisted was impossible for infernal creatures? And that his mother hadn't just abandoned him in Aszath Koth but had tried to take him when she ran? Had wanted to *keep* him? That changed everything.

Lycoris was staring past Damien's shoulder, holding very still. He looked back to see Amma and Rapture standing just behind where he sat. He had no idea how long they'd been there. Rapture was returning Lycoris's intense gaze, communicating silently, but Amma's eyes were wholly on him. He immediately stood and turned away, announcing that they were leaving.

If Amma had heard anything, she was gracious enough to keep it to herself, and Damien abandoned all his own weighty, existential thoughts and questions in the shadows of the karsts.

"Where to?" Amma's voice was lighter the moment they exited the mouth of the cave, sunshine falling on her as she took a deep breath of fresh air. She threw her head back and smiled up at the sky, and Damien was lost. Where to indeed.

"Eirengaard!" spat out Kaz, scrambling out of the boat and up onto the rocky shore. The imp had shown up when they were ready to leave, full of a new and annoying vigor. At least someone had been successful in the den. "The dark lord awaits! We cannot leave him in the crystal to waste away!"

Damien huffed, scratching his head as he stepped out of the small boat. "Well, that is the plan. Eventually." His waning interest in helping Zagadoth was easier to ignore for now. They'd emerged without separating the talisman from its vessel, and there was no point in going to Eirengaard without it.

He extended a hand, and Amma slid hers into it. Her fingers were warm, still human, still alive. She didn't blush when she grinned at him nor when she added in a playful voice, "Thank you, Lord Bloodthorne," but that touch of her hand knotted his stomach with the memory of how skillfully she'd created friction between the two and how soft her thighs, her breasts, her *everything* had been. She would remember those things only as a dream, and from her demeanor, she'd been pleased rather than vexed by them, which was strange. If she had tied him up and left him to plead with no relief, he would have been very frustrated. But then that hadn't been all. He had also said…things.

"The horses!" Amma sprinted ahead, her hand leaving his, and with it a tug at his chest. She made her way around the lake and up to her ginger mare, which was munching on grass beneath a tree a few paces off from where it had been left. Beside it, Damien's dappled stallion had its legs folded beneath it, lying in the warmth of the sun. He was not expecting to see either again, but he supposed they liked Amma more than any of the bumbling idiots they'd been lifted from.

He chuckled as he made his way over to where she was heaping praise on both horses in a sugary, sincere voice, because of course she was; she knew no other way to speak to dumb creatures, which was appropriate as dumb creatures seemed to like it quite a bit. He certainly did.

Maybe Damien would find a way to tell Amma those things again when she wasn't intoxicated, when she would have the opportunity to remember. Maybe.

Perhaps, if he found some way to repeat the sentiment he'd been trying to express the night before, she would even respond, and if he was lucky, she might even use some of those disgustingly syrupy words on him. But that could never happen if he left her behind. Basest beasts, what would he have done if she'd chosen to stay with the vampires? What in the Abyss had he been thinking, taking her in there at all?

"Damien?" Amma's eyes were on him, brow knitted in concern. "You're...smoking?"

He flipped his hand over, noxscura festering in his palm. He scoffed and flicked it away, pushing the arcana back inside where it belonged. "Just feeling for the best route," he lied. "I don't have an exact destination in mind."

Amma then carefully stepped away from her mare and up to him. Even dressed in those clothes that made her breasts so prominent and with a crossbow strapped to her back, she looked too sweet, too innocent, with her hands clasped and toying with a hesitant look on her rounded features.

"Yes?" he asked in anticipation of whatever impossible-to-say-no-to thing was coming.

She gnawed on her lip. "Well, I was thinking..."

"Dangerous."

"What do you know about witches?"

Damien grinned widely, feeling something open up inside him, like leaves unraveling and spreading themselves out to reach the first day of spring. "I know it's said they're in the Innomina Wildwood."

"So Lycoris said I should go see them because of the...the *old arcana* inside me"—this she said in a voice that he supposed she thought sounded like Lycoris and then went on quickly as if needing a good excuse—"and maybe they can help get the talisman out in a way that leaves me a little less dead?"

"That would be quite convenient," he said carefully and paced over to his steed, attempting to coax it up by its reins. It only glared back at him.

"Come on, Peter, up," she said, and the stallion stood under her gentle command. "So we can go?"

Damien clicked his tongue. The horse—Peter apparently—still glared at him, but on its hooves at least. He looked back at Amma. "Why not?"

Kaz moaned loudly, but even his exhaustive grumble couldn't damper Damien's spirits with the smile Amma gave him.

CHAPTER 18

DAMIEN

Attachment Issues, A Case Study

WHAT WAS KNOWN AS simply the Wilds was a sprawling place that had quite lax borders between its named regions, east of the proper realm of Eiren. Damien had been through it a number of times and had been to the more specific Innomina Wildwood as well. There were no roads there, not like the ones in the realm that were marked and sometimes patrolled. The flora and fauna were different too, less predictable and ever-changing, with untamed arcana seeping into everything.

Damien warned Amma of these things as they headed toward them on horseback, Kaz sulking on his stallion's rump since they didn't make a direct course for Eirengaard. "Now, I might be acquainted well with the vampires in Lycoris's den, but witches are not as friendly."

Amma hadn't stopped smiling since they'd set out, but at this, her lips faltered slightly, and she squinted at him. "Oh, not so keen to, what was it? Engage in intimate activities?"

Damien tried to scoff, but it caught in his throat. "I've only met a few, and they indeed had no use for me, magically or otherwise. They like to keep to themselves, and my presence in their forest was not exactly welcome, but that's typical once my heritage becomes apparent."

"Well, what makes them witches?"

"They pull their arcana from the earth."

"So they're just earth mages?"

Damien shook his head, not terribly capable of defining the reason why. "Mmm, no. They don't worship any of your gods."

"Neither do you, but you're still a blood mage."

"Their magic is also a bit...folksy? Superstitious? I'm familiar with some of their customs. The oldest ones are more ritualistic, and they take steps we don't necessarily need to anymore because magic has evolved. Mages have tamed it, and..." He turned then, feeling Amma's eyes on him.

She was frowning. "How else are the witches different from earth mages, Damien?"

"I can sense your demeanor has grown irate"—he straightened on his steed—"and I'm unsure there is anything I can say that will not worsen it."

"I'm not *irate*," she said unconvincingly. "Unless you tell me that they're all women and that's why they can't be called mages."

"No," he was quick to retort, then hesitated. "Though I do think most of them are women. But that's not *why* they're called witches, certainly. At least I don't think so. Is it?"

Amma only laughed at him then and changed the subject, asking after what kinds of creatures and plants they would likely see, the forest growing denser around them as the day wore on. She had always been inquisitive, but she was different now, engaged without underlying fear or suspicion, and he was thankful she'd finally decided to entertain the magic that was so clearly inside her.

Damien had felt it, that time in Xander's tower when he passed the spell through her to send a raven to Laurel. After witnessing what she'd done in the Grand Athenaeum, he knew what he was looking for, and it prickled up, a strange arcana that dwelt so deeply below the surface. It wasn't in her veins, and it wasn't tinged with the infernal or celestial plane—it just *was*.

And now it propelled her deeper into the Wilds and away from everything else. He knew she ached for Faebarrow when they were relegated to the Accursed Wastes, but returning home no longer seemed high on her list of desires.

Darkness, what he would do to get hold of something as solid as a list of Amma's desires when she was completely in her own mind, free of intoxication and magic.

It would take a few days before they found the Innomina Wildwood. However, they wouldn't know until they were already deep within that they were there—the place just sort of happened around one—and so their first day of travel ended in what could only be considered a rather ordinary forest. With a fire stoked and Kaz deep asleep so that he could take on the night watch, Damien and Amma bedded down, still apart but closer. If Damien had reached his hand out and she did the same, they would have touched. Not that he dared.

"Damien, can I ask you something?"

He chuckled, staring up into the darkened, leafy cover overhead. "I am sure you will, whether I say yes or no, so I suppose you may."

Amma did not respond for a few moments. It was perhaps a mistake to repeat exactly what he'd said to her that night she'd gotten drunk in the Faebarrow tavern and he had admitted to wanting to do things to her that made her wriggle and moan just at their suggestion.

"Yes, Amma?" he said louder to snap her out of wherever her thoughts had gone.

She made a contemplative sound, then hesitantly asked, "I was wondering if there was maybe something that you... want?"

Yes, there was absolutely something Damien wanted, from her specifically, but she couldn't be asking *that*, could she? "I'm not sure I follow."

"I mean, besides the talisman and freeing your father and wreaking havoc on the realm or whatever, is there anything else? Because I was just thinking, we're going to the Innomina

Wildwood for me, which already takes you farther off course, and I remember you saying you've devoted your whole life to making the talisman, so maybe there's something else that you want to go looking for that you haven't had the chance to yet? Or maybe it's a...a someone who went missing?"

Ah, so she *had* overheard at least some of his conversation with Lycoris in the den.

Damien's jaw tightened, but no growl came, and no hot anger bubbled beneath his skin. This was just another of Amma's attempts at being helpful, like when she'd been concerned about Rapture's intentions or the dangers for him in Faebarrow, and Damien was finding it increasingly difficult to be angry with the things Amma did.

"She isn't really missing," he heard himself say. "My mother chose to leave. She does not want to be found."

Amma shifted onto a shoulder. He could feel it, the way she looked right through him, even in the dark. He wanted to hate it, but vexation didn't come, leaving him with only a tug at his throat, coaxing him to say more.

"My mother entered into a deal with my father. She would bear him a child and raise it in return for asylum, from what, I do not know. She kept to the bargain until I was four years old, so my memories are very unclear of this time—I do not even remember what she looks like—but she eventually abandoned us, and then things took a turn in Aszath Koth. My father was imprisoned by Archibald right after, and I only just learned from Lycoris that these things were related. It makes quite a bit of sense now, to be honest." Damien sighed as he let the information wash over him again. "Zagadoth is usually an enthusiastic storyteller, but when it comes to the specifics of how he became confined and anything about my mother, he's always vague."

"If your father's trapped in a stone in Eirengaard, how does he tell you stories?"

Damien's hand went instinctively to the satchel he kept the occlusion crystal shard in. He couldn't tell her, not now anyway; she would probably want to meet the old bastard. "There are ways to communicate with him. Infernal ways." It was infernally annoying at least.

"Oh, like your raven," she said, nodding, and Damien noncommittally agreed. "So he doesn't like talking about your mom? Laurel's parents are sort of like that too. Did he tell you anything else?"

"Only that I should not expect her to return when I asked, that she didn't…that she wanted to be alone. That knowledge made things easier, but he never mentioned that she had taken me when she left or that coming after me himself was what got him trapped by Archibald."

Amma moved quietly on the soft grass, and he could feel her getting nearer but still much too far off to touch. "So she didn't exactly abandon you?"

Damien squinted up at the dark sky between the branches overhead. "That's what Lycoris says. And apparently she took Xander too."

"Xander?" Amma sat up with a start.

"Right?" Damien gestured wildly to the forest. "I told that

asshole I had a very specific memory of the two of us in a different place, one that he had to have remembered better than I could. Though I suppose he didn't actually deny it." Damien clicked his tongue, seething at the thought of being left on his back without answers after their sparring match. "He and Birzuma made their home in Aszath Koth after I was born. For a short time, my father at least put up with the two of them, especially as Aszath Koth was meant to be a sanctuary for those of our persuasion. Xander was a few years older than I, but he was a playmate with matched skills and was around often. Why my mother would take him too is even more of a mystery, but perhaps it was for the best as Birzuma is the one who eventually returned both of us to Aszath Koth."

"Birzuma," Amma repeated hesitantly. "So Xander's mother, the demon, brought you and Xander back?"

"Yes. She ended up trapped by Archibald too, but many years later in an unrelated incident—unrelated as far as I know."

"You must have a lot of questions for your mother," Amma said.

Originally, he had only wanted to see his mother again to know for certain that he was human too, but there were questions now, yes, which grossly complicated things. "Do you think I should look for her?"

She was still staring at him when he chanced a glance over, bottom lip caught between her teeth. "If you're prepared for whatever might be said, I think you should do what your heart is pushing you toward, Damien."

My heart, he thought, wanting to scoff but without the will to do so. Amma was right, of course, but damned annoying too.

For a long moment, the two lay in the early darkness, crickets chirping and the fire popping. And then Damien found himself speaking again, against his better judgment. "It's just so strange, isn't it? To take me with her? Lycoris even told me that my mother was *happy*. She said my mother and father were like salamanders in a volcano. Do you know how much a salamander would adore being in a volcano, Amma?"

"How much?"

"Quite a bloody lot!" He threw his hands up, then let them fall back on his chest with a great sigh. "Breaking their deal when it was simply a business contract at least made some sense, but if they were involved? Why—*why* would she break off their deal? Why steal me away and betray my father like that? They were married, for darkness's sake!"

Amma made a small, thoughtful sound but said nothing. If ever he needed her to say something, it was now.

"What do you think, Amma? Truly?"

The dim firelight illuminated her worried frown, eyes averted now. "Well, you know more about these things than I do, Damien, but you're pretty proud of not being completely human, and I expect that's because you think we're weak. In comparison to you, a lot of us are, so that's probably fair. And then there's the way you talk about demons and the Abyss and being a villain…"

The fire popped loudly in the wake of her voice, and Damien felt his jaw go tight again. "Please, finish your thought," he said, more aggressively than he meant.

Amma's voice wavered as she approached her next words with extra care. "Well, you threaten people with just the *name* of your father, and he is a demon after all. Saying your mother abandoned or betrayed him might not be all that accurate. Maybe your mother, I don't know"—Amma took a deep breath—"maybe she took the two of you and actually escaped."

As if the sky had opened up and dumped a deep darkness upon him, Damien's vision tunneled, and his body felt crushed to the forest floor. Amma's point was not foreign to him, but it was something he had pushed away any time it crawled cruelly into his brain to fester at the edges and infect his perception of his father and of his own existence.

And he'd never heard it said aloud before.

He pushed himself up from the ground, standing so fast it made him dizzy, and he ran a hand over his face.

"Damien?" Amma asked, voice quiet. He took a sharp breath at its sound, too kind, too sweet, too human.

"Up. Be on guard," he said, giving Kaz a nudge with a boot that could have been a kick if it were any sharper. The imp blinked and righted himself. "Stay here, both of you." Damien knew the bite to his words was enough to keep Amma from following—a good thing, as the enchanted Chthonic word to order her about was especially hateful at that moment. He turned and stalked off into the darkness of the trees.

Damien knew his father was evil—demons were minions of the dark gods, born of the infernal plane that fed them their powers and sustained them for as long as they could manage to stay alive—but Zagadoth was never evil *to* Damien. He encouraged Damien and guided him, he didn't allow others to treat him poorly, and he was… Darkness, what was the word?

Kind. Zagadoth was *kind*.

But then, demons were known to be deceivers. Birzuma had been exactly that, acting as a caregiver for Damien when his family had splintered, only to consistently play nasty tricks on him, berate him, punish him for things he hadn't even done, and encourage Xander to do the same. She'd ultimately been run out of Aszath Koth and marked a sworn enemy of Zagadoth's when the shard of his prison was returned to the Sanguine Throne, but Zagadoth hadn't been surprised by any of it—that was simply what infernal beings did.

The darkness was pushing in on Damien as he traipsed farther into the forest. There was plenty of moonlight streaming down between the branches as he went blindly forward into the night, but there was a murkiness to his vision, and it swam.

As much as Damien expected that Zagadoth had at least been cordial to his mother, there was always the possibility, no matter how painful and uncivilized it was, that the demon had simply captured and kept her. Zagadoth said there was a deal between them, but that could have meant she was only allowed to live in trade for providing him with a spawn. Not every union between infernal and human beings produced a blood mage—there was forethought in it and a bit of luck too. Something about his mother had been ideal to create offspring with a demon, a servant who would be utterly loyal, bound by blood, cursed with noxscura, so was it fate she happened upon Zagadoth or calculation on his part to seek her out and trap her?

Something caught Damien's foot, and he stumbled, catching himself on a tree. His breathing had gone shallow, heart pounding too hard against his ribs. He squeezed his eyes shut, though it changed little in the way of his vision, trying to slow it and failing. Behind his lids, an image formed: swirling fog, a pool of murky water. He opened his eyes again and pushed onward.

Zagadoth was never reticent about assessing the worth of others. Appraise everyone, waste no time on those who would be useless or those who would take advantage. Damien failed at this sometimes; once, for a very long and ludicrous time, he'd been with a woman who had nearly killed him. But it had proved to be good advice, advice he trusted in. It was, in fact, the initial reason he'd kept Amma around—she was useful as a shield, even when she was irritating him. Had Zagadoth felt the same about his mother? Saw a use for her and held her captive?

The trees were different suddenly, moving as if they were standing columns of thick, viscous liquid. And the ground felt soft, as if he would be sucked down into it if he didn't keep going forward himself. But it was getting increasingly difficult, his body heavy, breathing labored.

Why not just tell him? If Zagadoth had gone to the trouble of keeping some human around just to bring Damien into existence, why not just admit it? How was that different from slaying a village or corrupting a temple? It was just imprisoning one woman.

One woman who was his mother. The woman he remembered holding him, however foggy the memory, and really, truly loving him—the only one who ever had—the way only a human could. If Damien had ever experienced love, purportedly impossible for the infernal, it was through her. Zagadoth couldn't tell him he had hurt that human, not if he wanted Damien's loyalty. And he did indeed have Damien's total loyalty—a whole lifetime of it working toward his freedom.

His hand pressed against the satchel on his hip, fingers too clumsy to open it, to retrieve the shard of the occlusion crystal. What would he do if he had it? Throw it blindly into the forest? Crush it in his palm? Call on the demon and demand an explanation? For what? For a *feeling*?

Damien tripped again, and this time there was nothing there to catch him. He fell to his knees in the dirt, hands splayed out as they sank into the wet earth. His vision was blurrier than ever, but he could make out the blackness seeping from around his fingers even in the colorless shadows of the night. It spread away from his shaking arms at an uncontrollable rate, climbing over every rock, every fallen leaf, every tree trunk.

There was a mad dash from the sleeping creatures all around him, a slithering of snakes who had been in their dens, a skittering of furry things, and crawling of many-legged insects. Something larger bolted into the trees, and then the frightened call of birds, wings beating with terror as they broke from their sleep and through the branches to take to the sky. If the trees could get up and leave, they surely would have, but they were the only thing left for Damien's merciless release of noxscura.

The clawed fists of infernal arcana wrapped around the trunks in every direction. Damien watched it, trying to hold it back for fear it would keep going and never stop, but it stole his very breath and even the beat of his heart, quite literally killing him until he was forced to allow it to wreak its hateful havoc. The noxscura squeezed, it crushed, it strangled, and the trees cracked as they imploded, snapping and filling the sky with terrible groans. Arms no longer capable of supporting him, Damien collapsed, and the sounds were swallowed into nothing.

But Damien could breathe again, the thumping in his chest restarted, and his body was once again his own. He was alive.

He was unsure how long he lay there, something like sleep trying its best to take him, but his strength returned so that he could push himself onto his knees. Like he had fought a long battle, every muscle in his body ached. Something told him it wouldn't be this way if he hadn't held back for so long, but when he looked about at the trees around him, vision returned to normal, and under the brightness of the two moons above, he knew he should have tried harder to keep it in. This was no good.

Splintered, dry, dead—it was as if the area about him had been burnt, but there was no smoldering, only a stench too similar to death to be anything but.

Rot.

It spread out in a circle from where Damien had fallen, killing everything in its path, but what was left behind wasn't just a husk of what had been. There was potential there, a vessel for something else, and the ground felt pliable still, as if with the smallest portion of his will, he could cut a fissure into the infernal plane wider and deeper than any he had ever seen.

Breaking into another plane and summoning demons and dominions was not meant to be easy, but Damien knew in that instant it would have taken very little to bring almost anything into their world. It was a skill that even he should not have had—not like this.

Damien pushed back up onto his feet and staggered over to the nearest broken tree. The closer he came to it, the more it felt alive again, but in a way that was wrong. Arcana vibrated off it, infernal and dark. He couldn't do it again if he tried; there was no spell he was meant to know that would turn a tree into *that*. Nothing he had wanted to know. And yet here it stood, strangely his, both dead and not, like the darkness come to life.

This was demonic energy, his father's gift to him, but it had never come so quickly and completely unbidden before. If he could do this to a tree, what could he do to a person? To Amma? His heart pounded, and sweat broke out on his brow as horror ran cold in his veins. He may have been half human himself, but was he any different from his father if he too was keeping some woman bound to him? Was Xander right about what he had said? That he was meant for evil and nothing else?

Amma would grow weary of being kept, of being a pet with no true choices, and she would want to leave him too, eventually. Especially when she learned how he felt—how he had been so relieved when she'd chosen to remain with the talisman inside her even though he knew the alternative was no real choice either. She wouldn't have wanted to stay with the vampires, to have that cold, undead existence for eternity, out of the sun and away from the trees she loved best. It was a game, a deception, the illusion of a choice. And soon she would want a real option. Soon she would be faced with something that would work, that would finally free her of him, and what would he do then?

He ripped himself away from the tree, stalking back the way he'd come, escaping the ring of darkness he'd created. Just passing out of it brought a lightness to his chest. He took a deep breath, eyes lifting up to the sky. The moons were there, both of them, the moving one passing ever closer to the static one. Those lights had not been visible before, but his own darkness had ripped down enough of the forest to uncover them.

But he was free of that now, and in his limbs and fingers, there crackled a renewed energy. Whatever had been lost in the expulsion of arcana, he had regained it. He could breathe, he could see, he could think. He was himself again, whoever in the Abyss that was, and if he wanted to remain the version of himself he thought he knew, he would have to return as if none of it had happened.

CHAPTER 19

AMMA

On Finding and Being Found

Amma had known it was a mistake the moment it left her mouth, but Damien had asked, and it felt worse not to tell him the truth when he seemed so desperate for her thoughts about his father. She hadn't gone after him despite wanting to, but she'd sat up, waiting, staring into the dark, afraid he'd never come back. When he finally did, even the shadows couldn't hide the exhaustion on his face, and without a word, he fell asleep. She'd only dozed off herself after hearing his heavy breathing, assured he wouldn't traipse into the woods again and disappear.

The next day, though, Damien acted as if the conversation about his mother and father had not happened and seemed happy enough to answer her questions about the

Innomina Wildwood instead. Of course, Damien didn't know the names of most of the plants, but he did his best to describe them. After he'd told her about a flower as large as a man that could cloak itself to match its surroundings and she asked why the region was so different from Eiren despite being so close, he dropped his voice lower. "The Innomina Wildwood is untouched in a way your realm or even places like Aszath Koth aren't. Arcana has been left here on its own for far longer, and that sometimes manifests in gateways to other planes, the magic there leaking out. This is the only place I've ever been able to access the Everdarque."

Dread knocked on the back of her spine at that. "The Everdark?"

"No, the Everdarque," he repeated slowly.

"Yeah, that's what I said. You've been there?"

"Unfortunately. To collect components to make that thing you've got inside you."

Amma touched her chest, shivering. "There are fae components inside me?"

"Yes, and it's a bloody nightmare getting them back to this plane without disintegrating." He seemed quite annoyed with the idea. "Turns out you have to intend to take the thing back with you, not just assume it will come."

"Damien, you stole from the fae?"

"It was just a bit of sand." He shrugged. "It's not as if they count every grain. Trust me, they're quite busy with other, equally pointless things. But you know, you're the heir to a place called Faebarrow after all."

"Well, it's not like we have any fae there. It's just named that because there were all these little mounds spread out over the place that's the liathau orchard now, and long ago, the people used to think fae who blessed the earth and helped the trees flourish lived inside them."

"I thought the trees were a gift from your goddess?"

"Well..." Amma tapped her chin in thought. "Yes, Sestoth gave them to us, but the stories are kind of convoluted. Something like she had good fae working for her, you know?"

"Good fae?" He scoffed quietly. "That doesn't sound like a thing fae would do, not without a cost anyway."

Amma swallowed, not wanting to ask what he thought the price might be. Stories were told about the Everdark, some of them lighthearted warnings, others horrific and nightmare-inducing. None had the same elements—sometimes they were about winged beings who spirited off children, sometimes about creatures made of sagging skin and twisted bones that ate the hearts out of cattle and left the rest—but they shared one theme: No one went to the Everdark and came back whole, because going there at all was not something one was meant to do.

But Damien apparently had. And of course, he'd found it simply annoying.

"I guess you don't like them very much, but you also probably don't think they're very frightening, huh?"

"Frightening? They're all childish, petulant creatures with too much power and too little appreciation for death. But they're not our concern, just a thing that should be avoided if you come across any strange doorways or tempting food sitting out in a place it ought not be. Anyway..." Damien blew out a long, fraught sigh. "Oh, the Wildwood is also home to these very small, yellow frogs with blue bumps all over their backs that are—"

"Delicious!" injected Kaz.

"I was going to say hallucinogenic, so they shouldn't be touched." Damien laughed from the back of his throat and actually grinned at the imp. "See, aren't you looking forward to this detour?"

As Kaz debated the importance of edible amphibians versus serving his master, Amma was filled suddenly with a tickle that worked its way from her toes up to her nose in a flash. It came up on her all at once, and she squeezed her eyes shut, threw a hand over her mouth, and sneezed.

When she opened her eyes again, the old, barely visible path they'd been following was gone, the ground covered in sprawling ferns in all directions. The trees had changed into thicker, foreign species and were covered in ropy vines and colorful flowers. A bird was calling out from the much higher canopy in a rapid succession of the same low noise, and an insect buzzed past Amma's face, making her pull back from the size of it.

"We are...here," said Damien about as helpfully as she supposed he could. They hadn't found the Innomina Wildwood; it had found them.

The horses came to a stop, and Amma slid off her mare to alight on the ground, spongy beneath her boots. As she took a few steps deeper, sounds filtered around her: birdsong calling out and echoing back in bizarre tunes, the unbroken buzz of insects, water dripping from somewhere unseen. Ahead, light broke through the trees in hazy patches, glowing orange over beds of brightly colored flowers amongst the warmer greens of the flat-leafed plants that covered the forest's floor. It was autumn in the realm, trees were losing their leaves, and creatures were gorging themselves and slowing down as the world grayed around them, but summer was still in bloom here.

Amma breathed in deeply, letting a misty warmth settle in her chest. A breeze blew up from behind her, on it the pungent scent of decaying forest, of rich soil, of things fresh and ancient all at once, and she wondered if she had ever really taken a full breath before in her life. Nudged gently forward, she reached out to caress the spread of a leaf wider than both of her hands and banded with maroon stripes, smoother than silk under her fingers. She wanted to feel more, to run hands over the roughness of the bark the plant twisted around, to pull off her boots and sink into the dampness of the earth, to shed all her clothes and absorb the pulsing heat from what was decaying to become new again in the shadows below the flora. With another breath, the urge to run forward filled her lungs, her stomach, her veins.

"This is where we must part."

Amma spun around, heart shooting up into her throat, and froze. Damien's voice had been so calm, such an easy thing for him to say, despite the fact that it stabbed through her with a frantic and paralyzing fear. Her throat tightened around the words that were about to be blurted out: *why* and *no* and *never*.

But Damien was only speaking to Peter, his horse, not her, as he stood beside it and awkwardly ran a hand down its snout. The horse pulled away from him, and Damien sighed. "Yes, I know, you are very torn up about it."

"We can't take the horses?" Amma shook off the fear that had taken her at the thought of Damien leaving, but her voice still wavered.

"Traversing this place is better on foot, and without plains to gallop through, they are little more than clumsy prey here." Damien stepped back from the stallion as Kaz skittered down off its back, jumping to the ground where he immediately began to grumble about the wetness.

Amma said her goodbyes to the two, leading them back a few steps. The forest, however, didn't change around her again, only more of the thick, new jungle in all directions. "Will they figure out how to get back?"

"Only your gods would know," said Damien, then he cleared his throat. "I mean, yes, I'm sure." He waved awkwardly to the animals.

Amma left them, hoping they wouldn't wait this time as she imagined they would never find this exact place again. The thickness of the foliage swallowed up the horses as they trotted off in the opposite direction. "So there are, what, packs of wolves out here? Or bears?"

Damien smirked. "Not exactly."

"Worse," said Kaz as he scampered out before the two of them, throwing his claws up and baring all his fangs.

Amma made a worried sound in her throat, pushing past a leaf with saggy edges, beautifully yellow-green and as long as her arm. It was lovely, but she was suddenly worried about what could be hiding behind it. She quickly ran over the steps in her mind to load and shoot her crossbow, simultaneously checking for the dagger strapped to her thigh.

"Yes, worse," said Damien. "Terrible little creatures, just like Kaz here, with pointy teeth and bad attitudes."

Amma took a stalwart breath, more of that heady air filling her lungs and with it something like courage. Damien clearly wasn't afraid, and she need not be either. "All right then. How do we find the witches?"

"I'm not sure we do," mused Damien, eyes narrowed on the way ahead as he pushed past a fern. "Much like the Wildwood, I think they find us. That is what happened to me before."

"When you came to break into the Everdark?"

"The Everdarque. But no, I was unfortunate enough to run into them the time before that when I was seeking out unique blood," he said casually. "That was long ago. I think I was sixteen?"

"When I was sixteen, I was perfecting my chain stitch," said Amma with a huff. She'd always known she was lucky to be relatively safe and more than provided for with her station in life. However, imagining she could have been *here* doing *this* instead of embroidery almost a decade ago sparked jealousy in her chest.

"I did almost die. Twice," he told her as if the admission was painful. "You would be surprised just how many things are poisonous out here and how quickly they can affect you, even if you're meant to be an expert at filtering toxins out of your blood. Which reminds me—anything that color, leafy, scaled, or furry, will almost definitely paralyze you."

Amma had just been eyeing the exact magenta flower that Damien pointed out. "Noted. Was the blood for the talisman?"

"No, no, this was before I had the idea of enthralling Archibald. Back then, I was just honing my senses, exposing myself to as much as possible. The things here are different, as we discussed, and their innate arcana is often hidden, which makes it harder to identify since it's older and more primal. Apparently, I did not do a very thorough job, though, as I missed it in you."

Amma came to a stop. Old, primal, innate arcana? Inside her? She laughed. "Well, there probably just isn't that much in there."

"You made a tree," he said plainly.

She hummed, heading toward a cluster of blue mushrooms that were suddenly the most interesting thing in the world to her. "Well, you know, I had an acorn on me."

Damien swept around to stand before her, stopping them both short. "Amma, you *made* a tree. I saw it. You are more capable than you think, and I'd wager it's because you believe the ability is coming from outside you—the acorn or liathau wood—and not from within."

She shrugged. That was the case after all.

"I've been pondering an experiment," he said hesitantly. "Something I've been wanting to try if you'd be willing."

Intrigued, Amma eyed him, waiting for more. Damien had experimented with her before, when they'd sent the raven, and she'd quite liked that.

"Do you think you could resist the talisman?"

The creatures called out in the thick foliage around them. Something slithered through the underbrush, and there was a flutter of wings above, but Amma ignored it all. "You mean, like, overpower *you*?"

"Ah, yes, I suppose?" It was his turn to shrug, as if it were such a simple thing.

"Well, I doubt it," she blurted out. "You've got decades of training, and I don't even know what this is."

"That's fair, but you would not be using an exterior conduit for once. I could attempt to enthrall you, and you could use your arcana to defy the order."

Amma's instinct was to tell him no, that she wanted desperately to forget the talisman even existed because it meant there was still something horrible left undone that he hadn't given up on.

But he was also right: She couldn't use a door or a seed to withstand the order; it would all come from inside her, and she hadn't considered that possibility yet. And if she could fight it off, then Archibald certainly could, and the talisman might be useless.

Amma took a breath. "Okay."

Damien nodded, brows knitted, and he began fidgeting, awkwardness still peculiar on him. He looked about, then eyed Kaz. "Go busy yourself with something."

The imp grumbled but stalked off into the trees.

Hands on his hips, Damien took three long steps back from her, appraised the space between them, and then his face fell back into brutally decisive and just a little irked. "Are you ready?"

Amma bit her lip but kept from shaking her head. Instead, she closed her eyes, let her arms dangle at her sides freely, and insisted to herself that relaxation was possible. With a breath, she nodded. The first thought that swam into her emptying mind was *I should have asked what he's going to make me do*.

"Sanguinisui, come here."

Amma snapped to attention, a jolt shooting down through her spine and taking over the entirety of her body. When she opened her eyes just a moment later, she was standing right before him, vision level with his chest, and as the spell flooded out, leaving her sore and squirmy, she groaned. "Shit."

Damien tried to stifle his laughter. "Apparently, you were not ready. Again?"

She shuddered but this time did not close her eyes. Amma squeezed her fists, tensed her muscles, and focused hard on not moving. "Yes," she whispered.

"Sanguinisui, take my hand."

With a wave of arcana that simply nudged her elbow, her fingers unfurled and slid over his outstretched palm before she could even think to hold still. There was the magic again, slimy and irritating, but it scrambled back out of her when she had complied with his order. Amma clicked her tongue, pulling in her shoulders and scrunching up her face. "I can't," she groused, holding his hand up in front of his nose.

"Are you even trying?"

"Yes, of course!" She released him and crossed her arms. "I mean, it might make it easier if you order me to do something I don't want to do."

"Well..." Damien averted his eyes, and she was glad, realizing what she had admitted a moment too late, but then his jaw tightened, and he frowned. "Fine. Are you ready to try once more?"

Amma's heartbeat quickened at how intent he'd gone. She took half a step back, planting her feet firmly in the soft earth, flexing her fingers as she uncrossed her arms. Her body still prickled with the magic, uneasy as it slithered beneath her skin. She nodded.

"Sanguinisui," said Damien, "stab me in the chest."

"Wha—" Amma's voice was torn from her along with all her breath as she moved lightning quick, hand falling to the dagger holstered on her thigh, fingers wrapping around the hilt, and brandishing the weapon like she'd never done before. With abandon, she swung, a scream caught in her throat behind arcana that flowed through her as violently as she plunged the dagger forward.

No, stop, don't! her own voice shrieked in her mind, the blade but a glint of silver through the air until it came to an abrupt halt, its tip just nicking the leathers across Damien's chest. A tight hand was on her wrist, holding her at bay, but Amma was still pushing forward, feeling the urge to stab, to kill, in her body, but none of it in her mind or heart. Sweat broke out on her neck, a second burst of energy exploding through her as she tried to wrench her hand away from him and thrust back at a different angle, but he held her still.

Fight it, she said to herself, but there was no change, even as her entire body began to tremble, and she brought her free hand up to slam atop the other and drive the weapon into him. *I don't want to do this. I can't.* Tremors ran through her as she practically hung off the knife, digging her feet into the ground and sliding, going nowhere. *Oh gods, make it stop.*

"Damien," she choked out, "please."

"Sanguinisui, stop."

Her silver dagger fell to the forest floor, disappearing into the ferns, and she collapsed, the world blurring behind tears that sprang painfully to her eyes. Damien caught her, hands under her elbows to hold her up, but it wasn't enough. With her muscles so spent, her knees went out, and he staggered back into a tree, holding her right up against him as she began to truly weep.

"Amma, it's all right," he said urgently.

"No, it's not!" Her voice was hoarse, burning her throat. She balled a weak fist and blindly struck his chest with no real force. "Don't ever do that to me again!"

"I-I won't," he stammered, squeezing her waist as she continued to sob.

Her head hung, pressed to the top of the place she'd been trying to stab. She could hear her own voice, feel herself moving, but the surrendered sensation in her body wouldn't abate. She hated it, fumbling to regain command of herself as she repeated increasingly senseless blubbering that devolved into pitiful begging. "Please, Damien, don't."

His grip around her steadied with one arm, and he brushed a hand up along the side of her face, tipping her head up to him. "Never again, Amma," he said. "I'm sorry. Never again. I promise."

She drew in a ragged breath, blinking tears out of her eyes, fists loosening. The arcana was finally gone, but it had left her feeling betrayed by her own body. "What if I'd done it?"

His dark brows knit while fingers eased hair back from her temples. "What if you'd stabbed me? Well, I was already prepared—I gave you the command, and I am wearing a bit of armor. My skin does mend itself fairly well too, if you remember." The corner of his mouth twitched up. "Also, you know, I am significantly stronger than you and well-practiced at this point in fending off your advances."

A strange fear rose in her, but she reminded herself she was safe in the Wilds with a blood mage. She didn't realize the fear was due to the amusement in that blood mage's voice and his strange choice of words. "What's that supposed to mean?"

Damien looked alarmed for a moment, then he grinned. With just one arm around her middle, he lifted her, and her eyes went wide, feet suddenly off the ground. "I could just toss you over there if I really needed to."

She wiped at her eyes. "You wouldn't."

The soft forest floor was back under her boots, but he didn't release her. "No, probably not even to save myself from impalement, as pathetic as that is."

They lingered in the moment until Amma finally regained herself. But then Damien began to squirm.

"Ah, your dagger," he said, gently pushing her away as he knelt to retrieve the blade. Handing it off, he went to back up but knocked into the tree. Uncomfortably, he stood there, trapped before her, face falling stony once more. "And you do have my word that I will not use that Chthonic one again."

Amma took her dagger in two hands, hating it for a moment but knowing the blame did not belong to the weapon. It was her own fault. The fact was she wasn't strong enough, regardless of whether he compelled her with magic or not.

She nodded, head down, and they continued into the Innomina Wildwood.

CHAPTER 20

AMMA

No, Well, Maybe, Probably, Yes, Definitely

AMMA EXPECTED TO WAKE exhausted and confused in the Innomina Wildwood, but instead she felt renewed, like she had shed a weighty skin and could move freely for perhaps the first time in her life. That attraction returned too, the one that lured her deeper into the wood the day before. The night had been cool despite the protected hollow at the base of a massive tree she and Damien had slept in, closer to one another but not nearly as close as she would have liked, but the morning was balmy and enticing, and Amma was eager to venture farther in.

With no real direction as they went, Amma simply kept her eyes peeled, careful not to touch anything too beautiful or sharp, though she longed to run fingers over the green and gold world around her. Damien had taken to keeping half a step behind, and she naturally took the lead, chasing glimmers of light that broke across the thick underbrush, listening to the calls of birds and chittering creatures as if they were directions in Key. When vines hanging from branches swung in unfelt breezes, she followed in kind, and when the flowers ahead were not blossoming under the afternoon sun, she turned to find another way.

Then she put out her hand and placed it on Damien's arm, stopping abruptly. The bird calls had quieted, and the leaves no longer rustled. In the eerie silence, she peered ahead, instinct telling her to look up, but she saw nothing despite her skin pebbling with goose bumps.

Beside her, Damien shifted, and Amma turned. A set of yellow eyes stared out from the shadows, suspended in the thick, leafy cover above them. Amma's stomach clenched, the two caught in its unmoving gaze. It was difficult to tell, especially with its entire body obscured, but whatever was there was big.

A sound broke into the quiet, hanging in the air, small but distinct. Kaz came tromping through the low ferns from behind them, head down, face smeared with gore and the limp body of something reptilian in hand. The imp was chewing, and gleefully at that, completely oblivious. At least he would be slightly amused in the moment before he died.

"Kaz," Damien said in a low rumble, "hold still."

Even with his great batwing ears, the imp didn't hear, still twenty paces off, trudging loudly and chewing even louder.

"Kaz," he repeated, and the imp finally looked up, watery eyes huge and unaware, but only for a moment.

Either from the looks they were giving him or the intense aura that had settled on their patch of the Wildwood, Kaz sensed the danger then. He froze, foot hovering over the ground in his next step forward, wings pulled in, tail stiff, but all a moment too late.

The shadow in the canopy burst like a dense fog had been blown away, the leaves brightening as a form sprang off a thick branch. Muscled and long, the creature was covered in black fur, run through with russet stripes like dagger slashes. It moved impossibly fast for such a huge thing, clawed paws leading its pounce downward. Its elongated jaw was not unlike a horse's, with a flat bridge of a snout, but its fangs were entirely feline.

Damien had his dagger out, slicing down his arm as he called up a spell, but the creature would be on Kaz in a second, and the imp would be ripped in two. Amma slapped a hand onto the nearest tree without thinking, knowing only that Kaz had to be anywhere but exactly where he stood. There was heat under her palm and a yank in her chest that nearly pulled her off her feet.

The ground beneath Kaz split, knocking the imp forward. A thick root burst upward from the forest floor, catapulting Kaz right toward Amma to land squarely in her arms. The muscled creature alighted on the ground gracefully, as if it hadn't been intending to swallow Kaz whole, but then it yowled as Damien's blood blades carved its shoulder.

The animal, so like a cat but larger than a horse, dug claws into the wet ground, a pool of shadows growing up from its talons as it sank its head low and disappeared into a cloud of blackness. Only its eyes glimmered, narrowing, and then a spray of vile orange liquid shot out at them. Amma clutched Kaz to her chest, jumping away as Damien did the same. In the place where they stood, the orange-covered ferns burnt into nothing, the earth bubbling and melting into darkness, and a stench like acid filled the air.

Damien was cutting into himself again, the word coming out too calmly: "Run."

Amma squeezed Kaz, and the imp didn't even try to escape, long clawed arms wrapped about her neck. She bolted, legs pumping hard as she sprang over a fallen log and slid against the wet earth when she landed. There was a screech behind her and the feel of arcana lighting up the forest, and Amma came to a stop.

What was she doing? Running away to leave Damien to fight off that monstrous beast alone? When she had a crossbow?

She whirled back around, Kaz clinging tightly to her, and grabbed for the weapon strapped to her back. Damien had called up a spell, or at least she thought he had, as there were even more shadows descending on the place they had been. She gripped the end of her crossbow, but it was no use; there wasn't even a target to try and focus on. A blur of movement in the illusory darkness told her something was inside, but she couldn't decipher if it was man or beast.

She waited through a shallow breath, but even that was too long, so she dropped to the ground and planted one hand flat on the forest floor, the other holding on to Kaz. She dug her fingers in, pushing past decaying leaves and wriggling down into damp soil, feeling for something her mind told her was there, just not clarifying *what* she was meant to find.

As her eyes were locked on the shadows, there was another blur of movement, the muffled screech of a cat, and finally her fingertips grazed something smooth that jumped into her grip. The world around her sharpened, the sounds inside the cloud of darkness louder, and she knew Damien was there, alive, because she could feel his blood spatter across the forest floor. With an urgent thrum in her chest and a jolt down through her arm, the ground around her hand pulsed, and the earth cracked in a jagged line as it ran away from her, headed for the shadow.

There was a sound like splintering wood followed by two loud thuds, an animalistic cry, and the surprised yelp of a man. The cloud of darkness dispersed, sun breaking down through the trees above, and Amma sprang back to her feet. "Damien!"

He was on his back, covered in vines, utterly bewildered. Only a few paces away was the beast, similarly covered, similarly stuck, but it would likely last but a moment with its immense size, its black tail the only appendage free to lash through the air.

Damien's dagger rent through enough of the vines to free his upper half. There was blood on his face as he sat up, but his eyes were wide, and he pointed at Amma with the blade. "Did you just—"

"No!" she said too quickly, then sucked her teeth. "Well, maybe."

The big cat let out a hiss, more of that horrible orange liquid spraying through a band of tendrils and freeing a paw to slash. Damien jerked himself away, tripping out of the mess of vines that had been looped around the rest of him. He called up another shadow, backing toward Amma as the beast struggled to escape her earthen snare.

When he came closer, Amma saw he had wounds down his back that were not his own doing, the fabric of his tunic hiding the worst of it. "Go," he called to her over his shoulder. "This thing is strong."

"But you're bleed…" Amma's vision blurred. She took a step backward, legs heavy, foot slipping on a stone. She fell, and Kaz scrambled out of her arms just before she hit the ground.

Up against her back, the earth wasn't as hard as it should have been, but all the breath was knocked from her anyway. She tried to push up off it, but her own weight was too much. Her palms slid in the hot soil, too hot, burning, and the treetops overhead spun. She was sinking, being dragged downward, a whisper in her ear to give in, to rest, to stay.

Then the earth was no longer at her back, and Amma was scooped up against Damien's chest as he ran. She could see nothing, only flashes of light behind her eyelids, but she could feel the heavy breaths he took and wetness falling on her.

A voice broke into her muddled senses, not Damien's but not the screeching of the big cat either. This was human, and it called out so loudly the forest itself seemed to perk up and listen. With it, Amma felt Damien skid to a stop, his arms tightening around her. He said something, his voice muffled but vibrating through his chest and into hers.

And then, a tree.

Amma was sitting at the base of it, and she was…fine? She didn't know how she got there, but she wasn't worried about that—she wasn't worried about anything. Her gaze ran up the trunk's length, though where it crested, she couldn't tell. The tree went on and on, somewhere well above the rest of the forest's canopy. As she stared harder into the sky, the vision blurred, but she finally saw its leaves, pink and red.

Weak, starved, exhausted, Amma's limbs went impossibly heavy as everything melted back into darkness around her. Even the rise and fall of her chest was labored. The ground was beneath her again, holding her, but the ground wasn't Damien, and with that realization, Amma panicked. She tried to jolt upright, forcing her eyes open, but only made it halfway, mumbling out a weak cry and collapsing backward again. Something soft caught her head before it slammed into the earth.

"You were not ready," a voice said, not at all happy with her.

Tanned skin and black hair in long, thick braids hovered overhead. Features sharpened, drawn down into that disappointment Amma had sensed, thin lips curved into a frown, nostrils flaring. But the woman's hands were on Amma's arm, rubbing her bicep, and lightness flooded the limb, a significant improvement over the rest of them.

"Where is—" Amma's voice caught as she rolled her head to the side to look for Damien, and her gaze instead fell on a huge wet nose. Hot air chuffed over her face as whiskers twitched, the muzzle of the giant cat inches away. Amma froze, but instead of its golden eyes being narrowed and threatening, the pupils were huge and crossed as it watched her with a kitteny intrigue.

"You are lucky," the woman said with a biting laugh. "If Soot didn't just want to play, you would have been dinner."

The creature called Soot rolled her head against the earth, flattening an ear; the other had been sliced through, the blood on it now drying. She lay on her stomach, claws retracted so that only soft paws curled before her—paws as big as Amma's head. Damien had been injured by those hidden talons. Her strength had returned from the woman's touch, but Amma's need to find him in one piece drove her to sit up.

About ten paces from Amma's feet sat Damien, legs and arms crossed, looking about as irritable as she'd ever seen him, which was quite a bit. He was glaring at the other woman, blood still spattered over his face, leaves in his hair, and a tear in his tunic, though there were no dripping wounds. Peeking out from behind him, Kaz had his own black eyes trained on the big cat.

Then Damien's gaze flicked to her, and his face softened. He dropped the petulant pose, pushing up onto his knees. "Amma, are you—"

Before he could come closer, the woman threw out an arm. "No. Stay. Don't touch her."

He shot her a nasty look but froze.

Amma expected arcana to fly any moment as Soot too sat up with a trill, but no magic came. "What's going on?"

"Infernal creatures are tainted," she said, turning from Damien again and tending to Amma's leg like she had her arm. "You manifested more than you were prepared for, and now you are weak. If he tries to drain you, you will die."

"I don't drain creatures," Damien growled, eyes lidded heavily with annoyance. "You're thinking of ubi infernals."

The woman huffed, not bothering to look at him. "Well, excuse my precaution, but after you wounded Soot—"

"She attacked us first," he cut in.

"Regardless, you used such a dark spell that I can only assume you are an incubus or worse, pretending to be human." She tapped Amma's thigh and then dug into a pouch tied at her hip. "The planes leak sometimes, and awful things come out. You must be very careful."

Damien sat back at that, clicking his tongue and rolling his eyes.

"Damien is from this plane—he's a mage," Amma said, hoping the explanation was enough. "Are you an earth mage?"

For the first time, the woman smiled, albeit derisively. She brought the bud of a flower out of her bag, its tightly wrapped petals the color of a late evening sky. There was a scratch on Amma's forearm she hadn't noticed until the woman pressed the bud against it. A gooey paste squeezed out, and the woman ran a hand over the goop, hardening it with a pulse of arcana. Then she extended an arm, and from the ground, a root shot upward with a twist, forming a staff that placed itself just into her hand.

It was impressive, but it told Amma very little. "So that's a yes to the earth mage thing?"

"Amma, this is who we've been looking for. One of them anyway." Damien gestured to her vaguely, his upset still palpable. "Witch, this is Lady Ammalie, and I would advise you to answer her questions."

Amma's eyes widened, but the woman didn't appear bothered. In fact, she snickered as she stood. A band of faded blue cloth wrapped around her chest and crossed over her shoulders, but her muscled midsection was uncovered. Amma could tell from the stitching that it had been something else once but repurposed as a top. From her hips hung a long skirt, its intricate pattern hand-painted on a thick fabric. "You were summoned here just as I was once, so you tell me what I am." She extended a hand, and her firm, callused grip pulled Amma right up onto her feet.

She wavered a moment. "I don't know if I was actually summoned—"

"Yes, you do. Come on, I'll take you where you want to be."

Damien was quick to get to his feet too, but the witch swung her staff and connected with his chest. "No touching."

He grunted, and Amma held her breath, but he only glared at the woman he'd called a witch. Readjusting Amma's crossbow over his own shoulder, he straightened and rubbed the spot she struck. "No touching," he mocked under his breath.

The big cat rolled up onto her massive paws too, following silently at the stranger's side. Amma hesitated, but Damien gestured for her to go ahead, leaving space to walk farther behind, and Kaz, still in his imp form, scurried up Damien's back to ride on his uninjured shoulder.

Amma caught up to the woman. "Hey, hello, sorry about all this, but I really don't know if *summoned* is the word for how we got here. I was *told* about you guys by a vampire who said she felt some old magic inside me, which I'm also not sure is completely accurate, but sometimes doors unlock around me, and I might be able to talk to trees, so I wanted to see if you could help me figure out how to, well, not pass out like I did back there."

The woman quirked a brow at her. "Told, brought, followed your instinct—it's all the same. This place showed itself to you, and you're here." The woman tapped her staff against a tree, and Amma felt the forest around her wobble.

"The elves do that," she said in a hushed whisper, remembering how they had quickly stepped through the Gloomweald while traveling to Faebarrow.

"And they learned it from us."

"Who'd you learn it from?"

Another tap, another wobble. "Now, that's a good question."

The woman used her staff to push aside the torso-sized leaves that hung before them and revealed a stone structure that rose up out of the earth. Two columns of stacked blocks stood twice Amma's height, and at their top was suspended a single long piece of stone. The structure was draped in vines, with thick moss lying in patches at its base and corners. Symbols carved all along it that had been worn away over many years peeked through, the language indecipherable.

"I learned it from whoever built this," said the woman, taking just a moment to glance up at it before passing underneath. "But then the gods threw a tantrum, and this place was razed to the ground. Though it hardly matters. Someone did it before them too, and someone will long after we're gone."

Through the archway, a clearing was laid out, the forest floor replaced with massive slabs of stone, cracked long ago so that moss grew between them. Columns had once existed here and there but were broken and crumbling, taken back by the earth and serving as planters and pools of water in which brightly colored birds bathed. A furry creature with long arms and a curling tail skittered down from the remnants of a wall and came to a stop just before them, looking up. The size of a squirrel, it had a nearly human face surrounded by a halo of ruddy fur, and when it pulled back its lips in a smile, it revealed long fangs like something infernal.

The woman invited it closer, and it scurried up her arm to land on her shoulder, wrapping itself around her neck and peering from behind her braids to watch the rest of them with eyes that didn't blink. From Damien's shoulder, Kaz leaned toward it, and then in a puff of red smoke, he looked identical save for his jutting underbite.

"Oh good, you found her!"

Amma hadn't seen her appear, but an aged woman stood amongst the columns then. She carried a similar staff but was actually using it to hold herself up as she took a hobbling step toward them. Graying hair was bundled into long coils atop her bent head, and she was grinning so that the lines all over her face deepened.

"I don't know what help she'll be," said their host, sighing a long, put-upon breath and scratching under the chin of the monkey on her shoulder. She gestured for Amma to come closer. "She did bring a problem with her though."

The older woman chuckled, meeting the two of them in the center of the ruins. "The trees said she'd *bring* help, Kalani, not that she'd necessarily be it."

Amma's stomach twisted at that, but the distraction of a small girl sprinting down the notches of one of the trees stole her attention. Barefoot but dressed in clothing Amma would have expected to see back in Faebarrow, she moved like an animal, jumping from branch to hollow until she was on the ground. Just behind her, a pair of older girls walked out of the leafy forest, identical and lanky, with the pointed ears of elves. None of them spoke, but they looked at one another and waited. Amma's stomach twisted again. "The trees told you about me?"

"Well, they said someone would come who needed us as much as we would need them." The elder woman leaned fully on her staff, flowers sprouting off it, and when Amma looked closer, she saw they were sprouting off the woman too. "We're to provide you with some assistance, and in turn, you will give us something too." Her gauzy eyes shifted to where Damien stood, leaning against the arch at a safe enough distance to avoid another thwack of the staff.

"Oh, I didn't bring him here to give away," Amma said quickly.

"We don't want him," the woman called Kalani scoffed.

"Well, good, because you can't have him." Amma had been louder then, catching Kalani's eye, and the woman was taken aback only a moment, her surprise turning into delighted approval.

"Only to borrow." The old woman chuckled. "Come on, let's make a bargain, shall we?"

CHAPTER 21

DAMIEN

Defining What Constitutes a Chore

DAMIEN HATED A CAGE. Unlike the joke the elves of the Gloomweald had thrown him in or the bedchamber in Faebarrow that he had plotted from, this prison was much more absolute, even though it looked like a quaint dwelling. With walls and a floor constructed from thin branches that had been molded and woven together and the whole chamber suspended well above the ground in one of the larger trees that surrounded the ruins, the hut was at least impressive. It was sturdy and well enough furnished and had enchanted facilities, appearing to be exactly like the other homes dotting the trees. But if he wasn't allowed to leave it—and that woman, Kalani, had been very clear he was not—it didn't matter if they gilded the thing: It was still a cage.

At least Amma was a good negotiator, and annoyed as Damien was to be left out of whatever bargain the witches were making with her, he trusted in the outcome, especially after she'd insisted they could not keep him. It wasn't a thing he was truly concerned about—the cage, as burdensome as it was, *would* be temporary—but it had tickled him to hear how fierce her words were nonetheless.

He chuckled to himself as he washed the blood off his face and shoulder in the enchanted basin, then ran a hand over where the claw marks had been. They'd healed, but it was unfortunate he'd gotten them at all—cats usually liked him, and with Soot's ability to conjure shadows, it should have been a foregone conclusion that they would get along.

As he pulled his tunic back on, he heard the now-familiar skittering of Kaz and that furry little monkey clambering in through the window. They'd taken a liking to one another since Kaz had mimicked his form, and they ran up and down the tree Damien's cell was attached to. Upon their latest entry, the two had armfuls of fruits and nuts and sat together on the floor, nibbling and trading with one another, and Damien sat himself on the foot of the hut's bed to watch, wondering where Amma was.

The witches were unlikely to hurt her, but they would push her; he could see that in their eyes and hear it in their unspoken words. Amma was strong enough to endure it, and they might even get the talisman out, though as that thought struck him, Damien's unease spiked. If they managed to free her of it—of him—what would she do? The Innomina

Wildwood was much better suited to Amma than the karsts; she'd been drawn to the plants and the place's aura the moment they'd been invited inside. Would she choose to stay?

The chamber's door opened then, and the elderly woman stood there, the one who said she'd heard from the trees that Amma was coming. Slightly hunched, she didn't appear out of breath despite climbing her way up the stairs built into the trunk. With such folded skin and milky eyes, she had to be close to one hundred, but she stumped into the hut with her staff a head and a half taller than her and covered in little white petals, and she grinned up at him with the pep of at least a seventy-year-old.

But then that grin broke. "What's wrong with you?"

Damien's frown only deepened. "Oh, what isn't?" he groused.

"You're restless. That's at least part of the problem, and I've got a solution for that." Voice like dry leather, she cackled, taking herself over to where Kaz and the monkey were still sorting their goods.

"Do you?" Damien dragged himself up from the bed and went to the small window to peer out to be sure she'd come alone. The clearing in the ruins below had a few others crossing through it—none of them Amma—but the way up to his cell was clear.

"Your keeper tells me you're a blood mage."

"Look, I understand you don't want infernals here, but I'm not leaving without her, and she needs to stay until she's satisfied, so—"

There was a *thwack* as the woman's staff banged into the wall beside him. He recoiled from it, glad not to be under it but surprised she'd missed. Kaz and the monkey crept closer to one another. "You need to listen before assuming the worst." Then she chuckled. "Though I am sending you away."

Damien growled, and the room's furry creatures gathered the last of their snacks in their arms, ready to bolt.

"Your keeper has loaned you out to us in trade for our guidance."

"She has?" Damien's shoulders relaxed, and he actually grinned, not bothering to argue that Amma didn't have that authority, which, he supposed, might actually mean she did. A loan wasn't forever, and if it helped her, then of course he would do it. "Who do you want me to scare off?"

"Sickness," she said. "There is a corruption in the Wildwood, and it needs absolved."

At this, Damien squinted back at her. "You want me, a blood mage, to *cleanse* something? Have you confused me with the son of a dominion?"

"The trees said the newcomer would bring us the help we need—clearly, that help is you. It's up to you how you might rid us of this problem, cleansing it or otherwise."

Rolling his eyes, he went to get his armor. "Lead the way."

"It's a few days from here. I've arranged for the others to take you."

"A few days?" he balked. "And what about Amma?"

"You said she would stay until she's satisfied. When you

return—*if* you return, I suppose—then you can ask her how much longer until she gets the help she came for."

He couldn't argue with his own words, but he could be cross about them, and as he finished dressing, he was. Perhaps it would be easier for Amma if he were out of the way.

The small band of witches he'd been saddled with intended to leave immediately. While they finished gathering supplies in the middle of the ruins, he waited, both Kaz and his monkey companion running in circles around him. Just as he assumed he would be dismissed without so much as a wave, Amma came darting down from another of the huts set high in the trees.

Distress sneaking into her features, she stepped close to him, voice low as the others tarried nearby. "You will come back, right?"

He blinked down at her. "You are the one sending me away."

"Not forever, just on a little chore." A green moth flitted between them. They watched it bob toward a flowering plant, land, and immediately be crushed in the cerulean petals. Amma groaned. "Maybe this isn't a good idea."

Damien leaned in, hands behind his back. "If you're also ordering I return, then I will."

Her blue eyes flashed up at him. "Make sure you do."

Damien bit back a smile at that, hands falling lax at his sides and feeling oddly empty. But before he could figure out what to do with them, Kalani nudged him in the back with her staff and told him it was time to go. He was knocked off-balance while the vexation was knocked right back into him.

His party was made up of three witches, Kalani at the head. She moved like wind through the trees, climbing and disappearing as swiftly as her Soot did. There was also a man, Fior, the first he'd seen amongst the witches but clearly accepted as one of them. Broad-shouldered and stout, he refused Damien's hand when they met, instead listing off a number of rules for their travel together, none of which Damien committed to memory. Their third was a skinny young girl called Nell, who had little if any concern for much at all. She skipped along beside them, sometimes climbing atop the big cat's back, sometimes scurrying off without a word from the others and reappearing with fruit or nuts that she handed out to everyone, including Damien. She was the only one not wary of him and, in turn, the only one Damien thought to be wary of.

Kaz had come along as well, as had his new monkey friend, and for once, the imp was not complaining but chittering and scurrying about playfully. It was an interesting change, and Damien felt the arcane pull of the Wildwood himself, but without Amma's presence, there was a hollowness too that no sunshine could fill.

As Damien walked alongside Fior in the humid jungle, the witches' camp left behind hours prior, he regretted not saying something more when she had instructed him to return. He *would* come back, even if he was the only survivor of whatever terrible thing they needed someone infernally born to cleanse. But knowing he and Amma were to spend a number of nights so far apart made him wish he'd imparted some sentiment, not that he was entirely sure the things one was supposed to say when they felt however it was he was feeling.

"...do there?"

"Huh?" Damien pulled himself from the cloud of words in his mind, dense and disorienting.

"Where are you from, and what do you do there?" Fior repeated, slower, like Damien couldn't comprehend simple Key. It was the first time he'd made an effort to converse and not just bark out some command that Damien didn't intend to follow.

"Oh, I'm the demon lord of Aszath Koth's son. I'm supposed to oversee the city, but I've got people to do that for me while I work on releasing my father from prison."

Fior came to a stop, features slack like *he* might not understand simple Key.

"Too honest?" Damien asked Kaz, who still fancied himself a ginger monkey, sitting atop Soot's back.

"Master always speaks the truth unless deception serves best," he said, a little squeakier than normal from his fanged mouth.

Fior took a step back from the creature that he was sure shouldn't be able to speak.

Damien shrugged and continued on next to Nell.

Kalani had disappeared into the trees above them, and Fior eventually caught up. "They said you had infernal blood. The planes have been more active lately, and it's been a problem."

"Ah, some information," Damien said bitingly as he stepped over a log. "Do tell."

"It's too hard to explain. You'll see."

With a grunt, Damien looked to Nell, her hair in two long braids flopping about as she scrambled up and over the log. "I don't suppose you want to tell me what we're doing?"

Her dark eyes only gleamed, and she offered him a berry from her handful of spoils. He chanced that it wasn't poisonous and swallowed it with a shrug.

It was like that for the next three days, Fior cryptically hinting at a complication from some other plane, the little girl having a fabulous but silent time, Kalani disappearing and reappearing with no warning, and Damien refusing to ask more questions out of sheer spite. The four sat in silence when each evening came, took turns sleeping, and remained unbothered by large, Wildwood-dwelling creatures thanks to Soot, who eventually warmed to Damien, nuzzling into his hand after a proper apology.

Then they came upon the place they'd set out to find, and Damien did indeed see, as he'd been told.

A spire jutted up from the earth. It could have been a tree once, but Damien wouldn't call it that now. Blackened, it was as the old woman had said: a thing of rot and corruption and needing absolution. It was a strange thing to concede for someone infernal, but Damien agreed nonetheless when he saw it towering in the midst of the Innomina Wildwood.

Deadened and gnarled branches reached up leaflessly into a barren patch of the otherwise dense jungle. The twisted bark of this particular species, normally pleasant enough to look at, had turned grotesque and ropy, like a trail of intestines wound up and around the trunk to squeeze its life away. It wasn't dead, Damien knew just from looking at it, not yet. It certainly smelled of death, of inching closer to a state that was no longer living, but it hung on, perhaps trying to survive the rotting stranglehold all over it—or perhaps because of it.

When Damien took another step forward, he sank into a black ooze, and when he pulled his boot out, it was covered in a viscous sludge. The rot spread away from the spire, which had already infected two smaller trees on either side. Each bent away from the source, the far side losing its color while the closer half turned black and gruesome. There had been a third too, he presumed, but it was already crumpled in on itself, the strangest way he'd ever seen a tree fall, inward and into a wet, pulpy pile like it was so full of sludge it had nowhere to go but down.

The similarity to what Damien himself had done a few nights earlier was not lost on him, but that had occurred outside the Innomina Wildwood, and while that had been its own brand of horrific, if he had done *this*, he would have expected to have not survived.

"We're meant to set this right?" Damien asked, unsure if they really could. "Have you tried burning it?"

"It won't catch," said Fior. He remained ten paces back with the others; Nell frowned for the first time.

"Let's try a little infernal fire." Not entirely convinced himself, Damien gestured to Kaz, and the imp hustled over, his form shifting back, the ginger hairs falling away, and his leathery skin revealed. Fior made a face—he hadn't seen Kaz any other way—but it was more one of tired acceptance than horror this time. Kaz's shift at least brought a little cheer to Nell, who clapped.

With a deep breath and intense focus, Kaz whipped his tail hard at the tree. The flames caught, but only for a few seconds, crawling upward and then seeping in. As it fell into the spire and disappeared, only a ghost of the flames was left, and then that too was gone.

Kaz began to whimper out an apology, but Damien waved him away, continuing to circle the thing, his hand rubbing his jaw. "How long has it been here?"

"At least a moon," said Kalani. "It started small. We thought it was just a new Everdarque portal, so we ignored it."

"This isn't fae magic," Damien said, though that was clear.

With no other choice, he finally reached out and touched the spire. The bark didn't move, but beneath his palm, there was a squirming, like hundreds of worms writhing over one another, followed by the sharp pain of pinpricking claws. Arcana tried to work its way into him, to read him just as he so often did to others, but Damien had spent a lifetime learning to be difficult to read. As the arcana tried to rend its way in, noxscura answered in kind, pushing back and then reaching inside to explore for itself. And then everything went dark.

Damien's vision left him, the sounds of the forest were silenced, the damp air no longer against his skin. Left with nothing but the wet writhing under his hand, that sour, dead stench filled his lungs and settled over him. The noxscura had to go no deeper to discover what the spire was; it came right out and told him.

Fear.

Chaos.

Destruction.

Damien stood on the parapet of the keep of Aszath Koth, looking down at the city. It should have been a comfort to see it, lights dotting the dense roadways in the dark, but there was only panic—he knew what was coming, and he couldn't stop it. A set of hands grabbed him, pulling him into a shadow. There was a face too, and though he'd had this memory before, the woman was different this time, but then it was gone.

The world around him flew by. A pinch nipped his stomach as he was translocated far from Aszath Koth and then thrown to the ground and chained there. He looked down, but his hands were small and useless. He couldn't protect himself; he couldn't do anything but cry for his mother.

And then Xander was beside him.

Damien struck out, and the vision was gone like a hand through smoke, leaving him in pitch-darkness again but with his heart racing and sweat breaking out on his neck. *Fear.* Whatever it was, it wanted him afraid, to terrorize him instead of letting him see the truth, but he knew that was just a memory, and a foggy one at best, that had pushed forward before.

The darkness changed again, but there was no vision of

his past this time; there was just the grotesque tree and his hand pressed to it, but it was sinking in. The bark melted around his fingers, swallowing up his wrist, his arm. He couldn't pull out of it; it happened too fast, and soon he was covered in it, completely absorbed.

He was inside the thing that had been a tree; he *was* the thing, it was him, and the world was a chaotic amalgam of shadows and grotesque shapes suspended between life and death, never to be escaped. Damien's mind spun, falling over and into itself, nausea roiling in his root-like guts, a scream beating at a mouthless throat, legs that no longer existed wanting so badly to flee.

And then the noxscura reminded him: He was still himself. *Pathetic*, he spat into his settling mind, though whether it was at himself or the thing's attempt, he was unsure.

Damien squeezed his eyelids shut until there were flashes of light and opened them again to see the spire and his hand, touching but separate. He looked to one side and then the other. He was alone, and the Innomina Wildwood was… gone. No, not gone. Destroyed. Reduced to burnt-out stumps, piles of ash and sludge and rot surrounding him. The ground was gray, the sky was gray, the whole world was gray, devoid of life or even its possibility in some hopeful, far-off future.

But the tree. Damien dug his fingers in, the wood giving way with a squelch. He clenched a fist around the wet pulp that had once been bark and tore it back. It ripped away like parchment, leaving a hole surrounded by dripping splinters and, in its center, a sheet of glass. No. Water? No. Blood.

Smooth, the liquid surface rose upward but did not spill out. His face was reflected in the crimson like a mirror, so stark against the grays all around, and he saw what a mess he had become, drenched in sweat, teeth bared, deep circles under his eyes, and veins pulsing blue as the noxscura drained out of him. The effort was killing him to push through the defenses of whatever this was and to remain there, to see it, to *know* it.

And it told Damien then that he did *not* want to know It.

His reflection shifted, eyes blackening, features blurring, and the face that stared back at him from the bloody pit was no longer his own but one with a too-wide smile and gaping holes for eyes. Breaking free of the tree, the blood seeped out to form clawed hands to grip the edge of the hole he'd made, the figure contorting as It birthed Itself from the rotting spire.

Stuck to the spot, Damien could only watch Its dripping and oozing neck crane, face brought just up to his own. Breath reeking of centuries of decay fell over him, hissing through a grin so pleased he could only assume It, whatever It was, had already won. And It knew.

One of Us? It asked in Key and Chthonic and Ouranic and every possible language all at once, though Its mouth never moved and Its voice was not words but the sound of buildings crumbling and bones raking over shale.

Damien's throat constricted around a gag as he opened his mouth, but he swallowed back a retch and told it "Fuck off."

Ripping himself backward, Damien's hand broke away from the spire, and he staggered out of the oozy, rotting ring.

The stench was still all over him, the voice still ringing in his ears, and the feeling—the fear, the chaos, the destruction—prodding at every bit of him.

But the birdsong was back, the wetness in the air, the life. The Innomina Wildwood was still whole save for that cursed spot, but it had seemed so real—*all* of it—even as Damien knew it wasn't. He raked his hands through his hair, pacing outside the circle, counting his steps as his boots fell on solid earth, fearing they would sink in with the next hateful step. He fell to his knees, trying to tether himself to the plane, the one he'd been born in, and not that place, not to whatever that had been.

He wished Amma were there, to hear her voice, feel her touch, even as he was glad she was far from the horror he had seen.

"What is it?" Fior's voice called, and the mania of the moment subsided enough for Damien to peer up at the others.

They were huddled together, all of them, but Kaz carefully stepped away to approach Damien. "Master?"

He touched the imp, a thing born wholly from the infernal plane, and he knew then that It was beyond even the place from where imps and demons came.

"That is an ancient evil," he said, careful, deliberate, his voice surprising him with its hoarseness. It wasn't accurate, not entirely, but it was the best explanation he had. Calmer, he stood, clasping hands behind his back to think.

Kalani stormed up to him, grasping the shoulder of his tunic and squeezing hard. "But what *is* it?"

He shifted his gaze down to her hand, and she released him, but her face demanded an answer. He hated to admit it, but the name was on the tip of his tongue, and it fell out before he could stop it. "E'nloc."

She scoffed, backing up from the ring, too close to it for comfort. Even Damien's innards squirmed standing there. "You know this thing by name?"

Damien scratched at his neck and tugged his collar. "Yes, I suppose that now, I do. Though that thing can't be It entirely, more like a tendril of It. Regardless, It needs to be banished. You would be better off with a divine mage who can manipulate luxerna, but the four of us will have to do. Come, darkness knows how long this may take."

No matter how skilled Damien ever grew to be, there were base rituals he had kept with him since childhood. There was rarely time to pull them out for use, never in battle certainly, but the older and more primitive and more time consuming, the more powerful. And power was exactly what they needed.

Damien instructed the others to gather sticks and vines from outside the rot, things newly fallen and still full of life, and to arrange them in a circle outside the spire's reach. He pulled the parchment from his pouch, the translations of the Lux Codex he had carefully been reworking to counter his own magic. He wasn't willing to risk testing it on Amma, but on this, he had no qualms. Hurting whatever It was would only be a boon.

As the witches set up the ritual, Damien was alarmed to see the ring of rot had grown. He couldn't know for sure if he was one of the Us that It questioned him about, but there was a similarity, a link to the noxscura that was still beating at his insides to go back and discover more. But It had been distilled, a purer evil, beyond even something wholly infernal like Kaz or his father, and It had fed off him. Had E'nloc been truly whole, It might have swallowed Damien completely, but there was no time to dwell on that.

When they had created a new ring of good, warm, living things around the corruption, Damien passed the parchment to the others, showing them the original spells from the Lux Codex. For hours, they discussed which to use and how to modify the spells to make up for what they lacked until finally night had fallen and they were set to begin.

Damien sliced just below his collarbone, and the blood trickled down his chest, creeping out to the circle and easing into it, filling the protective barrier they'd made with noxscura as the witches pumped their own magics in alongside it. Again, there was blackness, jolts of chaos and fear, and a heavy sense of pending destruction. He could feel the others there at the beginning, their strange earthen magic mingling with his own, but It fought back to isolate each of them, and Damien was left alone.

But he was not alone, not really. There was someone he had to return to because she told him he must, and though it had felt endless, the darkness finally cleared. The double moons hung low in the sky as dawn broke over the Innomina Wildwood. The spire collapsed in on itself, a heap of melted wood and sickly rot, and the forest was free of It.

Nell was still sitting up, eyes open but weary, while the other two had fallen backward. Soot licked Kalani's face, and the monkey tossed pebbles at Fior until both witches mumbled and stirred to confirm they were not dead, just spent.

Damien touched inside the circle, but E'nloc was gone. He lay back and closed his eyes too, falling asleep as the sun rose. When the four were whole again, they covered what was left with fallen leaves and dirt and began the long trek back to the witches' camp.

CHAPTER 22

AMMA

The Immutable
Wisdom of Trees

Every day had been the same, and every day had been frustrating. Amma was woken early to walk through the Innomina Wildwood with Em, the elder witch, asking questions but getting very roundabout nonanswers. That was a thing older people did, and Amma knew this, expecting it had something to do with the fact that there either weren't answers, or it would ultimately be more profitable to find them on her own. It was no less annoying, though, that Em wouldn't just say *that* instead of "Well, you know, a tree is a lot like a loaf of bread when you think about it," which was probably true but also definitely wasn't. Then she would change the subject, pointing out a poisonous lizard or a cluster of mushrooms that would lead to the Everdark.

Amma would spend her afternoons with a number of the other witches inside a burrow beneath the base of a tree, up in someone's incense-filled hut, or sitting in the middle of the ruins, attempting to enter into a state they called *hessach*. At first, Amma had simply sat amongst the rest of them while they were closed-eyed and motionless, minds wandering off and leaving their bodies to visit *hessach*, the place that wasn't a place. It was the state of pure arcana, they somewhat explained, and also the sound the wind made as it blew through leaves. Amma was supposed to "go" there because if she was there, she wouldn't pass out, she guessed. As the days went on, she was able to close her eyes too, to fall still, and to see things. Sort of. At least she thought it might be working, or she was slowly falling for the huge prank being pulled on her.

But it was silver things specifically that Amma was seeing, and though no one would tell her exactly what *hessach* looked like, she had enough experience with arcana to recognize magic when she saw it.

Evenings were spent trying to call up roots from the ground to form a staff, an "easy" thing, they all said, but Amma couldn't do it. She could touch flowers and make them bloom, and she could force things to grow larger and fuller, but that wasn't what the witches wanted out of her, and by the sixth day, she was beginning to worry she would never get it.

Which was rather silly—six days wasn't long enough to do anything, even for a heroine, but Amma didn't know this about herself.

When night came on that sixth day and she was to return to the small hut she stayed in alone, she opted instead to remain in the center of the ruins while the others dispersed. She'd intended to sit for only a few minutes more to watch the moons come out through the canopy, and she lay back on the mossy stone floor to wonder if she would get a handle on anything well enough to justify whatever Damien was doing out in the Wildwood. The nighttime sounds intensified, insects and frogs chirping and calling, and the dusky deep blues and greens melted into darkness behind her closing eyelids.

Amma was barefoot. Her toes gripped the earth, feeling every stick and leaf and rock against the soles of her feet. She took herself forward through the Innomina Wildwood right to the base of a liathau tree. She'd seen this one before, and while it wasn't as thick as some, it was the tallest one she had ever come across, dwarfing even the elder liathau in the Faebarrow market district.

When Amma touched its trunk, there was a crawling against her palms, itchy and weird, but she knew the unpleasantness was necessary, and she endured it for what would come next. A yellow light peeked out from under her fingertips and then shone brighter and brighter as she pulled her hands back. Like many embroidery threads, the light ran from her palms back to the tree, tethering her to it.

The brightness of the threads illuminated her naked body in the twilight, though she wasn't concerned with that. She pressed her hands to her bare chest and felt that thready light sink into her skin. It wrapped itself around her lungs, her heart, her tongue, her mind, wholly warm and blissful, and she knew she could step into *hessach*.

Then the threads went taut, and Amma was jerked forward. Tangled up in everything inside her, there was no severing them, and she panicked at their sudden, violent independence. Yanked another step closer to the tree, Amma struggled to keep her footing, her next breath shallow and sharp. A new light, crimson, was glowing from beneath her skin. Wrapped up in many thin threads, it was wrenched right up against her chest, bulging outward from between her ribs.

Amma cried out, slapping her hands to her chest, struggling to hold it in place. Pain seared through her as it was pulled, and she pushed back, trembling with the effort. Wetness bubbled up from beneath her fingers, blood seeping out and running down her stomach.

"No," she choked out, more blood flooding her mouth as the threads around her lungs and throat tightened. "You're supposed to be good," she managed in a pained whisper. "Aren't you good?"

The tree did not answer. It only stood there, massive, uncaring, bending only to the wind.

"Please, I don't want this," she rasped, pressing into herself and spitting a mouthful of blood to the ground. "You can't! Stop!"

The pressure on her chest broke all at once. She inhaled sharply, falling to her knees on the wet earth, and waited, but she wasn't dragged forward again. The golden threads detached themselves and slipped off her skin, one by one. She watched them recede toward the tree from her place in the muck and wrapped her arms around her naked body. Still covered in slick blood, there was now a scar running between her breasts, though it looked old, and she could just see the crimson light as it dimmed, sinking back where it belonged.

There was a *thwack* at Amma's side, and her eyes sprang open. Brightness blinded her from her spot on her back on the mossy stones in the middle of the ruins. Morning had come, and she hadn't moved, but she also wasn't covered in blood.

"Ready for our walk?" asked Em, a haloed shadow against the day's light.

Amma tugged her tunic down to see her chest unmarred and mumbled, "Bloody dreams," before pulling herself to her feet to begin the day.

She didn't tell Em about the dream, but she had a feeling she already knew, especially since the old woman had said she had practically become a tree herself—whatever that meant. Her gauzy eyes were brighter though, and her steps through the thick jungle were quicker.

"This magic isn't really different, is it?" asked Amma, nibbling on a nail and eyeing a cluster of teal mushrooms that seemed suspect.

"What do you mean?" Em was almost dancing as she went, tapping her staff and humming.

"All of it. Whether the gods have blessed someone or if they have demon blood or if it's the elves talking to the trees, it's all the same, right?"

"You know, that's a theory," said Em. "And when you come right down to it, you're either making something or destroying something, and there might not be a whole lot of difference between those two acts either."

Amma screwed up her face. "Are you really arguing that if I make a tree sprout out of an acorn, it's the same as if I chop one down?"

"The tree you make won't last forever—maybe it was better off as an acorn? And if you do fell one, then you're left with the space to make something new, not to mention the fallen tree to create from." Em hummed a little more. "But it's not that simple, is it?"

"Most people think it is," Amma said with a sigh. "They believe certain kinds of arcana are evil and others are good, and that's it."

Em chuckled. "Well, they're probably not right. I'd reckon you've seen some evil magics do at least a little good—I know I have. And it's not like the arcana knows what it's doing, just that it wants to *do*. It's mostly neutral."

"Neutral," Amma repeated, kicking at the ground and then falling still. There, where her boot had just mussed the tendrils of a fern, was a leaf she recognized—a pink one. Amma grabbed it up from the floor of the Innomina Wildwood, feeling every inch of it carefully, running fingers over the veins, tracing its shape, and breathing in its citrusy, floral smell. "It's real," she said, whipping toward Em and holding the leaf out. "You have to take me to it."

"To what, dear?"

"The wild liathau!" Amma's heart sprang at hearing herself say the words, the impossible idea solidifying in her mind. It had seemed ludicrous when Laurel suggested the others would search for the trees somewhere else in the realm, but now Amma was standing with the evidence in her hands. "*This* is why I'm here. The help you said I was coming for? It's not for *me*, it's for my people, in Faebarrow. We grow liathau there. Our whole survival is based around its cultivation, and our orchard was decimated. They don't grow anywhere else, that's what we've always thought, but I need seeds, and this one"—she shook the leaf—"this one will have them!"

Em took the leaf from her with weathered hands, easing fingers over it. "Liathau, you called it?"

"From Sestoth." Amma was nodding and grinning ferociously.

"This tree is here, and you are right, but there is only one, and it's so old." Em twisted her lips. "I'm unsure if it even still bears fruit."

"I don't care. I have to see it!" Amma wound her hands over one another. "Please, take me there."

Em cackled, dropping the leaf and hustling ahead. "Well, can't say no to that, and now I'm excited too."

With taps of her staff and wobbles through the Wildwood, they came to a new part of the jungle, one that was really just like the rest of it but felt fresh. Amma's heart hadn't slowed, and when she finally laid eyes on the rich, twisting bark, it nearly exploded from her chest. The wild liathau tree was real.

At its base was a ring of darkening leaves, pink and red,

spattered over the greenery like beautiful droplets of blood. This space... It felt like home.

The liathau was tall, much taller than everything around it, and the rest of the trees were already four and five stories high, the canopy dark and clustered. Em stepped right up to it, a hand on her hip, head tilted back. "Oh boy."

Amma was broken from her long look up the trunk by the woman's sigh.

"What?"

"No, no, nothing, dear. Just...go on."

Amma pressed a hand to the trunk of the tree, eyes closing, heart opening. Holy gods, it was like standing in the orchard, the sharp, sweet smell sweeping over her, and for a moment, she could hear the gentle *thunk* of harvested seeds, the chirping of sparrows, Laurel's laughter.

What do you want?

Amma's eyes almost popped open. *E-excuse me?*

What. Do. You. Want.

Amma swallowed. *Uh, hi? You're the...the liathau, right?*

Yeah, sure, what else would I be? The voice in Amma's head was not distinct, but it was there, like the words were projected onto her mind, though it was clear they were irritated, to say the least, which was rather unbecoming of an ancient, blessed tree.

Luckily, Amma had a lot of practice dealing with the easily irritated. She cleared her throat despite the fact that she wasn't speaking aloud and smiled despite the fact that she wasn't sure the tree could really see her. *Of course, so sorry to bother you, but I had to come when I saw one of your leaves in the Wildwood. I was only wondering if maybe I could trouble you for just a few of your lovely seeds?*

Seeds?

The word was like being struck right up against her head, and Amma actually staggered.

I'm over fifty thousand years old, and you want seeds?

Um, yes? Please?

Fuck off, said the tree, and Amma actually gasped, eyes popping open.

"What happened, dear?"

"The tree told me to fuck off."

Em threw her head back and cackled.

"No!" Amma snorted, slamming her palm back against the trunk. "No, I'm here for a reason." *And this is it. You have to give me some seeds; I need them. Why else would the Wildwood show itself to me? I have a duty, and this is how I'm going to fulfill it.*

The tree tsked at her even though it presumably didn't have a tongue.

Look, do you have seeds or not?

Yes, it said after a moment, begrudgingly, *but you're not equipped to—*

Amma held up her silver dagger in her other hand.

Oh, well, maybe you are. But if you want them, you're going to have to come up here and get them.

"Fine, I will." Amma pulled her hand back, sheathed her dagger on her thigh, and took another long look up the trunk as her stomach dropped. Liathau typically grew their seeds in clusters at their peaks, and she'd been climbing them to harvest since she was seven years old, but the orchard's trees never grew much more than twenty feet. *Oh boy* was right.

"Going up there?" asked Em.

"You know it," said Amma, taking a few steps back and eyeing the first branch.

"The canopy of the Wildwood is quite different from the rest of it, you know."

Amma nodded, readying herself, but something felt wrong. She looked down at her boots and quickly kicked them off until she was barefoot, feeling the ground beneath her feet. The calluses she'd developed walking across the realm helped, but her soles were still sensitive to the sharpest things as she planted her feet firmly and then sprinted for the trunk.

Jumping into a small hollow, she propelled herself upward, arms stretching and grabbing the nearest branch, and with a swing of her legs, she was up and over it, falling onto her stomach with a huge breath. Amma lifted her head and peered back down at the ground, and there was Em, only a foot or so below.

"This seemed a lot higher from down there," she said.

"Oh, it is." Em gestured with her staff and hobbled to a fallen log to sit. "I'll wait here. You take your time."

Amma glanced upward and then pushed up to stand, the bark rough underfoot. The next branch was closer, and pulling herself onto it wasn't nearly as difficult. She went on like that, carefully, just as she had done back in Faebarrow, and though this tree was narrower at its center, it had many more footholds and branches to climb up. Amma quickly found a rhythm, and by the time her arms began to ache, she finally took a look down.

Em was a dot on the earth, but Amma was still not close.

A shiver ran through her legs as she crouched on a branch and stared up the lofty trunk. Gods, what was she thinking?

Can't do it, can you?

Growling, Amma stood, looking for the next branch. Too high to be reached. She couldn't find another way up, but other plants had grown about the liathau, including thick vines that hung from the far edges of the tree. Sitting, Amma wiggled her way out onto the branch and grabbed the vine. Heavy but pliable, it was easy to loop the length over her shoulder until she had enough. She then shimmied her way back to the trunk.

Unraveling half its length, she tossed the length of vine so that it would whip around the trunk, but it insisted on only making it halfway before falling. Again and again, she tried, and it continued to only go so far. Arms already sore, she gripped the vine tighter and closed her eyes. Arcana flowed through the tendril, and she struck out a final time, the vine snapping around the trunk but clinging on, slithering over the far side of the tree, and then its end fell into her other, outstretched hand.

Holding both ends tightly, she squealed and tied them together. "Don't have anything to say about that, do you?" she asked the silent tree and ducked under the loop she'd made.

Pressing her bare feet into the trunk, she gave the vine a whip to clasp on higher and pulled herself up. Suspended, leaning back, she held herself aloft with tension, took another breath, and continued straight upward.

Amma took breaks on thick-enough branches until she came to the canopy. The world around her had grown darker with time and the denseness of the trees. Many thinner branches extended toward the liathau, their lighter-colored bark and brilliantly green leaves in contrast to the deep brown and pink she was climbing, but they were a help as she continued upward, more handholds that allowed her to abandon the vine. The branches of the liathau itself were much wider as well, and she found she could walk on them with ease, footing steadier, even finding a place where they wound around like a set of stairs.

The canopy was different, as Em had said, other plants living off the liathau, winding around and hanging by ropy tendrils, but a bright, magenta ball of fluff caught Amma's eye. Damien's warning about poison popped into her mind, paralysis this high up being especially inopportune, but she ventured closer to see.

The creature was about as big as Amma's hand, its body covered in dangerously purple fuzz. The little thing reached to its limit along the bark but got nowhere. Excess veiny skin stretched along its arms and sides like wings. Its back half was wrapped up in a thin tendril that traced back to a beautiful flower, but Amma had seen similar ones in the last week in the Wildwood and knew they were carnivorous.

"Oh dear," she said quietly, inching closer. The thing chirped when it saw her, its eyes too big for the rest of it, snout twitching madly. She could feel its panic as it struggled, gaining an inch and then being pulled back. "I'm not sure whose side I'm supposed to be on here, but…" Amma placed a finger on the tendril, avoiding the venomous creature, and there was a jolt of arcana beneath it.

The tendril recoiled, releasing the magenta rodent, and with its freedom, it squeaked triumphantly. With one look back at Amma, it spread its arms and dove off the branch, sailing through the air with that excess skin pulled taut like wings, and it disappeared into the canopy.

"Sorry," she said to the flower and continued upward.

Enveloped wholly in the liathau's smell, Amma stretched her arms overhead, trying to loosen her aching shoulders. She'd climbed a bit more and had to be close, so she took a break against a limb that bent upward. There was relief in her muscles at the shifting pressure of the limb on her back as if someone were giving her a massage.

But trees didn't rub backs.

Amma twisted around and nearly fell right out of the tree. A plated body slithered past, as thick as her torso. Mesmerized by its length and the muscles rippling under the green scales as it undulated away, she stood stupidly for far too long, and then there was a hiss.

Tongue, jaws, fangs. Amma screamed and ducked, scrambling over the branch and away from the snake whose head was big enough to swallow her whole without even unhinging.

There was a blur of movement beside her, and she jumped away from it, across a gap in the branches. Amma landed on a thinner branch that bobbed under her weight, arms flapping to stay aloft, bare foot sliding and then catching.

Heartbeat in her throat, she crouched low just as the snake struck over her head. Its sinuous body caught on the branch that was her next target, and she changed course, springing away and toward the trunk of the liathau. Which, of course, left her nowhere to go.

Amma spun, grabbing the strap of her crossbow and pulling the weapon over her shoulder. Releasing an arrow from where it was stored, her hands worked on instinct as her eyes followed the snake coiling slowly over dark brown bark and between pink and red leaves until it pulled the entirety of its monstrous length up and away.

Back pressed to the trunk, Amma gulped at the air fast and hard, crossbow lifted, ready in arms that somehow remained steady. She scanned the leafy canopy, a spattering of colors that the huge creature too easily blended into. The birds had scattered, but there were other sounds, louder than they should have been, and then silence.

Maybe it had gone. Maybe the snake had only been frightened and would leave her be.

Or maybe it was determined to make Amma its next meal.

Amma shrieked again as the diamond-shaped head dropped down just before her, unhinging its jaw and striking. She squeezed with precision, though, and her arrow connected with the thing's throat. The snake stopped mid-strike, its hiss cut off, dropping but not dead.

Sprinting away, Amma grabbed for another arrow. There was a branch, one that was too far up to jump to, but she tried anyway, kicking off the trunk, and somehow there was bark beneath her feet. Like steps forming themselves as she went, the tree molded itself to where she needed to be as she dashed upward and slammed another arrow into place. The snake struck out again, and she squeezed off another shot mid-run, this one less measured, and it didn't hit.

Amma swore and kept running. She darted down a branch and dove off toward another, foot landing with a snap, and then there was nothing as she fell.

Throwing her free arm out, she clutched the closest vine, the thick tendril pulling free and ensnaring her back. Amma's body swung, jerked through the air as the vine went taut before she slammed into the liathau's trunk. Pain burst up her spine, stars in her eyes, and her shoulder twinged as she hung from one arm. The crossbow was still strapped to her and in hand, but she had no way to load another arrow as she dangled like a piece of fruit, ready to be plucked and devoured.

Glinting scales caught the filtered light as the serpent's head rose up from below. Slowly, it twisted its head as if to show her the arrow that still pierced its throat. Amma groaned and dropped the weapon to let it dangle from her back, useless now.

The snake hissed, jaws lengthening as its eyes bored into her. Amma reached backward, swinging herself in a last effort to scramble away, clawing at the bark and wishing she could stop the fangs that drew nearer to piercing her.

Rough wood pressed hard against her palm, and she wrapped her fingers tightly around a new weight. Yanking her arm back, she discovered she was holding a staff. Beautiful, twisted, and as dark as the liathau's bark, it was dotted in tiny pink leaves, and in its deepest fissures, the slightest glint of something silver and liquid.

She would have liked to marvel at the arcane staff for hours, to celebrate herself for finally conjuring it, to throw her arms in the air and shriek with joy, but…fangs.

Amma thrust her arm forward just as the serpent snapped its jaws. Fangs cut through the air like arrowheads at her sides, the wet heat from its mouth spraying her as the staff caught. Amma hung there, legs pulled upward, and the snake recoiled, mouth stuck open. The staff bowed but refused to break. Wrenching its head back and forth with a furious confusion, the snake's body slipped, its weight pulling it downward in its tumultuous writhing.

Amma saw her chance, swinging her other hand upward. The tree reached out, bidden by her arcana, to lift her to the next branch, and she broke free of the vines to run. The greenery all shifted to pink as she sprinted upward, through the crisscrossing, thinner branches, until there was a bright speck of light ahead. Amma was breathing heavily, her muscles sore, but her heartbeat propelled her toward the light.

Breaking through the final layer, Amma's head crested the leaves, and she fell still. Her lungs filled with air so cold her throat began to seize—and the sight was enough to take the rest of her breath away.

Trees stretched on for miles, the greenery bending in the wind like a gentle sea. The sky was brilliantly blue, clouds rolling in it, fluffy and white, and far off were mountains, misty in the distance. Despite her fear seconds earlier, Amma was filled with the deep serenity of the earth spread out before her, the distance to be covered, and what she had already passed through, so much seen, so much still to see, and then *death*.

The serpent burst forth from the canopy, maw gaping. Amma shrieked and ducked back beneath the safety of the leaves, and the snake crashed down behind her, sanctuary obliterated. Her bare feet steadily gripped the branch as she sprinted toward the liathau's center and whirled around, crossbow in hand. Treading backward, she loaded the bow with her last arrow and aimed, shoulders slamming into the trunk. There was the snake, undulating toward her, jaw open. And then it froze.

Amma waited, breath held as the snake twitched, its thick rope of a body sliding sideways, weight shifting in a strange way. Then its head fell forward, not striking but collapsing, slamming down onto the branch and nearly knocking Amma off with the vibration.

She pushed back into the liathau trunk, nowhere to go, but the serpent was already doing the going for her. Its body lost its tight coil around the branch as if it had no control over itself, and once the middle of its weight had slid off, the rest could only follow until the entirety of the huge serpent fell right out of the tree.

Amma dropped to her knees to watch the snake fall as if dead, slamming into every unavoidable limb as it went until its limp body was swallowed up by the trees. Arrow still loaded, she glanced at her weapon, then out at the canopy before her. A tiny magenta speck stuck out from the dappled green, sailing off with those veiny wings. She gasped, looking back to where the snake had fallen, paralyzed.

Paralysis this far up was definitely no good.

The snake's body had made quite a bit of noise as it fell, so Amma was unworried about Em still on the ground, but once the sound of snapping limbs was gone, she turned back to the trunk and blew out a breath, looking at it expectantly.

Yes, all right, they're just over here, she heard the tree say, the voice coming right up through her feet. Amma found the small cluster of seeds, three of them, and she wiggled with joy at the sight. Ripping off the bottom of her tunic, she used her silver dagger to carefully collect the seeds and tie them up, placing them in her pouch, and then she finally sat.

Teary-eyed, she placed both hands on the liathau but spoke aloud. "You don't know how much this means to me."

Yes, I do. I know more things than you could ever imagine: I'm fifty thousand years old!

Amma clicked her tongue but chuckled and gave the branch a pat. "Regardless, thank you."

Don't thank me yet, said the tree. *You still have to get down.*

Amma grimaced and groaned, moving to stand.

Ah, ah, wait just a minute. Isn't there something you're forgetting?

There was a tug in her chest as if an extra weight there were being pulled downward. "The talisman," she said, dread balling up around her heart, the sensation strange but not misplaced.

Shall we?

Amma slapped a hand over where she had dreamed the slice had been. The panic that flooded her veins eclipsed even the panic of becoming snake food. "Tomorrow," she squeaked out, standing. "I'll come back, and we can, um…we can do it then?"

The tree sniffed even though it didn't have a nose. *No bark off my trunk either way.*

Amma was exhausted and achy, but her descent to the forest floor was quicker than the climb. She tried very hard not to think about what the tree had offered and tried even harder not to linger on the fact that she had declined. Only until tomorrow, though, she told herself. In the back of her mind, there was a sound like laughter, but it was only the rustling of leaves.

CHAPTER 23

AMMA

Well-Placed Exposition

It was evening when Amma returned to the witches' camp, and she was completely sapped. The only thing she would have liked more than taking a long soak in a bath and crawling into the comfort of a big, fluffy bed would have been to see Damien, but when she and Em hobbled across the mossy stones of the ruins, there was still no sign of the party that had set out a week prior.

Too tired to join the others amid their evening meal, Amma simply ravaged a piece of fruit on her way to the private hut she'd been given for her stay. Two monkeys were chasing one another around the tree's base, and she tossed them the rind of her fruit, wiping at her mouth before ascending. She pulled off her crossbow as she pushed through the vines that covered the entry. She didn't want to think about what she intended to do the next day, but the sooner she went to sleep, the sooner Damien would return. It had to be soon; he'd been gone so long.

It was dark inside with the sun down, and she placed her crossbow against the wall, yawning with a hand over her face, and when she dropped her arm, there, bare-chested and rubbing a linen against wet hair, stood Damien. His eyes fell on her, and then he smiled, really, truly smiled in that rare way that lit up her insides.

Amma sprinted across the hut faster than when she had a giant serpent on her heels, then pounced. As she threw her arms around him, Damien stumbled only a step, inhaling sharply, then fell very still. She hung from his neck, feet scrambling as they scuffed the floor, squeezing relentlessly with her head buried in the crook of his shoulder, all while the realization of her overeagerness set in. *Oh gods*, she thought, *what am I doing?*

And then the linen fell to the floor, and Damien's arms pressed in around her middle as he bent to embrace her fully. His skin was warm, still slightly damp, and it smelled so good, she sighed right up against his neck, body melting to his. Damien clung more tightly then, fingers curling into her sides. He took a deep breath, the expansion of his chest pressing into her.

Amma's body flushed, warmth running from the center of her chest and into every limb. They'd never embraced like this, never touched one another so intimately without almost immediately pulling out of it, yet it felt exactly right.

I missed you ran through her mind, unable to be spoken when the words mingled so complexly with the more amorous ones. *I want you.* She reluctantly leaned back to look at him but didn't let go. No one had told her what he had been away doing, only that it was dangerous, but she could see a change on his face. He was exhausted, that much was clear, and perhaps relieved as well, but there was something else.

It had only been seven days they'd spent apart, but each night she'd thought of him, imagined hearing his breath beside her as he fell asleep, recalled those violet eyes, that knowing grin, the painful-looking scar she had come to adore. His face had burned itself into her mind, and now that it was before her again, she knew something had changed.

"What happened?" she asked, voice a whisper as she touched his cheek.

He turned ever so slightly into her palm. "Oh, nothing, only a bit of banishment," he said, voice a rumble. "Have they been good to you here?"

The threat in his tone sent a shiver through her. "Yes, of course. And were they kind to you, or do I need to put a crossbow bolt between someone's eyes?"

He let out a single low laugh. "Darkness, no, but be careful with those offers—I might concoct some falsehood just to see you do it." Damien's grip on her tightened, the mischievous grin melting off his face. "It certainly wasn't like being with you though."

She slid her fingers up over his temple and into his hair, gently gripping and pulling him closer. "If you hadn't come back…" she heard herself saying, voice cracking and trailing off, unsure how she could explain the hollowness in her chest at just the thought of him not returning.

If he hadn't returned, she would be free of him, of the villain who had her arcanely chained to his side, so how had it come to this? To getting absolutely everything she needed—the Brineberth soldiers run out of her home, her pending wedding struck from possibility, seeds from a wild liathau to repopulate the orchard—and feeling as though none of it mattered if she didn't have what she *wanted*. If she didn't have *him*.

A shadow shot in through the small, frond-covered window at the front of the hut with a shrill cry, and the two started. There was a scraping of talons on wood as a mess of feathers came to land on a table just inside, a raven skidding to a stop and nearly toppling over the edge. Wings spread, it ruffled itself and gave a final indignant croak before it fell still.

"Wonderful bloody timing," Damien grumbled, straightening as his hands came off Amma. A chill replaced where they had been. "Corben, you look awful."

The bird cawed in protest as a roll of parchment fell from his beak. His mouth remained open as he panted, and even as his feathers relaxed, he did look a bit chunkier than when last they'd seen him. Corben's plumage wasn't quite as full as before either, and the hop he attempted was very short.

Amma clasped her hands behind her to keep from grabbing Damien again as he left her side. Seeing him barechested made it even harder, but then he retrieved his tunic from the foot of the bed and, disappointingly, pulled it on, and Amma was able to refocus on the raven. "He does look a little different. Does that mean something went wrong?"

Damien had reached out for the bit of rolled-up parchment on the table but hesitated, eyes flicking back to her and brows knit. "Are you prepared to find out?"

She nodded, hurrying to stand beside him and assess the bird.

He unraveled the small parchment, eyes flicking over the writing. Amma squinted at it, but it definitely wasn't Laurel's messy handwriting; it wasn't even in Key. Damien groaned. "Is it time again? Seems we just had one." He rolled it back up and stuck it in a pocket.

"Wait, what is that?"

"Just a...well, it's sort of an invitation, or perhaps more like a summons."

"To?"

"Yvlcon," he said simply, like she should know what that meant. "Parchment's enchanted though, so it may come in handy. Corben's return to us was at least partially deterred fetching that. Now, are you ready?"

He held out a hand, and she took it, and with his other, he ran fingers through the raven's feathers. A familiar tingling sensation ran up her arm and into her mind, and Amma had the distinct feeling of walking back through the doors of Faebarrow keep as words followed in Laurel's bright but sharp voice.

Well, I hope this is how this is supposed to work, but you should know I've never talked to a crow like this before but—oh, okay! A raven, yes, so sorry, sir. What was I—oh, Amma! I am so upset I missed your exit! The drama of it all, my gods, I am going to need all the details when we see one another next! I, of course, never doubted for a moment that you were completely fine, but I didn't let on. I even faked a quite convincing swoon at the news, and you can guess who I made catch me.

Laurel's laughter lit up Amma's mind, and both she and Damien snorted out "Tia," simultaneously.

But anyway, things here are actually going shockingly well. Those skeletons cleaned out almost every single Brineberth bastard, and get this—they'd kill one of the soldiers, and then the body would just stand up and join the horde. It was amazing! Cedric did unfortunately figure out how to get out of the city without getting stabbed in the dick, the rotten, fucking asshole, but a lot of them didn't. Small victories, you know? All the undead soldiers are still here, by the way, but without anybody left to fight, they're just kind of hanging around. It was weird at first and a little spooky too, but they do whatever Tia says, and she just started giving them mundane jobs, and turns out they're a lot of help, not just watching the wall but with everything. I even taught one to sew for me, and it's hard to tell when they don't have skin or anything, but I think he's enjoying it.

Damien's brow pinched like he wasn't sure whether to be pleased or not.

Tia's pretty good at bossing people around, as you know, and it doesn't seem to matter if they're dead or not, and with the added help, Faebarrow's doing okay except for, ya know, the no-trees thing. I got that sapling to Nicholas after we got him out of prison, and I told him I'd kill him if he didn't take really good care of it, but I didn't tell him how, so he's extra anxious, but the baby tree is doing great. Your mother and father are predictably flustered and flaky, and they're a total mess about you being gone again, but I know I can't tell them you're safe, which is, like, really eating away at me or whatever, as you can imagine. I'm fine, I just miss you! And so does Perry, of course. He's hemming and hawing about the Osurehm exams, but you know I'll get him there one way or another. Anyway, I think that's everything.

Damien sighed and opened his mouth, but Amma held up a finger for him to wait.

Oh, right, one more thing! Tell Sir Scary-Surname that someone got into Cedric's quarters before me and practically cleaned the whole place out. I only found this half a parchment with writing on it I can't read, but I've got it, so don't worry. And tell him I know he's not going to do anything nefarious to you, but you better do something nefarious to him, and remember every detail because I hear blood mages use their tongues to—

"Oh, by Sestoth, Laurel!" Amma squeaked, covering up whatever profane thing she had said. Damien's eyes didn't leave the bird, but his smirk grew.

Well, I think that's actually everything. Bring me home something exciting next time, okay?

Amma chuckled, heat leaching out of her face. "They're all fine," she said in a breath. "I thought—"

Laurel's voice broke into Amma's mind again. *You're still here? Go on, go back to Amma! Take her my message!*

Damien clicked his tongue. "Hmm, I suppose I forgot that it takes some arcana to actually send Corben on his way."

Still here? Laurel's voice groaned. *You've got to be getting hungry, huh? Here, have some of this. Oh, you like sweet rolls? I have plenty!*

Corben's feathers fluffed, his chunkiness making a bit more sense.

Well, it's not that I don't like you here, but this is Perry, and he's going to send you on your way.

Amma giggled, and then there was Perry's voice, quiet and questioning: *I-I am?*

At this, Corben shook his head and croaked as if to signal there was no more to be heard.

"It seems your acolyte indeed figured things out. Maybe he'll make a better priest than I imagined," said Damien, removing his hand from the raven. It shook its thick neck and hopped in place.

"Perry used infernal arcana? Wait, no, you said Corben's actually divine, didn't you?" She reached down to scratch along the raven's fluffy neck, and he gently nibbled at her finger.

"He's not really any one thing." Damien ran his thumb up Corben's chest to reveal the one white feather nestled in and hidden by the others. Then the raven actually pecked at his hand. "Excuse you, that was not meant to be an insult."

Corben hopped closer to Damien and snapped at the pouch on his hip.

"What? What could you possibly want?"

Amma went to a small cabinet and pulled out the remains of a loaf of bread. "Probably food. He worked so hard."

"Well, he's not an actual raven. He's an amalgam of arcana and the idea of—"

Corben snatched the piece from Amma and gobbled it down.

"Dark gods, you greedy little monster. Haven't you gotten fat enough?"

Amma snickered. "Actually, I have a job for him that might help." She dug into her pouch and pulled out the ripped-up bit of tunic tied in a bundle and held it like a sacred thing for Damien to see. "Guess what I found."

His thin brows raised.

"Liathau seeds."

"What? You didn't. How? I thought they were a gift from your goddess? Wait, did you actually conjure them? Amma, this is—"

His excitement made her laugh. She waved a hand at him to stop. "No, no, I just climbed a tree and got them. There was a snake in it, but nothing I couldn't handle. Do you think Corben can take these to the greenhouse in Faebarrow?"

Damien looked as though he didn't entirely believe her but nodded, and he threaded a hand back into the raven's feathers, the other taking hers. The rush of magic that filled Amma then was so like being home, even without Laurel's voice, that she nearly cried. Corben left them with the small sack gripped safely in his talons, and then, when they were alone, the two turned to one another.

"I do hope that was...satisfactory," said Damien.

She nodded, smiling so wide it hurt her face. Just hearing Laurel's voice, and Perry's to boot, had brought such joy to her heart, let alone what she'd been told. "The barony sounds safe, Cedric's gone, and if the remaining liathau have some time and special care, they might be okay, and you"—her breath caught as she swallowed back the lump in her throat—"you did that."

"No, I only assisted *you*."

Amma shook her head, biting her lip, heart racing. There was no use in hiding her eagerness for him anymore, and Laurel had said it as plainly as anything anyway. She closed the space between them, no longer needing corked-up confidence. Amma had noticed a change in Damien, but she too had changed in their short time apart, and now she felt truly free. And what good was freedom if it wasn't put to use?

"Bloodthorne!" a voice called loudly from down in the broken ruins outside. "Show yourself!"

CHAPTER 24

DAMIEN

Tracking and Trespassing

I F DAMIEN HAD ROLLED his eyes any harder, they would have fallen out of his head and bounced right down into the Abyss—at least that's what his father would have said.

He was going to kill them this time, pity be damned. Irritating him was bad enough, but the Righteous Sentries' latest interruption would absolutely prove to be their last, not least of all because the ravenous look Amma was giving him had shifted right off her face at hearing their voices. He could already see the Sentries in his mind, mangled corpses floating in pools of blood in the last light of the evening down in the ruins below. He dropped the frond and whipped away from the small window in the hut to pull on his leathers.

"How did they find us *here*?" Amma was bent at the waist,

peeking around the edge of the window. Her skin was still flushed, and she was breathing in that way that made Damien feel like a predator going after a small animal. He almost dropped his armor right there and pulled off his tunic again but shook the temptation to pounce on her away.

"Oh, who bloody knows. Luck has apparently smiled upon them, but it will prove to be misfortune when I'm finished." He strapped on his bracer, ensuring his dagger was in place, then paused. How *had* they found them? The group was little more than bumbling idiots playing at being heroes. They couldn't track a query in the middle of an open field, much less through the Wilds and into the Innomina Wildwood.

"They're getting a little cranky," warned Amma, gnawing on her nails.

Damien hopped over on one foot, pulling a boot on the other. She'd moved just enough of the dangling leaves away to reveal the ruins below. That elven mage had called up a ball of fire in his palm, bright and licking dangerously high; the knight's sword was glowing with that ridiculous holy light; and their priestess was even looking more confident, the three of them standing back-to-back in the center of the ruins. Predictably, their sneaky one was nowhere to be seen.

Damien yanked the last strap of his armor with a grunt. What if they'd shown up even half a day sooner, before he had returned, and gotten their hands on Amma? He had spent enough time apart from her for a lifetime—*no one* was taking her away from him again. He balled a fist and there was already noxscura there, pliable and hot in his hand.

At the edge of the ruins, Kalani appeared, her staff held defensively and glowing at its end. The set of identical witches stepped in from the opposite side, hands empty but looking menacing with their dead eyes and stiff postures. The Righteous Sentries called out that they were looking for Damien specifically and that the tribe of witches violated orders of the realm by harboring a criminal.

"We don't serve the realm," called Kalani, and Soot padded up beside her from the shadows, ears back and hackles raised.

Beside him, Amma's skin was warm as she placed a hand on his arm. He swallowed, looking down at it, then to her. "I don't want anyone getting killed because of me," she said, words laced with the same delicacy as her fingers on his sleeve. "No one else, not over a misunderstanding."

Fuck, why did she have to go and say a thing like that? As if she knew exactly what he meant to do and the power her words held over those actions. "But..." He sighed. *I really want to* was perhaps not the most stalwart thing to say at that moment, even though it was exactly what ran through his mind.

The small shake of Amma's head was all he needed.

"Fine." He couldn't manage to keep the drip of disappointment out of his words. "But stay hidden here. I will see to defusing the situation."

Amma gave him a wary look but then nodded. He hadn't proven himself a good negotiator in their history, but before Amma, he'd worked his way out of worse situations. Anger never helped, but cold calculation did, and he paused in the hut's doorway to collect his thoughts. If nothing else, he needed to find out how the Sentries found them so it wouldn't happen again. And then, perhaps, reason with them.

Stepping through the thick vines, Damien scanned the ruins below. Four enemies, one still unseen, six potential allies, depending on which way the witches would be swayed, and Amma hidden. Kaz was included in that number, still disguised as a monkey at the base of the tree, watching with big eyes.

The elven mage saw Damien first, pointing with the flameless hand but not releasing the spell. He'd learned something at least. "Bloodthorne!"

"Hello," he drawled, waving with a play at amicability as he slowly took the bent pieces of bark that served as steps down along the trunk to meet them.

"Where is she?" spat the knight, sword raised.

"Who?" Damien clasped his hands behind his back and tried to stand as unmenacingly as possible, difficult at his height and with his natural demeanor. His eyes swept over the lot, catching Fior's leery glance as the man stepped into the ruins. That was one ally tipping away from him already.

"The Lady Avington," the knight called as if they'd all forgotten. "You absconded with her nearly a moon ago from Brineberth."

Damien shrugged. "No, no, I never absconded with anyone from *Brineberth*—in fact, I've never even been there. But how *did* you find me out here in the Wilds?"

"What's going on, blood mage?" Kalani's smooth voice was not as accusatory as her words could have been. She cocked a brow, standing tall and jutting her chin out.

"A misunderstanding," he said, echoing Amma's words, though he wanted to say it was idiocy and blind loyalty that led to the current annoying situation. He paced a few steps around the edge of the ruins as casually as possible. The three of them shifted right along with his movements but still held their attacks. Arcana was heavy in the air.

"He's a criminal and a kidnapper," the priestess, Pippa, said, voice only shaking a little. "Whatever he's told you is undoubtedly a lie."

Damien felt the witches turn toward him, some expectant, some critical. Apparently, banishing the greatest evil he'd ever come into contact with as a favor wasn't enough to gain their full trust, nor was their opportunity to spend uninterrupted time with the supposed abductee. He groaned, focusing on Kalani and squeezing a fist around the noxscura to keep it at bay. "Again, things are not entirely as they appear. These... *fine* adventurers have been sold a bill of goods from a questionably righteous marquis and have been following me—the how of which I am very interested in, if I might say again."

"We had help," the knight announced with a stark laugh.

"Help?"

Pippa made a face at the knight, and the mage cleared his throat. "Your help," the elf clarified. "You left a trail of infernal arcana easy enough to follow for someone with my adept skills." It was then that Damien realized he wasn't holding his book, but it was hanging from a chain on his belt instead, the weight of which threw him slightly off-kilter.

Damien sniffed. The ring in the forest that had resulted from his...*tantrum* was bad enough, but this was something else entirely. He'd made himself trackable? And by these idiots? Basest beasts, what was happening to him? He rolled the arcana in his fingers just for comfort, just to know it was there and that he still commanded it.

"We have no evidence of misdeeds here," Kalani finally said, reasonable as she tended to be, brows knitting as she looked at Damien. "In fact, just the opposite, albeit shrouded. Why don't we let the evidence speak for itself?"

She wanted to bring Amma out, and as much as the Righteous Sentries were total fools, they were all ready to attack, as were the witches, and he didn't want to pull Amma into the center of that.

"Safety," he said.

"Or her imprisonment?" Kalani frowned at him. Too reasonable. Damn it.

The arcana in Damien's hand flared. He was not imprisoning Amma, and he had come to abhor the idea, but it was an incredibly difficult thing to argue.

Especially since he actually sort of was.

His heartbeat sped up, his nerves not letting him think straight. A well-aimed spell would blind the three Sentries, all bunched up so close, and Amma had only asked they not die—she'd said nothing about maiming them. He could follow up with a few broken bones, maybe slice off a limb or two, if only to slow future pursuit. And it might be fun to make them choose which they would be forced to lose.

The three stood there, still poised to strike but holding back. That was out of character as well, especially for the big bastard in full plate. He glared at them each in turn, but when he got to Pippa, he saw that her eyes were just darting back to him. She'd been glancing up at the hut—the hut where Amma was hidden.

Damien wheeled around, raising a fist full of arcana. There on the top step stood a shadow brandishing a weapon. Before he could react, the vines in the hut's doorway were swept aside, and Amma stood there with her crossbow raised, tip of its arrow an inch from the sneaky one's nose. The Righteous Sentries' thief threw up her hands, and she jerked backward. Amma advanced on her to keep the weapon—the thief's own stolen weapon—at an unmissable distance.

"That's my girl," Damien murmured, satisfaction running like arcana through his veins as he closed his fist around his magic again. After seeing how steadily Amma held the weapon, he'd kill every last person in the whole of the Wilds just for a brief moment alone with her.

"He's enthralling her!" called out the priestess, and a ball of white light burst forth from the symbol she wore, straight at Damien. He enveloped himself in arcane smoke just as there were other flashes—the mage's fire, Kalani's spell, the glint of the knight's sword, a gust of infernal fire as Kaz scurried up—before everything went dark.

Damien dismissed the shield quickly, needing to see the

aftermath, but the knight stood before him. Impossibly fast, the man brought his blade down, arcana crackling behind it. Damien ducked away, but his blood was spilled from a painful gash that should never have been able to cut so deeply, let alone land.

But then blood was exactly what Damien needed. He swept a hand down the burning slice and actualized blades to throw at the armored man, carving into the plate and knocking his heavy form back onto his ass.

The mage was next, far off but calling up more fire. Kaz shifted course to take the brunt of his spell, but when the imp hurled himself at the elf, the priestess intervened with a fire of her own. The spell was white hot and full of divinity, knocking Kaz to the ground and causing him to skid into one of the ruin's broken columns so that it crumbled around him.

Damien's anger flared as a searing and foreign pain ran up his arm. He called up a strangling darkness around the two casters. Hemming them in with shadows, hearing them both cry out, seeing the fear in their eyes before it was blotted out—it was utterly delightful. Darkness squeezed them from both sides, and they gasped, the mage scrambling for his book and the priestess for her symbol, but he trapped their arms, crushing them, bending them just to the point of breaking.

But no—death wasn't what Amma wanted.

"Damn it." Damien called back the shadows, and the two collapsed. From the corner of his eye, there was a glint of metal, and the knight was almost right on top of him again, ready to cleave him in two. He moved to raise his arm and call up his own arcane sword, but an agonizing pulse through his shoulder blinded him with pain.

Damien staggered, breath catching, his own magic twisting inside him, uncooperative. With the knight still advancing, he would have to do the cowardly thing and run from the sword that had already dealt him a potentially fatal blow.

"Enough!"

The ground rumbled, and Damien's attempt to flee the knight's longsword was halted, his boots caught in place, followed quickly by his arms. He'd be sliced right in two if he couldn't get away, the only option left to cast, but the sword never came, and the spell fell away from Damien's palm in confusion when he saw the knight frozen before him, trapped in a tangle of vaguely familiar vines. He looked down to see that he too was trapped in those same thick, green tendrils. They were even sprouting flowers.

The elderly witch woman was standing at the base of the tree Amma and the sneaky Righteous Sentries member had just descended. Her staff was pulsing, and where its base touched the earth, hundreds of veinlike roots were crawling away, the source of what held Damien and the knight as well as the priestess and the mage. Amma was still holding up the last of them with her crossbow, but the old woman shook her head, and both slowly put down their weapons, each taking a step back. Behind the last Sentries member, Fior showed up, poking his staff into her back, and she fell still.

"Now, what is all this, dear?" the witch asked, much more politely than the others deserved.

Amma slipped her crossbow over her shoulder. "They're here to bring me back to where they think I belong, but I don't want to go."

"She's enthralled," called out Pippa again hoarsely.

"I am *not*," Amma snapped back, a venom to her voice that made it feel as though the vines around Damien had tightened. She took a breath and focused back on the old woman. "I'm not, you know this," she said, the softness settling back into her words as she touched her own chest. "But it may be ordered by the crown of Eiren that I return."

Damien's heart raced, arcana crackling at his fingertips, though weaker than it should have been.

"We don't answer to your crown," said Kalani. She was nursing her arm as if she'd been injured. "The Wilds are exactly that, and they are our only mistress."

"I know, but the crown won't see it that way. We brought this to you, and we should take it away. I'm sorry." Amma bit her lip, blinking over at Damien, then back. "Just give us a head start."

The old woman's thick brows rose, skin wrinkling around them fiercely.

"You shouldn't be forced to get involved, but I need this last favor from you. Let us leave, and hold them. They can follow right after, just let us be gone first."

The witches traded glances across the ruins. Many more of them were holding staffs, keeping the vines in place. Amma carefully walked through them, past the bound-up mage and priestess, past Damien and the knight, and to where Kaz had fallen. He was in his imp form, but his red skin had lost its brightness, and when she scooped him up, he was limp and groaning. Amma cradled him to her like she had the infant back in Durendreg, and he didn't protest.

"Yeah, okay, we can do that," the old woman said, shrugging at the others.

"You're interfering," the mage warned, whiny voice pained.

"And you're trespassing," Kalani replied, the tip of her staff glowing as the vines around the elven man tightened. "If you just disappeared out here, no one would know."

The vines about Damien loosened, and feeling flooded back into his arms and legs, though he wished it wouldn't; his injured bicep was so painful he actually reeled. He rolled his shoulders, anxiously noting the wound still wept, and gave the knight a sideways glance. A vein bulged in the man's neck as he growled. As awful as the wound felt, that made it sting a little less. But then his eyes trailed down to the weapon that had managed to injure him and the arcana pulsing through it. He hadn't come up with that on his own, nor had the priestess—they had help.

Amma went quickly to Damien, turning back to the others. "Thank you," she said, voice shaking as she rubbed Kaz's back. "Thank you for everything."

The old woman nodded to her, nearly hidden eyes shifting to Damien in the dark and then away.

Amma turned, free hand grabbing Damien's good arm and tugging, and they slipped into the thick line of trees beyond the ruins.

It was immediately much darker with such dense cover, and the night sounds of the Innomina Wildwood came up all around them. From behind, the glow of the ruins still shone, but with every quick step away, it lessened until only the moons lit the way when they chanced to break through the trees. Damien didn't like the dangers the Wilds presented when they weren't being chased by a small band of idiotic mercenaries, but now, at night and with his wound not healing, their odds seemed impossible.

Yet Amma was determined, her hand wrapped securely around his wrist, pulling him along. Kaz blinked his eyes open over her shoulder, coming back into consciousness. "Master, I have failed you." His voice was weak, the divine spell that had hit him taking a much bigger toll than anything the priestess had ever cast before.

Damien shook his head, understanding more than he could say, and the imp closed his eyes again, head falling lax on Amma's shoulder. "We should stop and discuss this," he said carefully to her.

Amma glanced back in the darkness but made no move to halt. "We can't. I don't know how much time they'll give us."

"Exactly." He stumbled over a root, struggling to keep his footing, nausea roiling in his gut at the pain that jolted up his arm and was beginning to prod at his chest. "We need a plan. Anything could be out here, and I don't think we'll be able to outrun those morons."

"We don't need to. We just have to hide."

Damien retched, and not just from the pain he was still

trying to ignore. "Amma, I do not hide." He peered into the shadows for moving creatures or shining eyes, but she had them moving too quickly to tell in the dark. "And unfortunately, those imbeciles have somehow found a way to track me, so I do not think I *can* hide."

"I know, I heard them, but I have an idea." She turned sharply, and the ground began to slope downward. Her footing was impressively steady as they went, though Damien stumbled a second time, trying to keep up.

"Perhaps you could be sweet enough to enlighten me?"

The ground leveled out, and Damien blew out a relieved breath. There was a faint glow ahead. Amma led them toward it and finally came to a stop, a small cluster of mushrooms at her feet. She spied another group of the shining fungus and went to it. "It may be a little...challenging," said Amma as she reached a larger cluster of mushrooms.

Damien swallowed hard, casting the spell to search his surroundings for the blood of other creatures so weakly it was useless, though it should have been simple. "This is no time for a challenge, Amma."

In the dark, the Innomina Wildwood all looked the same, but Amma had brought him to a spot that was slightly brighter, blue mushrooms clustered about to form a ring that the two had entered, a tree standing in its center. There was a smell, like well-spiced meats but with an undercurrent of something unpleasantly sweet, and when Damien squinted into the dark, the shadows moved like they were in a gentle wind even though the air was stagnant.

"I know it might be a questionable idea," said Amma, releasing his wrist and kneeling at the base of the tree as she shifted which shoulder Kaz lay against, "but we could use the Everdark."

"Oh, fuck." The realization of what they stood in hit him all at once, eyes falling on the pitch-black hollow she knelt before, shocked he hadn't sensed the intensity of the shifting magic sooner. Again, he tried to ignore the wetness still dripping down his arm.

"Em has been pointing the portals out to me," she explained, staring into the unending darkness at the tree's base like she couldn't look away. "She says they close behind anyone who enters them. We won't be followed if we go in."

"Portals like this close so you can't get back out," he scoffed. "It's another plane, Amma, and it's bloody dangerous. I should be leading those idiots away, and you should take Kaz and go back to the witches, where it's safe. If the Sentries are only able to track me, I can lead them out of the Wilds at the very least, and—"

"No." Amma reached up and grabbed his hand once more. "We're not separating."

The squeeze of her fingers was almost painful, but it was adamant. "It *is* dangerous though," Damien reiterated, softer. "Magic is different there, and the fae are different—they don't know death like we do—and when we find our way out, we could end up anywhere in existence. *If* we find our way out."

Amma had set her jaw hard, staring up at him with her

obstinate and beautiful face under a pall of silvery moonlight. "We will find our way out. When it's safe."

It was absolutely foolish, but Damien believed her.

A branch snapped in the darkness beyond them, and be it one of the Righteous Sentries or something bearing fangs and talons, it made Amma tug Damien to his knees beside her, and they both moved toward the hollow. He hated that it was their only choice, but with his unmending wound and the forest's looming threats, he supposed the fae could be somehow less bad. If they were lucky, they could immediately find an exit and be sent back in the realm somewhere too far for the Reckless Simpletons to catch up.

"It's going to be a tight fit," mused Damien, squinting at the narrow tunnel.

"Well, if experience has taught me anything," said Amma, handing Kaz over to him, "a little preparation makes a world of difference." She pressed a hand to the apex of it, and the edges of the entrance actually swelled wider, the tree groaning loudly into the other sounds of the night. Amma gestured for him to go first.

Damien laid Kaz over his shoulder and, on all fours, with excruciating pain up his injured arm, went forward into the darkness. The ground was wet and soft under his hands as he angled downward, and the meaty smell intensified, undercut by a sweetness like overripe fruit, yet it made him nearly salivate. Fae magic, he thought and pushed the hunger out of his mind. On his shoulder, Kaz mumbled and shifted, still alive but clearly regretting it.

If it had only been a hollow under a tree, he would have already reached a very angry critter at its bottom, but instead Damien's hands pressed into firmer, dry earth, though it was shockingly cold. His next blind touch fell on a too-smooth surface, and with the angle, his arms began to slide.

Damien pushed up onto his knees to keep from toppling forward, but the movement was too quick, and his head slammed into the earthen ceiling. "Fuck!" His knees, however, just kept going, and the very sudden steepness took him.

He tried to steady himself against the sides of the tunnel while buoying Kaz against his chest, but everything was slick and frozen in the pitch-darkness. He tightened his grip on the imp as he slid, but then there was nothing below him, and Damien was falling.

CHAPTER 25

AMMA

A Court of Ice and Irrationality

IT WASN'T THE FALLING that was bad, even though one's stomach shot up into one's throat and one's mind flooded with fear. No, it wasn't the falling at all but the landing.

For Amma, at least she landed not on the hard ground but on the slightly less hard form of Damien, who had found the earth first. That didn't make it not painful, just less so, but for Damien, she imagined, significantly worse.

"Sorry," she croaked out, rolling off him. Then the cold hit her. Frigid and wet, her hands sank into the soft ground differently than they had on the pliability of the jungle floor.

"Bloody wonderful." Damien groaned. "Winter." White crystals fell from his shoulders as he sat up and dusted his black hair.

They'd landed in the middle of a wide trail lined on either side by pines, everything covered in a blanket of white. The snow hung from the boughs like linens, still in the breezeless air. Amma's breath swirled before her as she blinked up at the night sky. Though dotted with many stars, there were no moons, yet the snow that coated everything shone with its own faint light. The hollow they'd fallen through was nowhere to be seen.

As they slowly stood, snow crunched beneath them, the only sound in the frozen stillness all around. The prickle of unseen eyes climbed up the back of her neck with each too-loud movement. Amma tried to fall as still as the trees that were tethered in place by their heavy white cloaks. The road stretched smoothly away from them in both directions, undisturbed by tracks since the last snowfall.

Something fell at her side, and she sighed at the splintered wood that had once been a crossbow. At least she still had her dagger.

"This is the Everdark?" she asked, never imagining it to look so much like the world she already knew.

"The Everdarque, yes," Damien said, picking up Kaz awkwardly with one arm from where he'd landed. "Still alive?"

Kaz managed a noise of sorts, though he only seemed to have the energy to shiver.

"Poor thing." Amma wrapped her arms around herself, cloak abandoned at the most inopportune time.

"That divine spell got the best of him, it seems, but he has no pressing injuries. He will only need time to recover. Here, keep one another warm." Kaz made no complaint, only tucking in his wings and tail as Damien handed him to Amma. He still gave off plenty of heat though his leathery skin was cold to the touch.

"You have pressing injuries though," she said, clasping Kaz with one hand and taking the other to Damien's arm. His tunic sleeve had been shredded, and a gash ran up the length of his bicep, deep and oozing.

"Their arcana was slightly stronger this time," he grumbled.

She gently moved a bit of ripped linen away, the damage worse than she'd ever seen it. The cuts Damien made to himself were bloody, yes, but shallow. This time, his skin was split gruesomely, no sign it intended to mend itself, and there was an angry bubbling at the edges of his flesh like it had been burnt. "I don't like this. Why aren't you healing?"

Damien gazed out at the way ahead, the wide trail bending away, trees hemming in on either side with blue-gray shadows. "Magic becomes uncooperative when you change planes, and it isn't always *right* here anyway." He dipped a finger into his wound with a wince and swiped his hand through the air. Trailing behind was a hazy line of smoke, and then all at once, the smoke expanded as a wall of blackness burst forth before them. Amma jumped back from it, and it dissipated harmlessly into nothing. "You see, I didn't intend for that to happen, but my arcana is chaotic here."

Amma grunted, then looked down. Crimson bloomed over the glittering white beside his boots. "We have to take care of that."

"Damn it." Damien kicked snow over the blood and tore at his sleeve. He tried to wrap the loose fabric around his arm but struggled, and Amma took over. She knotted the linen tightly at his elbow, the excess soaking up the blood. "Good enough," he mumbled. "It would have been better to end up somewhere less frigid, but Winter may be for the best since it's purportedly desolate. I would cast for a return portal, but our eyes are more reliable than magic for now."

Their boots crunched along down the trail, a sound that would have been otherwise pleasant but was now too revealing in the quiet. "You're saying Winter like it's a place?"

"The Everdarque is broken into four territories, though they are governed in no rational way. The fae are simply enthusiastic about their aesthetics and prefer to live in their so-called seasonal courts unendingly. They even give themselves nonsensical titles." He put his hand out as they walked, and a snowflake fell into it, melting away into nothing. "I've only been to Summer, but the fae there spoke of Winter as an abandoned place."

Each step had them sinking into the snow, but it glowed from below like daylight. Up against the darkness of the pines and the night sky, it was like walking through a dream. If it hadn't been so cold, Amma would have appreciated its beauty. "So you're friendly with some Summer fae? Maybe we can find them?"

Damien chuckled, though there was no real amusement in his voice. "I would not say I'm friendly with any of them, no, but I allied myself with a viscount or a margrave or some such out of necessity while there. Fae are too fickle to have friends, not that I would be one if they did—blame the boredom that comes along with immortality."

Amma watched him grip his wounded arm, trying to hide the look of pain he wore. She wanted to believe that it was just the strangeness of the Everdark that slowed his ability to heal, but that same sense that something hidden was watching them told her Damien's injury was worse than he was letting on. "The fae are immortal like the vampires?"

"Neither have a natural end to their lives, but vampires can be killed. Death doesn't stick to fae. They purport to not have been born either, which I suppose may be true since they don't seem capable of reproducing."

There was no wind, a blessing with the cold, but no other sounds of birds or scurrying creatures either. Amma held Kaz a bit tighter. "You mean it's just been the same group of them forever?"

Damien shrugged his good shoulder. "If you manage to kill one, they just come back and go on with their interminable life. They have no concept of the permanence that death is for you or me. That's what makes them so dangerous."

They came around a bend in the trees, and the firs opened up to reveal a valley of untouched, sparkling whiteness, a frozen turquoise lake in its middle. The sky was like a swath of velvet, dotted with hundreds of silver specks and spread out over the world, and rising up into the blackness from the lake's center was a palace of ice.

"Oh wow." Amma sighed, her breath's heat misting before it was swallowed up by the cold.

Dozens of spires drove themselves upward, every surface sharp, threatening the very sky. But the colors glinting off the spires were the softest whites and teals and pinks. Glassy and beautiful, the castle unsettled Amma deeply.

"Of course." Damien grunted at her side, a deep frown creasing his face, and then he gritted his teeth as he clenched the fist of his wounded arm. Even in the dark, Amma could see his skin had gone more pallid than usual. "Let's go back. I'll cast for a portal instead."

"Damien, you're getting worse," she said. "Shouldn't we see if they can help?"

"Help?" He snorted, but even that looked to hurt him. "A fae could just as easily be our undoing as it would deign to assist us."

"Why not both?"

The voice was like frost forming on the back of Amma's neck, crawling frozen fingers over her scalp and turning her head. Behind them stood a creature as tall as Damien at its shoulder, but it loomed well above them as its antlers sprouted in all directions. Body covered in white fur like an extension of the snow itself, it stood on four slender limbs and would have been majestic if its head were not so horrifying. As starkly white as the rest of it, the deerlike skull rose up out of a furry neck, antlers wider across than Amma could reach with both arms extended, and though it had no eyes, it thrust its head to look down on the two.

So grand a creature would have eclipsed a lesser rider, but the being on its back was just as striking. Clad in white furs, the matched skeletal face also sprouted prongs, slightly smaller if much more ornate, covered in silver threads strung with red gems that glittered in the snow's light as they swayed. The recesses of their eyes, though, were not empty hollows; something more peered out from behind them.

The rider shifted and, with a graceful swiftness, alighted on the ground beside the beast. Damien's hand gripped Amma's wrist covertly, squeezing her, and she was thankful for its warmth, even the stickiness of his blood a comfort.

Footsteps crunched much lighter than they should have for the rider's large frame approaching them. Long—perhaps slightly too long—fingers slid beneath the chin of the antlered skull they wore, and then the mask dissipated into snow, gems and all swept away on a sudden gust of wind.

Beneath was a man—no, the portrait of a man laid over a fae's face, though something in Amma lit up like she would have known, even without the descriptions from the fairy tales, that she was looking on a fae regardless. Strikingly gorgeous with long silver hair slicked back and eyes as crystalline blue as the frozen lake behind them, he was so beautiful that the oddness to his hands—what was that, an extra row of knuckles? No, it didn't matter; he was too pretty to be in possession of anything wrong about him at all.

"You've come so far," he said, voice as deep as the cavern in the karsts, and nodded toward the palace behind them. "Why not beg a favor from the fae king himself?"

Damien's grip tightened. She knew he wouldn't react kindly to that word: *Beg*. "King?" Damien's voice, however, was lighter than she expected, and he cocked his head. "Is the Winter Court no longer ruled by a solitary prince?"

The fae held his features very still as he assessed them with unmoving eyes over a pleasant if cold grin. "And who told you this?"

Damien squinted, thinking, then the name came out slowly. "Scot?"

"Scot?" the fae repeated, stony.

Amma cringed—that did *not* sound like the kind of name a fae would have.

"The Margrave of the Summer Court," Damien clarified, nodding and clearing his throat.

"Ah, Scot." The name was a hiss on his breath as recognition passed quickly over the fae's face with the arching of one thin, snowy brow and a smile that revealed quite a few pointed teeth—not that there was anything amiss about that. "Well, even a prince grows weary of his title eventually. Come, human friends of Margrave Scot, let us see how the fae king may aid you from his throne." He parted the thick furred cloak he wore to gesture toward the lake.

The fae stepped away from his mount, and it too disintegrated into powdery snow, swept away on a breeze that died out as quickly as it came. Damien never let him out of his sight as he passed by, and there was a warmth Amma wasn't expecting when the fae came close, like stepping out into the sun from under a shadow.

Amma glanced over to Damien. He looked thoroughly annoyed as his violet eyes trailed the fae, but the circles under them deepened in their darkness, skin going gray. "Come on," she said quietly, slipping her wrist from his grasp to take his hand instead, careful not to tug on his injured arm. He relented so quickly that it confirmed everything she feared.

They followed, finally reaching the lake. The fae continued out over the frozen surface, and Amma confidently went along behind him. Damien still held on to Amma, fingers clasped, and it proved necessary when they both immediately lost their balance.

Amma's heart shot up into her throat, arm still tightly around Kaz as she took shallow, nervous breaths. Then she tried laughing, awkward and stilted, as she looked at Damien, who sardonically snorted back. They were stuck.

The fae did not look back as he traversed the slick surface with no difficulty, but he made a vague gesture, and a fall of snow appeared along the ice in a trail behind him. Grumbling, Damien tested it, and the two were able to cross, the slickness underfoot diminished, but danger still lurked with every step.

The palace lay atop a wide and exhaustingly tall staircase that grew out of the ice, the steps transparent, glowing turquoise, and then shifting to stone at its apex. When they reached the peak, the remainder of Amma's breath was stolen by the beauty of the palace's doorless entry. The fae continued ahead of them, and though he was tall, the tunnel he entered dwarfed even him. Carved from the ice, its walls and ceiling were jagged but reflective with colored lights. Dull yellow, rosy pink, seafoam green all moved across the walls like ghosts of the world when it was alive, source unseen, then bleeding away into nothing.

The tunnel went on, its ceiling impossibly high, and there were thinner places to allow the starry night sky to come through, sharp shapes of deep black twinkling with silver. Deeper in, the walls were smoother, archways layered upon one another and reflective so that the corridors leading elsewhere were dizzying. Their footsteps on this floor, no longer ice but a smooth, blue marble with a vein of silver running all through it, were too loud, just like when they crunched through the snow.

At the far end of the grand entry hall were more stairs that led to a dais, immaculate icy columns flanking it in varying heights and a plush seat with a high back in its center. The lone piece of furniture in the otherwise bare room was covered in brilliant white fur, a hint of softness surrounded by the harsh, slick walls. Behind the throne, a wall of icicles hung thin and glimmering as they constantly dripped in a trough that reflected more starry light.

Amma took another tentative glance around, noting no attendants, no courtiers, no one at all, including the supposed king. Winter was as empty and desolate as the rumors purported, it seemed.

The fae ascended the dais, shrugging off his heavy furs as he went. The pile turned to snow as it hit the stairs and was swept away into nothing by another unseen force. Beneath, he wore a gown of thin powder-blue material that clung to his form, collar high and train long, covered in silver filigree. He took the throne, sinking down into the fluffy softness.

His hand opened, long, slender, maybe-extra-knuckled-but-not-quite fingers splaying out, then each finger curled inward, and the water from the trough behind floated upward to form a crown of icicles that sat itself atop his head. "So beg."

Damien's jaw clenched in the exact way Amma expected it to. "Fuck." He closed his eyes and tipped his head back, readjusting his wounded arm.

"You stand before the King of the Winter Court, and if you would like a wish granted, I would like to hear you beg. Is this proposal offensive to you, human?" The fae king sat forward with a quickness, gripping the arms of his throne, fingers digging into the plush covering with an odd crack.

Damien only groaned, taking a deep breath as if, despite what loomed before them, he could fall asleep right there, standing up.

"Perhaps you ought to have thought of your hubris before siding with that treasonous Margrave Scot."

"What?" Damien's eyes opened slowly as he bobbed his head back forward. "Siding? I barely know—"

"Any friend of a pawn of the Emperor of Summer is an enemy of this court."

"There's a bloody emperor now?" Damien grumbled as a bit of life flared in him even as his shoulders drooped. "I'm fairly certain I did *not* say I was his friend."

The fae leaned forward even farther, limbs appearing to lengthen, lips pulled back to reveal more of those curiously pointed teeth. "You did not deny it," the king hissed. "Perhaps he has sent you as spies? Or assassins?"

Amma's mind sparked—she had been accused of something similar before. Her eyes pinged from the drained blood mage to the incensed fae, where she noticed something new: an excitement growing on his features he'd not had before.

Damien wasn't flustered by the fae's changing appearance though. "Look, we'll just go if it's a problem."

A slam reverberated through the entry hall, a rush of freezing cold climbing up their backs. Amma spun to see that the tunnel was now obscured with a thick wall of ice, disfiguring the world beyond it and run through with cracks. When she turned back, the fae king had settled into his fluffy throne, head held high.

"There's no need to go flitting off," he said as if he hadn't just made it impossible for them to leave. When his smile returned, his teeth were not so pointed, and there was a definitive change there—no longer knowing insistence but something like desperation. "Perhaps we can still work things out."

"With supposed assassins?" Damien tried to gesture with both hands, forgetting his injury and actually sucking in a pained breath.

"We're not assassins." Amma laughed, though nerves tinged her voice as she shifted Kaz to her other shoulder. "But we actually do require aid. Clearly."

"Amma," Damien whispered, "do not make us appear weak."

She eyed him sharply. "*I'm* not."

"What I am hearing," said the king as he rose back to his feet, slim form swaying, "is that you would humble yourselves before the Winter Court for a favor and that you would remain here to earn it. Yes?"

Amma handed off Kaz to Damien's good arm and took a step forward, curtsying. "Your Majesty," she said in her sweetest voice, "we would be honored if you would host us in this trying time."

The fae king steepled his too-long fingers, peering down at her. She held herself in gentle supplication, waiting, and then he smiled again. "The court shall see what it can do."

CHAPTER 26

AMMA

The Care and Curing of Blood Mages

"I HATE THIS." DAMIEN'S voice was as surly as ever, echoing out into the chamber they had been ushered into.

"Yes, I know, I know." Amma took Kaz back from him, eyeing a divan not far from the door. She laid the imp in a bundle of furs there and tucked him in. Kaz snuggled down with a sleepy yawn, the cutest she'd ever seen him, uneven jaw notwithstanding, though the fact that he wasn't talking certainly helped.

Amma took stock of the rest of the room. Walls of shimmering ice reflected the room back at itself, cloudy and blue and carved into with intricate patterns over every inch like a gaudy, colorless wallpaper. Furniture grew directly from the icy walls: a wardrobe, a dresser, a desk, each smooth, with elegant designs and sharp corners, impossible without magic. From the ceiling hung a chandelier covered in frost, the drippy, frozen snow illuminating the space with a gentle white glow but no flames. Similarly, a fireplace was built out of one of the walls, mimicking a traditional hearth though made of ice. Blue flames danced in its center but gave off no warmth. The chamber's center held a bed, its frame similarly cast from ice and raised up on a frosty platform, though thankfully covered in many pillows and fluffy linens. But—Amma swallowed—there was only the one.

The Winter Court's king had agreed that they could retire for the evening and conjured another creature from snow, this one short, web-footed, kneeless, and adorable. It was perhaps some sort of bird as it had a beak, though it waddled rather than flew and gestured with a flipper-like appendage. They followed it through the reflective, empty halls of the palace and were left in guest chambers, though no other place appeared to be occupied.

They would need their rest, the fae king had ominously said before they were led from the hall, but they would find everything they could possibly need where they would be taken. Amma hoped that meant something to treat Damien's wound.

There was an adjoining bathing chamber, and Amma tugged Damien by his still-intact sleeve into it. A basin of ice was jutting out of the wall, and when she placed her hands beneath the spout, it ran with clear water. The shock of the cold made her pull back, but she gritted her teeth and cleaned away the dirt from her palms and then stoppered it. As the basin filled, she opened a narrow larder and found a stack of thin linens and a row of transparent boxes, strikingly familiar.

Amma picked up the central glass box, parchment wrapped just about its middle, the label written in Ouranic of all things, but then below that, a translation in Key: *For healing the unmendable wounds of surly blood mages.*

"Well, that's convenient," she said, flipping it over to look at the back and another label there that read, in much smaller script: *May cause drowsiness.*

The blood mage in question was sulking as he leaned against the chamber's doorway, apparently not feeling the ice his head and shoulder rested against. "You were awfully nice to our captor," he said miserably.

Amma rolled her eyes. "Well, that's what I do." She held up the jar. "And it got us this."

"I don't want that. I told you, I'll heal eventually. It may just take until we're out of the Everdarque, which is what we should be trying to do—finding a way out."

"Oh, you'd prefer we run away?" She gestured to him and the edge of a big block of ice that served as a bathtub of sorts.

"No." He grimaced, following her direction and taking a seat before her. "But no good will come of this. Fae are mercurial and ill-humored, and that one's no exception."

"Well, you would know," she mumbled and began working at the shoulder straps to his leathers. "Come on now. You might be okay with all that bleeding, but I'm not."

The pinched anger fell off Damien's face as he used his

good arm to assist, and they managed to remove his chest armor. Amma tugged at his tunic after, and he did his best to slide out, but she could tell nearly half of him was paralyzed at this point, so she eased it over his head and then down the damaged arm, discarding the bloodied thing on the floor.

The wound itself was unchanged, deep and dark as it ran from his shoulder to his elbow, and it still gave up blood, but the skin around it had blackened more than she'd noted before.

Amma ran a finger over the dark veins that were crawling away from the mark. She couldn't imagine enduring a wound like that herself. "Help me, Isldrah."

"Hmm? Who is that?" Damien's eyes had gone glassy as he peered up at her. "Do I know her?"

Amma shook her head, turning from him to dunk a linen in the water basin. "She's the goddess of health. One of my mother's attendants worshiped her and would say that whenever I'd get hurt. She does birds too, I think."

Damien sucked in a sharp breath when she wiped at the drying blood, eyes jolting open. "You don't invoke divinity," he said, voice strained as he looked away.

"Sorry, sorry," she said tenderly, taking even more care to apply as little pressure as was needed to wipe at the blood. "This just seems especially bad. I know you weren't healing before we climbed through the burrow."

"Observant." He tipped his head back to watch her, and she could feel his muscles relax under her hands. "The magic the Sentries use has always been rudimentary, but this time it was as if it were tailor-made to damage someone with noxscura in their veins."

Amma traded the dirty linen for a clean, damp one. "And they found you too." As she pressed the cold fabric to his arm, the bleeding finally ceased.

He made a thoughtful sound, opened his mouth, and then a yawn caught him.

"You're tired," she said quietly, assessing his arm, which was clean of blood and looking marginally better.

He glanced wearily out the doorway to the big bed in the room's center. "I don't trust that fae enough to sleep."

"If what you need is sleep, you're getting sleep." Amma opened the container, the smell of mint and citrus hitting her as she dipped a fresh linen into it. When she touched the linen to his cut, he pulled back with a gasp. "Oh, stop it."

"But you're hurting me," he whined, and she almost laughed as she grabbed his arm, only distracted for a moment by how hard his bicep was.

"Well, I'm not trying to." She touched the white salve to the edges of his wound again, holding him still.

"Yes, well..." Damien was pouting, looking away from her as he struggled for the words. "It's just unnatural, you... hurting...anything."

Amma cocked a brow at him, but he didn't look back. Much more carefully, she smoothed the linen over the wound, and the irritation seemed to seep out, the darkness to his veins lessening. "This can't be as bad as when you slice yourself open," she said gently as she worked, "but it's only for a moment more. Be brave for me, all right?"

Damien snorted but cracked a grin, squinting his eyes shut, and his face actually reddened.

Amma chuckled, taking a final linen and wrapping it around his wound. She was careful to lift him by the elbow, not wanting to cause more pain, but even wounded and pallid, his body, strong and imposing, didn't seem like a thing she could harm. She smoothed the linen down after tying it off, running her fingers along the muscled tautness of his skin, then pulled back suddenly when she realized she had been touching him without excuse.

Face flushed, she laughed nervously and busied herself cleaning up the used linens. "There, that wasn't so bad, was it? You did so well."

He looked like he might protest, but another yawn caught him.

"And now you need to sleep."

"Can't," he said, eyes half-lidded. "Dangerous."

She turned back to him, hands on her hips. "Unless there's a sudden change in temperature, I think we'll be just fine in here."

His head was bobbing down, but his brow had gone all knitted again. He was leaning forward, elbows on knees, hands flexing like that could help to keep him awake.

Amma returned to stand just before him and cupped her hands under his chin. As she tilted his head up, a gentle curiosity took his features, and they softened. "You'll be all right, Damien. I'll take care of you. I promise."

He swallowed hard. "You will?"

Amma looked down at him, and for the first time, Damien seemed small. Her mind filled with the sapling in the greenhouse, the acorn on the road, and the seeds from the wild liathau. Most things started out that way, tiny but with a whole world of potential inside, and they really only got big with at least a little help. "Of course I will."

All at once, Damien slumped forward against her, and she scrambled to grab him as he slid to the edge of the bathtub.

"Okay, well, I didn't mean fall asleep right this second," she groaned, slipping hands under his arms and pushing him back up. "That salve sure works fast, huh?"

With a hefty tug, she managed to pull him onto his feet, and that roused him enough to be walked into the main room.

"Gods, you're heavy. You better never make me drag you around when we're in real danger." With a shoulder under his arm and a hand pressed into his bare chest, Amma did her level best to drag Damien across the chamber, his feet barely helping. "Come on, we're almost to the bed."

Like he was drunk, his eyes opened, one and then the other. He grinned sleepily down at her, mumbling something nonsensical but suggestively eager, and he finally managed to help her help himself up onto the frosty platform to collapse on the mass of pillows.

Amma blew out a breath, then started tugging off his

boots. He mumbled something else, and she answered, despite not knowing at all what he was saying. "Oh yes, very interesting, Lord Bloodthorne. Tell me more." He did go on, a groan followed by a few muddy words, but they trailed off into nothing by the time his boots were off.

She kicked off her own and climbed up onto the bed to kneel beside him. His eyes were closed, and his mouth was open—was he already asleep? She eyed his hip pouch, too bulky to sleep with, but remembered the last time she tried to lift something off him that was strapped to his waist while he slept.

Well, this wasn't that; she wasn't stealing, only trying to make him a little more comfortable, so she undid the buckle while struggling not to think about how close her hands were to making him comfortable in a slightly different way. Amma gave his belt a tug, but it didn't come out from under him, though he didn't stir either. She yanked at it again, but he only made a small sleepy noise while the belt remained firmly in place. With a silent countdown, Amma pulled much harder, but the leather simply slid out of her hands, and she went flying backward.

Damien barely murmured, though she'd practically hurled herself off the bed. Sitting up and sweeping her hair out of her face, Amma nearly gave up, then had another idea. Gently, she touched her fingertips to his side and then dragged them toward his waist. Damien giggled sleepily, eyelids squeezing tighter. He squirmed just enough for her to slip the belt out from under him, though she nearly missed her chance, so distracted by her own laughter and the frankly giddy sound he'd made.

Finally free, the belt was warm in her hands, and her grip tightened as she looked down at him. To see him so peaceful, all the surliness put away, was rare, and she eased his hair out of his face. "Damien?"

He only took a heavy breath, eyes still closed.

Amma bit her lip, gaze lingering on his sleeping form, his chest rising and falling. She put his belt and pouch down on a side table and took a deep breath. "I hated when you were gone. I tried to do my best, to learn things, but the entire time, I just wanted you back. I know it's selfish, but I..." Her voice trailed off, but telling him how she had failed to get the talisman out *again* when he definitely wouldn't remember wasn't right anyway. She shook her head, checking the bandage on his arm once more, and when she was satisfied, she turned to climb off the bed and find a suitable place to sleep.

Plucked from the spot like she were a pillow herself, Amma was suddenly dragged backward by her middle. Breath caught and balance lost on the squishy surface of the bed, she found herself on her side, Damien's good arm clamped around her tightly. Heat came up against her back as she was pulled into his chest, his knees pressing to the backs of her own as he curled and fit himself around her.

"Stay with me," he mumbled into her hair, words clear so close to her ear and breath warm—all of him so warm.

"Damien," she whispered, trying to look back but caught in his tight embrace, "did you really mean to do this?"

"Just stay," he said again, nuzzling tighter against her.

Amma really had no other choice—not that she would take it if offered—but she did listen for more, just in case. There was only his heavy breathing and the warm pulse of his chest against her back. His arm was heavy over her, still holding on, but had lost its urgency. She could have wiggled away, but she felt herself only relaxing and then her own eyes closing, and soon Amma was asleep too.

When she woke, she found Damien's arms still around her, his breath still heavy as it fell over her face, but she'd flipped toward him, nestled against his chest. She blinked up at his face, expecting him to wake alongside her, but he remained heavily asleep even when she pressed up onto an elbow and ran a finger over his nose.

No reaction, just the gentle rise and fall of his chest. She whispered his name but got no response. She pulled up one of his eyelids, and a violet iris stared back without seeing her. Amma wiggled herself out of his arms and assessed the bandages, now darkened, and quickly left the bed to gather clean linens and the salve from before. As she opened the container, she noted the Key that she was sure had read *May cause drowsiness* before had changed itself to state *Most definitely will cause hibernation for at least three days*.

She clicked her tongue, but when she unwrapped the old bandages from Damien's wound, the salve had done its job quite well, the skin mostly mended and his veins nearly back to normal. She cleaned his skin, reapplied the salve, and rewrapped the injury in new linens. He remained unconscious, but Amma still explained what she was doing as she worked, just in case he could hear.

Then the hair on the back of her neck rose, and Amma sat up very straight. She snapped her head to the side, just catching a set of bulbous, black eyes leering over the foot of the bed. "Oh, Kaz, you're feeling better?"

The imp grunted, claws coming over the icy edge and pulling himself up. Over his shoulders, he had tied one of the furs like a cape, and it dragged along behind him as he planted himself firmly on the foot of the bed. "What did you do to Master?"

"I'm taking care of him," she said, running a hand through Damien's hair. "He's hurt, like you were."

Kaz made a wary, irritated noise.

Damien remained unmoving, and Amma pulled a thick blanket over him. "Look, Kaz, I know you don't trust me, but I'm not going to hurt him. I care about Damien, all right?"

"Humans say lots of things like that," Kaz grumbled, absolutely not believing her. "But they lie. And they leave."

She huffed, standing from the bed, and smoothed down her ripped-up tunic. "I've had a lot of opportunities to leave, Kaz. I could have run away while the two of you were gone in the Wilds or left with the Righteous Sentries either time they came around. Even back in Faebarrow, I could have just stayed. The vampires offered me a place with them too. But I'm still here."

The imp glared back at her, and if he was considering anything she said, he didn't show it. "Because you are ordered to be."

"Because I want to be," she said so quickly that she didn't realize the words had come out at all. Amma cleared her throat and focused hard on pulling on her boots. "Now, you can stay here and watch over Damien while he sleeps, or you can come with me to make sure I don't do anything you disapprove of, but I'm going to go and barter our way back to our plane, somewhere safe for all of us, you included."

Kaz's arms uncrossed, underbite moving around in thought. "Master would want me to keep an eye on you."

She nodded, checking on Damien once more and tucking him in before heading for the door. "That's fine with me." With the imp just behind her, she let them out into the chilly hall. "Together we can go speak with the fae king, and I'm sure we can come to some reasonable agreement."

Just as Amma pulled the door shut behind them, a freezing gust blew down the corridor. Her vision clouded as snow swirled past her, and then it was gone, leaving behind the King of the Winter Court in all his beautiful, sparkling glory.

"Reasonable," he said, voice like a cracking sheet of ice. "I have been called much worse."

CHAPTER 27

DAMIEN

The Incessant Desire for a Passage Back

The world was cold and empty and dark, but there was a flicker of warmth, a small source of heat, and Damien reached out to it, pulling it close. It cuddled back into him, and he was, for perhaps the first time in his life, completely content.

"Stay with me," he said, and she did.

But as he tightened his grip, the warmth shrank. He tried to catch it, but it slipped away, leaving him to curl in on himself, empty again and alone.

The darkness around him shifted, a shadow in it, familiar, frightening. Then a laugh, so like Xander's, and the glint of a sword, swinging down at him with a divine light. It slashed into his chest, opening him like some prey animal gutted by a wolf, and life flooded out as he crumpled to the ground.

He lay there in nothingness for a long time, maybe forever, feeling all the pain and none of it at once. Then a nudge, just enough to make him move again, and the warmth returned.

It's only a dream, a voice cooed directly into his ear with a sweet lilt. *You're safe. It's all right.* He couldn't respond, though he tried, but he knew it would protect him; it had promised, and he simply reached out again and held on.

That warm sweetness lasted until it again disappeared, and Damien found himself on his knees. He was naked, the wound on his stomach and chest healed, but when he lifted his arms, they were covered in every slice he had ever given himself. Hundreds, thousands maybe, all risen to the surface, angry and ugly and weeping blood.

Movement in the darkness revealed the long, slim lines of a woman's body. She stalked from the shadows and stood over him, smiling down, but there was nothing kind in that look, only joy for what she was about to do. His stomach dropped as she raised a dagger to her mouth and snapped her teeth down on its tip.

Delphine, no, please!

Damien threw his hands up, and she struck out but didn't cut into him. The weapon had been turned, the hilt offered up. He took it from her, every muscle aching in protest of what he was about to do as he raised the dagger to his own face. Blood, hot and wet, spilled over his cheek, the blade slicing through his skin with a sluggish agony he could neither stop nor quicken. And then he was awake.

Heart beating madly, body covered in cold sweat, Damien jolted, the brightness of the room blinding him. Everything ached, pinpricks and arcana pulsing through his limbs, and his stomach roiled. He groaned, running his good hand down his face, and then reached out as if his fingers should have found someone, but the space beside him was empty.

Blinking, he sat up, the chamber a cloudy shade of blue through sleepy eyes and smelling of mint. He couldn't quite recall where he was, when he had fallen asleep, or how he had gotten there, but he did know he desperately needed to take a piss.

He wavered as he got to his feet and instinctively traipsed across the room to the smaller attached bath. He found the latrine, and as he stood there waiting for his bladder to empty as if it had been filling for days, he tugged at the linen wrapped around his arm. He worked at the knot, done so well by nimble fingers, and it eventually gave way, unraveling to reveal only a thin line left running up his bicep. The wound had healed nicely, considering how deadly it had been. And then he suddenly realized why.

Damien willed himself to finish, hopping in place, and shouted for Amma. There was no answer other than his own voice echoing back off the icy walls of the chamber. He ran across it, seeing no sign of Kaz either, and burst into the hall.

The Winter Court palace was massive, and he could scarcely remember the way they'd been brought—the ambush in the Wilds, the fall into the frozen Everdarque, the meeting with that fae, all a jumble. Damien called Amma's name again as he raced down a reflective hall, his own shadow passing him by. No answer.

His mind swam with what could have happened—that so-called king could have her in any of the rooms in this place, a tower, a dungeon, his bedchamber. At that, he growled and moved even faster, turning down another hall that spilled into some grand chamber, a table in its center, much too small for the rest of the space. It was strange, but he had no time to consider it. Basest beasts, had Amma been whisked away to another court?

Before he let himself spiral deeper into frenzied concern, he closed his eyes and reached out with his mind. His arcana sparked, chaotic and confused. There was only a vast wasteland of nothing, though noxscura plucked at his senses, pulling him in every direction and willing him to stay right there.

And then he found the blood that he needed, with its curiosity and its liveliness and its human warmth. Amma. Her heart was pumping madly; she had been running, screaming, but the presence of her was all around and nowhere at once.

"Fuck!" Damien's eyes sprang open, and there, standing just ahead of him, was one of those fat, little not-birds the fae had conjured. "You!" He pointed at the egg-shaped creature. "Show me where they are."

The flippered being turned on a webbed foot and waddled away. Damien sprinted after but quickly caught up, and though it was clearly doing its best, Damien fell into a walk so as not to pass it up.

"Faster," he demanded, and a beady black eye roved up to him before it flopped down onto its rounded belly and suddenly propelled itself over the smooth stone at an astonishing pace. "Didn't realize you could go this fast," he barked, bolting after it.

The creature led Damien right out to the massive throne room, straight down the entry tunnel, and through a passage cut into the block the fae had used to seal them in. He dashed outside, down the palace's steps to the lake, still glowing turquoise under a constantly darkened sky. The dusting that made it possible to walk across was still there, the fishbird propelling himself even more quickly across the ice.

Damien hurried to the bank, his arcana impossible to call up properly, senses blurred by the Everdarque, but Amma was close, and he opened his mouth to yell for her once more.

Freezing wetness slapped Damien in the face, shocking her name off his tongue. He turned, and there was Amma, half-hidden behind a mound of snow, a bright shock of color draped in a pink cloak amongst the white and blue shadows of the Everdarque's wintery night. Beside her was the fae king, as silver and sharp as the world around him, both blending in and jutting out, a ball of packed snow hovering over his hand.

"You got him!" Amma squealed and then propelled herself over the bank. "Damien, you're finally awake!" She ran with the same speed she'd had in the hut in the Wilds but stopped short of embracing him, hands covered in thick mittens as she threw them up like she might have grabbed him about the neck under other circumstances. Instead, she carefully set the soft mittens against his arm. "And look, you're healed, but you must be freezing."

Only then did Damien feel the elements, and the cold bit at him, but his heartbeat settled as he surveyed her shrugging off the long fur-lined cloak. "Why are you out here? Are you unharmed?"

Amma nodded. Beneath, she was wearing a dress of velvety fabric, skin completely covered, but her face showed no distress beyond a sudden concern aimed at him. She threw her cloak over his bare shoulders and pulled it tight around his neck, brow pinched, round lips pulled into a pout. Damien knew that look, and it used to make his chest tight and annoyed, but this time his heart squeezed in a different way. "We were just working on the finer details of having a snowball fight. I have *so* much to tell you."

The fae king strode up behind her, looking tall and beautiful and smug and exceedingly punchable despite the fact that Damien knew aggression toward any fae was ill-advised at best.

"Ah, the sleeping prince has finally woken," the king drawled.

Damien would have sneered at him, balling a fist covertly beneath the cloak, but a round bundle of animate sweaters waddled up. "Kaz? Is that you in there?"

The imp made a gurgly little noise through a slit in the knitted fabric, barely able to move arms and legs that poked straight out, but he was solidly protected from the cold and didn't even shake. Amma laughed sharply, and Damien chuckled, his ire subsiding for the time being.

Back in the relative warmth of the palace, Amma guided Damien over to a hearth glowing with an actual fire despite being carved from ice. He was sure it hadn't been there before, but it was central to the throne room now, huge and elaborate with a stone ledge hovering over the flames holding a small number of pots. "You were asleep for three days," Amma explained as she picked up a thick linen from a tray and retrieved a teapot from the ledge.

Many things could happen in three days. Damien glanced over at the fae king. He was on the other side of the throne room, distracted with Kaz, who had gotten himself stuck in the many layers, working with the imp to peel them off. "I did not intend to be."

"I know, but I'm glad—your wound needed it." She offered him a cup of what was in the pot. "Taste this, tell me what you think."

Damien took a sip of the tea, senses filling with the scent of pine, its heat lighting up his throat and blooming in his chest agreeably. "It tastes as though you've boiled the northern forests."

"That's good?" She squinted, lip caught between her teeth.

He took another sip, the feeling returning to his hands around the copper mug. "Absolutely."

Amma's grin warmed him even more than the drink. "Hemlock pine tea, like Laurel taught me to make."

"Is this what you've been up to? Perfecting the recipe?"

"Um, no, that's just hot needle juice." Her lip biting turned fidgety, and her gaze shot to the fae who had managed to get Kaz out of one sweater and was tugging on the next, which was caught on Kaz's talons. Voice much lower, she leaned in. "Did you know his name is Wil? Just Wil. Well, King Wil of the Winter Court, but still. Isn't that sort of silly? I would have thought fae would be named, you know, long, pompous-sounding, nigh-impossible things."

Damien chuckled lightly. "You certainly are judgmental about other peoples' names, considering."

"Considering what?"

He shook his head. "Never mind, Amma. Fae can't give you their true names or else your mind will devour itself, or so they insist. Tell me about your time with *Wil*, if it was not just boiling needles and throwing snowballs."

"Right, well, he's apparently been alone in Winter for quite a long time—I guess he lost some game or something, and everyone left—and it's gotten him a bit down, but it turns out fae don't really do any of the fun, snowy things, which explains why the others won't come back to Winter. So I've been showing him some of the things we do in Faebarrow when it's cold, and he *loves* them." Her eyes lit up. "Especially the kind of things you do to keep warm afterward."

Damien's stomach knotted. "What kinds of things to keep warm?"

"Making hemlock tea, having actual fire, boiling big pots of stew, you know." She gestured to the hearth and its many pots, then dropped her voice even lower. "They seemed fairly obvious to me but sort of extraordinary to him, so I thought at first he had gone a little mad with no other fae around since all he does is sit around playing with himself."

The copper mug in Damien's hand almost gave way under his grip. "He *told* you that?"

She shot a covert look over at the fae and then pointed through an archway to an adjoining room, the one Damien had found himself in on his search of the palace with the strange table. A chair was placed on either side of the table, each carved from ice. "Yes, practicing the game I mentioned that he lost to someone named Norm, of all things—that's the Emperor of the Summer Court. Sounds like a jerk to me though, honestly. Anyway, Wil tried to show me how to play, but I couldn't get the hang of it. The pieces need magic, and it's like all mine is suddenly gone." Amma's mouth turned down, hands held out and small fingers flexing.

"It's just the plane," Damien assured her.

"Maybe. Anyway, King Wil won't exactly admit to it, but he is *dreadfully lonely*." Her eyes went exceptionally wide, the blue of them glassy under the frosted chandeliers. "It's why, you know, he sort of imprisoned us when we got here."

At this, Damien grunted.

"I know, I know, not an excuse, but it *is* a bargaining chip." That sadness in her eyes sharpened, like a furry forest creature turning feral.

Damien slowly took another sip, brow pinched over the

mug's rim as he watched Amma's mouth twist up. What a quick shift—when had she become so dangerous? Something in his chest twitched fondly, and then there was another twitch, lower, and he was glad for the pink cloak even if he did look ridiculous in it.

"So Wil and I made a deal."

Hot tea came out of Damien's nose as he tried to hold back the outburst that came anyway. He hurried to put the cup down and wipe at his face. "Amma," he choked out, "you made a *deal* with a *fae*?"

"She did."

Even as the frosty voice rippled up Damien's back, a blazing fury took the rest of him. Tugging at the knot Amma had made around his neck, Damien pulled off her cloak and pushed it into her hands, whirling around and snarling. "You'll get whatever it is you think you've tricked out of her when the Summer Court freezes over."

King Wil was taller than even Damien, and though he was thin, his presence was menacing. That was how fae were: ethereal, delicate-looking things until their intentions came to the surface, followed swiftly by their true visage. Shadows fell in the hollows of his face, features so cutting Damien could practically feel the welts forming on his own skin. "I have promised to give her anything she requests," said the king in a voice deeper than the chasm in Bloodthorne Keep. "She has not yet named her desire, but I've assured her that I can fulfill whatever it may be."

Amma's fingers were cool against the heat of Damien's

skin as she touched his arm. "And I only promised to help bring the other courtiers back."

Damien swallowed, eyes still boring into Wil as he addressed her. "You mean to say you promised a fae that you would *sway the will* of other fae?"

She snorted with irritation, a thing she so infrequently did that it pulled Damien's gaze back to her. "Oh, Damien, it's not that serious. We're throwing a party, for goodness' sake, that's all."

"Which, I must say, there is much left to do before the festivities on the morrow." The king's face had gone softer again, but his smile was all fangs. "We should return to planning while the demonling roots about in the kitchens for sustenance, as I do believe your bodies wither away without food. It appears to be already happening."

Damien glanced down at himself, bare-chested with his pants falling low on his hips but far from withering. He puffed out his chest and snarled, but a pang in his stomach made him deflate again. Amma's hand taking him by the elbow, however, was enough to make him back down.

After being dropped off in the nearly bare but enormous kitchens, Damien found he had to scrounge for sustenance, but Kaz remained with him. Alone, Damien questioned the imp as he ripped into some dried meats and continued to poke about in every cabinet.

No, the fae hadn't touched Amma, Kaz confirmed, but yes, Amma seemed to like him. "Explain," Damien demanded.

"I do not know, Master"—the imp clacked his talons together nervously—"but she *smiles* and is *nice* to him."

Well, that certainly described how she was with nearly everyone.

Damien took a breath, peering into the emptiness of the larder and swallowing the salted mystery meat. "And at night? Where does she go?"

Kaz's tongue shot out, and he gagged, and Damien glared at him. "Back to your chamber where she gets in bed with *you*, Master."

Damien's body went hot, but not with anger. Yet another reason to pity himself for not managing to wake sooner, preferably in the middle of the night. He stuffed the rest of the meat into his mouth and poked his head into the oven to completely conceal the grin that threatened it.

"But," said Kaz with a strangling apprehension that drained all the pleasure out of Damien, "she always changes your bandages first, just like in the morning, and she has to blather to you the *whole* time even though you're clearly unconscious. She calls it *taking care of you*, as if a blood mage would ever need *that*." He jumped up onto a counter and lifted the lid off a massive pot to peer inside. "What are we looking for?"

Damien's lips quirked up while Kaz was preoccupied, but he swallowed back all the other strange, fluttery feelings in his throat. "An exit. A way back to Eiren or the Wilds or even Aszath Koth could be anywhere."

"I haven't seen one of those." The imp's voice echoed into the cast iron.

Damien sighed, standing straight and taking a long look around. Ice everywhere, blue and cold and dreary. Amma would not want to stay in this place, no matter how attractive that fae king made it or himself appear to be. She was smarter, more ambitious, too enamored of living things to remain in a world destined to hibernate forever. A place like this. Or, he thought suddenly and depressingly, a place like Aszath Koth.

Damien frowned, taking a breath and testing his arcana again. Gently, slowly, carefully, he felt the palace around him, not looking for anything in particular this time but only feeling the weird, wobbling magic of the Everdarque. It truly was empty, not a living creature anywhere, though the entire place buzzed with magic. Of course, everything was constructed by that fae. His dizzying powers equated to naught but illusion, but there was a stronger ping now that he was open to feeling for anything, and he went toward the source.

Wandering out of the kitchen, Kaz on his heels, the two passed through a long dining room and then straight into a second one and a third, each variations on the theme of blue and white crystals. Ridiculous, useless, a grand show of nothing but pointless wealth and opulence, he thought as he followed that magical hum back to the throne room, which was equally big and ostentatious and stupid.

A little like the throne room back home.

Damien shook his head and passed into that strange chamber Amma had pointed out, the one she'd innocently said Wil had been "playing with himself" in, following the strain of magic that tugged at him right to the table. Carved into the table's frosty top was a map of sorts, though the labels were all in Ouranic. Of course fae favored the language of the gods—they thought very highly of themselves.

He placed a hand over one of the words to feel the carvings, but an unexpected pulse shot back up at him so strong he was knocked right back into one of the icy chairs. Damien's hand smoked, noxscura angrily buzzing over his skin to mend the blistering that had been done to it, his magic working a little better, but only just—he hadn't sensed how powerful the table was. Nauseated like when he had been in that temple in Durendreg, he leaned forward to keep the room from spinning. "What the fuck?" he murmured to himself, pushing back his hair from his face.

Beneath sat two buckets, predictably made of ice as well, but not for vomiting into when one was shocked by the arcana in the table, apparently. Instead, each was filled with small figurines, the one nearest him giving off a golden glow. Damien very carefully pulled one out, and it pulsed with a similar magic to the table, but the arcana was contained by its glass exterior. It was in the vague shape of a human and had a flat base to set it upright but no discerning characteristics. Inside its hollow form was a swirling yellow liquid.

No, not a liquid. Luxerna.

His eyes darted to the second bucket, and its silvery glow told him that the figures inside it were similarly filled with noxscura. His stomach twisted itself into knots. One hundred and forty-two knots, to be exact, but there was no time to count. It was one thing to have noxscura swimming in his own veins, passed down from his father, filtered through his blood, slipping out as smoke and winnowed down to be weaker than its origin, but to see it like *this*? Holding a pure and unbridled source of arcana was harrowing, even for a blood mage.

But of course, that was how the fae would see noxscura and luxerna—just a pretty decoration and part of some silly game. Damien always knew fae were dangerous, and the discovery didn't shock him, but his thoughts immediately went to Amma. Wil had tried to teach her to play—what if one of the figures had broken? Chances of her surviving direct contact with the stuff were abysmally low, and if she did? That may have been worse.

He stood, wanting to be far from the chamber, and strode out its back entry into a courtyard, a dark, moonless sky above. Kaz followed dutifully, sniffing around and poking at everything. The courtyard was free of snow, a few benches scattered about, and holly bushes lined a path to its center where a grand fountain was spouting more ice.

Beyond the courtyard lay another grandiose chamber, visible through sheer, icy doors, and he could just see the forms of Amma and Wil walking beside one another, pointing to the ceiling and speaking together. Despite the cold, sweat had gathered on Damien's forehead, and his heart had yet to completely settle. Amma turned, and her eyes found him through the door. She was smiling at first, but then that look turned to worry, and she took a few steps toward the courtyard.

Damien shook away the sickly feeling of the too-pure arcana from the other room and instead pushed his way into the ballroom, ushering her back the way she'd come. "Fine," he said, answering a question that hadn't been asked and grinning at the fae king. "How goes it?"

Wil turned up his lip, displeased at Damien's arrival, which only satisfied the blood mage.

"Better than your search for appropriate attire apparently," Wil snapped, and a thick tunic appeared in his hand, which he passed to Damien, then pointed vaguely to the room with those long, spiderlike fingers. "We were discussing garland. Just here and here and here."

"And maybe a tree," said Amma, eyes glittering.

"Inside?" Damien asked.

"It can be done with magic, can't it?"

King Wil grinned. "Yes, of course, anything can."

Damien remained close as they traversed the rest of the palace, discussing décor and menu items and activities and dark gods knew what the fuck else until Amma eventually insisted they had to retire. She had been yawning for some time, but the fae was hard-pressed to let them go, no sign of exhaustion himself. Damien was relieved when they finally reached the bedchamber, as was Kaz, who cuddled up on the divan by the door and fell asleep right away.

Damien too was feeling exhausted, not quite as healed as he would have liked, and he pulled off his boots as Amma did the same, murmuring to one another about the length of the day and being bewildered by the constant darkness. Without much thought or propriety, Damien had mostly undressed, and Amma had nearly done the same, both making their way to the single bed in the room's center, and then they stopped short.

"Oh." Amma's eyes went wide, the sleepiness run out of them. "I just thought—well, I've been, um…" Her face turned the most glorious shade of red.

"You've what?" he asked, pretending to forget everything Kaz had told him.

"Well, you were there…" She giggled nervously, pointing to the bed. "And I guess I sort of, you know, wanted to make sure you were still breathing at night."

Damien made a thoughtful sound in the back of his throat. "I appreciate your concern."

"You put out a lot of heat when you sleep." She couldn't seem to look at him, throat bobbing as she swallowed.

"No need for either of us to be cold," he said quite logically and gestured to the bed.

Amma had taken off the velvety outer dress she'd been wearing, a shorter linen dress beneath. It wasn't the tiny chemise that had been burned into his mind, but her legs and arms were bare and would need to be kept warm.

She finally nodded, mostly to herself, and climbed onto the bed, hugging the far edge as Damien went around to the other side. Settling in, even beneath a shared blanket, there was enough room between them for a whole pantheon of gods. If only he could remind her of how bold she'd been not so long ago. The Chthonic word would do it, but he had promised her he would not use it again. As they lay there, the room's lights seemed to know, dimming themselves.

"Damien?"

"Yes?" he answered too quickly in the dark.

"I'm sorry that I got us stuck here in the Everdark when we could be out looking for your mother instead."

Damien's breath caught. He had put that thought completely out of his mind. "This was our only alternative," he struggled to say.

"I'm also sorry for what I implied about your father."

"Please, don't be." He stared up at the chandelier above them, the only source of light in the room gone shadowy and blue, reflecting over the icy ceiling like stars. "I requested your honesty, and you gave it."

"But it upset you, and I don't want—"

"It's all right." He couldn't think about it—there was no forest for him to storm off into this time with spare trees to accidentally infect. In fact, just the opposite: There was a room with what amounted to tiny bottles of unholy arcana that he could... Bloody Abyss, he had no idea just what he could do with them, but it would be nothing good. His stomach balled into a knot. "I do believe we should leave here as soon as possible though."

"You don't like it here." She shifted in the darkness. "And you really don't like King Wil."

"No," he answered earnestly, "but I would also like to return to other business."

The quiet lingered, as wide as the space between them, and then Amma's voice peeked into it with a slight rasp. "I have a confession I need to make to you."

"About the fae?" He heard his own voice, uncomfortably flat with barely contained jealousy.

"No." She displaced the blankets, fidgeting. "It's only about me. Something I did that may have been sort of bad."

Damien silently thanked all the dark gods and demons and basest beasts—and may have even sneaked in a gracious prayer to that Sestoth Amma admired so much—that the chamber was dark and they were far apart so that she could not see how his interest, among other things, had suddenly piqued. He cleared his throat. "Oh?"

"Yeah, um, so." Amma rolled toward him. There was still an ocean of mattress between them, but it felt like the tide had just gone out. "Lycoris offered to take the talisman out of me, and I turned her down. I know I shouldn't have, but—"

"No," Damien stopped her. "I hoped she might have had another way besides changing you, but it would not have been acceptable to trade your current life for the talisman. I never intended for you to stay there with them, unless you wanted to of course, but that decision was..." Damien rubbed his face. "I am sorry I even placed it before you."

"There's something else," she said, tracing a finger along the blankets. "I had this dream."

Damien nearly sat straight up, but he bit down on his tongue and kept himself flat on his back. He could scarcely believe she was about to tell him.

"It was about a tree."

Death could have come for him right there in the form of disappointment, and Damien wouldn't have known the difference. "I imagine you have a lot of dreams about trees, Amma."

She sat up then, and he watched her pull her knees to her chest and wrap her arms around them in the dark. "Well, I ended up meeting the tree from this dream, and it told me how to get the talisman out."

Damien's brow shot up. "It spoke to you?" He too had talked to a tree recently. Sort of.

"It said removing the talisman was something I should be able to do to myself, and it offered me help to do it right then." She took a deep, shuddering breath. "But I'd dreamt about purging the talisman before, and it hurt *so* much, Damien. I didn't know dreams could do that, make you feel pain like that, make you think you were dying, but it was like being cut open and having my heart torn out, and I couldn't go through with it. I want to help you—I mean, I don't want you to unleash a demon on the realm and destroy it, but I *do* want you to have your father back. But I just couldn't."

Damien swallowed back a lump in his throat, shaking his head. For all Amma had been to him and all she had done for him, it was the thing she hadn't that suddenly struck him so deeply. Damien had been privately glad not to have the talisman readily available—it meant he could not follow his father's orders just yet—but more than that, unburdening Amma of the talisman so that she could make choices based solely on what she wanted also meant dissolving what tied the two of them together. What had at first been a hateful and cumbersome chain had grown into a tether he desperately held on to, an anchor he relied on in an arcanely dark sea so easy to become lost in, and as selfish and terrible as that was, the thought of severing it pierced him deeper than any blade ever had.

But he couldn't tell her any of that, no matter how reassuring it might have been in the moment. She was so concerned with him, with his pain, his worries, his *feelings*, that she didn't need yet another reason not to make a decision that she wanted to make.

Her voice broke back into the quiet. "I'm sorry I was weak."

"Do not be sorry, Amma," he said with none of the usual exasperation of that sentiment, pushing himself up to sit as a distraction from the other things, the syrupy, heartfelt things, that he wanted perilously to say.

"But you still don't have the talisman."

"I would rather have—" Damien cut himself off, eyes wide and staring into the darkness of the room. *You.* That was the answer. But it was also the problem. And telling her would be no gift to either of them. He cleared his throat and turned to her, words careful. "I would rather have you not be in pain."

"It wasn't just the pain," she said, eyes glassy under the dim lights. "I was afraid of losing…of losing everything."

Damien reached for her without thinking, and she moved to meet him in the middle of the bed. He pulled her right up against him, and she didn't resist, but she did crumple like a small, fragile thing in his arms, burying her face in his chest. Amma clawed gently at his shoulders, a desperate creature rooting around for safety, and he held on to her as if she would be torn away at any moment.

How he could offer her comfort that she suddenly clung to so tightly and simultaneously be the source of her pain, he didn't know, but he pushed his disgust with himself away as he heard a sob break out of her. Of course she was afraid of losing everything—her home, her family, herself. Damien and his plans were a threat to everything she'd ever known, and he was asking her to play a pivotal role in the destruction of it all.

"Amma, don't do this to yourself," he said softly into the top of her head. "You are not weak for wanting to stop malevolence. To stop me."

"Please don't," she whispered, her breath hot against his chest. "Please don't say you're evil."

Damien certainly felt evil then, though in a wholly different way than he'd always imagined his deeds playing out. The insistence hammered at the back of his skull like a twisted arcana forcing its way into his brain, and he wanted to take her face in his hands and tell her just that, but then she'd so sweetly made a request of him, and he was so completely enthralled by her, he could do nothing but oblige. "For you, anything," he said, the words some of his most dangerous and also some of his most honest. "But for me, you mustn't cry."

She tipped her face up at him, cheeks tear-stained and eyes red-rimmed even in the icy-blue light, but she set her mouth hard, lips no longer quivering.

Dark gods, did he want to kiss those lips, to press them to his own like he had back in the karsts when she was needy and excited, to rip away all this indecision, to make her his, loyal only to one another. He ran fingers through her hair, and there was a flicker of joyful Amma in her bright blue eyes.

Damien gently pulled her head back against his chest and settled the two of them down into the bed, eluding her tempting lips. Amma's fingers curled around his neck, tracing thoughtless circles on his skin and sending tingles along his body. How could she do that, make her touch so kind and enticing and painful all at once? The feeling lingered like arcana in his veins long after her hands fell still and her breathing became heavy, falling asleep across his chest as if she could trust him, as if she were safe in the arms of a blood mage, as if he had never threatened to end her life.

It was almost funny how perfectly she fit in his arms, so bloody humorous how comfortably her body tucked into his own like they were built just for one another. Even here, in the ridiculousness of the Everdarque, with ruin looming so close by, it felt like a fucking joke how *right* it was to hold her and be held. And he knew then, unequivocally, that losing all of it—losing her—was going to be even more painful than never having Amma to begin with.

CHAPTER 28

AMMA

Broken Vows and Fixed Numbers

Amma woke, glancing up to see a sliver of Damien's violet eyes gazing down at her. It was not the first time she'd woken in his arms, but it was the first time he'd been completely aware of what he was doing, grin deepening as he squeezed her even tighter. It was already warm, nestled amongst furs and one another, but a new heat flourished in her chest. The lingering embarrassment at the night before was nudged out by contentment and safety and that other thing, that thing she wouldn't say because feeling it for Damien was wickedly dangerous, but she knew it was there too.

And then something else prodded at her, also quite warm but stiff too. She shifted her hips against it to maneuver around and cuddle up even closer, but Damien's eyes flew open, and his fingers tightened on her skin. Instead of deepening their embrace, he released her and rolled away.

Amma pushed up onto an elbow, sleepy mind waking up as she grinned at him. *Oh no, you don't*, she thought, but before she could pounce, there was a fervent knock at the door.

As if caught in the midst of unacceptable behavior, both jumped from the bed and scrambled for their clothes. Kaz started squawking, tumbling out of the nest of blankets he'd made himself on the divan and going for the door.

"They're on their way!" King Wil announced from the threshold, filling up its entirety with his slender frame, arms out, excitement palpable.

Amma had just pulled the thicker dress over her head and realized as she tugged it down that it was backward, chest and neck too tight, but she tried to put on her brightest voice, hearing it crack with hoarseness. "Oh, how many?"

"Every single one!" The king twirled into the room, steps light, then eyed Damien. "Even your friend Scot."

"I thought he was a traitor?" Damien's tunic was undone but sadly on, and he ran a hand through his black hair to push it back but only mussed it up further, like a raven's wing in a storm. Amma's insides turned to mush as she watched him fidget.

"Defector, loyalist, what's the difference?" The king danced over to Kaz, gave him a pat, and then went back to the door. "There are new cloaks for you in the wardrobe. Be quick, there is still so much to do!"

As Wil hurried out of the room, Amma pulled open the opaque door of ice on the huge piece of furniture built right out of the wall. A white fur-lined cloak hung before her, quite long, deepening in color to sapphire at its base and run through with silver filigree. Beside it, a black velvet cloak shimmered amethyst when it moved in the light.

"Show-off," scoffed Damien, and Amma snickered, moving them aside to reveal a third in the warm tones of changing leaves and just Kaz's size.

The palace had been populated with hundreds of those short flippered birds, presumably all conjured by the fae king. They waddled everywhere, carrying trays and making last-minute adjustments under King Wil's direction, which was of course odd, since he could change anything he liked to look precisely as he imagined with just a flick of his hand. That was how the entire castle and indeed even the world beyond it had come into being, as Amma understood it, but it kept him busy enough to not fret much more over the impending guests.

Amma herself was anxious enough, but between the fae king's constant buzzing questions and the crooked, playful grins Damien was sneaking her, she didn't have much time to wonder if the deal she'd made would be considered complete after this. She'd wanted to tell Damien the night before that she kept the talisman inside her, not to stop him from doing something awful with it but to stop him from leaving her to go do it. But it was shameful that she cared more about keeping him around than about the whole stupid realm.

There would be time to feel guilty about all that later though. For now, they had a party to throw. As she was giving one of the conjured not-birds a boost so that he could adjust a garland of pine boughs and holly berries over the throne room's massive hearth, Amma got a very strong whiff of something sweet and floral that tickled her nose and made her turn.

A flutter of pink and yellow petals swept down through the tunnel of the palace, plastering themselves to the icy walls and creating a pastel carpet. The air was bright and filled Amma's chest with warmth and the urge to skip about, like playfulness itself had been invited to the castle.

"Rosi, darling!" called Wil, and he swept across the throne room to meet the fae who led the small entourage entering. She was draped in a gauzy pink material that clung to her full curves and floated about her like the wind was at her constant beckoning, which was entirely possible. Flitting about her was a small contingency of butterflies, coming to rest on a shoulder now and again, and atop her head was a wreath of thin sticks and vines, though on closer inspection, the crown was more of a nest on account of the eggs that sat on the dome. She didn't appear to feel the cold, but she was also glowing like the sun itself, skin a shade of gold and a mane of coiled hair to match.

As Amma took in the others behind her, she realized that Wil's frosty skin and silvery hair were practically ordinary compared to the rest of the fae. Green, blue, mottled, striped—the skin of each fae was entirely unique and dizzying, and though they were each human enough in appearance, there were hints beyond a shock of violet hair or an arm covered in white speckles that these creatures were far removed from Amma. They moved about with little to no concern for the space around them, as if already at home, and greeted Wil as if there had not been an "eternity of silence" preceding the party. Or so he had claimed.

But then the one called Rosi turned to where Amma, Damien, and Kaz had sequestered themselves, her golden eyes flickering. "Oh, you have some human visitors, Wil?"

The Winter King swallowed, a nervousness shimmering over his icy features. "Ah, yes, you know how it is. They fall in sometimes, and if you do not take care of them, they die, and then things get complicated with the veil and everything."

"Of course. We have a few of our own as well." Rosi gestured over her shoulder, and a pair of nervous-looking young men poked out from the crowd of fae, significantly shorter than the rest. At that, Amma exhaled and pressed a hand to her chest, and things felt as though they might actually go smoothly.

There were thirty-nine fae by Amma's count, plus two humans that came in with the Spring Court, each given thick cloaks by the conjured waddlers in colors and styles that enhanced their unique appearances. Amma could not speak, only watch, trying to take it all in, until her eye was caught by a specific fae who was laughing brightly at how one of the flippered birds was chasing a rogue butterfly. She had deep-brown skin and long, soft waves of hair the color of dawn at its pinkest.

But a cool breeze blew through the tunnel, stealing Amma's attention. The petals left along the floor dried out, turning crispy as their colors faded, and a shadow formed at the tunnel's end. A pack of red foxes barreled into the throne room, kicking up petals that caught with warm licks of fire before burning away, filling the air with a smoky, charred scent. The Autumn Court had arrived, forty-five in total, carrying in the colors of fallen leaves and the twilit sky.

The throne room should have been too crowded, but it appeared to expand, and Amma and Damien pushed themselves farther back to keep to the wall as the fae greeted one another, but then a fae calling herself Retta, with a very generous chest and the most cheerful laughter Amma had ever heard, insisted they mingle, pressing slices of hot, fresh bread into their hands, and they were swept into the crowd.

It was all going quite well—until it wasn't. There was a flash of heat, and the tunnel shimmered so brightly Amma thought some arcane blast would ruin them all, but the ice only ate away at itself, melting so that the entrance widened even larger and the floor became a pool. Over the water, silhouetted by the blinding light at his back, a fae rode in on a long, slick board, arms out and chest bare. His tan skin and well-built physique glittered as the light at his back faded, and he twisted to come to a halt in the throne room, water cutting up before him and splashing outward in a huge wall toward the others.

King Wil was there, and he threw an arm out, freezing the wave before it crashed down over the rest of them, saving the other fae as they gasped in a horror Amma could not decipher from genuine surprise. Surely they could have all done something about it to save themselves, but they each traded looks, some thrilled, others shocked, and there was a voice just behind Amma, deep and feminine, that simply said, "That would be Norm."

The Emperor of the Summer Court peeked out from around the frozen wall with a grin of white teeth, none of them pointed but glaringly bright against his cinnamon skin. Golden hair flowed down his back, and his body was muscled, adorned with ink in various shades to create patterns rather than clothes. As his wave crumbled into tiny flecks of ice, the two rulers met. Behind Norm, there was a large contingency of fae, many of them adorned in bright colors, but there were others who Amma could tell had once belonged to the Winter Court. When Amma counted, Norm and his courtiers were fifty-seven strong. The fae stared at one another, and then Norm offered his hand. They clasped wrists, and just as quickly, Wil whirled back to the rest of them, announcing that the festivities would begin.

Amma had thought she would have time to rest then, maybe even getting a few quiet moments with Damien, but Wil insisted on making her his assistant. Together, they demonstrated for the others how to pack the perfect snowball, how to lie in a bank and wiggle about to make a snow dragon, how to best sit before sledding down a hill. It all felt incredibly elementary, and Amma had to bite back laughter each time a fae asked if they were doing something correctly, as if there were a right way to have fun. Hours passed in a flurry of frigid activities that wore down Amma much sooner than any of the fae, but eventually the entire contingency retired to the ballroom to gather around many popping fires and long tables of foods laden with fat and spices.

The Autumn Tsarina, a made-up title if Amma ever heard one, was a fae with hair like a maple's leaves and pupilless eyes. She had whisked Damien off to fawn over him with a few other fae dressed in black cloaks while some of the Summer Court were cheering for Kaz as he toasted various foods with his tail.

Amma had finally taken a seat at one of the tables across from a pair of identical pale fae who spoke in tandem but were apparently from different courts. The two introduced themselves to Amma with the names Ontsumn and Omenbanca. When she stared back, alarmed that they had given her the "true names" Damien had spoken of that caused madness, they laughed in unison and explained that "our other names were taken," though it wasn't really an explanation at all.

A warm body took a seat beside Amma, making her straighten. The pink-haired fae from the Spring Court leaned an elbow languidly on the table, resting her head on her hand and staring right at Amma, waiting.

Amma's pulse quickened from being so close, but the fae's easy smile sparked relaxation deep in her bones. She lifted a hand, dark skin rich like soil, and a sprout grew up out of her palm. From the new bloom's center, a bubble formed. It expanded, taking on an odd shape until there was a tiny pop, and it detached, the stem beneath withering away into nothing, and a glass figure dropped into the fae's hand. She offered it to Amma.

"Don't worry," she said, voice like the rustling of wind through the trees. "You're not in trouble. Promise."

Amma's eyes flicked to the figurine, identical to the pieces on King Wil's game board and filled with a shimmering, golden goo, and then back up at the fae.

"You're meant to take it."

"I-I can't play," said Amma, her own voice hoarse and cracking. "I don't have the magic."

The fae chuckled lowly. "Not to play with."

"What do I do with it?" Amma tipped her head, bringing her nose close to the piece, vaguely human shaped but without features.

"I'm not sure. Tertius just says you can't leave without it." The fae pointed with her other hand to a fae who was laughing at another table, skin blue and a divot in the middle of his forehead. "He doesn't really know why, because he's given away almost all his powers, but when he tells us something, it's only when he's almost completely certain."

Amma reached out, and when she picked up the piece, its innards sloshed, starry speckles riding the waves of gold inside. "I feel like I'm not supposed to have this."

"Don't worry. If anyone should have it besides me, it's you, but Tertius says you won't have to watch over it for very long. Keep it close to your heart for now."

Amma's reflection in the glass stared back at her, and then she swallowed hard and tucked it into the neck of her dress.

"Mind if I borrow her, Rea?" King Wil appeared over the fae woman's shoulder, and she flashed Amma another comforting smile before flitting away.

Amma was relieved when the Winter King led her out of the ballroom and into the courtyard, the space quiet even with the large doors open between them and the party. She took a deep breath of cool, fresh air, steam swirling before her as she let it out. Snow speckled the dark sky as it fell, a very fine dusting of white over the stone benches and glossy leaves of holly bushes that circled the yard.

"I must express my deepest gratitude, Amma," said the fae king, gesturing to her with the slightest bow. "I have for too long languished in these halls, wandering them with nary but my own good company, but you have resolved the ache in my chest without even knowing it."

Amma's brows shot up, and she plastered on a smile, all teeth and restrained giggles. "Oh, I did? I had no idea you felt that way." Thankfully, sarcasm was completely lost on the fae.

Wil touched his chest with those too-long fingers. "I owe you our agreed-upon debt."

"Safe passage," she said quickly, thrilled that her end of the bargain appeared to be fulfilled, "for me and Damien and Kaz. We need to get back to Eiren."

The humble smile on the king's face faltered. "You wish to leave? All this?"

She followed his spindly fingers waving over the courtyard. It was beautiful, the snow sparkling like gemstones in the darkness, the serenity, the magic that answered every whim. Kaz even seemed to enjoy himself. In the days that Amma had been helping Wil, she had contemplated what staying there would be like if it became necessary for longer than a few days. It was comfortable, safe, and she had a bedchamber—one she shared with Damien—though she had always planned to leave.

But they *could* stay there, couldn't they? The two of them, forgetting about the world beyond the Everdarque. Neither she nor Damien would have to go home to be beholden to those there. And they could keep sharing that bed.

King Wil's face changed again, lips curling upward. "Your mind wavers. Humans, so fickle." He let out a small laugh. "What else could you wish of me? I can give you anything, you know, though humans often ask for the same few things: riches, love, power. Why not all of it? I could make you a queen."

Amma felt her skin go warm. She'd seen Wil conjure everything in the palace from the robe she wore to the massive hearth in the ballroom, the pines, the lake, the very snowflakes falling on her eyelashes. She blinked up at the fae king's smile of too many pointed teeth, a smile that spread over his tapered jaw and reached right up to his icy irises, filling them with a mischievous expectation. He *could* do anything, and if Amma had the opportunity to get exactly what she wanted…

"You can make me powerful?" she asked in a voice that was so quiet she was unsure she had spoken at all.

His grin only grew, and like that, it seemed too wide, extending beyond anything human. "More powerful than you could ever imagine."

Amma's throat felt thick, and her heartbeat slowed. She could be strong enough to will the talisman out of her and leave herself whole, to return to Faebarrow with power unimaginable and ensure her people's safety, to help Damien in some way that didn't force him to bring destruction to everything around them. And maybe if she could show him just how strong she'd become, Damien would see her the way she wanted him to.

"I'd like to be strong," Amma said, though her voice was still soft, fingers clenching, tears pricking at the backs of her eyes at just the thought. "How would you do it?"

The fae king laid his hand flat, and the snow that gathered in his palm lifted up, swirled about, and in its place sat a transparent cup, frosty, the liquid inside thick and silver.

"What is that?"

"Power," he said simply.

"This is what makes fae powerful?"

"Well, we have always been this way. But for a creature like yourself"—he chuckled, and the cup rose up from his palm to float before her—"it *could* be existence altering."

Amma put her hands out, and the icy chalice set itself on her palms. The shining surface inside moved exactly like the streams of silver she had seen in the fissures back in Aszath Koth when the Brotherhood had summoned Kaz, that image, so beautiful, still stark in her mind. The mirrorlike surface of the drink showed the deep violet of the sky, every fleck of snow as it fell, and her own face when she brought it close.

The girl who looked back was afraid. She was naive and frail and pathetic, and if only she could be stronger, bolder, smarter—but all that was in the cup, wasn't it? It was within her reach to be a better future baroness, to be a better friend, to be a better woman, and all she had to do was drink.

"Sanguinisui, stop!"

Amma froze, the cup to her lips. The smell hit her then, smoldering ash and metallic blood, and her mind fizzled. Bloodthorne's Talisman of Enthrallment pulsed through her, and her body reacted without her mind's permission, holding completely still, but her knees were weak, and she was sure she would faint.

The cup was snatched from her hand and thrown, shattering somewhere in the courtyard, but Amma could see none of it, ordered by magic not to move.

"What do you think you're doing?" Damien was beside her. "That would have killed her!"

"Oh no, you cannot know a thing like that for certain." The fae king held his hands up, laughing. "It only *could* have killed her!"

Damien growled, hands clenched, and then he rounded on Amma. "And you," he said with a bite, "what in the Abyss were you thinking?"

Amma's heart fluttered like a panicked moth. She was still trapped under the spell, muscles aching, her breath refusing to come. He had told her to stop, and she had, unable to move, to even breathe, until he released her, but he was so angry, he didn't even notice.

"I'm sure she was thinking that she was about to get exactly what her heart desires," said Wil.

Damien turned to him again, away from Amma and the spell he was leaving her under. "She did not ask you for *that*," he spat. "She intended to request a return to our plane."

The fae king smiled fiendishly. "Oh, but she didn't."

"Yes, she did," Damien growled and then whirled toward her again. "You did, didn't you?"

Amma tried to speak, but nothing came, throat not moving, tongue frozen, head feeling like it would explode as her vision tunneled.

Then Damien realized all at once what he had done—using his arcana in the Everdarque, where it would not fully listen to him. "Amma, sanguinisui, be…be normal?"

Amma stumbled, arms falling, head heavy as she sucked in a huge breath. Damien grabbed her, but when she was steady, she shook him off.

"Oh, that was a fun little trick!" Wil clapped. "Do it again!"

Damien had his hands out, looking at them like they'd hurt her. "I didn't mean… Amma, are you all right?"

She rubbed her temple, shaking her head.

When no one obliged his request, the fae king clicked his tongue. "Expecting her to die from just a taste of pure arcana—how little you must think of her."

"I didn't say—" Damien cut himself off again, the frustration mounting as he tried to contain another outburst. "Even if she'd survived—*if*—she can't be exposed to pure noxscura. It will change her."

"Can she not make that decision for herself?"

"No! Not this! Never this!" He couldn't contain himself anymore, as close to frantic as Amma had ever seen him, shouting at the fae who stood there, so composed. Black smoke was curling around Damien's limbs, his own magic, and it sparked off into the night. Around him, fissures broke, and silver swirled in them before closing back up.

"Well, I suppose not, as it seems she doesn't make *any* decisions for herself. Not with that fun little spell you've got on her. But, Amma, dear, this is your chance to get whatever it is you want. A blood mage is no match for the entirety of every fae court, and we have a bargain; I must abide by whatever request you make."

She glanced over her shoulder, the snow falling harder now, but through it, she could see the other fae gathered at the doors, peeking over one another to watch and whisper. Kaz slipped out from the crowd and scurried up, eyes wide.

"I want to go," Amma said breathlessly, reining in every angry, explosive, petulant thought. She had to make the right choice—someone had to. "I want to leave, the three of us, together."

The fae king's face changed in a flash, suddenly dark and pointed and terrifying, and she swore he grew an extra foot in height. "Leave? You want to leave? With him?"

"You promised me whatever I requested," she said, shoring herself up, breathing hard but staring back at him as his features twisted. "I have fulfilled my bargain. Now you will fulfill yours."

The king looked like he had been struck, and for a moment, she feared he would take it all back. His arm swept down through the air, limb long with too many joints, as a freezing wind tore at her, the snow caught up in it blinding. "Fine, then go!"

The ground beneath her feet gave way, and Amma's heart shot up into her throat as her body fell, down, down, and then she slammed into the hard ground.

Amma lay there for a long, brain-addled moment, the breath knocked all out of her, everything dark. Death—this was death, she thought, choking for her breath, but then a speck of light, and then another, and she was staring up at Ero and Lo in the night sky. Two moons, the moons of her plane, shining back down on her.

Aspens, maples, pines. A forest, dense and dark, surrounded them, free of snow but with leaves fallen. They'd been returned to somewhere in Eiren, somewhere in the midst of a chilly autumn just as they'd left it, but where exactly, she could not tell.

Damien was beside her, picking himself up with a grunt and rubbing the back of his head. "Fucking fae," he mumbled as Kaz mimicked him with his own cranky grumbles. "I told you none of them are good. At least we are finally free of that place."

She glared at him as she sat up, the only words she could think to reply with a jumble of anger in her mind.

"What?" This he spat too angrily at her, but she swallowed down what she wanted to say yet again, simply getting to her feet.

Amma wiped the pine needles from her breeches, the velvet dress and the furred cloak gone, though there was a small pile of snow where she had landed. She felt around on herself, her hip pouch in place and the glass figure from the fae Rea still stuffed between her breasts.

"He was tricking you, you know," mumbled Damien, checking the straps of his armor. He was returned to his old clothing as well, tunic still torn up his once-injured arm. "He didn't care if you were poisoned, if you died. It was just a game to him, like everything is to those fae."

Amma blew out a frustrated breath, turning away. She did not need to be lectured—she knew what she was doing, and she had made the right choice in the end. Hadn't she?

"He only wanted to play with you, to keep you like a doll." Damien was grumbling to himself more than to her, but he certainly wasn't being very quiet, and it made her blood boil.

He spoke as if she cared about the fae king, but she didn't, not really; she only cared about what she had potentially lost in the power he'd offered. The power Damien had taken away.

"That fae would have locked you up had you given him the chance, and—"

"Locked me up?" she exploded, rounding on him. "Is that what *he* wanted to do to me? To keep me like a plaything and make me do whatever *he* wanted? To not let me make any of my own decisions?"

As she waited for her answer, Damien's face changed, the scowl falling off it. Beside him, Kaz's eyes went wide and worried too. "Amma," Damien finally said, softer, "this is not the same. You don't understand—"

"No, *you* don't understand!" she shouted, voice quickly going raw with distress. "You don't know what it is to be weak and afraid. I just wanted to be powerful, Damien, and I was doing it for you!"

"What?" His hands were held out, face screwed up. "Why?"

"I wanted to be strong, to be something that you would think more of, that you would respect, but you—you couldn't even keep your promise to me that you wouldn't use that spell again." Amma sucked in a breath and pressed a hand to her chest. Her heart beat with an anger and ache that she hated so viscerally, she would have rather it stopped altogether than go on like this.

"Amma, I—"

"I'm going for a walk," she said, eyes falling to the forest floor and voice falling cold. "And you are *not* going to follow me. You're going to be the one to sit here and not move, and you can wait and wonder if I'll come back. Then, for once, you can feel all the awful things that go along with being ordered around and left, if blood mages even *can* feel them." She turned and headed off into the darkness of the trees, alone.

CHAPTER 29

DAMIEN

The Very Sinews of Villainy

DAMIEN WATCHED AFTER WHERE Amma had gone for a long time. The shadows amongst the trees deepened, the sounds slipping into night, and he could only wait in the spot he'd been left, sitting on the ground, hoping she would eventually turn around. He wanted to believe that she would because she was kind and sweet and forgiving, but it was unjust and stupid to think Amma had no limit to her patience. He was a bloody fucking idiot; he had broken the vow he'd made to her and somehow convinced her that he didn't even have the capacity to care.

But he did care, and he did feel, blood mage or not, all those impractical human emotions that had been pounding on his chest and he had finally let in. And it was awful.

"She'll hate me now." Damien didn't recognize his own voice when it broke into the quiet, thick with defeat. "Won't she?"

Kaz had been waiting patiently up on a rock, tending to his leathery skin to be sure there were no lingering snowflakes, smart enough not to say a word until then. And still, he was even smarter, only lifting his shoulders with a hesitant glance back at the blood mage.

With no cutting words from the imp about how they should both be glad to be free of Amma's presence, Damien knew he had truly fucked up. With a nonsense sound that came right from his chest and echoed out into the world uselessly, he fell onto his back, the ground coming up to meet him not nearly as painfully as he deserved.

"Master?" Kaz skittered down the rock, landing in a crunchy pile of leaves. "Amma does not hate you."

Damien lifted his head to see if the imp's underbite had twisted into a smirk, boldly about to break into some sort of joke that would surely end his life, but he looked only hesitant, claws tapping against one another.

"You've never called her by her name before," Damien said.

The imp made the beginning of a retching noise but stopped. "She made sure I was warm," he mumbled and then shook his head, great big ears flapping. "Master, the point is I don't think she hates you. I don't think she *can* hate you."

"I know, I know, I'm a dark lord with the infernal power to compel and enthrall, and I can make her do whatever I want."

Miserably, Damien dropped his head back to the ground to stare up at the dark sky, the two moons drawing ever nearer one another as if one would eclipse the other and soon. He touched his hip pouch, arcanely returned to him through the fall out of the Everdarque, and he could feel the latent magic of the Yvlcon summons inside.

"I don't mean that, Master," said Kaz. "I think it's that she's—"

"Pathetic."

Damien flew to his feet. The voice—Xander Shadowhart's voice—struck him, and he whirled around. There stood the blood mage, casually leaning against a tree, pouting and looking like an absolute asshole.

"Where in the Abyss did you come from?"

"The better question is where did *you* come from?" Xander pushed off the tree like the effort was overwhelming, rolling his head on his shoulders. He was dressed in a red suit this time, bright even in the dark and much too festive for how Damien was feeling, only adding to his annoyance.

"Lost you for a bit," Xander said, "but I did *not* expect when I finally found you that you would be all alone, sprawled out on the ground and looking so sad, though I am pleased to have you to myself."

Kaz skittered back when Damien unsheathed his dagger. "I'm really not in the mood, Shadowhart. What do you want?"

Xander smiled viciously. "Well, at first, because of that little stunt you pulled in Durendreg, I wanted blood. But then I realized that was a bit too cliché, you know? And if I were in your boots, I might have betrayed me too. In fact, I might have even done it just for funsies. But you—you had a reason, which is annoying, really, because it was probably something stupid and righteous and put in your head by that girl." At the mention of Amma, Xander's smile fell off, and Damien's grip on his dagger tightened. "But then I realized, whatever the reason, it was enough to make you abandon your best chance at freeing Zagadoth, at getting what *you* really wanted. So I dug a bit deeper and decided that, as much as I'd like a spot of revenge, what I *actually* want is more important."

Damien swallowed, eyes darting out into the forest. Amma hadn't taken the opportunity to return at the worst possible moment, so keeping Xander there with him was for the best. "And?"

Xander dropped himself down onto a fallen log, crossed his legs, and gestured between the two of them. "I want this."

"What?"

"You know, the thing you said. Fondness? What is it… friendship?" His tongue came out like there was ash on it.

Damien rolled his eyes. "Don't play games with me. I told you I'm not in the mood."

"Games? Me? Why would I do something like that?" Xander propped his chin up on a fist and smiled, and for once, it wasn't entirely wicked, though it did look like it pained him. "You know I've got a special place in the hole where my heart ought to be for you, so I just thought I'd give you one last chance before I really turned my back on whatever *this* is, this thing you insist exists."

The muscles in Damien's shoulders loosened a bit, and he clicked his tongue. "How's that meant to work?"

Xander shrugged. "I dunno. Maybe we just…chat?"

They both grimaced.

But then Xander let out a deep sigh. "So, things, how are they?"

With another long scan of the darkened tree line but seeing no sign of Amma, Damien shuffled in place and ran a hand over his face, the answer coming out despite himself. "Bad."

And that made Xander smile yet again. "How delightful and felicitous! You know what might cheer you up? Yvlcon!"

Damien touched his hip pouch again where the scroll was tucked away. "It's already begun, so I'm obviously not going, and apparently neither are you."

"It's a summons by the Grand Order of Dread, Bloodthorne. Of course you're going, and so am I. In fact, I'm there right now myself." Xander chuckled, bobbing his head side to side as if what he said made any kind of sense. "Unless you think you'll never need them again? Or that the help they've given you means nothing?"

Damien ground his jaw. He had been assisted by the Grand Order a number of times in acquiring components for the talisman—the talisman that needed to keep itself hidden out in the forest until Xander finally decided to fuck off. Skipping Yvlcon did potentially jeopardize a number of alliances. But Amma absolutely could not go.

Xander sighed wistfully. "Well, not that you asked, but

I'm wonderful. I've been terribly busy perfecting translocation. Now I can use living targets to pop in on strange and new places, provided I've marked them, and send other beings to locations based on where they've been. Oh, you should have stuck around, really. Even without the *ancast erfind*, I've come such a long way since our study sessions. I even had some extra time to figure out how to work that divine resurrection spell from the Lux Codex!" He was really grinning, and Damien couldn't possibly bring himself to believe him. "But back to you: Daddy Zag's still locked up in his crystal, I presume? Mother is as well until I find someone who's been directly down into Archie's vaults and will cooperate."

"You found a way to break the binds on the occlusion crystals?"

His fingertips drummed over his chin. "Maybe?"

"Liar."

"You got me!" Xander laughed, loud and long, throwing his head back. Damien hoped Amma heard him and would stay out of sight. "No, of course I haven't—but that brings me back to the point of all this. See, I lied back at the tower too—I did quite like our little study sessions, your pet's presence notwithstanding. I finished translating the rest of the book, by the way."

Damien scoffed. "Yet you stand here in one piece. Malcolm was more powerful than you, and he couldn't survive being alone with the thing."

"Who says I was alone?" Xander's brows waggled. "It's funny, the allies you make when circumstance calls for it. But

I still need that talisman of yours, and since Kitten's not rubbing up against your legs and purring, am I to assume you've finally..." He slid a finger over his neck.

Why did he even ask? Xander knew the answer. Damien just grunted.

"Oh, what has happened to you, Bloodthorne? You haven't slit her throat yet? Haven't impaled her? Not even a *little*?"

"Well, almost," he muttered under his breath and looked away.

"And to think *I've* been fantasizing about ramming a blade into her heart since you told me that talisman was there for the harvesting." He sighed like it were some mundane task and not killing a woman—killing Amma. "Just the thought of holding that thing, covered in her blood, waving it around in your face—it just gives me chills!"

Damien didn't feel the noxscura come this time; it was already surrounding him, seeping out from every pore. Even free of the Everdarque and back on the plane he belonged, Damien's control over the stuff was too closely tied to his disposition. Xander could see it, could likely *feel* it, filling up the forest around him, and yet he stood and paced forward.

"To see your reaction then—would it be like this? All riled up and on the verge of losing yourself? Or would it be sadder? Softer? If I gut her in front of you, what would you do? Would you cry?" Xander draped a hand over his chest, eyes rolling back into his head. "I don't know if *I* would survive that. I'd probably die right along with her from pure joy."

"You would certainly die," Damien managed through

gritted teeth, voice low. If Xander wanted, Damien would make it so.

"Promise?" Xander took another step toward him. "A pity I won't kill her, not if I want the sweetness of knowing you've had to do it yourself. I only hope I can be there."

Damien's hands clenched, the hilt of his dagger burrowing into his skin. But then he took a breath, reining in the arcana. Amma still wasn't anywhere to be seen, and even with his threats, as bold and hateful as they were, Xander couldn't do anything to her if he was here and she was not. Now that he was closer, Damien could see the lump beneath his tunic, two vials hidden around Xander's neck, not just one. He'd brought much more blood than he needed, prepared for a fight. But Damien wasn't going to give Xander what he wanted—what he *really* wanted—which was to force him to lash out so that when Amma did show up, he would be useless to protect either of them.

No, he wouldn't let Xander do this, wouldn't let him take advantage. Damien had already let his anger hurt Amma; he wouldn't endanger her further. He would simply let the self-absorbed asshole talk until he grew bored enough to fuck off.

Xander's dark eyes flitted about, presumably watching the arcana disappear, and he frowned. "Oh no, I like you best when you're on the edge. You're not better than that now, are you? Has she truly left, and you've moved on?" His lips twisted around in thought. "I suppose time heals all wounds. Or most of them anyway." He gestured vaguely to his own face and then to Damien's scar.

If he let Xander keep going like this, if he started talking about *her*, he might lose his hard-won grip again, so he spat out the first thing that came to mind. "Do you remember my mother?"

That made Xander falter. A laugh caught in his throat, and he cocked his head. "Your...well, yes. She loved you. It was disgusting."

Feeling stuck, Damien didn't move.

"Not enough to stick around, obviously," Xander stuttered.

"She took us," he said, tongue thick, "to Eirengaard. I know you remember."

Xander fidgeted about, lips turning up in annoyance.

"And then Birzuma brought us back."

"So you're indebted to her," Xander snapped, "and you're willing to work together again, yes?"

There was something tempting in Xander's words. He was skilled, as much as Damien hated to admit it, and dedicated. But he was also deceptive, he always had been, and much worse, he was Abyss-bent on Amma's death.

Xander continued. "We're in the exact same predicament—you said it yourself, and I would be lying yet again if I said I haven't been fantasizing about the two of us teaming up since your proposal, which you so ineloquently snatched away like some nefarious cocktease. Imagine it: The two of us, releasing our parents, maybe even convincing them that they would make better lovers than enemies." He chuckled, the sound so amused at first, but then it fell away and his dark eyes went cloudy. "Then we'd finally be brothers like we always should have been. Wouldn't that be nice, Damien?"

Damien. Xander never called him that. He swallowed.

"And all it takes is skinning one little kitten."

But not that. Never that. "My brother would be willing to find another way. One that didn't shed so much blood."

Jaw hardening, Xander glared back at him, coming close enough to gut. "It would have made for an intriguing tale, the two of us, but it's not the one being told, is it? You're so wrapped up in the fiction you've got going with that girl, but that's what it is—fiction. A lie you're telling yourself." There was none of Xander's normal nonchalance in his words, the bite to them venomous. Damien had been wrong when he'd tried to convince himself Xander would eventually grow accustomed to Amma's presence, maybe even like her. The truth was she got in the way, and he loathed her for it. "You know if your blood put the talisman inside her, it is only by your blood that it's coming out."

For perhaps the first time, Xander was being entirely honest with him: What he wanted was to work together, but he wanted that work entirely on his terms, like the selfish, spoiled child he was. "Then I suppose it's not coming out."

With a hefty sigh and a huge step backward, Xander clasped his hands behind him. "Oh, Bloodthorne, how you've disappointed me! But not surprised me, I suppose, since I took proper precautions." He paced backward from Damien, squinting at the sky. "I'm sure you'll forgive me eventually.

Or come after me relentlessly. Either way, I am excited to see what our futures hold."

"What in the Abyss is that supposed to mean?"

"Well, I preemptively wanted to give you a little breathing space. With a side of distraction. Maybe a teeny, tiny portion of revenge too, for myself. You asked me what I wanted by coming to see you, but it's too bad you forgot to ask about my new associates. See, I needed someone to replace you, and I found them—four of them, actually—and in trade for their assistance with the Lux Codex, I gave them a few gifts and promised to lead them to their quarry." He held up two fingers, between them a colored stone. "Gave them one of these too so they could deliver it. By now, I'd say they're already in that coastal march of Eiren. What was it called?"

As if the world had been torn out from under Damien's feet again by a malevolent fae, his stomach dropped, and all the breath was knocked out of him as he choked on the word: "Brineberth."

"That's the one!" Xander dropped the translocation stone, the plane tearing itself open before him, so much more powerful than before as he stepped inside. "Oh, that face you're making. I cannot *wait* to see it when she's actually dead." And with one more step, he was gone.

CHAPTER 30

AMMA

The Various Shapes and Sizes of Heroism

AMMA HAD, FOR MOST of her life, found it easy to push away that which was uncomfortable and frankly unacceptable to feel. Those sorts of emotional outbursts were to be hidden in favor of amicable acceptance and an even temperament. But Damien had done something else to her, inspired something new, and while she shouted at him and said some cruel things, it was more than just *anger* that had bubbled out of her.

Feelings, being inherently frustrating and messy, are also often vindictive. It is one of their worst traits, which is really something that shouldn't be thought on for too long—feelings having feelings—but just quietly accepted as the truth of things. After being denied and bottled up and misconstrued, feelings too have a limit, and if they find they cannot be expressed in their natural, honest states, they will resort to putting on the cloaks of other feelings, adopting new accents and a little makeup, and when they are finally convincing enough, roar out into the world disguised as something completely different.

The darkness and solitude of the forest were meant to help. Amma certainly expected them to when she stormed off, but then she'd been trudging through fallen leaves with no regard for the sounds she made, grumbling to herself, and by the time she'd come to a stop, her limbs ached and her mind was perhaps an even fuzzier blur than when she'd left.

She'd been power hungry, that Amma knew for certain. She'd read about such a thing and even suffered through others' surrender to it, but when it came to her own hunger, power made a different kind of sense. She spread her fingers out, feeling the icy cup in them again, smelling the silvery liquid so close to her lips. She told Damien she was doing it for him, despite the fact that saying so was a mistake, because she knew he would ask why: *Why, Amma, would you take a risk like that for me?* If she had to answer him, she could never hide away the truth again, and then when he told her having affection for an infernal being was foolish and wasteful, she would just...

Amma slapped her hands onto the nearest tree and dug her fingers into the bark. There was a shudder that racked its way down her arms, her stomach rolling over itself and bile rising in her throat, and then a long, low creaking as the branches curled downward toward the forest floor. She didn't know what she was doing, she didn't care, she just needed to get whatever pain was inside her out, and she felt her magic drain away—the magic she thought she had lost—into the tree, its limbs growing heavy with the burden of her arcana.

Staggering backward from it, her mind spun and vision flickered in and out. Even in the dark, she could see how vibrant the maple had become, blooming new leaves to replace the fallen ones and growing twice as many branches. "That may have been a mistake," she mumbled to herself, pressing a hand to her stomach and stumbling forward. She had to stay on her feet, had to keep from fainting out there alone.

Amma swallowed, pushed herself straight, and turned around. That was enough. She could go back now, and she wasn't confident what she would do when she returned—apologize, yell, cry, confess—but by the time she got there, things would figure themselves out, surely.

And then she knew something else entirely was wrong.

Amma had felt Damien's arcana many times, and she thought she could recognize it, but the crackling of magic in the air confused her—infernal, yes, but was it Damien?

"I told you not to follow me," she said, louder and with more bite than she anticipated.

There was no answer.

"Kaz?" She turned slightly, one direction and then the other, not wanting to lose her orientation so that she could find her way back.

There was no sign of the imp. But there was a twig

snapping and movement just behind her, and before she could turn around, something pointy pressed into her back, making her breath catch.

Amma instinctively reached up for the crossbow, but it wasn't there, broken and abandoned in the Winter Court. Instead, her raised wrist was grasped and twisted painfully behind her, and then the other arm was trapped too. As she screamed, there was another sound, laughter somewhere far off in the forest, and then another hand clamped over her mouth. Arms caught and secured behind her, she instead bit down hard.

"Ow!" The hand came away, and she sucked in a breath, ready to scream again, but a linen was shoved into her open mouth instead. She tried to thrash, but she was shoved backward into the hard wall of a body, and a second linen was pressed over the gag to hold it in place as a figure finally came into view.

Short and slight, the woman Amma had held up with her own crossbow in the ruins of the Innomina Wildwood solidified right out of the shadows before her, the knot she'd just made at the back of Amma's head tied tight. Amma squealed in the back of her throat, barely a muffle against the choking linen, and thrashed away.

"She bit me!" The knight's booming voice was in Amma's ear, the one who had so brutally maimed Damien with his arcane sword. No wonder the squeeze on Amma's arms was so painful that she thought her shoulders would pop as he shook her. "We're trying to help you, damn it—calm down."

How is this helping? she attempted to scream, but it only came out as a muffled warble against the gag.

"It's not her fault, Barrett." The wavering voice of Pippa, the priestess, sounded from Amma's left as the woman stepped out from the darkness of the trees. "Remember, she's enthralled."

Amma screamed soundlessly against the linens. The hands that were holding her finally fell away, but her wrists were already bound at her back, and she stumbled forward. She tugged at the rope, but the knot was too good, and she sneered at how proud the smaller woman looked.

Desperate to explain, Amma could say nothing, words coming out nonsensical and muted. Her eyes darted from the priestess who had her hands out as if pleading to the mage who had wandered toward them as he flipped through his book. Panicked and frantic, Amma fought against her binds and shouted noiselessly until her throat burned.

"Hurry up, El," said the smaller woman, winding her hand at the mage. "You were supposed to be ready to translocate us as soon as we got her."

"Well, I prepared this suppression spell for Bloodthorne, but he's not here, so I don't know what to do with it."

Barrett was massaging the hand Amma bit. "Oh, who cares? Just use it on her. Xander probably thinks we're already in Brineberth by now."

Amma froze. Brineberth? Xander? How in the Abyss the two had anything to do with one another, she had no idea, but she was not willing to find out. She turned and fled as fast as her feet could take her.

"Hey!" The voice of the knight followed after, and then so did solid footfalls on the forest floor.

A blast of arcana crashed into her back, knocking her to her knees, and she felt every muscle, including ones she didn't know she had, seize up. It wasn't pain, but it was close, the thing that flooded through her, like liquid metal filling up her veins, and she knew that even if she hadn't just expelled so much magic into that tree, she wouldn't even be able to make a seed crack open then.

"Stop trying to run off. We're the good guys!" Amma was lifted as if she weighed nothing, and Barrett hoisted her over his shoulder. When she slammed down onto her stomach, the breath was knocked from her and stars burst in her eyes, but she did hear him mumble, "stupid bitch," which didn't just keep her conscious but invigorated a new rage inside her.

Amma's sluggish limbs kicked, but Barrett trapped her legs too. Though her vision was wobbly, a golden glow appeared in the darkness, rushing past her upturned head, and then there was a *thunk* in the leaves.

"What's this?" Pippa picked up the figure that the soil-skinned fae, Rea, had given Amma, the sparkle of the goo inside reflecting in the priestess's eyes. "Oh, Xander will want that."

Amma groaned, sucking in a deep breath through her nose, the gag too tight against her mouth and the knight's shoulder digging into her stomach, head upside down as she hung over his back. Those fae, Rea and Tertius, had been right: She hadn't kept hold of that for long at all.

Tears sprang to Amma's eyes as she continued to try to scream, but even the minuscule sounds she was making were dying away, devolving from threats to pleas. *Don't do this*, she tried to beg them. *Please, don't take me away.*

But even if they could hear her, they never would have listened.

"Hey, this is nice," Barrett's voice sounded as his hand moved over her thigh, and then a pressure against her leg was removed. Her silver dagger—by Sestoth, why hadn't she thought to grab that when she had the chance? "Here, Kori, have it."

"Here we go," the mage announced, and there was a scramble behind Amma, a flash of light, and suddenly the whole world flipped upside down.

Amma's vision sharpened in the brightness that followed. It was still night, but the moon's glow, undisturbed by tree limbs, was like daytime compared to where they had been. Dropped back down onto her feet, Amma staggered. The land laid out before her was flat and windswept, spotted with thickets of heather and a few copses of twisting trees. Beyond that, the nearly empty moor stretched far into the dark distance.

At Amma's back, there was a low rumble that came and went, and she turned into the briny breeze behind the lot of them. She had never been to this place, but she knew the smell of the ocean and that Brineberth March ran all along Eiren's westernmost border, separating Faebarrow from the sea. Before her, the moor continued on, running into the ocean, and just on its edge, a building.

With a rough shove, Amma was pushed toward the stony keep one hundred paces away. It was a blocky thing, older too, made up of solid, militaristic walls and lacking all the pomp and size that a marquis's castle should have had. She tried to ask where they were, but her voice was once again a quiet muffle against the linen that was wedged into her mouth.

"Oh, you think we should remove that?" Pippa asked, carefully walking up beside her.

"No." Barrett gave Amma another shove so that she continued along the dirt roadway that carved across the moor. "She's a biter."

"Well, she looks like a captive," the smaller woman, Kori, said.

"According to Pippa, she's enthralled. That's not our fault." El, the mage, flipped through his book as they went. "I don't really have anything to get rid of that, but you'd think that suppression spell would help, huh?"

The priestess shrugged. "Maybe we can reason with her. Kori, could you please?"

Kori reached up as they continued along and undid the knot against the back of Amma's head.

Amma spat out the excess ball of linen that had been choking her, taking a huge breath, mouth dry and throat burning.

"Sorry about all this," Pippa said, a gentle hand touching her shoulder. "But it's for your own good."

Amma's nostrils flared, and she flashed angry eyes at the priestess, trying to form words, but they came out in an unintelligible growl.

Pippa jerked away, and Barrett took Amma roughly by the upper arm again, her hands still bound behind her, so the tug threw her off-balance. "Don't even think about it."

Think about what? she wondered. Running? Fighting? She was struggling to just get her voice back, even the muscles in her throat sluggish from the arcana still sludging through her veins. The keep was getting closer, moonlight illuminating the banners emblazoned with the red lion-fish hanging above its entrance, and her feet stopped, heart following suit. She'd heard them say Brineberth, but seeing it there in front of her was like a cold dagger pressed to the throat. If she went inside, it would be the last thing she ever did.

But Barrett's patience had run out the moment her teeth had pierced through his glove. He dragged her forward, ignoring how she stumbled and squeezing her arm so much harder that she cried out.

"Careful, Barrett, she's not our enemy," Pippa cautioned, keeping her distance with a wary eye trained on Amma and a hand up defensively.

The one called Kori scoffed. "Yeah, the marquis isn't going to want his wife back all bruised up."

"I'm not his wife," Amma rasped, eyes locked on the banner fluttering in the wind. Not yet anyway.

"Betrothed. Whatever." Kori had Amma's silver dagger out, flipping it over in her hands and feeling the weight.

"Though I guess we can blame it all on Bloodthorne. I'm sure he's done worse to her."

The rope around Amma's wrists was cut, the tension on her back gone, but the knight's thick hand was still wrapped around her arm, dragging her ever forward at a quickening pace. With Kori behind her, dagger out, Pippa prepared with a spell at her other side, and El leading the way ahead of them, there was nowhere for Amma to go, even if she could run.

"I'm surprised he really wants her back, being used goods and all," Barrett grumbled. "There must be other baronesses."

Even without the linen in her mouth, Amma felt a gag at the back of her throat. Cedric was too invested in what Amma represented—a legitimate claim to Faebarrow—to break their engagement, no matter what imagined slights he thought she'd done to him while she was gone.

Kori scoffed again. "He better—I want my gold, and this hasn't been easy."

"I don't know," El said, glancing back at the others over his shoulder and holding up a hand, a ball of red arcana forming there with a jagged line of black running through it. "I think we already made out pretty well." The magic in his palm sparked then, and he yelped, quickly putting it out and laughing nervously.

Kori rolled her eyes. "I just want paid."

"Shadow walking not enough for you? Or is it just Pierce you miss?"

"That's right!" There was a pointy nudge at Amma's back. "Where's my crossbow?"

Amma's head was tipped up, the banner looming over all of them as they reached the entry to the keep. "The Everdarque," she said in a whisper, all the breath pulled out of her as the massive wooden doors swung open.

"The Everdark?" Kori's voice fell low as they crossed into the keep. "Guess that enthrallment makes everything she says a ridiculous lie."

The inner courtyard was surrounded by a high, thick wall, the moonlight pouring down into its center, but the darkness of the corners was so black it was like staring into the Abyss. Unlike any other keep Amma had been to, the grounds were covered in many trails made by heavy boots in the muck. There were no well-kept hedges or fanciful fountains, only workstations and efficiency, and it smelled of hot coals and sweat.

A drunken cheer rose up from a group of men off to the side of the courtyard's entrance. They celebrated as one of them fell hard to the ground and another threw up his arms in triumph. Amma was glad when the guard El had spoken to guided them away from the brawl, but then a set of robed figures passed by—priests, especially ominous in the dark— giving her the chills.

They trampled over wet earth in the courtyard's center, her stomach sinking right along with her boots, dread crawling up her spine. But there was no sign of Cedric Caldor, and for that alone, Amma was able to stay upright as Barrett drove her toward the building at the keep's back.

The hall in the largest structure of the simple keep

looked to be meant for dining and meetings. Braziers along the walls were lit with unarcane fires, and small, high windows were rare, lending the place to safety but also allowing smells to linger—salt, grease, human—and Amma's already toppling stomach roiled again. She was propelled between old, scratched tables lined with benches where a few men sat playing dice and finishing meals. Their conversations stopped as the five made their way through, and one man, a familiar man, got to his feet.

"Lady Ammalie!" Roman Caldor rushed across the hall, and Barrett's hand released her arm just as Cedric's older brother embraced her. "Oh, I prayed to Osurehm for your safe return, and here you are!"

Amma was going to have a number of nasty words for Osurehm when she finally met him.

When Roman pulled back, he took her by the arms, squeezing where Barrett had only just released and making her wince, but he didn't notice. "You must be so scared and so happy to be home."

Amma could only blink back at the face that looked so much like Cedric's but held none of the knowing malice or faux sympathy. She hadn't seen Roman in moons, but he had been to Faebarrow a few times and was just the same as she remembered: bigger, stronger, and decidedly a whole lot dumber than his brother. Because of this, he didn't really act the way a marquis was meant to, but at least he was nice.

"Actually, there's a little problem," said Pippa, and Kori elbowed her.

The elven mage rolled his eyes. "She's been enthralled, so she thinks she's not supposed to be here."

"Enthralled?" Roman's brows pinched and lips twisted up.

The elf nodded. "Yes. Arcanely."

When no one explained it further but Roman's eyes didn't sparkle with understanding, Amma sighed. "It means I'm supposedly mind controlled by magic."

"Oh! Ammalie, that's unfortunate."

"Well, I'm not ac—"

"But you've brought her back, and that's what's important to my brother. When Ced gets back, he's going to be so happy!"

Kori pushed past El and stuck out her upturned palm, saying nothing.

"Payment, right. Uh, Jervis? Can you handle this? And get Gilead?"

As an older man motioned for the Righteous Sentries, Amma was led away and through another door into a smaller chamber. Thankful to be away from the others, she didn't fight, her mind working hard to take in the keep, searching for a means of escape, but then the door was closed behind her, and she was in a small office filled with ledgers and a simple desk, no windows, and no way out but through Roman.

And Roman had no idea.

"I'm sorry Ced's not here to welcome you, but he should be back any day, and, oh, Ammalie, you must be starving! What am I thinking? I'll have something brought in, and—"

"No, Roman, listen!" She grabbed his arm before he could

go back for the door, hand frozen on the handle. Voice raspy and wavering, she shook him, forcing him to look her in the eye. "You have to let me go. I can't be here, not when Cedric comes back, not at all. He's going to kill me."

"Kill you?" Roman's face was painted with utter confusion, even more so than what was typical. "Ammalie, Cedric would never. He loves you, he wants to marry you."

"Gods, that's even worse," she groaned, squeezing his forearm harder. "Please, listen to me. It's an act, all of it. He doesn't care about me; he just wants Faebarrow and the liathau. He's already wrecked so much of the barony, he's turned the whole place upside down since you were last there, and—"

"Ammalie, no, no, that wasn't Cedric." Pain made his brows tighten. "That was the skeletons, remember? The ones that your captor released. Ced told me all about it. We've been trying to liberate Faebarrow since." He said this with such conviction that Amma almost believed him.

But she shook her head, hard. "No, Roman, listen! The skeletons are good; Laurel told me through a raven. It's Cedric who's bad—he was arresting people for pottery and chopping down all the trees, and my parents will be sent away or killed, and I'm—" Her breath caught, terrified at just the possibility of what he might do.

"Arrested for pottery? Talking ravens?" Roman laughed nervously, and to be fair, her words may have been difficult even for someone with more advanced faculties to follow. "Boy, you really are in thrall, huh?"

"*Enthralled*," she said through gritted teeth.

"Aww, yeah, that's it, but it's gonna be all right, I promise. I'll have Gilead help you, and if that doesn't work, I'm sure when you see my brother, you'll snap right out of it because of love and stuff."

Amma's heart was pounding, the mention of Cedric again making her panic. Her eyes darted around the room, falling on a small plant on the desk's edge. She grabbed it and squeezed, willing its tendrils to flourish. "No, Roman, I don't love your brother, and he definitely doesn't love me." She sucked in a full breath, focusing intently on the arcana inside her, not wanting to hurt Roman but willing to do what she had to for freedom.

Roman's eyes pinged down to her hand, wrapped about the plant, then searched the ground madly like some explanation would spring up from the stone floor, like it would be revealed this was all some elaborate trick, and everyone would be laughing in mere moments. "You don't want to marry Cedric?"

Amma could only shake her head in desperation, her focus on the plant and the magic she was forcing into it.

"But...but you said you did?" He was really struggling.

She let out a ragged breath. "I know, but I can't."

"What...what are you doing?"

Amma looked back at the plant. Her hand was squeezing the stem so firmly that it had snapped, but there was nothing. No growth, no vines ready to ensnare and throw him out of the way, no arcana at all. She squealed, "I'm going to kill that elf if I see him again!"

The door behind Roman opened with a low creak. When he moved to the side, Gilead was there, the mage that Cedric always had following at his heels and doing his bidding. Sallow-skinned and perpetually smiling with a jagged jaw of gray teeth, he set pale eyes on Amma. "I've been informed we have something in our guest that needs to be broken?"

CHAPTER 31

DAMIEN

When One Considers the Alternative

XANDER WAS GONE, TRACELESS, just like he'd arrived, except he had cut right into Damien without even touching him. If he was to be believed, then Amma was gone too.

Damien broke into a run, calling her name as he flew through the trees. His dagger fell into his hand with a rapid flick, and he ripped it thoughtlessly over his skin, using his blood to strengthen his seeking spell. He reached out, blood dripping from his arm, sending his senses wide. She would be there, she *had* to be—Xander was nothing but a slimy fucking liar, and this was only some trick.

But Amma's presence didn't come back to Damien. Woodland creatures that scattered, birds that took to the sky, slithering things that hid in their holes—they were everywhere. But there was no human—no sweet, kind, beautiful human—no matter how far out he desperately pushed his arcana.

"Master!"

Damien stopped short, kicking up leaves and whipping around.

Kaz was bounding toward him, wings flapping as he ran to clear more distance. "Master, she's been taken!"

Damien's heart dropped into his gut, the blood draining out of him. He already knew, in truth. He knew when Xander said it, and Kaz would not lie, not about this. But as his own spell continued to crawl away, not finding her, it did identify a lingering infernal arcana, the fizzling out and burning off of a spell so like Xander's translocation.

He homed in on the sense, following it. "Who the fuck took her?"

Kaz hustled to keep up. "Those Righteous Sentries. I only found them when they were stepping into a portal with her."

Damien stopped suddenly, stomach lurching. *Don't follow me*, she'd said, and her eyes had been so angry, so...disappointed. He'd hurt her, he knew that—he'd been hurting her since they met—but this was different. This had cut her to the quick, and she'd finally walked away from him. Perhaps she had seen her chance and chosen not to turn back.

"Did she..." Damien swallowed hard, the spell to chase after Xander's magic wavering. He stared out into the darkness ahead of him, seeing her walk off again, wishing he'd had the courage to beg her to stay. "Did she go willingly?"

Kaz had the tip of his tail in his clawed hands, worrying it. His big eyes held the answer, and he gulped. "No," he groaned, all gravel and regret. "They tied her up and carried her off. She looked very, very angry."

Damien blew out a relieved breath—she *hadn't* wanted to leave him after all, thank all the basest beasts—but then caught himself. The only thing he really knew for certain was that she didn't want to go with them to Brineberth because *of course*. But regardless of whether she wanted Damien, she would want to be in Brineberth even less, and he wouldn't leave her there. He pushed off the tree, following the last dregs of his arcana.

When he found the place the translocation spell had been cast, he noted how the fallen leaves had been disturbed, signs of a struggle that made his insides twist, and then the burnt spot where the stone had been dropped to rip open the plane. He pressed a hand to the soil, feeling as it continued to thrum. Even better than Xander's previous spells, this one was so clean, so good, and had nearly erased itself already, but it had also been exceptionally powerful.

He focused his arcana into the remnants of the spell, trying to read it. He knew they went to Brineberth, west of Faebarrow, but he had no idea where he currently stood— Damien had seen to making Amma too angry to request a specific destination from that ridiculous fae.

The blood dripping from his arm pooled into the earth, and then it was found, the memory of five presences, four of which he cast off for the familiar one, the warm one that made his heart ache, grabbing on before it could slip away. Eyes closed, he could see her, and then there was a sense of distance, a vague impression of the miles between them, before the ghost of her was gone.

He glanced up at the moons, their shapes broken by the branches of the trees. They were closer together than he'd last seen them, but he could still orient himself and headed in the direction the spell had pointed him. He strode through the forest, direction unwavering, and Kaz followed. It didn't matter how long it took, he would find her, and he would make it so Marquis Cedric Caldor could never do this again.

When Damien broke through the trees, he spied a fire burning low beside a rocky outcropping with sleeping bodies and a small contingency of horses about it. He strode up to them, ignoring the voices as the watchman for the group called to wake the others. A bowstring was pulled taut, but Damien swiped an arm through the air blindly, and he heard the weapon snap. Someone ran at him, but he called up a shadow at his back, hearing the surprised cry and *thunk* against it. Choosing the sleekest and sturdiest-looking horse, he threw himself atop it, Kaz clamoring up its haunches just in time for Damien to dig in his heels and speed off.

The animal thundered across the open field, forgoing the roads to drive forward as westerly as possible. He should have been feeling weary, but he'd been renewed with purpose. There would be no stopping until the horse refused, and then he would find another, but his stomach twisted at the thought of how long this would ultimately take. He needed to aid his journey with arcana if he would ever get to Amma in time.

But then arcana and Amma aided him instead.

CHAPTER 32

AMMA

A Eulogy for Alleged Chivalry

UNLIKE ROMAN, GILEAD WASN'T stupid. The mage had every opportunity to learn what Cedric truly was, to hear the vile threats he made, and had still always shown him loyalty, so there was no use in Amma pleading her case to him. Instead, she screamed, she kicked, she scratched, but she was still dragged up a wide flight of stairs and then a second winding one where she was tossed into a tiny room. Gilead didn't bother attempting to remove any enthrallment spell from her; he only assured Roman that with time, she would calm, and a guard should be posted outside her door for her own safety.

With a promise that "Marquis Caldor will deal with you

when he comes back" and then a shouted half prayer as he left, Amma finally found herself alone.

She paced the small chamber, only a simple stuffed mattress on the floor, a washbasin without water, and a chamber pot inside. The place was unswept and had none of the modern amenities of even the taverns she had stayed in on the road. It certainly wasn't fit for the future wife of a marquis, a thought that made her gag but should have been questionable to the others. But none of the men had even blinked when she had been dragged back out into the dining hall and upstairs, except to comment that whatever infernal spell she was under had turned her into a feral animal.

The keep was old, serving as some sort of barracks for a small contingent of soldiers and mages, though the lack of arcane lights and running water suggested the place had been disused for quite a while previously. There also didn't seem to be much around beyond the walls to support the keep—no village for commerce in sight, nor even a single farm to produce food.

And there were no women. She wondered how long the men had been here without families or outside contact and why in the Abyss Cedric thought this was the right place for her. Whatever the reason, she needed to flee.

There was only one small window in the room, a narrow slit in the stone good only for peering out and shooting toward the sea, and she couldn't have fit through it if she tried. Even if she'd managed to get her shoulders and hips through, it was a very long way down the side of the keep, then the wall, and finally the cliff to the rocky shore below where the waves broke endlessly under the moonlight.

Her weapons were gone, magic drained and suppressed, and there was nothing else in the room to use. She hadn't even been given any utensils with the bowl of food left for her, not that she could stomach looking at it. Her fingers clenched, surrounded by stone, linen, and clay.

Clay.

Amma fell to her knees on the lumpy mattress and upended her hip pouch. The broken shard of pottery she'd gotten from the square in Faebarrow when that artisan had been dragged away fell out, thick and sharp at its corner. A slip of soft blackness that made her heart shoot up into her throat followed the broken pottery.

Amma lifted the feather, holding it like a sacred thing in two hands. She ran a thumb up its length, its shine iridescent in Ero and Lo's light. Elderpass felt like so long ago, when Damien was still harsh and when Amma was still plotting to get away from him. It was laughable when he'd handed it over, telling her it would bring him to her if she got lost.

Why would I want you to find me if I ran away? she had asked.

I'm sure there are some *things in this world worse than I am.* Damien had been wrong then—it was not some things, it was all of them.

She grabbed the piece of pottery and felt for its sharpest edge, bringing it to her forearm, then stopped. Damien said she would need to spill her blood, but she couldn't risk anyone else seeing the cut. She remembered then the light when the talisman had gone inside her, how it had glowed red before receding under her skin. She tugged her tunic down and didn't hesitate, aiming just to the left of her sternum, gritting her teeth and digging in.

Crimson bloomed on her skin, and she inhaled sharply at the pain. How Damien cut into himself so stoically, she had no idea. She dropped the piece of pottery back into her bag and took the feather to her chest, covering it with her hand. Her heartbeat thumped hard under her palm, the blood warm, the feather soft. Amma was all out of magic herself, expelled and stifled, and her body exhausted. She wavered and then lay backward, hand still snug up against her heart.

But Damien had told her she didn't need to do arcana, she only needed to want him. And by all the gods and arcane things in all the planes, dark ones included, she did want him, so the magic came on its own.

It was like a whisper that coursed through her body, sweeping out through her fingertips and toes, feeling every inch of the room and racing back to gather once again under her palm. For the slightest moment, she thought she felt him, the touch of Damien's fingers on her wrist, the warmth of his breath on her cheek, but then it was gone. When she lifted her hand, the feather was gone too, leaving only a smear of blood on her palm and chest.

Eyelids closing, her hand fell away, the cool, briny air of the tower room stinging the open wound. Would it be enough? Enough to...gods, what did she expect exactly? For Damien to rush into the heart of danger, into a keep full of soldiers under the sword of a man he'd stolen from? To come to her rescue *yet again* at great peril to himself and everything he'd worked for? He would surely be sick of how *abductable* she was by now—she was certainly sick of it.

In the dark, her mind slipped in and out of consciousness, dropping her into nightmares of Cedric returning, of pain and blood, and then waking her with reminders of her failure. How could she expect Damien to come after she'd yelled at him? Told him to sit and stay like some dog? For all Damien knew, she had just left! Walked off with no intention of ever returning to him. She may have still had the talisman in her, but his interest in it had been waning anyway, and he was resourceful; there were surely alternatives, and he had friends who could offer them. Friends like Xander.

Another nightmare followed of people she loved who had turned on her, this one pulling her so much deeper that when she woke from it, she had forgotten where she was. The dim light coming through the narrow window had changed, brighter with very early dawn, but it was enough to remind her: She was trapped and still alone.

She shifted, and the cut on her chest stung. *What if he just doesn't want to come?* Amma thought, drawing in a deep breath, eyes squeezing shut and fists balling. Sleep didn't come again, but there were visions: stabbing a werewolf, hurling that animate book in the Grand Athenaeum, shedding blood to wake Lycoris, scaling the largest, wildest liathau in existence.

Amma sat upright, eyes wide. *Abductable*. The word flashed into her mind, and a burn flared in her chest. Amma had been abducted many times, it was true. People who would do her harm were stronger than her, and they were resourceful and manipulative too. But despite being spirited off so frequently, Amma had yet to remain truly kept. She glared at the tiny tower room and huffed. This abduction would be no exception.

It was quiet outside Amma's door while the sun rose, but Cedric wasn't to the keep yet, which meant she still had time to sit and listen and wait. The soldiers believed she was enthralled—a funny word for crazy, more like—but she could hear the guard outside her chamber being changed, and the new one had hopefully not seen her being carried off like a madwoman the night before.

Amma waited until there was quiet again, boots falling away down the spiral steps of the tower. She brushed fingers through her hair, pinched her cheeks, and straightened her tunic to make sure the slice was properly covered but that her breasts were being as supportive to her plans as possible. She poised her hand to knock—what a joke, knocking to get *out* of a room—and then paused.

She flipped her hand over and imagined arcana there, and the faintest emerald light shone in the center of her palm. She clenched a fist around it. El's spell had finally worn off.

Hand hovering again, she tried to smile. It felt so odd, so wrong, that it actually hurt. She scrunched up her face, working her jaw, and tried again. More awkwardness, more discomfort. Then she imagined opening the door and seeing Damien.

The watchman who answered her knocking eased open the entry to find a sweet, smiling, sane Lady Ammalie Avington, and this seemed to throw him completely. Perfect.

"Hi," she said, breathy and beaming. "It's Jon, right?"

He was young and wide-eyed, and his baldric was a bit too big for him. "Right," he said, then shook his head. "Uh, I mean, no, my lady. Sorry, it's Arthur."

"Arthur." She touched her chest, keeping her voice low. His eyes darted down to her hand, then back to her face, still holding the warmest smile she could. "Of course it is. Apologies, Artie, I'm having a very, well…confusing morning." She worried her features and bit her lip.

Arthur made a small noise in the back of his throat.

"It's embarrassing, really." She fidgeted from one foot to the other, clasping her hands and squeezing her arms inward as she took a heaving sigh. "But I don't exactly remember how I got here, and I was hoping, Artie, that you could tell me where I am?"

"You're in Brineberth, my lady," he said with apprehension. "Krepmar Keep."

"And where is my…my beloved?" She swallowed back the bile that rose in her throat.

"Marquis Caldor is meant to return today. He will be so relieved to see you, especially if you're feeling better."

"And I really, *really* am. Oh, Ced, how I miss him *so*." Amma pressed her hands to her chest again, wincing when she accidentally bumped the cut but covering it up with a lovesick moan. "I just wish I could be with him right now, but, oh, Artie, maybe you could help me?" She blinked up at him with a hopefulness that was actually sincere.

He glanced over his shoulder to the winding stairs and back. "My lady?"

Amma took a big breath. "Well, I am just a mess, and I can't greet the marquis like this. Is there somewhere private I can clean up and perhaps wait for him?"

"Oh, um?" Arthur looked to be thinking very hard. Good, she wanted this to be difficult. "The well inside the keep has gone dry, but Salwel has blessed us with a second, outside the walls. I can have some water brought up?"

Ah, so he was also pious. "Could you really?"

"I can call for—"

Amma chanced touching his arm, and that silenced him. "Could *you* bring it to me?"

It was Arthur's turn to bite his lip.

"It's just..." She sniffled, though no tears were coming. "It's so embarrassing how dirty I've become. It's an affront to the gods, really. I was under a terrible spell, and I was so unruly and confused, and the marquis will already be so upset and disappointed. But if you could help me, as a favor, I would be eternally grateful, as would Salwel, I imagine, as the god of wells and...and water?"

"The coast."

Amma nodded with a grin. "Exactly!" She fetched the empty washbasin and brought it back to him.

"I'm not supposed to leave my post," he said hesitantly, even as he took the bowl.

"Oh, I know, and I hate to ask you to do something like this since your duty is so important." She stared at him earnestly. Perhaps it was unfair—Amma had been on the other end of manipulation like this before, but duty was too powerful a thing to let go to waste. "However, if you think about it, Artie, you're serving Marquis Caldor directly if you do this for his future wife, who he loves and cherishes so much, and the gods too, since cleanliness is next to godliness." She repeated the popular aphorism, knowing full well it wasn't meant to be taken so literally.

Arthur began to nod but didn't seem entirely convinced.

Amma grinned, eyes darting to the door. Wooden. Of course. "And don't worry, I understand that obviously you will lock me inside when you go for my safety, because that's your duty, Artie, and you would only ever be totally loyal to Brineberth and to the crown."

"I would," said Arthur, and the corner of his mouth hitched up. "I will."

The door shut and clicked, and Amma listened hard for Arthur's footsteps to fall away, difficult to hear over the thumping of her heart in her ears, but when it was silent, she pressed both hands to the door and asked it nicely to unlock. To her utter delight, it did.

With the door swung open, the winding staircase stood before her, dark and narrow. There was nowhere to go if she ran into someone on it, but Amma had braved a similar structure in the Grand Athenaeum, and she could do it again. Amma bolted from the room and took each step with quick but careful silence. She hugged the inner wall and then slipped through the arch at its foot onto a landing.

Straight ahead lay a walkway, open to the floor below at one side and a wide staircase in its middle down to the dining hall. She crept to the edge of the banister to peek downward, just catching a set of men entering the hall, their gruff voices shouting at one another and making her duck back into the dark. She would be completely exposed if she took the stairs, but behind her was another hall and perhaps an additional way downward.

The shadowy space appeared simple, with only four doors off it. The barracks for the soldiers were elsewhere in the keep, but if these were private chambers, they were likely reserved for those who ranked much higher. Amma's memory sparked with Damien's request via raven to Laurel. He'd wanted the paperwork out of Cedric's office, but it had already been removed.

With no way to tell which room was which, she pressed a hand to the closest door and tried it. Locked. Biting her lip, she wrapped one hand around the knob and placed the other flat against the door and let out a long breath. *Open*, she thought, and there was a click.

Inside, the trappings were nicer than in her little tower quarters but typical: a bed, a wardrobe, a desk, a washbasin, but there was also a set of dress armor for a Brineberth soldier in the corner for someone massive. She took a few steps toward the desk, peering down at the figures spread out over it, some atop horses, some with swords, others with hands out to cast. Amma had seen things like this before, used to strategize battles, but the way they were set up here was…different.

The figures were lined up in rows, almost like a battalion, but there was an aisle down the middle. At the front was a single figure toppled over with yet another standing behind it, facing all the others. When she tipped her head to look at the parchment below the scene, she could see it was once an old map, the entire realm of Eiren laid out, but had since been scribbled on.

In terribly poor Key, something like a eulogy was written out for a Sir Bran the Brawniest, praising his past triumphs in battles, including beheading a dragon in one fell swoop and rescuing a cartload of puppies before it tumbled off a cliff. Amma groaned: This was definitely Roman's room, and the likelihood of it holding any kind of indicting secrets was low. Gods help the people if Cedric ever turned over any part of Brineberth to him officially.

But then a much neater Key, the one of the original map beneath the scene Roman had drawn, caught her attention. "Krepmar Keep," she whispered to herself, finger sliding over the name written in the forgotten southern corner of Brineberth she knew she had to be in. There were three other places marked in the same way, one in the southeast nestled into the Wilds, and another marked in the heart of the Kvesari Wood, northeast of the realm, with an additional note of *Briymari's Tunnel*. The elf they'd met in the Gloomweald, the one concerned about chaos and end times, had spoken of trouble in the Kvesari Wood. There was a fourth location on the opposite, northern coast where *The Temple of the Void* was written, and beneath that, *Catacombs*.

Since it was much too big and covered in things to take, she committed the map to memory and crept back to the door, pulled it shut as she slipped into the hall, and willed it to lock behind her. There were no voices when she listened, so she scurried across the landing and tried another door. This one would not budge, her own magic coming up against something strange that actually pushed against her senses, but she did smell incense and burning metal when she pressed her shoulder against it, so she doubted it led to more stairs.

Frustrated, she clicked her tongue and considered venturing to the wide staircase again, but as she approached, she heard more voices, men piling in and complaining about breakfast being late. Amma backtracked down the hall and pressed her palm hard into another door. *Please unlock, please unlock, please*—The knob gave way, and she slipped inside.

CHAPTER 33

DAMIEN

The Spoils of Servitude

DAMIEN PULLED HIS MOUNT to a violent stop, kicking up dirt in the darkness of an open field. The arcana against his hip was all in a panic, and he dug into his satchel to find the source of the disturbance. There, at the bottom of his bag, lay a feather.

"Amma, you bloody wonderful genius, you remembered," he rasped, lifting the magicked feather to his face, feeling the arcana thrum through it like a beacon. Wind whipped around him as if it was already pulling him toward his target, and his face broke into a smile, his dagger sliding down into his other hand.

The raven feather was an older magic, made years ago with Xander's assistance, of all the bloody bastards in the realm, but it was well before the skill he had apparently gained now. To use this magic, he would need a source of power that wasn't just his blood. That was how it was designed—it needed a life.

Damien dismounted, gazing up at the horse, spent from galloping. It was a powerful beast, but it was no knoggelvi, not arcane in the least. His focus shifted then to the ground and the little figure that had just scrambled down its back. With claws folded over one another, the imp blinked big, watery eyes up at him.

"Kaz," he said, the name heavy in his throat. "Ever-loyal, never-relenting minion of darkness. My most faithful servant."

The imp's eyes widened, chin lifting, terrible little grin growing with all its plucky, ill-pointed fangs. His batwing ears twitched, and his actual wings fluttered at the shower of compliments. "Master?"

"I am so *very* sorry," Damien said, and in the strangest turn of events, he actually meant it.

Kaz's tail came around him, and he gripped its end, worrying the triangular point.

"I need your help, little one." Damien knelt, feather in one hand, dagger in the other. "For Amma."

Kaz predictably pulled a face at the mention of the woman. It wasn't truly up to the imp; Damien wasn't going to give him a choice either way, especially if he took much longer than a moment to relent, but there was a voice in him, one that sounded curiously like Amma's, that told him to do this right, to try and be...*kind*. Or as kind as one can be, he supposed, when carving the heart out of something.

"I need your life, Kaz." He spun the dagger in his hand and shrugged. "Is that...is it all right?"

The imp's forehead crumpled, eyes on the blade as it caught the moonlight. "For her?"

Damien ground his jaw, then took a breath. One second more of patience, it was all he had, and Amma would want him to use it. "Yes. For the woman who taught you to make snowballs and kept you warm and never had an unkind thing to say about you."

Kaz's gaze fell to the ground. "This is what you want, Master Bloodthorne?"

"I want her back," he said, the words falling out with a desperation he was finally unembarrassed by. "You above all other creatures, I think, understand why."

Then Kaz puffed out his chest with a big, shuddering breath, and he nodded.

Damien's stomach twisted, and he wondered if it might have been better if he'd had to wrestle Kaz to the ground and stab the life out of him, messy as that would be. At least Kaz would be returned to the infernal plane again, where his servitude would no longer be required, though he had a feeling the end of his service would actually disappoint the simple beast.

Damien clicked his tongue at his dagger. "Ready?"

The imp nodded again, but his little ears shook. Damien put a hand on the tiny creature's shoulder, realizing for the first time how much bigger than the imp he was. He pressed the dagger's point right to the middle of Kaz's chest, taking his own deep breath. It had been so much easier when he just kicked him off the parapet in Aszath Koth. But this? This felt *bad*. "At least you could come back." Damien offered him a crooked half smile.

"Uh-huh…" Kaz's eyes were turned down to the blade, bravely standing as still as possible.

Damien swallowed. "Thank you, friend." And he plunged the dagger in.

It was quick—Damien knew how to end a life efficiently, especially one so small—and the pain Kaz felt was likely fleeting. A last breath, fear on his wretched face turning to shock and stiffening, and then he was no more.

Imps weren't truly made to be on this plane, so his body wouldn't last long, talons already disintegrating into ash as Damien carefully laid him on the earth. He sliced down through the chest and cut out the imp's heart, a puny organ, black with many veins and full of a thick, viscous blood that sizzled when it dripped, but it was brimming with the arcane life he needed.

When the heart was free of its shell, Kaz wasted away much more quickly. Damien was glad—he didn't want to leave the body there, nor could he spare the time to bury it— and soon there was only a small pile of ash and goop that would be swept away on the wind. Damien cut into his own hand, placing the feather atop the wound and the imp's heart atop that, and then he squeezed.

Arcana flooded directly into his veins, a burst of vitality filling him wholly and wrapping itself around every limb, every organ, every drop of blood. He'd only done this spell once, the change still strange, much stranger than illusion, but he willed it on faster, forcing the magic to take him as quickly as it could. And then it did, wind sweeping past him, the earth falling away, and he wasn't a blood mage anymore but a bird.

A raven, to be specific, because Damien Maleficus Bloodthorne would have it no other way.

He rose up, black wings spread, the spot where he had ended Kaz's life too small to be identified as he headed west. Winds bent around him to aid his travel, faster and higher still, and he reached the warm current that would speed him onward. Infernal magic tunneled about him, the world sharper with a raven's eyes and yet a blur with the speed.

The slight feeling of loss and guilt tickled at him, but it was eclipsed by something even more foreign: hope. He couldn't yet see it, but he knew he was headed for the ocean. The feather would guide him to where its mate called from, where Amma would be.

The world continued to darken, and time grew meaningless when he was surrounded by warm currents and magic, until the ocean finally came into view, the sun rising at his back. He slowed as he was pulled down by his arcane lead, a moor spread out before him. There was little around, and it was clear why: Something here was wrong.

The land appeared to be normal under dawn's pink and

orange lights, even from above where he should have been able to pick out some pattern or irregularity. The heath stretched out toward a cliffside that dropped into the ocean, no sign of life about except for an old keep. Damien, though, was reminded of the Wilds, the chaotic energy that flowed beneath that place and often through it, the magic that was untamable. And then he felt something more, something deeper, something he would not have understood had he not been so intimate with it already.

His raven form shuddered, coming up against the magic that was too similar to the ancient evil he had put an end to with the witches to not be the very same. His own powers weakened as he was suddenly struck with fear. The face he saw during the banishment of that evil flashed in his vision, and the stark memory of being a child, alone, batted against his mind like a caged sparrow.

But there was that keep, the only building for miles, its gate open to allow a small contingent of soldiers inside its courtyard. He knew Amma was being held within, and there was no time to let fear distract him.

CHAPTER 34

AMMA

A Second Lesson in Futility

THE CHAMBER AMMA HID herself inside was large, and yet it was cramped by its massive trappings. The bed was central, a dark wood four-poster that had feet intricately carved to look like lion paws. The posts rose to the low ceiling in fang-like points. Opposite it stood a chest with gaudy relief images of what else but attacking lions on each drawer. A desk was squeezed along the far wall, the lion motif continued in its curving legs and sleeker taloned paws. There was a theme here, and it screamed Cedric.

She pushed off the door and went right to the desk, flipping through the papers atop it. A list of names and ranks of men in Brineberth, those available for promotion to fill spots that had recently been left vacant. Amma cringed, knowing many had perished due to the Undead Army, but put the papers and her guilt to the side—they'd been occupiers after all.

She pulled open a drawer, and a tingle shot through her arm. *Liathau*. It was lacquered to be shiny and extraordinarily smooth, but it was liathau wood beneath her hands and all over the room. Cedric must have had the pieces made recently and brought there. The effort that had taken and the self-absorption to have it done at all twisted in her gut. Yes, the wealthy often had furniture made from liathau, but never so much. Amma's fingers skimmed over the expertly cut edge of the desk, and when she got to the end, a tiny pink leaf sprouted into being under her thumb.

"Sorry," she whispered to it and rifled through the open drawer. There were only a few maps, one with the now-desecrated orchard in Faebarrow marked and others with potential Brineberth pastures planned out. Perhaps there was something there, intention at least, but he already had the trees cut down, and her mother had said it was by order of the crown, so that had apparently been no crime.

Amma turned for the rest of the room, checking swiftly behind the furniture, under the bed, inside the wardrobe. The chamber was filled with Cedric's fine things, meticulously arranged so that she had to inspect them delicately and replace them with a care she would much rather turn into a rage, ripping them up, breaking them into pieces, throwing them about the room. With each tunic she touched, each boot she moved, each linen she refolded, her hatred for him grew, fed by the sunlight and water of vengeance. She wanted to strangle him with his pressed tunics, smother him with his Clarisseau-imported blankets, crush his skull with his dire wolf leather boots.

But then there was a sound from the hall, and she slipped herself into a hollow between the far side of the chest of drawers and the wall, crouching down to stay hidden. Amma barely breathed, listening, footsteps coming closer, and then there was a hand rattling the knob. The door remained locked, a voice called to another on the other side, and the footsteps fell away again.

Amma's body slid fully to the ground, shaking. They were looking for her, and what in the Abyss was she doing? Crouching on the floor of Cedric's personal chamber, looking for a clue she might not even find?

"There must be something." She grunted and ran her hands over the chest of drawers at her side. There was a soft click, and Amma's mouth fell open, hand darting to the underside of the chest. Already on her knees, she ducked down. A wooden ledge had popped out, hanging down on a small set of hinges, and atop it, parchment and a tray filled with coins.

Amma grabbed the paper with none of the care she'd been using, falling backward to lean against the bed's footboard, eyes wide, taking in the images finally in her hands. Two rings, one inside the other, and between them hundreds of dots and lines. She'd seen something like this in theology class many years ago. It was a star chart, and along the side, there were words written in a language she shouldn't have been able to recognize, but she knew from her extracurricular studies translating the Lux Codex with two blood mages that it was Chthonic.

Cedric should not have this—not as a divine mage of Osurehm, certainly, or really even as a citizen of the realm. Chthonic was evil, or so it was said, and Cedric had always branded himself as so holy, so righteous, so upstanding, a descendant of a dominion many, many generations earlier. He was one of Archibald's *chosen*, whatever that meant.

It was only one piece of parchment, but it was enough. Amma hugged it to her chest, a wave of relief breaking against her ribs, and then rolled it up to stuff away in her small pouch. She was careful again, popping the hidden ledge beneath the drawers back into place. Now, to get out.

Amma stood and crossed the room to its only window. This one was much larger than the arrow slit in her tower prison, the shutters on it open. Out over the water, the sky was bright with the new day, and she leaned slightly forward. Though she could easily fit through, nothing about the side of the keep was scalable. There was only a smooth, unadorned wall and the craggy cliffside leading down to a rocky death. The sounds of crashing waves enveloped her, the smell of the ocean and the salty breeze on her face feeling, if only for a moment, like freedom.

"Ah, what a lovely if not pleasant surprise."

Amma spun, heart so quickly in her throat she choked. The click of the lock had been lost in the sound of the waves.

"Abandon the search. I've found her," called Cedric

Caldor over his shoulder just before he shut the door behind him, closing the two of them in.

Amma pressed her back to the cool stone of the wall beside the window, breath stolen, sweat already breaking out on her neck.

Free of his armor, Cedric stood in a tailored dress suit and took to the buttons on his coat with a sigh. "I received word you'd been delivered last night, but when they said you had gone missing upon my arrival this morning, somehow I knew—I just *knew*—exactly where you would be." He didn't bother with the faux bravado he used around others, his distaste for her plain even as he smiled. "So eager to once again be in the arms of your betrothed."

Amma's mouth went dry, eyes pinging around the room for a weapon, but she'd been through every drawer and knew there wasn't anything within reach.

"I must say, I'm surprised, Ammalie." He shrugged off his coat, the tunic beneath crisp and clean, and he paced around the bed toward her, hands clasped behind him. "I had no idea you were so daring. It's a shame, really—you could have been put to such better use." Cedric ran his hand along the smooth grain of the liathau footboard. "But then again, your family name is your most valuable asset, and we can't compromise that, can we?"

Swallowing, Amma heard the crack in her wavering voice before she even spoke. "My parents will want to see me."

Cedric came around the bed and stepped up to her, eyes trailing the floor, lips curled up in a smirk. "And how are they to do that after the little stunt you and that infernal abomination pulled?"

She pressed harder into the wall and away from him, chest tight, every muscle taut, terrified. "What stunt?"

"Don't lie to me!" Cedric's hand wrapped around her throat, pinning her. "I didn't fall for your games before! I didn't bend to your will simply because you promised yourself to me."

Amma gasped in a shallow breath, a foot scuffing against the wall as she tried to pry his fingers from her neck.

"Do you think your words mean *anything*?" He released her throat, and as she sucked in a breath, he took her by the arms and jerked her sideways.

The wall at Amma's back was gone, the space of the open window making her stomach drop as her arms flailed, one of them catching the ledge, the other wrist caught by Cedric, forcing her to remain dangling out over nothing.

"I would throw you to your death right now for what you've done, for the fool you tried to make of me, if it weren't for the misplaced fealty those morons in Faebarrow have for you. They love their ridiculous, filthy little baron's daughter who disgraces herself by working in the orchard, treating those lowborn, arcana-less peasants like equals. Disgusting." The accusations were spat at her as if she were treasonous, but they were not new. He'd berated her before for her desire to leave things in Faebarrow as they'd always been.

She remembered how, at first, he had seemed kind, open, willing even. How he had very politely courted her a year prior, and though she had felt nothing at his hollow compliments and meager attempts at endearing himself to her by way of bragging about his reputation, she had gone along with things because it had been asked of her. Because it was her duty.

Even with her trepidation at witnessing the tiny breaks in his mask, the moments he would say something suddenly cruel and then insist it had been but a joke, or when he would make heartless suggestions and then urge her to understand she had no place in deciding her barony's future, she had still agreed to marry him in hopes that he would eventually see the value in the way Faebarrow operated, in the prosperity of the people, the health of the liathau, and perhaps even in her own happiness.

But Cedric never changed, he only revealed his true self to her—a man who had no interest in the prosperity, health, or happiness of others, least of all Amma.

"Fuck you, Cedric," she rasped, and then she spat in his face. If he was going to call her disgusting, then that was exactly what she would be.

He sneered, releasing her shoulder to wipe the spit from his cheek. Amma flailed out over the drop, but his other hand held her firm, and then he snorted. "You pretend to be so demure and innocent—if only they knew." He forced his knee between her legs and shoved her upward to perch on the window ledge, leaning close, hot breath on her face and vicious teeth gnashing. "But I know. I know that you're nothing more than a whore. My fucking whore."

Amma's skin crawled. She'd do anything to get away from him, to not smell him, to not hear him, to not feel his hands on her. The waves roared and crashed below, and nausea flooded her guts. "Just drop me—I'd rather die."

"Of course you would."

Cedric ripped her back into the room and threw her. Amma hit the bed hard, but his hands were off her, and she twisted to scramble away. When she was grabbed again and Cedric's weight pressed into her back, she screamed, clawing at the linens but going nowhere, ensnared but refusing to surrender.

A hand came around her face, seizing her by the jaw and yanking her head back, lips just against her ear as her throat constricted. "Scream all you like, bitch, no one is coming to help. In fact, some of them are looking forward to hearing it themselves. When I leave for Eirengaard, you'll be staying behind since whores are so hard to come by out here."

Amma flailed an arm free from underneath him in her frenzied panic, twisted, and wrenched her elbow into Cedric's side. He grunted, wincing, and enough pressure was taken off her that she could drag herself out from under him and kick backward. Whatever she connected with made him groan in a much more satisfying way, and Amma grabbed the bed's footboard, gritted her teeth, and pulled herself forward.

But Cedric was incensed, and the pain seemed to only spur him on. He lunged for her and, taking a fistful of her hair, ripped her backward. "You've got a lot more fight in you now," he snorted as she tried to twist out of his grip. There was a crack in her ear as his hand made contact with her face, and she was blinded.

White-hot pain bloomed across her cheek, and the taste of metal coated her tongue. Amma spat, vision returning to see the blood trailing from her mouth to a spot on the white imported linens, but the pressure of Cedric's fist in her hair was gone. She dug fingers into the footboard, clinging so tightly she knew she had to be crushing it, as Cedric grabbed the front of her tunic and pushed her down onto her back.

There was another crack, but this one came without pain, and then another, loudly echoing into the room. Cedric halted the yanking he'd been doing to her clothes, looking up with knitted brows. A rumbling beneath them wiped the vile pleasure from his features, followed by a long and low creak like the groan of branches in a coming storm.

As Cedric sat back, Amma pulled herself right over the footboard, slamming into the floor. Ignoring the pain, she tried to scramble back farther, never enough room between herself and the marquis, and came up against the chest of drawers. The bed was no longer a static piece of furniture, though Amma could barely believe her eyes. It was shuddering, stiff and odd as the layer of lacquer over it cracked, and the bed shook itself out.

Cedric realized slower than Amma, his confusion twisting into horror as he raced clumsily backward into one of the posts. It squirmed behind him, and he shrieked, flailing off the bed's edge. Behind Amma, there was more shaking, the chest moving against her back like a great beast of an animal taking breath-like pulses. She shifted off it, crawling to the room's corner as the desk too began to groan and move.

The overwhelming creak of the sturdy wooden furniture overtook Cedric's shouting as it came to life around them, each piece rising up, taking heavy, wide steps on the paws their legs had been carved into. The chest of drawers moved itself in front of the door before Cedric could bolt for it, its top drawer lunging out at him, backing him toward the far wall where a small side table jabbed him in the back.

Amma watched wide-eyed as the bed doubled itself over and angled its headboard posts forward. Their fang-like points twisted, resin shedding off them to leave the dark wood naked, jagged, and sharp, and even without eyes, the bed found Cedric. The marquis should have called up his arcana or tried to run or even begged Amma to make it stop, as useless as that would have been, but instead he stood in awe of his luxuries turning on him. The bed struck out then with one rapid movement, and the spiked post impaled him squarely in the chest.

A wet, gurgly, unbecoming cry dribbled out of Cedric's mouth with a sputter of deeply crimson blood. His features were drawn back, still in shock, as shaking hands pawed at the liathau post penetrating him just under his ribs, too wide a wound to be healed as it affixed him right to the stone wall.

Amma slapped a hand over her mouth, pushing her back into the opposing wall, a shudder running through her. Under her other hand, there was slight movement, but she wasn't afraid, the desk nudging her thigh gently. Warmth thrummed through her palm, the liathau telling her it was still there and that she had given it life to protect her. Her arms shook and her knees went weak, but she never blinked—she couldn't look away, just in case. She had to see it. She had to know.

Cedric Caldor had always been so sure he could never be felled, and then there he was, run through, not by a sword but by his own possessions. His eyes had gone glassy, not really finding her, just searching the room with a sluggish haze.

Just die, she thought, watching an arm grasp weakly at the air, desperate for saving.

The bed pulled itself back, blood flooding out of Cedric's massive chest wound as he wailed pathetically, and the post thrust forward once more, pinning him to the wall as his body fell completely lax.

A weak laugh broke out into the silence. Amma was surprised to hear it come in her own voice from behind her hand, but then another followed, and it felt *right*. Not because it was funny, the sight of a dead man, slumped over the weapon that had taken him, a pool of blood and gore growing beneath his feet, but because it was a relief.

Though they still shook, Amma's hands came to her clothes, straightening her tunic and nervously touching every part of her. She was still whole, as whole as she had ever been, and she was alive.

And Cedric Caldor, Marquis of Brineberth, occupier, tormentor, villain, was dead.

CHAPTER 35

DAMIEN

The Illusion of Safety

T HE MAGIC OF THE shapeshifting spell was waning, and fast, as Damien homed in on his target. He wanted to swoop in one of the narrow windows, shrouded by the shadows on the keep's far side, but the shift wouldn't hold, and at this rate, he would fall hundreds of feet out of the sky not as a bird but simply as a man. He may have been more than just a man, but blood mages didn't have wings, and the solidness of the ground was a terribly good equalizer no matter what barreled toward it.

Damien dove down short of the keep, aiming for one of the very few clusters of trees amongst the moors. The branches came at him fast, and he was about as well-versed at being a bird as a bird was at being a human, so when he tried to brake, he just slammed into a thick crisscrossing of branches. It struck him then nearly as solidly as the tree's limbs that he should probably put his talons out and beat his wings backward. Erratically flapping and clinging to a thin branch, he finally came to stillness in the tree.

Beak open, he let out a breath, and then all at once, his form shifted back into that of a full-grown man. The twig that had sufficiently supported a hollow-boned raven gave up completely, sending him straight to the ground.

Rolling onto his back with a groan, Damien glared up at the broken branches he'd hit on the way down. "I don't know what Amma sees in you," he muttered up to the tree that couldn't hold his weight, and once he remembered how human limbs worked, pulled himself to his feet.

Farther from the keep than he would have liked, Damien peered out from the clustered copse. There was no cover out on the moor, not that Damien envied an opportunity to skulk about. No, for this, he wanted to call up every dark and demented force he knew, tear fissures into the infernal plane, and welcome evil to serve at his whim. He would burn the place to little more than a smoldering pile of ash and personally slit every throat he came across save for Cedric Caldor, whom he would mount alive on a pike and watch leisurely bleed out as he begged for his life. Then he would sweep Amma into his arms and profess…well, he would figure out exactly what he'd say later.

But it might not matter, even if he could come up with the perfect words. If Amma saw him bury his dagger in every being complicit in her capture, she would surely suggest that at least some of them didn't deserve it, and since he only knew the face of the marquis, he would, however unfortunately, have to leave the rest alive.

Because he *did* care, and he *did* feel, and he was going to bloody well prove it to her.

Along the dirt pathway, a young man in soldier's garb was strolling away from the keep, carrying a large bowl. There was no one else about, and he veered off the path and into the thick brush. Infernal arcana still tingled intensely in Damien, the shifting feather and Kaz's heart invigorating rather than draining him. He could disguise himself as this man, but he had to get rid of him first. But not kill him. *Fuck.*

Trickery it was then.

Damien hid himself completely within the copse, feeling like an idiot—blood mage, son of a demon, *hiding behind a tree*, but it was necessary—and then whistled, high and sharp. He waited, but no footsteps came nearer. Damien chanced a look around the trunk, the man fifty or so paces off and standing near a well but looking about curiously.

Damien whistled again, higher, sharper. The guard stepped toward the darkened copse of trees blanketed in shadows with the sun now completely risen but then stopped. Damien pressed his lips into a thin frown, annoyed and prepared to whistle again when the man began walking toward the trees again. Wonderful, he was finally coming and would make this easy, proving himself a moron already since he hadn't even unsheathed his weapon.

Damien pulled himself back behind the tree completely to wait. Any moment now, the soldier would stick his head in, and Damien would catch him about the neck and restrict his breathing until he stopped kicking. Whether he survived or not afterward was between the soldier and his gods.

The footfalls came to a stop, but the figure never made an appearance, and Damien almost poked his head out again when he heard movement just beside his hiding place. There was a shuffling and then the sound of leaking water and a very satisfied sigh.

"Oh, for fuck's sake." Damien stepped away from the stream of piss landing an inch from his boot, and the young man stumbled back from the hulking, black-cloaked blood mage before him. He might have screamed, might have even pulled out his sword, if there wasn't a root right behind his feet, but instead the guard tripped, landed flat on his back, and then failed to move at all. Damien waited a moment, nudged the fallen man's leg, and realized the dumb kid had knocked himself out. "Well, suppose I'll take that one for free."

It took a few moments to pull off the man's clothes and put them on over his own. The layers may have looked a bit strange, the soldier scrawny and younger, but when he shifted his appearance, it would mostly work. The only problem would be Damien's scar—when he cast an illusion on himself, the old wound wasn't going anywhere. Thankfully, blood on its own could assist with that.

After tying the man up in the middle of the trees so that when he woke he couldn't go running back to the keep,

Damien hustled toward the road in the soldier's clothing, the symbol of Brineberth across his chest and the sword strapped on a baldric over his shoulder. He'd cut himself more liberally than needed to cast the spell on his skin, shifting his features about to look like the younger man, and then smeared the excess blood over the unalterable scar on his face.

As the entry to the keep opened for him, another man stood there looking aghast. "Arthur, what the fuck? Thought you were just getting water?" He swept his eyes out on the moor behind him.

"Bird," said Damien, lowering his voice though he didn't know why—he had no idea how this Arthur he was meant to impersonate spoke—and pushed past the soldier and into the keep.

"Bird?" The man kept stride with Damien as he took stock of the courtyard, counting the others. A few looked up, but most paid little attention. "Were you attacked?"

"Yes, by a bird."

"What kind of—"

"Big one," grunted Damien, wanting to run him through with the very human sword strapped to his side but instead just trying to shake him. "Piss off and send someone out in my place." That was one way to get rid of at least one of the men in here, though there were so many that one might not make much of a difference.

The soldier fell back, mumbling about everyone's temperament going to shit lately. Damien walked with a purpose, acting as though he belonged while he took stock of the lean-tos where a few worked on armor and weapons, a pit where others were training, and a curious contingency of robed men having a whispered discussion.

There were numerous small buildings lining the outer wall of the courtyard, but he knew Amma would be kept in the largest one at the back—it seemed like it would be most difficult to escape, and Cedric wouldn't give her any chances, especially if he had any idea how wily she could be.

Damien strode across the courtyard's center, boots sinking into the wet earth, slowing him. Noxscura swirled under his skin uncomfortably, and then he was hit with another wave of that magic, the darkness he'd felt in the Innomina Wildwood, and his stomach twisted. E'nloc and Cedric were connected somehow; he'd known it since he'd glimpsed the name on paperwork in the marquis's office, but he had to focus to keep the mask of the guard up, so he pushed the urge to reach out and investigate away.

Inside, the small hall was lit lowly with braziers, fortunately darker than it had been outside, but there were a number of men sitting at tables and eating a morning meal, shouting loudly at one another in the cramped space.

"Aye, Arthur, lose track of time out on the moors again?" an amused voice called to him from the nearest table. "Thought you weren't on scouting duty this morning?"

He glared over at the man and made him start when he fully showed his face, the blood he'd smeared down it surely grisly coupled with the old scar that the actual soldier didn't have.

"Fuck." The man stood, dropping the hunk of meat he'd been gnawing on. "Is that Gilead's doing? I didn't believe Fergus, but…" The other two men at the table turned toward Damien, mouths hanging open, and the attention of the next table over was also drawn to him.

"Bird," repeated Damien. "Pissed it off."

When the men traded confused glances with one another, Damien continued deeper into the hall, past the long tables and benches, and cast his gaze up the stairwell to an open walkway above. The smell of greasy meat and burnt potatoes wafted from a closed-off room nearby, and there was another door tucked off to the side, looking to lead to someplace smaller.

Amma would surely be behind a closed door, but which one?

Damien chanced calling up arcana, reaching out for her blood beneath the roar of the voices all around, struggling to maintain his disguise and being sure to avoid alerting anyone who might be arcanely inclined like those robed men outside.

"You look like you could use some food, Art."

Pulled out of the spell, Damien growled and glanced at the man who had spoken to him, now at his side and offering a plate. He was shorter and slighter than some of the others, a bow strapped to his back.

"No," said Damien, concentrating again.

"Come on, ya never turn down a meal. What, you caught the crazies out here too? You'd be the third one this week, not counting the little lady."

Damien was about to walk away from him, but his blathering had finally come to something useful. "Lady?"

"Yeah, they brought the baron's daughter back, not that she acts rescued. You ain't seen her last night? No, I guess you were on duty, huh? Surprised you didn't hear her—she was screaming up a storm, mad as a cat in a wet sack—but at least we finally got some ass to look at around here."

Damien knew his disguise flickered when he eyed the man again. "Where is she?"

"Ha, well, I know the rumor going around"—he took a bite of the meat he'd been offering and raised his brows—"but me and you are gonna have to do some real heavy lifting if you think Caldor's gonna give either of us a turn with her before the general or—"

Damien grabbed the front of his tunic, jerking him forward, plate clattering across the floor. "I know that the restraint I am showing by not slaughtering you right now is beyond your minuscule comprehension, but understand that if you spew another word of that thought, I will bury this sword so deeply down your throat, it will only be retrievable by way of your asshole. Tell me where she is. Now."

The man's eyes had gone wide. "Gilead really did fuck with you, didn't—"

There was a scream that pierced the air, followed by the name Damien had come to loathe: *Cedric.* Though the voice was low and masculine, Damien dropped the scrawny man and followed its sound. A small retinue of soldiers had beaten him to the staircase, and more were on his heels, and they all fell in together, pushing their way down a hall to an open door.

Some of those around Damien drew weapons, others simply fell still, eyes wide and mouths falling open. From behind, more men gathered, calling out to learn what had happened, while one turned back into the group from its front, escaping the crowd and retching into the hall's corner.

Damien attempted to force his way to the front, equally jostled by the others, some of whom had filed into the room. Beside him, another man was calling for space, and a path was cleared for him, so Damien followed the robed priest, finally making his way to the door.

There was chaos, blood, and a body. Nothing about what Damien was seeing made any kind of sense, as if a storm had swept through only this chamber, every piece of furniture splintered and scattered about. The victim, who had been impaled against the wall, had fallen to his knees over the weapon of his ruin. And then he realized it was Cedric, run through and dripping the very last of his own blood into a massive pool on the floor.

Damien grinned slowly, only disappointed that he hadn't been able to send the bastard to the Abyss himself.

The mage who had pushed through them began throwing his arms about. He was a familiar man, the one from Faebarrow who had been in the Grand Athenaeum and apparently served the Caldors. He was yelling about the marquis's blood being spilt, and there was another behemoth of a man kneeling in the pool beside the body and absolutely sobbing.

"Brother!" he cried, throwing his head back and raising open hands to the ceiling. "Osurehm, how could this happen? How can this be?" He grabbed at the mage, dragging him toward the corpse. "Gilead! Heal him!"

"There's no healing this, Roman," hissed the mage, pulling his robes from the sobbing man's grasp. "We can only salvage now. And you—you need to protect yourself!"

He threw his arms out again, an absolute wreck, though how anyone could have such affection for Cedric was a mystery. "But how did this happen? Ammalie, how?"

Damien's heart squeezed, and he pushed farther forward, peering around the wall to see the small, disheveled figure of Amma in the corner, crumpled in on herself, just staring.

"Take her for questioning," Gilead called as he continued his frantic search of the ruins of the room.

Damien saw his opportunity to stride into the space, grab Amma, and pull her past the others under the guise of Gilead's order. Amma was so rattled she barely recognized being moved, her body allowing itself to be led through the men and onto the landing. He focused on the disguise, as it wanted to falter, illusion magic difficult enough to keep up, but with her finally in his grasp, his ability to hang on to the spell heightened.

She let herself be guided down the wide staircase, a scuffle overhead as the other men were ordered about to secure the room, and the wailing continued. Another retinue of men passed them at its foot, one of whom got in the way. "What are you doing with her?"

"Locking her up for safekeeping." Damien pushed past the man, an acceptable enough answer for him but apparently not for Amma.

Her body jerked suddenly in his grasp, and she screamed. They garnered only a few looks from the others as Damien dragged her along the back wall of the dining hall. She struck him, and he caught her free arm, but instead of rendering her still, her struggle only heightened to an animalistic attempt at escape.

"Put me down right fucking now!" she shrieked as he grabbed her about the waist, guilt striking him even harder than she had as he lifted her off her feet. "I'll rip it off and shove it down your throat!" Voice like a serrated blade, her need to get away from him was so strong that his softening heart almost let her. But then they'd finally reached the door in the dining hall's corner, and he tossed her inside, clearing it just enough to slam it shut behind him.

Amma turned then and lurched for the door in one last, furious attempt to escape.

"Amma," he hissed, voice low. "Stop—it's me!"

But she was feral and swung for his face. "Don't touch me!"

Damien took the punch right to his eye, and that was all he needed to drop the illusion. Knocked into the door with a hand slapped over his face, he groaned as she continued to pummel him, lifting a knee to strike him in the gut. "Ow, Amma, for darkness' sake, please stop hitting me."

The onslaught came to an abrupt halt as Amma's limbs went lax, and she took in a shuddering breath. Damien remained still, hoping she would recognize him, and when she didn't recommence her wild thrashing, he finally dropped his hands.

"Damien?" Her voice was barely a whisper in the room, weak and unsure, but her blue eyes were as wide as they'd ever been, finally really seeing him.

He pressed a hand to his stomach where her knee had nearly knocked him breathless. "Basest beasts, Amma, for someone so tiny, you certainly—"

Amma threw herself at him, and he reared back, expecting to be attacked once again, but instead, arms were slung around his neck, pulling him down to her, and lips were pressed to his own. She tasted of copper and salt, she was panting like a rabbit caught in a trap, and she was clawing at his neck so harshly she had to be drawing blood, but she was kissing him.

Amma was in his arms, she was safe, she was *kissing* him, and he was complete.

CHAPTER 36

AMMA

Despicable Callousness

DESPITE BEING IN THE most dangerous place she could imagine, Amma knew she was safe. Damien's arms were around her, his warm body pressed to hers, and his lips were kissing her back, tender and soft like she knew he could be—like she knew he truly was.

"You came for me," she whispered up against his mouth.

His fingertips grazed her temple, smoothing away hair that had fallen in her face, and he pressed another kiss to her lips. "You called. How could I not?"

"I thought…" The words fell away as she stared into a face streaked with blood, exhaustion pooling in the hollows of his eyes.

"You thought what?" He rested his forehead on hers, a

husk to his voice as a crooked smile grew over his mouth. "That I wouldn't? That I could possibly bear to lose you? That I am not utterly and unconditionally—"

The ground shook, and Amma would have fallen had she not been holding on to Damien. There was a snap and a groan as the earth continued to shudder, voices rising up from beyond the door, and a crack crawled its way up the wall beside them. The room fell still again.

Damien squeezed his eyes shut. "Amma, please tell me that just sometimes happens on the western coast of the realm."

She shook her head. "I don't think so."

"Fuck." He stood straight and looked about, hands still tight on her hips as the earth began to rumble once more. "At the very least, it's a distraction." Then his face contorted like he might be sick.

"Damien, what's wrong?"

He shook his head, grabbing up her hand, and eased the door to the dining hall open amidst the quake that was shaking the building once again. Men were streaming out into the courtyard, no one taking notice of either of them. A pillar in the room had cracked through, and a table was knocked over in the scuffle. Damien tugged her arm, and the two slipped in amongst the others to escape the failing building.

The courtyard was darkening under heavy clouds that had rolled in, though the sky had been clear that morning. Before them, a contingency of men spread out, and the gates at the far wall were open wide, but the two came to an abrupt halt. That—that wasn't supposed to be there, and it seemed everybody knew it.

In the center of the courtyard, there was...nothing. The ground had seemingly opened up, but not to the earth below filled with roots and rocks and dirt. No, the courtyard's center had become a massive pit of the inkiest blackness Amma had ever seen, darker than any shadow Damien had ever conjured.

Suddenly slick with sweat, Damien's hand squeezed Amma's as they were jostled from behind by more men fleeing the hall, but he didn't move, struck still. She tugged him away from the door and toward one side of the courtyard, knowing Gilead and Roman would soon come out. Damien's eyes never left the pit, but his legs began working again. Every face Amma could make out in the shadows was painted with terror, and she felt the dread that was emanating off the newly formed void too, but Damien's features twisted into disgust.

The two gave the pit a wide berth, but others were running to it despite their fear, weapons drawn. The ground still shook, shouts and the breaking of stone filling the air. One of the mages left a cluster of others and fell to his knees at the pit's edge, a place she couldn't imagine wanting to be, and he stared hard into the nothingness below. The rocky lip under his hands looked to crumble as he leaned forward, and Amma picked up speed.

There was a small structure along the side wall of the keep, and Amma led them toward it, open doors on both ends so that they could run through and end up closer to the keep's exit. Amma dodged around the men, Damien trailing after her, but just as she made it to the building, the stones of its facade gave way. With a terrible crash, it crumbled right before them, blocking their escape around the pit. Amma halted, skidding back away from the falling rubble and knocking into Damien.

His eyes had been locked on the void as he let Amma drag him across the courtyard. Pallid and sweating, he suddenly doubled over, grabbing his stomach. "This is wrong." He coughed when she tried to make him straighten. "The noxscura. The rot. How is it here too?"

Amma's heart couldn't pound any harder, but his words made her veins go cold. "What is it?"

"It was in the Wildwood too," he said, standing again, breaths heavy and face contorted with pain. "It took hours and the power of the witches to banish it, but there isn't time for that now. This is stronger, and it's...it's hungry."

At that, a tangle of black smoke coalesced over the pit. It rose up, distorting the air about it, sinewy and slithering, and then struck out. Its haziness solidified and wrapped around a body lying injured beside the fallen rubble. The man was jerked upward, crying out as his limbs went rigid, and in one swift move was dragged downward into the darkness. There was a sickeningly wet crunch. Blood spurted upward and then rained back down into the void.

"Oh gods," Amma whimpered, falling over herself to pull Damien back and put as much distance between them and the pit as she could. They were cut off from the exit by the destroyed building, with the only way out now along the void's far side, which meant going back to where Roman and

Gilead had finally emerged from the main hall. But the marquis and the mage didn't notice either Amma or Damien, as drawn to the horror of the chaotic pit as everyone else.

Queasy and addled, Amma tried to take a calming breath, but the briny air had gone sour, tainted with a gruesome aura. Another body was yanked into the nothing with a black tendril, smoke one moment, solid the next. Another scream, another crunch, another rain of blood. Beside her, Damien bent down onto one knee and placed a hand on the ground.

"What are you doing?" She tried to pull him back up. "We need to go."

"This can't be allowed." Damien's voice was hollow, brow heavy as he glared at the thing before them.

Amma dug her fingers into his shoulder, holding on to him so he wouldn't go toward it, as crazy as that would have been. Of the men still scrambling, one actually did stagger toward the pit and then thrust himself right in, no tendril needed. Amma's horrified scream caught in her throat, her grip on Damien tightening. She could feel it then, the way it thrummed, matching her heartbeat, and she knew.

Everything would cease to exist if It got Its way. Better than she knew almost anything else at that moment, Amma understood that every person, every creature, every tree, she, Damien, all of them, would be gone. Only then would It be happy. And then E'nloc would destroy Itself.

"What in the Abyss do we do?"

Damien turned up to her. "You have to go. Get as far from here as possible."

Her grip on him tightened as he stood. "And leave you?"

"I have to try and stop It."

"How do you think you're going to do that?"

He gazed out on the void again, that nauseated look taking him once more as his eyes went glassy. "I don't know how, not from the outside, but I think I know what It wants…"

Another tendril struck out from the pit, this time snatching a mage who fled past, pulling him in with a horrified scream until he was swallowed by the dark. Damien's face didn't change as he watched, simply staring, stoic, resigned.

"Not from the outside?" Amma glared at him hard.

"But from the inside."

"Don't be *ridiculous*." Amma shocked herself with her own bite, giving him a shake. "You're leaving this place now, with me. Do you understand?"

He blinked then, gaze shifting over the whole keep as if he'd just woken from some dream.

She snatched his jaw and turned his head to meet her gaze. "Tell me you understand, Damien."

His throat bobbed with a swallow, eyes finding hers. "I…I understand."

"Good." She squeezed his hand and took off, and he let himself be pulled along, passing behind Roman, who stood there slack-jawed, staring at the pit. She led Damien around a heap of rubble that had once been a makeshift armory, fire smoldering from the stones, and hugged the other side wall even as it shook and cracked. The main gate of the courtyard was open wide ahead of them, the last of the soldiers fleeing through it.

Damien picked up speed then, running along beside her, intent finally set on the way out, and together they sprinted for the doors, paces away. Soon they would be free, the pit behind them, the walls of the old keep falling into it, swallowed up and gone.

Then there was a pull at Amma's arm, and she was ripped right off her feet. Falling onto her back, the wind knocked out of her, arm extended over her head, she locked her grip on Damien's hand, refusing to let go. Amma rolled onto her stomach to see he had fallen flat, scrambling to get up just as she was, still holding on. Behind him, the pit appeared both far off and too close. A tendril had crawled out of it, solid and black and stretched long across the courtyard to wrap itself around Damien's ankle.

Amma swung her other arm overhead to grab his wrist, knowing what was coming a second before the two were ripped toward the pit unrelentingly. She screamed, digging fingers into his slick skin, teeth gritted, eyes squeezed shut. She would sooner pitch herself into the nothingness than let go, but they weren't stopping, so Amma released Damien with one hand and buried it in the earth as they were dragged along. She felt for the arcana that she knew had to be there, even in this treeless place. Eyes shut, Amma reached out with her mind, with her heart, and then she felt it, the tiniest spark hiding in a sea of darkness, and she placed all her will behind it.

Shoots sprang from the wet earth all around them. Just thin roots, weak on their own, the vines climbed over their bodies, but together there were hundreds, maybe thousands, and while some snapped, others tightened down against the earth and held on with everything they had, slowing their ruthless advance toward the pit.

Damien too had a free hand and reached up to rip his dagger from its sheath. He dragged the blade down his outstretched arm, blood welling up through his sleeve and wetting the blade. Chthonic words fell out of his mouth, and blackness rose up around them both, encasing them in a dark cloud, and finally, the two fell still.

Inside the cloudy haze, the rest of the world was blocked out. Then the roots holding them in place began to turn from their wet whiteness to gray, thinning, drying, and crumpling into ash. They died rapidly as the ground beneath them became soggier, but Amma was able to scramble up onto her knees, crawling to Damien. His eyelids were fluttering down, but she screamed his name as she wrapped her arms around his bloody one, feeling the heat radiate off his cut as she pulled him upward. The cloud about them dissipated.

"It wants me," he told her, voice ragged as he stumbled up to his feet. "Something's driving It. It's calling for a...a vessel."

"Well, you can't—" Amma's eyes widened, ripping Damien back down to the ground with her. A black tendril struck out where they had just stood. It shot out with such force that it slammed into the wall beside the open gates. Rubble was knocked across the exit, and the tendril went wild, flopping over the earth as it pulled itself back into the pit.

Amma shot back to her feet. Across the void, there was Roman still, backed up into the main hall that had collapsed in on itself, still staring in disbelief, but there was another figure too, this one not cowering or afraid. Gilead stood just at the edge of the pit, blackness swirling around his feet and hands out as if he were somehow in control, though Amma knew whatever It was couldn't be controlled.

"There." She pointed, one hand still tight around Damien's.

He stood and found Gilead, eyes sharpening on the man, and then took his dagger to his skin once more. His hand shook as he did it, but he didn't falter, running a palm through the sticky crimson and throwing the droplets across the darkness. The blades formed themselves, flickered as they crossed the pit, and then hit Gilead squarely in the chest.

The mage stumbled back with a wet cry, the arcana around his feet crackling, and the ground rumbled again. More tendrils snapped out from the pit, but they were erratic and wild, flickering from shadow to solid form, slamming into the earth and sinking back into the darkness without ensnaring anything.

Amma and Damien turned back for the exit gates, one of the doors broken off and blocking the way out, the other side filled with crumbled stone. Amma searched for the best way through, but Damien just tugged her back. "I'll clear a path." He called up arcana, the air crackling, and Amma only thought to stop him a moment too late. With something to focus on, a single tendril shot itself toward the two.

Amma shrieked, tackling him out of the way and just over the arm of pure arcana. They slammed into a pile of rubble, and Amma watched Damien's eyes go glassy again, the spell fizzling out.

"Overdoing it a bit." He coughed, holding up the bloody dagger. "Fucking hole's sucking the life out of me."

Amma growled, eyeing the tendril flopping about as it blindly searched for him again. She would stab it if she didn't think that would only help it track them. "What do I do? There has to be another way to get us out of here."

Damien shifted beneath her, sticking a hand into his satchel and pulling out a scroll of parchment. "This is a terrible idea," he told her, "but it's the only one I've got."

She took the scroll with shaking fingers and unraveled it. "Despised Damien Maleficus Bloodthorne, son of Zagadoth the blah, blah, blah, you are callously summoned to Yvlcon," she read aloud. "Then there's just a bunch of squiggly symbols. How does this help?"

"It's enchanted," Damien groaned, "but it may take us somewhere worse."

Amma looked up at the pit of never-ending darkness that was almost certainly growing in size, the bloodied mage who was crawling to his feet and calling up arcana, the blackened tendrils that were clambering for a vessel to inhabit or eat or worse, and no way to escape any of it save for straight up the crumbling walls of a decrepit keep. "Nope, there's nowhere worse than this. Let's do it."

"Dip it in my blood, and read the rest of the words aloud."

She was already covered in his blood, smearing the parchment with it. "This is Chthonic—I can't read it."

"Yes, you can." His hand was squeezing her arm weakly, and she felt a tingle of arcana run through her. "You recognized the language, didn't you? Chthonic's phonetic anyway."

She took a breath and let the words come, the ground below them rumbling harder, the tendrils in the pit flopping about, senses sharpening, but the magic seemed to be sparking everywhere. She read as best she could, a language she didn't know, symbols she couldn't place, but it came out all the same, and then there was a freezing wind at her back.

Turning, she saw that there stood a doorway, nearly as black as the pit itself, a frame of silver, reflective and moving as if made of liquid metal. Damien struggled to sit up, and she hurried to help him, but he slid down again, legs weak, body going lax.

Amma tugged at him again, muscles aching. "Damn it, Damien, why are you so heavy?"

"You're just small," he groused, strong enough, apparently, to talk back but not enough to actually walk.

"Where's Kaz?" She heaved him toward the door with all her might. "Can't he get all big and carry you?"

"That," said Damien, scuffing back up to his feet and wobbling, "is for a future discussion when our lives are not in peril."

Behind him, a tendril struck out, headed directly for the two, but the last bit of Damien's energy seemed to run out, and he fell forward, landing on Amma, and they both tumbled into the frigid darkness of the doorway.

CHAPTER 37

AMMA

Summoned to Yvlcon

Amma's body ached, Damien's full weight atop her and not at all in the way she would have preferred, as he was unconscious and bleeding, but at least the dread that had firmly placed itself at the base of her spine had gone. She touched his face and whispered his name, wiggling out from under him while gently flipping him over. He was still breathing, and he made a sort of sound, enough to tell her he was alive, and she glanced about to see where they'd ended up.

The small chamber was doused in a blue light from crystals affixed along the base of the stone walls and silent too, a stark contrast to the chaos of where they had just been. There were relief sculptures carved on the surfaces, scenes of great destruction, death, and mayhem, so she tried not to look at them for too long. The ground was covered in circular carvings, symbols at even intervals that could have been Chthonic but were somehow prettier. There was also no pit of darkness trying to eat them. She breathed a relieved sigh and wiped a hand over her face and through the tangle that was her hair.

With a low creak, a dull light flooded the room, and Amma straightened. A hidden door swung open from the wall, and a figure appeared in it, low to the ground, with long limbs and big ears.

"Kaz?" She pushed up onto her knees, hopeful.

The creature stepped fully into the blue lights, and while it was almost definitely an imp with bulbous eyes and swirling horns, this one had maroon skin, better teeth, and much knobbier elbows than Kaz. It did, however, give her the same disapproving look she'd come to associate with imps.

"Late arrival," it said in a voice that creaked like a chain in the wind. "Who are you?"

"Um…" Amma looked down at Damien's still form, covered in blood and mud and bruises, then thrust the crumpled bit of parchment in her hands toward the imp.

He scowled at her even deeper but waddled up to take it. "Bloodthorne," he murmured to himself as he snapped his fingers and a slate appeared in his hand. He ran a claw down it as he mumbled the name to himself again, the sound terrible as it screeched into the chamber, and even Damien, near unconsciousness, winced.

"Ah, right here, Damien Mal—wait, really? What did *this*

to a blood mage?" The imp dropped the slate, and it disintegrated before it could shatter against the floor.

It was really too much to explain, so Amma just shrugged.

"I need a priest!" the imp called back through the door, crossing his arms and glaring at her. He waved the scroll in his hand. "The summons didn't mention a minion."

Amma opened her mouth, not sure what to say to that, but a figure appeared behind the imp, and she gasped instead. Slithering in on a serpent's body as thick around as a human's torso, the creature loomed well above them all, a long thin tongue poking out from beneath the hood it wore. Her instinct was to reach for the crossbow that was no longer on her back, feeling for nothing as the creature slithered farther into the room and went for Damien.

"Don't you dare," she growled, throwing herself over him.

Damien's hand twitched up against her leg, tapping her. "It's all right," he mumbled from beneath her, and hesitantly, she backed away just enough, eyes tracking the snake-man.

He reached human-enough arms covered in patches of scales out from his robe and laid them on Damien's chest. Amma gnawed at her lip, entwining her fingers with Damien's and squeezing so he would know she was there. Arcana pulsed through him, and all at once, the blood mage shot up like waking from a bad dream, breathing heavy, eyes wide.

"Amma," he husked out, "where are—" His free hand flailed, falling on her and grabbing tight, and then he blinked up at the hooded priest and the imp. The two creatures were still, the imp's features twisted up in confusion, and then Damien pulled both hands back from her, cleared his throat, and set his face stony. "Zagadoth the Tempestuous sends his dark regards to the Grand Order."

The snake-man fell into a bow and then slithered back out of the room. The imp nodded at Damien but was much more curt. "And the Grand Order begrudgingly accepts. But you're still late, and you are only registered as one. If you would remain here, Lord Bloodthorne, I will see to proper quarters and…approval. It will be but a few moments."

The imp bowed, awkward and put upon, and backed out of the room, the door sinking smoothly into the wall and leaving the two alone again in the small chamber.

"Oh, bloody, fucking Abyss." Damien dragged a hand down his face, slumping forward, then turned to Amma. The coldness he'd injected into his features was gone when he looked at her, replaced with something else, something she wasn't used to seeing. "Amma, are you all right?"

She glanced down at herself, clothes torn, covered in mud and blood, skin beginning to bruise. But she was alive, and most importantly, she was with him. "I think so."

Though he looked as though he didn't quite believe her, he nodded. "Things are about to be…" He swallowed and licked his lips, eyes darting around the room. "How can I explain?"

She looked about too, not seeing what it was he searched for. "Maybe you can tell me where we are?"

"If only I knew. This is where the Grand Order converges,

but they're never clear where exactly it is. I'm not even sure what plane we're on." He struggled to his feet, and she did as well, grabbing him in case he wavered. Damien collected himself though, and then took her by the wrists, pulling her hands off him. "Don't do that."

"Do what?"

"Anything that suggests friendliness unless I explicitly order it of you. Do you understand?" He was looking at her sharply, nothing like how he'd been moments before.

"Not really."

He released her and brushed his hair back out of his face, eyes pinging to the still-closed door and then back to her. "You don't belong here, Amma. You aren't a member of ill repute or a registered minion or even a genuine thrall. In fact, you qualify for almost none of the very few circumstances under which nonmembers are allowed at Yvlcon."

Amma swallowed. "Um, should we go?"

"We can't. There's no leaving until they hand over the translocation stones at Yvlcon's end. That is if there's still a realm to go to after that *thing*, not that there's anything to be done about it now."

"Well, if I'm not allowed to be here, and I'm not allowed to go…"

There was a sound from beyond the room's only door, and he grabbed her by the upper arms, holding tight. "Listen, you're my captive."

Amma pouted. "Well, yeah, I know, technically, but—"

"Not technically." Fingers dug into her biceps,

underscoring his words. "Do nothing, do not even speak, without my permission."

"What? How am I—"

"Ah, no, stop." His voice lowered, colder, darker, as he leaned down, the blue light shining upward and casting eerie shadows over his face. "What did I *just* say?"

She opened her mouth, then clamped it back shut, glaring at him.

He waited a moment, and then the corner of his mouth twitched up with just the ghost of a smirk. "Exactly."

"You must be feeling better."

"Amma," he snapped, and she quieted again, crossing her arms and twisting her features up into a snarl. He took a patient if irritated breath. "Bringing you here was the only way I could think to escape *that*, but this is hardly a safer place than where we were. If I cannot convince them otherwise, you will be seen as an interloper at best or a threat at worst. You're clearly not evil yourself, so they'll need to believe I've brought you here for…other purposes."

"What kind of purposes?" Amma's heart sped up, and her mouth went dry when his features creased with unease. "Not sacrifice-y purposes, right?"

He shook his head. "No, but there are certain expectations on me here, expectations I have not been meeting for some time, that I will have to—Look, you *must* play along if we're both going to survive this. Do you understand?"

She felt her brows knit, the specifics still unclear, but she nodded anyway.

"And don't do that."

"Do what?"

He gestured to his own face and put on a sour expression. "Look all cranky like that. I wouldn't allow you to do that."

"Wouldn't *allow*—If I wasn't cranky before, you sure are making me now."

He tipped his head, raising a brow.

She clicked her tongue but forced on a smile, eyes still narrowed at him.

"I know you can do better than that." Damien slid a hand up over her shoulder to the back of her neck, hot against her skin and tugging her close. "And you *will* do better than that for me," he growled, and then his lips were on hers.

Amma stiffened under his kiss, shocked, but then she melted against him, hands grabbing his tunic to stay upright. His mouth took hers completely, and a moan was drawn out of her throat as his tongue slipped over hers. When he pulled back, leaving her panting and dazed, she could only stare up into his eyes, and a lazy grin crawled up her face.

"There's my good girl." When he smirked, every inch of her skin burned, but she would have dropped to her knees right then if he'd asked her to—she would have done *anything*. But then his knowing look fell away just as quickly, and the grip on the back of her neck went much tighter as the creaking door to the chamber began to open once again. "And for what it is worth, I am deeply sorry for what is about to happen."

BONUS CHAPTER

AMMA

Alone in the Wilds

MIDDLE BITS ARE FUNNY things. Not funny in the way endings are in that they're not the thing they claim to be but funny in almost the opposite way in that they are *so* middley they often skip over their own beginnings, and sometimes their endings never come.

It wasn't likely that Ammalie Avington could be convinced of the humor in middles, especially the part about ends not coming. Then again, maybe she would learn to like that; it would just take the right set of hands and string of words to show her the light…or the dark, depending on which way one reads it.

But that would be later, and in the intervening time, she

had been plagued by the middles of things, or rather by the interruption of them.

Those interruptions truly began during her voluntary imprisonment in the Chthonic Tower. Amma was alone in the middle of the night, lying in the middle of a precariously comfortable bed, languishing in the middle of dangerous thoughts. Specifically, thoughts of Damien Maleficus Bloodthorne, which could be nothing *but* dangerous. Though there was little else on her mind when she lay in bed at any time, the broody, menacing, dare she think *cocky* blood mage was not at all helpful to get her to sleep.

It had only been a few days since fleeing Faebarrow, but they were torturous once Amma knew the feel of Damien's touch and was subsequently deprived of it. How tightly he'd gripped her waist, the fingers that had tickled her ribs, the hardness of his chest against her back—it was all so delicious, and then? *Nothing*. He'd withheld even the most chaste contact until the night he offered to send a message to Laurel. During the spell, Amma once again reveled in Damien's fingers as they grazed her cheeks, how his palms caressed her jaw, the way his body heat made her feel like a honey cake left out in the sun.

As he cradled her face, she had buried her fingers in his arcane raven's feathers, but she wished the silky blackness were Damien's hair instead. How she'd wanted to run her nails over his scalp and draw his face down to hers as she sank deeper into his hold. A hold she wished would constrict around her so that there was no way to escape.

Perhaps it had been the looming threat of what was to come or the lingering thrill of what had been, but nestled between those not so subtly euphemistic perils was an even less subtle hollow of elation that ached to be filled. So even in the volatility of the Chthonic Tower, when Amma was finally alone beneath the silky sheets and stripped of all her clothing, she had decided to take matters into her own hands.

She was no stranger to her own body, but it had been so long that it took a little exploring—no, not quite like that. Er, maybe the other way around? Perhaps if she wiggled deeper into the mattress.

No, she needed…inspiration.

Eyes closed, Amma could see Damien again and the intensity in his violet gaze as he cradled her face. It was so tender, his touch, and she could mimic that on herself, how his thumb had rubbed a faint circle into the dip of her cheek. When he cast through her, his infernal arcana slithered over every inch of her flesh, exploring its taut peaks and its soft valleys. She could do that too, even if her own hands couldn't coax out the fervor Damien's could. She imagined his grip sliding downward, fingers taking her roughly by the chin and an arm tugging her right up against him, the hard and unyielding length of his body pressed to hers.

The corner of his lips would turn up in that way it so often didn't, and his mouth would open as it closed in on hers, and he would whisper—

What the fuck was that?

Amma jolted upright at the sound of a crash. She clamped

her thighs around her hand, eyes wide as they searched the unfamiliar chamber while her fingers ceased searching the more familiar one. Movement in the room's corner made her already harried breath catch, but it was only a shadow imp. She'd learned they were harmless, but she'd forgotten how they hid in the darkest crevices and watched.

Even one observer was too many, so she snatched her hand from the death grip of her thighs and buried herself under the linens. Though her thoughts didn't absolve themselves that night, her fingers certainly did.

There would be another unfinished middle for Amma in the midst of the eerie karsts, surrounded by vampires in the midst of whatever came between life and death. Coupled with Damien's breathless appearance at her chamber door, the thrill was enough to inspire another attempt at an ending. It was close to perfect, once again in the comfort of a real bed with soft linens and…well, *almost* privacy.

Damien had been lounging by the fire, lazily sprawled over a divan. She'd never really seen him like that and wouldn't have believed the shadow through the draperies was him if she didn't know for certain. In fact, she would have thought he didn't know how to sprawl, but there he was, relaxed and unhurried. How she'd wished to take advantage of that, to crawl atop him and tease him until his restraint was shattered.

Despite that, she believed she had no such courage; she had gazed at his shadow, sinking into the reverie. The silhouette of his long fingers flicked through the pages he held and made her wish they were flicking her…ah, well, nothing, *of course*, because goodness gracious, he was in *the room*, and now was *not the time*, and oh great gods, what in the realm was she *thinking*?

So another middle came to an abrupt not-end, and Amma was left languishing until the witch's camp. There was privacy in the Wildwood, but exhaustion and worry were quite the mood killers. It was only when she had first heard the voice of the trees, had finally heard *hessach* and began to understand, that she realized she might have that thing she'd been chasing for so long: Amma might have power.

Damien would soon return from his journey into the Wildwood with the witches; she knew, she could feel it in her blood and in the budding magic inside her. So she took herself to bed unromantically but needy nonetheless, excited to tell Damien what she'd done.

"I'm powerful now," she imagined she could whisper to him the moment he arrived.

"Oh, are you?" he would ask, demonic grin and violet eyes immediately hungry—no, *starved*.

Amma would nod even if she weren't sure, because she knew what would come next—fantasy Damien was as ferocious as he was predictable. He would grab her by the wrists and skillfully throw her arms over her head, pinning her hands to the wall. "Care to tell me just how powerful you think you've become?"

Amma would wiggle then in a pathetic attempt at escape, not that it would matter because she wouldn't *really* be trying. "So powerful," she would say because the game would be too *fucking* fun. "More powerful than a blood mage, I bet."

Damien would bear down on her, her wrists still trapped as he pressed her to the wall so movement would be impossible. Every inhale would force their bodies to shift against one another, his breath warm, hers coming with a quickness. With his free hand, he would trace down the side of her face and then over her lips, the faint touch of just one finger so soft she could barely stand it. "Keep talking like that, and I'll have to fill that pretty mouth of yours with proof otherwise."

Amma would nod, unable to contain herself. She would want him to do whatever he wanted with her, and before the command even came, she would open her mouth, tongue spilling out.

"Eager, greedy little thing," Damien's voice would purr, and he would hook a hand behind her neck, tipping her head back against the wall as he taunted her with lips so close yet untouchable. "I think you know that's not how you get what you want."

She wouldn't be able to fight the grin his words would elicit, and he would know exactly what she was doing. "But I'm the daughter of a baron. I always get what I want," she would muster in that whiny voice that she could only hope would drive him mad. "And I say I might even be *more* powerful than you."

Then Damien would growl, and fear would flood in right behind the fun, her body pulled taut when he lifted her wrists, nipples budding and flesh shivering. "Is that so?" he would ask, running a finger down to the low neckline of her chemise, because of course that was what she was wearing, the less material between his skin and hers the better. "Are you powerful enough to stop me, Ammalie?"

Oh, her whole name—she *liked* that. And she liked the way his finger slipped across the tops of her breasts, taunting her with their release from the lace.

"Y-yes," she would stammer out, pouting a lip and trying her best to look defiant because she knew that was something *he* liked.

"Well, go on then," he would say, and he would let her go, which would be very confusing until she saw the shadows that had been summoned to replace his grip on her wrists, still holding her bound in place.

With the careful meticulousness she had seen so many times, Damien would unsheathe his…*dagger*—yes, definitely his dagger, because this was too good, and she didn't want it to be over just yet, which was another problem with middles: They were just too tempting. Then he would inspect the dagger's sharpness with hands she would be desperate to have back on her. His eyes would flick to her and his brow would cock.

Amma would swallow and cease the wriggling she hadn't realized she'd been doing.

"Still my defenseless captive, I see." Damien would take the tip of the blade to one strap of her chemise, and with the simplest flick, it would be severed. "And there is indeed much to see." He would cut the second strap, and the silky material would fall away, leaving Amma completely exposed to him. With her wrists bound overhead, she was exactly as helpless as she wanted to be.

His gaze would bring with it a flush that would spill over her body, lighting up her thighs, her stomach, her breasts, as he abandoned the blade. "So," he would say in that maddeningly cocky way as he crossed his arms and drank in her nakedness, "free yourself, oh powerful one."

Amma would bite down on her lip and tug at her wrists, but it would be no use. Despite the fruitlessness, she would try again, pushing onto her toes and reaching upward as if that might change things. The constriction would only get tighter as she squirmed, the result of Damien twirling a hidden finger and commanding the shadows, no doubt, his vicious grin growing.

"Oh, what*ever* is the matter, Ammalie?" he would say with feigned concern.

And she would know that her role would be to tell him she'd been defeated, that she was trying but she couldn't, but that wasn't what would come out of her. "I don't want you to let me go."

The truth would break like sunrise in her chest, and that burgeoning dawn would reflect in his gaze, because despite how simple the words, he would *know*. And whatever he might say would be...well, it would be soft and sweet and not exactly the thing that would push her to the edge, because of course that was what she was meant to be doing! Not wallowing in the melancholy of her heart but in the lasciviousness of her nethers.

"That is a very naughty thing to admit, Amma." Ah, there, *that* was better, and it wouldn't be delivered sweetly at all. In fact, Damien's voice would turn rough and punishing. "Sanguinisui, spread your legs."

Amma would gasp at the feel of her body acting of its own accord. There would be no fighting the spell she professed to hate—and she did hate it when it was used to hurt her, but in the safety of her mind, it did anything but. She would find herself straddling nothing but still bound to the wall, a chill shuddering through her as cool air caressed the exposed wetness between her legs.

"Oh, Amma," he would say, and the heat in her face would flare as his gaze settled on the shimmer dripping down her inner thigh. "I haven't even touched you. Not yet." Eyes would crawl up her body, and she would tremble as if his scrutiny were some palpable thing—and maybe it was. Maybe errant shadows would be sent to tease at the very fringes of her body, the backs of her knees, her elbows, her neck. "Is that what you want, Amma? A blood mage to manhandle you?"

Devoid of the ability to put a sentence together, she would only be able to nod and whimper.

"Only good girls deserve what they want," he would growl, suddenly much closer but still torturing her with space between them. "And I'm not sure you've been very good, teasing me, lying to me, and now you're not even using your words. Sanguinisui, tell me what you want."

"I want you to touch me, to lick me, to *fuck* me" would spill out of her with an urgency, the truth she needed him to force her to admit. "Damien, Master Bloodthorne, *please*."

Damien's fingers would sink into her then, and Amma would cry out in pleasure and pain both, the feel of him finally giving her what she wanted but the ache of needing more an agony.

"Sanguinisui, say it again."

"Master Bloodthorne," she would pant as his fingers circled her most sensitive spot. "Please fuck me."

Devious laughter would crawl up her neck as his lips pressed to her throat and his hand continued to chase the peak of her pleasure. "Not yet, Ammalie," he would groan against her skin. "Not until you come apart for me."

Naked and bound by shadows to the wall, Amma would buck and whimper and plead. Her fingers—er, his fingers knew exactly where to caress, exactly how quick and then how slow to stroke, exactly how deep to sink and curl. She wanted to give him what he wanted, what she wanted too, but she needed more of him. "Damien," she would say in a quivering voice, "please, *make* me."

"Sanguinisui," he would growl against the shell of her ear, and his breath would be…cold? And his voice would… change to a whisper?

A breeze blew over her skin and with it a sound, wind through the leaves, the voice of the trees, *hessach*.

"Huh?" Amma opened her eyes, and there was no devastatingly handsome and hungry blood mage looming over her, but there were ceiling beams and a roof made of wood. Living wood. But not *that* kind, and oh gods, now was *not* the time.

But she had been warned by the witches that eventually her power would come when she finally let it, and in that moment, when her breaths were heavy and she had pushed her body to its breaking point, she realized it had.

And Amma hadn't.

So another of Amma's middles reached its very middleyness, and that was where it was abandoned. But Ammalie Avington's story would go on, and satisfaction would probably come one day, her neediness no longer eclipsed by fear and frailty, though she wouldn't know it just yet.

**AMMA AND DAMIEN'S STORY
WILL CONCLUDE IN
VILLAINS & VIRTUES BOOK 3,
ECLIPSE OF THE CROWN.

ACKNOWLEDGMENTS

Something about writing the acknowledgments for *Summoned to the Wilds* has had me so stuck. I should have finished it months ago, but it's October 21, 2025, and this is my last chance to knock out this page before it ends up nixed from the book altogether. (Actually, I bet MJ would find me more time because she's cool like that, but I really gotta stop pushing my luck.)

I thought for a while it was the middleness of this book (oh, here she goes again) convincing me that since we're neither starting nor finishing the series *right now*, this part isn't necessary. That's obviously untrue. So many people have worked to bring the middle of V&V to life: illustrators, designers, formatters, editors (who have dealt with so much of my bullshit I don't know how they're still being nice to me in the notes), MJ (who has dealt with *even more* of my bullshit, all with a smile), marketers, printers, shippers, and loads of other people I don't even know about have all come together to get this book into your hands, and that's an amazing feat in no small part because things are sort of a mess right now, aren't they?

So really the thing I think I want to thank here is whatever it is that's keeping everyone going. Everyone who touched these pages in the process of putting *Summoned to the Wilds* together, and you too, touching the pages right now. Maybe it's your best friend, your cat, your morning cup of bean juice, or just your own indomitable spirit, but whatever that little spark of love is, I want to acknowledge that. It's doing tremendous work, so please hold on to it, nurture it, and don't let it go.

ABOUT THE AUTHOR

A.K. Caggiano is not a pen name—if it were, it would be more pronounceable and probably have "Violet" in there somewhere—but the real name of a woman in Vermont who likes to write silly little love stories and even sillier long-ass sentences. She perseveres solely because her cat demands Churu by the caseload. She can almost see Canada from her house.

Website: akcaggiano.com